The Dragonscale Comb

The Ardulum Series:
Ardulum: First Don
Ardulum: Second Don
Ardulum: Third Don
Tales from Ardulum
Ardulum: The Battle for Pruitcu
Ardulum: Mirrors of Andal

Other books by J.S. Fields:

Anthologies:
Distant Gardens
Farther Reefs
Lofty Mountains
Fiery Deeps
Lesbians in Space: Where No Man Has Gone Before
Lesbians in Space: The Sapphics Strike Back

Sci Fi
Queen

Fantasy
Awry With Dandelions

Myths of Yuro
The Rosewood Penny
The Dragonscale Comb

The Alchemical Duology
Foxfire in the Snow
Ocean of Fireflies

The Dragonscale Comb

J.S. Fields

Space Wizard Science Fantasy
Raleigh, NC
www.spacewizardsciencefantasy.com

Publisher's Note: This is a work of fiction. Names, characters, places, and incidents are a product of the author's imagination. Locales and public names are sometimes used for atmospheric purposes. Any resemblance to actual people, living or dead, or to businesses, companies, events, institutions, or locales is completely coincidental.

Cover art by Katie Cordy
Map by Katie Cordy
Editing by Courtney Brooks
Book Layout © 2015 BookDesignTemplates.com

The Dragonscale Comb/J.S Fields.— 1st ed.
ISBN 978-1-960247-52-0

Author's website: www.jsfieldsbooks.com

For Rosiee and Colleen. Thanks for sharing in my love of spicy monster literature. Will we ever be the same after those dinosaur books?

CONTENTS

Chapter 1 - Marani ... 7
Chapter 2 - Marani ... 26
Chapter 3 - Nuria ... 54
Chapter 4 - Marani ... 67
Chapter 5 - Nuria ... 86
Chapter 6 - Marani ... 100
Chapter 7 - Nuria ... 116
Chapter 8 - Nuria ... 128
Chapter 9 - Marani ... 139
Chapter 10 - Marani ... 154
Chapter 11 - Marani ... 166
Chapter 12 - Nuria ... 176
Chapter 13 - Nuria ... 188
Chapter 14 - Marani ... 200
Chapter 15 - Nuria ... 217
Chapter 16 - Marani ... 235
Chapter 17 - Nuria ... 244
Chapter 18 - Marani ... 251
Chapter 19 - Nuria ... 257
Epilogue ... 269

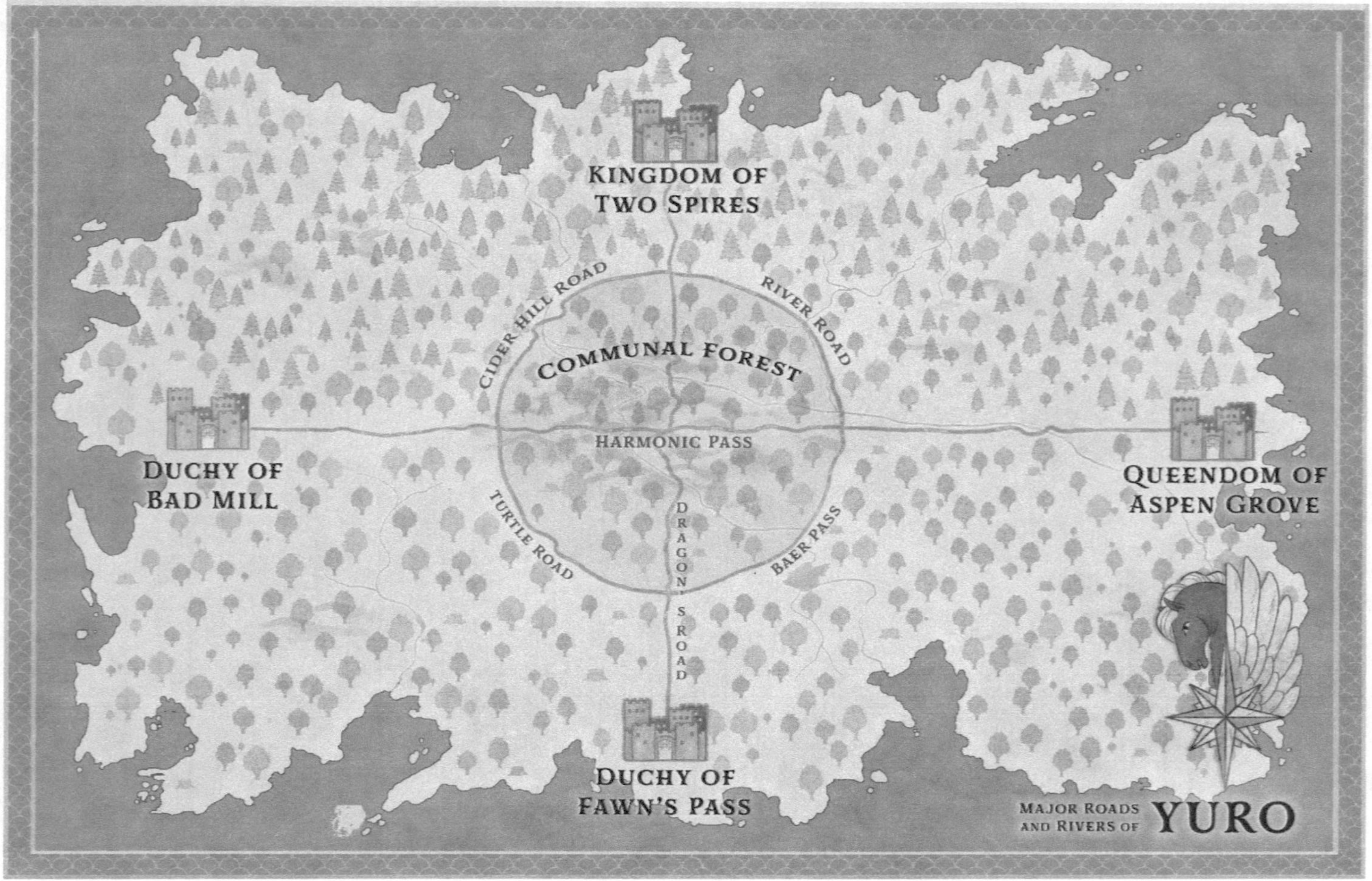

KINGDOM OF TWO SPIRES
DUCHY OF BAD MILL
QUEENDOM OF ASPEN GROVE
DUCHY OF FAWN'S PASS
COMMUNAL FOREST
CIDER HILL ROAD
RIVER ROAD
HARMONIC PASS
TURTLE ROAD
DRAGON'S ROAD
BAER PASS
MAJOR ROADS AND RIVERS OF YURO

Chapter 1 - Marani

A dragon is a creature of contradictions. Born in water, they mature in fire. Formed of feathers, they are made of scale and hide. They are an amalgamation of form, a confoundment of science, and are, arguably, the original settlers of our archipelago.

- A Political Protocol for Nonhuman Species, introduction

The air should have been freezing, so high above the forest, but Marani felt only the thrill of flight. She stretched as far out as her tiny frame would allow, the feathers on her kit-wings rippling in a rainbow of greens. They'd go brown, eventually she knew, like her mother's—eventually turn mostly to scale—but right now, *right now* she would delight in her feathers, and the brightness of an early morning sun, and that she was flying, *flying* for the first time in her life.

You're beautiful, little one. A beautiful little miracle.

Miracles shouldn't be cold. Had the sun gone behind a cloud? When had the sky turned silver? *Is it nighttime?*

Only for a little while.

That was a stupid answer, and the wind kept biting her, the gusts ripping off her soft hatchling feathers and abrading the still too-sensitive scaling underneath. Her fire, which had only just begun to kindle, snuffed from her belly—the absence as cold as hunter steel. It was the bald patch on her shoulder that hurt the most, and her mother still owed her an apology for removing a fresh scale-feather without asking first, especially before her first flight.

I want to go home. To the caves.

Her mother did not respond.

Marani brought her wings down, thinking to propel herself upward, to circle back to the safety of the nest that lay hidden deep underground, nestled next to the heart of a still-active volcano. Or perhaps they would head back across the ocean to her father's mountains, where humans were pets and occasionally, dinner. Perhaps, if she warmed and her fire breath returned, she'd be allowed to practice along the way, aiming at sailing ships that spread the human infection farther across the planet with each rise of the sun. Yuro—the small island she and her mother currently circled—had been the last place free of simian colonization. Now it was as dirty as the rest of the planetary islands, but still pretty, Marani thought, in its own way. There were cephel fruits to eat, and walnut trees to scratch your back against, and nettle tea, which tasted better than a thousand humans.

As she turned, her feathers flew and danced in the whipping wind, sheared off from whatever storm Marani had accidentally flown into. She pressed her wings down, down against the circling air, finally thinking she might gain height but...but when she looked down she...she had no wings.

She had no wings!

Where turquoise and lime feathers had danced against moss and olive, now there was...flesh. Hide. A sort of light, mud-colored, featherless pelt from which grew five useless worm-like shapes. *Fingers. Blech.*

Her flesh-bones scrabbled against the wind but without feathers, without wings, she fell. The only sound before had been her own delighted, childish roars, but now there was the horrible rushing of wind, the peal of her screams that sounded simian, *mammalian.* Gravity spun her tail over head but she had no tail, no, she had legs, like a bear, like a unicorn, like a monkey—featherless and meant for the ground.

The forest rushed toward her. Marani screamed for her mother using not snout but mouth, a sound that should have been "Errrrrrreeeecch!" but came out a strangled, high-pitched scream instead. The wind whipped her face, strangled her cries. She was going to die, impaled by a foreign forest she'd only just learned to crest.

Mother! Mom, help me!

"Marani? Marani love, wake up. You're having a nightmare."

The voice came at the same time that talons pierced Marani's shoulders. She screamed again, although her descent had stopped. Now it was only her blood that careened to the forest below.

"Marani! Wake up!"

Woosh woosh. Wooshwoosh. The sound of wingbeats. The sound of her heartbeats. The sound of her blood, pumping out of her, draining what warmth she'd managed to collect overnight. The sound of the flush rising thick in her head, preparing her to fight, to yell, to fall...

The ground came up, the tree canopy tickling Marani's new feet. She kicked at the branches in a futile waste of energy. The dragon—maybe—dipped them lower, lower, until its leathery, scale-less wings sheared the trees, severing the tops.

Not a dragon. That much she could tell. Dragon talons were sharp, yes, but also dexterous enough to hold a teacup. These claws held her as sloppily as a horse's mouth. Where was her mother!?

Beneath the treetops now, they shot down like a bird of prey. Marani saw reds of a sunset and a pool of her own blood on the ground and then, in the clearing just below, the unmistakable glint of unicorn horn. Worse than that, she saw the outstretched arms of a human woman, as if to welcome her to a life of the damned.

"Rawerrrrrrr!" The thing carrying her bellowed from deep in its belly as it released her. Marani fell again, descent broken by branches, cephel fruit, a horn raised to impale-

"Marani, step *out!*"

The flush broke.

The dream shattered.

Marani, still screaming, opened her eyes to gauzy sunlight and the very concerned face of Princess Nuria of Aspen Grove.

Her princess.

Her lover.

Her *human* lover. Because Marani was human or at least, partly human.

Right?

"Can you hear me, Marani?" Nuria's hand still gripped Marani's shoulder, right where the talons had dug in—horrible, hooked talons that shredded her newborn skin and dug at her soft bone...

Marani clapped a hand over her own mouth, though she could not stop the scream. The edges of the flush still held her even as the images of the dream bled away like watercolors in a rainstorm. She had fallen but she had not hit the ground. She never hit the ground. The dream always stopped right before unicorn horn skewered her chubby little human body, right before those horrid human hands grabbed her from the harpy claws...

"You're here with me," Nuria soothed when Marani finally stopped to breathe. Her face was a mess of saltwater. When Marani took her hand from her mouth there was moisture there, on her palm. She'd been screaming for minutes, if not longer. She'd be hoarse today. Again.

"Do you want to talk about it?" Nuria asked her, her voice coaxing.

Marani snarled in response. Not at Nuria, but at her overactive imagination.

"I see. That sort of morning, is it?" Nuria curled up next to Marani on the overly soft four poster bed and put a warm hand on Marani's bare belly. They were both naked because firstly, Marani had not tied herself to a solitary woman to not take advantage of the perks and two, she had a bad habit of shredding nightshirts while thrashing through her dreams.

Nuria continued with her low, soothing tones. "You're not falling. You're not flying. You're on a bed, in a stone castle, on the first floor. You are safe. Your brother Jacks is safe. Javad and Liu, everyone you care about, is safe."

"Safe," Marani managed to say as she sucked at the damp morning air, "is an abstract term when magic is involved."

Nuria kissed her forehead. "Are you sure it's a memory? These last weeks have been stressful. You've been buried alive, repeatedly stabbed, and lost your skin. Maybe this is just your mind trying to make sense of your...heritage."

"Through a recurring night terror?" Marani rubbed her eyes. "I hate it, whatever it is."

"What did you see? Anything different?"

"I saw. I saw..." She sat up and inspected both shoulders. Both showed only unblemished, unpunctured skin.

No, not skin. Scale. The dragonscale shone with a kindling fire, sparkling in greens and browns across the breadth of her body. Scales so sharp they tore the soft callouses of Nuria's fingertips, scarred Nuria's lips, and made palace silks impossible to keep in one piece.

Marani was a *dragon*. Partly transformed or not, that undeniable, horrifying fact was not sitting well.

"Oh gods," Marani groaned as she ground both her palms into her forehead. "I don't know how much more of this I can take. Dragon here. Dragon and human in the dream. I'm so damn tired."

"No one expected you to adapt in two days, lover. You've had longer breakdowns over break*ups*. Just...take your time. We'll work through this. We'll make sense of it. I promise."

Marani propped herself up on her elbows. The white cottons of the bed had scorched a brown silhouette of her body—a fun new effect when her temper, or a flush, flared. She was a kettle perpetually steaming with a pressure she dared not release.

"You're safe, Marani," Nuria continued to soothe.

But it was Nuria's previous sentence that glued itself to Marani's still sleepy mind. A caustic memory of Nuria's prophetic notebook—informed by her yearly soothsayer visits—flashed to the surface. Marani said, only half dangerous, "How many of my breakups have you witnessed personally?"

Pink tinted the tip of Nuria's nose. "You're deflecting. You're angry, but not at me."

"Ugh." Marani collapsed back onto the bed, trying to push the remains of the dream out with her exhale. "You're right. I'm sorry. I just...I thought I might have this sorted before you, we, left for Bad Mill. Your negotiations on Aspen Grove getting its own port and becoming a player in international trade would go a lot more smoothly if you came on dragonback. Bad Mill didn't have to negotiate before, because they were successfully breeding pegasi when no one else could. Now you have a *dragon*. Pegasi are irrelevant. Dragons you can ride *and* they can breathe fire. Plus." Marani winked at Nuria in an attempt to dredge up some of the charm that had worked on many a tavern girl. "Think of the chaos."

"Chaos is not how we get treaties signed, but I appreciate the visual. I'm sure arriving with you, regardless of transformative state, will have an...impact. Now if you could breathe *fire*..." Nuria took Marani's hands in hers and kissed the palms. A sharp edge of scale caught on her lip, drawing a bead of blood.

"Don't do that!" Marani hissed, but Nuria refused to let her pull her hands away. She stubbornly leaned in for another kiss, but Marani slipped out from hold, off the bed, and onto a blissfully heated stone floor. "Time to get up and seize the day. We're leaving for the Duchy of Bad Mill today, right? And you're going to lose a whole lip if you keep that up."

Nuria sat cross-legged on the bed, the pose exposing absolutely every inch of the princess. Heat rose inside Marani, but mercifully a blush would not show through scale. The hunger in her eyes she had no desire to hide. "If you think I'm going to let a little scale keep me from kissing you, Highwayman," Nuria said, "you are in for a big surprise."

The absolute royal confidence in Nuria's voice finally brought a smile to Marani's face. "Yes, Princess. Of course. Anything you say."

Nuria stuck out her tongue as she reached to the wardrobe and tossed a delicate seafoam-colored tunic at

Marani. "As you like, My Lord Dragon. The Queendom of Aspen Grove is at your service, although we would like to remind you that you have entered into a contractual agreement, and that it is dragons who do not break promises."

"None of the stiff dragon words, please. I hate it. Relics can all stay in the past." She watched while Nuria rummaged in the wardrobe for her own tunic, and only began her own dressing process once all chances of seeing Nuria's breasts had extinguished.

"To less acrophobic topics. Any word from Jacks?" Marani asked as they both proceeded to worm their way into lilypad-colored jerkins. Marani toyed with the neck of her tunic, the thick cotton hanging loose with the sudden thinness of her frame. They'd managed to leave so much back in Two Spires, but apparently coordinated clothing was an intra-island torture. That was likely why Queen Ndolo, Nuria's mother, was single.

Nuria brushed through the letters on her writing desk as they both entered the adjoining study, where their breakfast waited. "No. Plenty of others, however, from all over the island. We've already pushed back our trip to Bad Mill once, Grey," Nuria said, using Marani's highwayman name. "I don't think we can do it again. I don't know how we don't already have armies at our gates, especially with you being mostly scale and temper. Jacks is somewhere in the Common Forest. We're a day away, in Aspen Grove, and Bad Mill is another day to two days away, by horse. We have to proceed to Bad Mill without him."

Marani let out a long, long sigh that brought not just her breath, but a few orange embers, into her mouth. Not fire, just fire starter. She'd learned very quickly not to spit said embers onto the rugs. Unicorn pelt combusted faster than horsehair. "You couldn't spare half a day so I can go out looking for him?"

Nuria's hand fell, oh so delicately, onto Marani's shoulder. Mercifully, all Marani saw were seashell pink nails, and not killer talons. "He can take care of himself, love. No one knows that better than you."

"Maybe," Marani said as she slid away from Nuria while simultaneously grabbing a ball of rice and cramming it into her mouth. "But there is a big difference between invulnerability, and just the general concept of pain. For instance, laying down in a strawberry field might not kill him, but it will make him swell like a pufferfish and potentially render him unable to walk."

She grabbed another fistful of rice. Nuria shook her head. "We're not in your forest, Grey. Manners. Please."

Marani lifted her pinkie as she dropped the second rice ball into her mouth. "Whaf if he needfs me?" Jacks didn't need her, of course, not in the same way anymore. She'd spent most of her life caring for his hyper-sensitive skin and delicate stomach, just to find out that he too, was a dragon, and his sensitivities were barely skin deep. Underneath his human coverings, he was just as invulnerable as Marani was. She'd seen his yellow-green scaling herself only a few days ago. But all that knowledge couldn't erase a lifetime of worrying about her baby brother. Finding out they were both magical creatures in human skin wasn't going to change that. At least not overnight.

With exceedingly delicate fingers, Nuria picked up a sort of fancy leaf thing, tucked a small ball of rice in the middle along with a flower-shaped cut out of what Marani assumed was fish, wrapped the whole thing up, and took an impossibly dainty bite. "Do you still think he's at your old family plot? Even in two days, rumors will have spread. The sanctity of the Common Forest won't hold if there are *actual* dragons to be gawked at. Chances are good your homestead will be overrun now, with tourists and treasure hunters of all forms. If not now, then certainly in the next week. Do you really think he'd stay and...what? Play tour guide? You'd just stab them all. Jacks is more tempered."

"Tempered he may be, but we've got the same impulse control issues," Marani muttered. Jacks had not come back with Marani, Nuria, Javad, and Liu to Aspen Grove. Citing a need to 'just have a few days to sort this all out,' Marani had reluctantly agreed that he could meet them back at Nuria's palace before they all set out as one dysfunctional unit, to Bad Mill. It had taken them one whole day to traverse River Road and the East section of Harmonic Pass. Marani had spent the next two days eating every roasted game bird in sight and sleeping a solid fourteen hours a night—although said sleep was more tossing and screaming than rest.

Yesterday had been their agreed-upon day for Jacks to return. Bad Mill was expecting them late tomorrow, but for that to happen, they needed to leave in the next few hours. Nuria had sent a pega-letter advising their delay, but on the Jacks communication front, everything had been silent.

"Marani?" Nuria coaxed. "You're making that face."

"Am not." If Jacks was dead, surely Marani would know. If he had transformed, the entire island of Yuro would know. If he was tied up and being held captive by overeager royalty, or worse yet, too swollen to move because he'd slept on a horsehair mattress by mistake...

Nuria kissed her. Not as a light whisper this time, but forceful intent of lips on scale, delicately painted fingernails clinking across Marani's cheeks.

"Nuria, your skin—" Marani said, trying to step back. But the princess only pressed into Marani, driving the kiss for a breath-stealing moment.

The heat of the flush rose in Marani's cheeks, her scale warming enough that it steamed in the chill morning air. "Nuria—"

Nuria pulled back long enough to cock her hip and say, "You talk *so much* for a dragon. Please shut up."

Well then. Who was she to disobey a command from royalty?

Marani, conscious now of the rice-paper thinness of human skin, drove Nuria against the wall with hips and shoulders. It was only after she had the princess pinned that Marani slipped her tongue into Nuria's mouth, enjoying the softness while her hand, very delicately, cupped one of Nuria's breasts.

"Mmm," Nuria breathed as her hips rose against Marani. "Better."

"Something something about living to serve or whatever dragons are supposed to say to future queens." Marani dipped her head lower, moving her kisses to Nuria's throat. Her hand she refused to move, instead turning her touch to a feather tease across Nuria's nipple. "We haven't packed yet," Marani said as her kisses trailed lower, to the thin silk of Nuria's neckline, then down across her collarbone.

"Dragon," Nuria gasped as Marani's hand moved south, settling on the princess' hip, and her mouth returned to her favorite position over Nuria's breast. "I thought I tired you out last night."

"Don't starf somfing you canf finish." There'd been a time in Marani's life where an evening with a woman meant a night of deep sleep, and a cheerful morning. The past three days—every moment since the dragonscale comb had broken apart and unbound the magic of her body—Marani had found no method to contain her restlessness. The power inside her churned like a combustion engine without exhaust. Small things that had once mattered – the fall of her close-cropped grey hair, the intricate timeshare of highway robberies—had dulled to a nightfly buzz. In their place was the sharpness of desire, not just of Nuria, but of food, and movement, and *freedom*.

Breasts were, of course, also still very high on her priority list.

"Hey!" Nuria playfully batted at Marani's head. "No nipping sensitive areas unless we're in bed. We don't have time for me to change undergarments."

"It's unfair that you ever have to wear clothes," Marani grumbled. She stole a final kiss then stepped back to the breakfast table, enjoying Nuria's struggle to push a princessly veneer over her stuttering breath.

"Yes, well. I do have obligations." Nuria smoothed down the front of her tunic, frowning at the indents left from her pert nipples. "No more of that until we are alone again, please. It takes them forever to settle down."

Marani smirked as she ate another rice thing. "You started it."

Nuria snapped her fingers. "Dragon. Focus."

"I *was* focused." When Nuria's smile began to sour, Marani pivoted. "To the Jacks issue. Our family plot may be small, but the Central Forest isn't. There's kilometers of cave systems. There's an entrance right near where my parent's—" Marani nearly choked on both the word, and a grain of rice that had lodged in her throat. Nuria handed her a tall glass of pettian juice, which Marani drank without bothering to savor. "Where our family lean-to used to be. I'd bet you a unicorn he's down there, looking for his key. I can get lost in an orchard, but I've never lost Jacks. I can find him and be back here before you leave. At worst, I can catch up to you on the road." Marani probably should have been more concerned about Hans, and her bandits, and their unrealistic aspirations of pegasus and commerce dominance. With four monarchies about to combust, an exasperating but utterly enchanting princess in her bed, and a pending evolution of her body, Marani could not summon any extra mental space for whiny bandits.

"And you expect to find him how?" Nuria offered her another expertly wrapped rice-meat-leaf thing. Marani ate it all in one bite, knowing from experience that trying to nibble it would only result in jettisoning rice. "Sibling bond? And what if you transform on the way and dragon ravage a town or," her voice turned mildly dangerous, "the women of the town."

Marani pulled Nuria close, clasping her hands around Nuria's waist and whispering conspiratorially, "I have my own princess."

"Mmm. Starting something again? Can we please remember my panties?" Nuria's hands stroked Marani's arms once, twice, almost established a rhythm that could lead to a more horizontal position, before Nuria's touches turned to tickles.

"Not fair!" Marani yelled. She pushed Nuria away and scuttled back to toward the bedchamber. "You're taking advantage of new scale sensitivity." Marani let a wide shoulder of her shift slouch down, showing a breadth of shimmering brown and green scale. The little oval-shaped things—more the size and shape of a fingernail than what she'd seen pass for real dragonscale—sat flat in one direction when stroked, and raised like woodgrain in the other. Lift the scales up high enough from, say, an overeager tongue of a curious pegasus, and underneath were sharp, dagger-shaped scales that pricked Marani's fingers to bleed.

But a light touch—oh, that sent trembles through her. The sensation wasn't tickling in the strictest sense, but it did make her squirm and squeal in ways that were deeply inappropriate to a highwayman. Or former highwayman now reformed consort of the princess of Aspen Grove.

Marani, staying out of princess reach, said, "Why not come with me? If we leave after breakfast, it's just a small detour and we can circle back to Bad Mill after we visit the Communal Forest. I'm not sure I've ever seen a politik that couldn't wait until morning."

"You're not at all concerned about the poisoning of the Two Spires king, Princess Oksana's coup attempt and any potential living sympathizers, your unsupervised bandits, and that this *entire island* is now aware that at least two dragons still live? Time is very much an issue, especially when people stop drowning in disbelief and decide they need to come see the dragons themselves. We are working with a very narrow window of maneuverability."

"Okayyy," Marani drawled. It wasn't that she had forgotten about any of that, but rather that *she was a dragon*, and that whole concept was taking up significant portions of her mind. "But we'd be a lot harder to find in a forest."

Nuria shook her head. "You're impossible and—" She'd been toying with the stack of still unopened letters while they talked. The wax seal had come undone from the top letter but the stamp was undamaged—an imprint of a pegasus feather.

"Oh." Nuria brought the letter close to her face and read, fingers so tight to the paper that it crinkled, threatening to tear.

Joviality bled from the bedchamber.

"Nuria?"

"Mother...she sent for the soothsayer. My soothsayer. The royal soothsayer. She is set to arrive today, before lunch." Nuria looked at Marani and reached out, slowly, for Marani's shoulder. "I have so many questions," she said softly. "Surely you do, too?"

Marani's insides twisted. Tiny red sparks bled from the space between her scales. Corresponding lines of smoke twirled from inside Marani's seafoam tunic. Marani had *plenty* of questions for the mysterious woman who had gifted Princess Nuria yearly visions of Marani's life, starting with where the soothsayer's magic had come from, and followed quickly by what her business was snooping around Marani's private life. She was certain there would be yelling involved in the meeting, and, if Marani could push the transformation just a little further, fire.

"That's three tasks for the same time frame," Marani said as she forced herself to calm down. She still shed sparks, but these skated down her scales like rain, scarring the stone instead of the cottons she wore.

"I've managed worse. Settle, love. No need to burn down the castle over a soothsayer and her borrowed magic." It was a delight the way Nuria pressed her fingertips down as she stroked Marani's scales, treating each with the same ministrations she'd recently used on a very different part of Marani's anatomy. "It's your choice. I'd never force you. If the queen sent for the soothsayer, then I have to stay to see her. Take the opportunity to go find Jacks, if you want. Or stay and get a question answered, too."

"Jacks is my priority. The soothsayer can wait." Marani closed her eyes and let her head lean back against the wall.

"You wouldn't be afraid, would you? My brave bandit?"

Marani snorted but did not open her eyes. "I said nothing about being afraid. It's just that the soothsayer is…I mean…" Her left eye popped open. "You didn't have to stop. I'm not trying to be difficult."

Nuria's face held concern, not irritation. Her fingers had come away and she held her right hand to the window, the streaming sunlight casting rainbows from a silk-thin, pearlescent scale. "From your shoulder where the tunic dips," Nuria breathed. "More beautiful than your comb, even."

Marani couldn't muster anything more than thinly veiled disgust. "Am I supposed to shed?" She saw no gap in the scale of her shoulder to indicate injury. Queen Ndolo had asked at least six times if she might be able to buy shed scales off of Marani, although for the first time in her life she did not need money.

"Uh huh," Nuria said in a tone that suggested she had in fact not heard a word Marani had spoken. The princess ran her thumb—firmly—across Marani's jawline. At the tip of her chin Nuria brought a second finger up and very, very lightly, pinched the scaling.

Marani felt no pain, not even a real tug. But in Nuria's palm, held out for her to see, were six more scales, half old and thin, the others thick and shining with inner fire.

"So I'm molting? Like a pegasus? Is that normal?" Marani could help the hitch that snuck into her voice. She'd been half-dragon for *two days*. The Island of Yuro was maybe on the brink of pegasus war, her brother was missing, she'd not gotten to properly touch her princess this morning, there was a looming soothsayer visit, and now her skin was coming off. *Again.*

"Hush. We can sort it out." Nuria dumped the scales onto the breakfast table, on a plate of half-eaten rice, opened a small, hidden drawer under the table and retrieved a hand mirror. "If you were molting, there'd be skin underneath, right? That's not what I'm seeing."

After a few experimental tilts of her chin and the mirror, Marani finally caught enough sunlight to inspect what should have been her first dragon bald patch. What she saw instead was...what? Bone, maybe, if bone could be brown. She touched her own finger to her chin and felt the same striations that had been a part of her dragonscale comb—the same striations that she'd felt on every dragonscale she'd ever touched. But this chin scale was huge, comparatively. Marani saw no edges, just a plate, more or less, that seemed to run endlessly under her smaller, more flexible surface scale.

"Does it hurt?" Nuria asked. "Do you want some oil for it? Shall I get a, a brush or a towel and remove the other loose ones?"

"No." Marani ran experimental hands up her arms, tugging at the wiry musculature. She grabbed at the nape of her neck, massaging scale and bone. Then she bent over, rubbing her thighs, calves, and still bare feet. Thumbnail-sized scales flaked off as she went, leaving a narrow circle of glittering green and brown on the stone floor. The thick underscale that remained pulsed with a pleasant heat that did not reach Marani's insides. She shivered.

"Maran—"

Marani put a finger to Nuria's lips as she ran her tongue over her teeth. They were flat and very human, at least for now. But there was a molar at the back that, yes, if she pushed, wiggled ever so slightly. The same happened with a front bottom tooth, and an upper molar.

"What's wrong? What's wrong with your teeth? You're making a strange face."

Marani remembered how impossible it was to ignore wiggly teeth as a child. Wiggly scale was going to be a nightmare. "Another issue has just unfolded."

"Explain, please, Grey. I'm not good at parsing cryptic dragon."

Marani decided against making a comment about Nuria's familiarity with cryptic soothsayers. "Do you remember losing your milk teeth?"

"Of course."

Marani lifted up the edge of scaling that ran along her chin, where the small scale met the newly revealed plating. She pinched a line of scaling there and tugged, ripping them from their matrix.

It should have felt like pulling teeth. Instead, she felt more of the twinge of a hair-pull—a desperate moment of stretching before a quick burst apart. The pulled scales she placed with the others—might as well collect on Ndolo's offer—and then turned her chin to Nuria.

"It's still just the same brown scale," Nuria said, her fingertips soft yet still near bruising on the scale that had not yet been ready to be uncovered. "Just warmer. Are you suggesting this scale—"

Marani sucked in a thick breath of the humid morning air. "Our timelines may have to change." She slid a finger under the fine scale that circled her elbow and flicked four scales loose in quick succession. Though they were a monarchy away from the old grandfather clock of Two Spires, Marani swore she could hear the *tik tok tik tok* in her head. "This layover is coming to an end. And as much as we joke about me escorting you to Bad Mill in dragon form, I don't know if that is the best idea. I don't know if being in any sort of building is a good idea, at least not over the next few days."

Her words sounded flippant, which was not by design. Nuria's brow furrowed anyway. "No, I...I agree. Bad Mill isn't where you should be, when it happens. The balance of power is already in their favor, with their success in pegasi breeding. They have Yuro's only functional port. If they have the only dragon, we have nothing to negotiate with. Eastgate, Two Spires, and Aspen Grove might as well hand over their monarchies and get it over with."

"Agreed, but your negotiations with Bad Mill can't wait." Marani sank into one of Nuria's gilded fainting couches, her loose scales catching on an embroidered pillow and snapping stitches. "Right?"

Nuria stroked the loose scale on Marani's cheek. "Your logic is sound, but I would never command you to the forest, Marani. I will not command dragons, regardless of history."

"That's sweet, but it doesn't make being apart from you hurt any less."

"I know."

In Nuria's unspoken words, Marani heard the real argument. Not about the power balance of the island, but that Marani-the-mostly-human was (sort of) an asset, especially in the personal protection arena, but Marani-the-dragon would be nothing but deadly distraction. That the negotiations with Bad Mill, the legacy of Two Spires, those were delicate matters, and Marani was not a delicate *person,* so there was no way she would be a delicate dragon, and that setting fire to Bad Mill's port, or Bad Mill itself, was not a good way to start, or end, negotiations.

Despite the kissing, and fucking, and sweet words, they both knew Marani belonged in the forest, with bandits and feral horses, or in the sky, with the pegasi. She was in a princess' bedroom on a technicality of attraction, on a malfunction of love, and the fever dream of their romance was about to fall away as easily as Marani's dragonscale.

A maid knocked on the door and asked about the breakfast trays. Nuria went to the door and spoke to her—words muffled—then returned soundlessly to the couch.

They sat in silence for long moments, Nuria staring at Marani and Marani staring at the trail of her scales across the floor. When the cushion under Marani turned from wafting smoke to actively aflame, she stood, doused the couch in the remaining pettian juice, and said, "I'll go get Jacks and if I'm still...like this, after I find him, we will meet you in Bad Mill. With luck, I might even be able to find him and meet you back here before you leave, especially if your soothsayer visit runs long. Jacks can't be that hard to find. He is a dragon, after all. And if I go dragon along the way, well, you'll still have Jacks. He's a constant reminder of my humanity."

Nuria's brows knit together in her "are you sure?" look. Marani loved her even more, in that moment, for giving the space for this to be Marani's decision, not royal dictate.

Two more scales fell from her cheek and landed on Nuria's lap. Her tongue pushed on a back molar and this time it came clean off, a dagger-sharp tooth just emerging beneath. Marani turned and spit the tooth into her hand.

"Grey, was that a—"

"Scale? Yes. Hey. Um." It was time to exit the bedroom. If teeth were falling out, Marani had hours, not days, left in her body, and there was no way Nuria would leave for Bad Mill once Marani sprouted wings. "If you miss me maybe spend time thinking about how a dragon can drive negotiation tactics. I'm not opposed to eating your enemies. Or uh, if you have any fantasies you've been working on that involve a dragon in the bedroom. Really, that one we're going to have to spend some time with because I have more questions about dragon-human relations than I do about dragon-horse relations."

"Marani!"

Marani was already at the bedroom door, her mind as hot as her footsteps burning the stone in their wake. Prophecy had brought them together, and love should have kept them that way, but the magic of Yuro clearly had other plans and a very fast timeframe. Transforming into a dragon in your lover's bedroom was also a very bad look.

"I've made my decision, you've agreed, and it's time to execute. No time for mushy goodbyes. You'll unravel us both." Marani blew a kiss. Nuria's hands curled into the sides of her tunic, but Marani caught the tremble to her lip as well. "Princess," Marani said, softening her voice as she stepped out into the hall. "I'll find you in a few days, one way or the other. I have...not a lot of time left. Maybe hours. Maybe days. All I know, all I feel, is that this process, this unravelling of magic, it won't stop. Aspen Grove needs a trade treaty for your commerce stuff, and I need my brother. Because sooner, not later, Yuro is going to have a dragon again. I don't think either one of us have given any real thought to what that's going to mean, or how, exactly, we're going to contain it."

Chapter 2 - Marani

What effect has the human population had on magic? The most notable can be seen in the wild pegasus. Parented by both dragon and horse, the original human settlers to Yuro brought draft horses to help till the land. These were left alone. It was only when the affluent came with their show-quality Hackneys and Sorraias that the dragons found a new appetite.

- A Political Protocol for Nonhuman Species, Chapter 1: Colonization of Feral Forests

"Glad you still have your hatchet, but you look like shit. When you've got this sorted, you're coming back to the castle, right?" A very well-fed, well-dressed Javad dogged Marani's heels as she secured saddlebags and weapon holsters to her royal pony—a hunter who'd been bred for wild game sport—and who was still too high off the ground for general comfort.

"I'm a fucking dragon, Javad. The situation isn't reversible."

The short, balding man shot back, "And you're avoiding the question."

Marani hooked her left foot into the stirrup and paused, internally screaming at herself that she was invulnerable, and a dragon, and being scared of heights was embarrassing and juvenile. "I don't know," she muttered, both to the horse and Javad.

Javad stroked the dagger on his hip, his eyes squarely on Marani. "Well, I want to return, so you have to. Got it?"

"I didn't invite you along." Marani sucked up the courage to mount. The well-bred palace horse did not backstep, which almost helped. Once seated, she swallowed nausea long enough to glare back down at Javad. "We are not glued together. Your position at the castle is secure. You don't need me."

"Oh, I'm sorry. I didn't hear you over the memory of you needing a fucking rescue all of three days ago. Dragons flock, Grey. I'm as infected with Yuro magic as you are. You're not going to transform alone in the woods somewhere. Stop being a half-breed horse ass."

"I'm not. That's why I'm going to find Jacks." Marani turned her horse toward the highway. "Stay here with Liu. Or join Nuria's escort to Bad Mill. I'll be fine."

Javad snarled. He pulled a tiny dagger from his boot and launched it at Marani's head. It flew close enough to tickle her scale before turning forty-five degrees in midair, then embedding in one of Princess Nuria's carefully planted rosewood saplings. "I'd better not be this scale-headed when I transform. Assuming I do. I have to, right? This magic in me is the same as yours."

Marani gave him her best "I'm too busy to be bothered with your nattering," look.

"Fine. Focus on the now. Our guild still patrols the highways. They took a shot at you before, Grey. Don't forget who helped pull you from that ditch."

"Or who helped put me into it?" Marani looked back over her shoulder at her most trying, and most loyal, bandit underling. He was a junior member of the Aspen Grove knighthood now, whatever that meant, which was no doubt a reward for his help in taking down Princess Oksana's plotting during the Two Spires Harvest Ball. Javad did not share Marani and Jacks' skin issues, but his aim with knives, swords, arrows, and rocks was unexplainable except by magic. The dragons of Yuro had gone extinct, or gone into hiding, over a generation ago, but magic called to magic. Or so Marani rationalized when she wanted to keep her fist from Javad's face. Would Javad get a transformation? She had no idea. He'd need a key, certainly, and right now Jacks was the priority. "Do you *want* to come?"

"Don't sound so incredulous. I'm not going to leave this job no matter what bullshit you pull. My wife loves it here and has bonded over pastries with Liu. But, you know," he toyed with the bland-looking dagger at his hip. "You carry a hatchet, not a sword. Your body is a shield but your mouth is a liability. You need help. Jacks needs help. If the forest calls, Grey, I will answer, too." He pursed his lips, then added, "Is the forest calling you, Grey? Because I...I think it might be calling me."

Shit. "Do you hear a clock?" she asked. "Drawn to any glittering caves? Find an old trinket that you just can't put down?"

Javad shook his head. "No. But mornings taste like green leaves and honeydew. I fucking hate vegetables, too. Nights I dream of waterfalls and soft dirt." He wiped at his nose. "You started something, Grey. You awoke something, and it won't be put down. I'm not drawn to stupid shit. I'm drawn to you. Not in a creepy way."

"Yeah, I get it." If she was having flashbacks, it was a solid bet Javad was, too. And so she said, deeply against her better judgement, "I'll wait if you want to grab a horse and join me."

"Ten minutes," Javad said with what could not possibly have been a deferential head nod, and disappeared back toward the stables.

"If anything calls to you, like a comb, or a knife, or a butter plate, bring it along. No matter how silly," Marani whispered after him. That was the game at this stage, finding all their keys. Hers had been a dragonscale comb she'd thought belonged to her mother, but which had likely been made from one of her own scales. Breaking it had broken the spell that kept Marani in human form. Jacks was probably looking for his own key now. He'd always hated being a step behind Marani, even as a toddler chasing after her on unsteady legs as Marani ran the trails of the Communal Forest, foraging for enough food to keep them alive another day.

That there was magic was inside Javad, Marani had no doubt, but there was magic in soothsayers too, and probably a hundred other ways the Island of Yuro could infest its inhabitants. Marani was certain she'd seen Javad bleed before, but all three instances had been due to her stabbing him to make a point. If he was having dreams like her...they weren't about falling. What did a man with perfect aim dream about? Missing a target? Not going hungry, surely. Javad might not have always had access to a budding pastry chef and a castle of butter, but unnatural marksmanship meant he'd have always had a pheasant or rabbit or feral horse on hand to cook up. Dreaming about waterfalls and fruit made as little sense as her scale-skin.

"Ugh," Marani said. "Horse flesh. May none of us ever have to eat that again."

Because the island of Yuro clearly hated her, a pegasus whinnied overhead.

"No," Marani said without bothering to look up. "Absolutely not. No thank you. Go away."

Another whinny.

Marani scowled up at the sky and an absolutely enormous pegasus flipped over and started flying upside down in obvious amusement. Pink and orange wings flapped lazily in the late morning sun, and matching tangerine scaling covered the draft-sized horse from ear to ankle—whereupon the scales gave way to yet more feather.

"Grrrr." Marani bared her teeth.

The pegasus roared. The lips of her rounded snout pulled back, showing far, far too many pointed teeth.

"Just bite my head off and be done with it," Marani growled.

The pegasus, acting like it understood her words, sank slowly, slowly down, back hooves lower, front hooves up, until Marani could have reached out and slapped the golden things away. "I get it!" she yelled as her pony tried to rear. "You're powerful. You're curious. You're not going away. Just...go *up*."

The pegasus did one more pull back of her lips and then shot straight up into the air, far faster than any animal should have been able to.

"What was that about?" Javad asked as he cantered over to her, his quarter horse a midnight blue with silver scaling down the left side legs. A stunningly beautiful horse by all standards. Marani elected to not ask him if it was borrowed with permission.

"Pegasus antics." Marani waved her hand. "You know how they are."

"Not like that," Javad said. "I've never been within throwing distance of a wild one, and that thing up there flew close enough to taunt you." He smirked, slow and smug. "Maybe she's saying it's time for you to take to the skies, too."

"Someday, I may grow wings. Someday, I may breathe fire. Someday I might be a dragon the size of Aspen Grove castle. But *never* will I fly."

"You'll be a piss poor dragon then, won't you?"

"Thank you so much for the reminder of why I planned on traveling alone. We're going back to the preserve, and we're going to be quick about it. The goal is to find Jacks, then get our butts to Bad Mill. The less you talk during all this, the better."

Javad nodded, but his smirk remained as they led their horses away from the Aspen Grove courtyard, through the town, and back onto the roads they'd once controlled.

* * *

Potholes dotted the once immaculate Harmonic Pass, but both Javad's horse and Marani's pony were too well trained to complain about the inefficient path. When Marani had led the highway guild, she'd used a bit of their stolen coin to repair the roads, because no one was going to court bandits if they were also likely to lose a wheel. It had been a community service, really, as the bandits had only stolen from carriages and royalty, not commoners on foot and horseback. Marani had standards.

Hans, the man she'd left in charge, who had violently usurped her leadership, shot her and Jacks, and had both of them buried alive in a deep ditch right off the highway, clearly cared little for the careful balance of economics and banditry. Maybe it wouldn't matter, once pegasi travel became a feasible reality. But that was a decade off, hopefully, and right now, *right now,* although they'd not been attacked yet—the roads just looked like shit.

Three hours into their travel and the only sounds that had broken the silence were the beating of distant pegasi wings, and the occasional *clink* of a scale falling from Marani's body as she shivered, despite the newfound heat inside her, in the morning's autumn breeze. Javad took note, Marani noticed, every time one fell, but kept his mouth shut.

It was Marani who spoke, finally, right as the sun hit its zenith and her scale, sending sweat to bead across her forehead. This attracted the ever-present forest nightflies. She swatted and craned her neck, trying to squash as many of the irritating black insects as she could, and inadvertently looked skyward. The pegasus from the castle continued to nicker and fly in lazy arcs just above the tree line, her body movements as coiled and fluid as a snake. As a matter of fear and principle, Marani hated horses and pegasi, and found herself wondering if horse flesh would taste better as a dragon. Her entire role on the island could be containing the feral horse and pegasi population.

Javad grunted a question at her.

"You forget, don't you, how horrible these things are," Marani said as she again smacked at her neck. There was no need—the nightflies couldn't puncture her skin if they wanted to—but their buzzing was grating and they always seemed to find ways into the corners of her eyes.

"They flock to you like ants to honey." Javad brought his horse up next to hers and held out a very hairy, bare arm, upon which not a single nightfly rested or swarmed. "I've never had an issue with them."

"Shut up," Marani said, although her words had no bite to them.

"No. And as long as we are discussing swarms, what does your skybound friend want?"

"To irritate me?"

Javad nudged his horse to the front, then turned it so the horse blocked the road. "You used to make me shoot arrows through pegasus wings when they got too close to your forest plot so they wouldn't take off the heads of any of your thieves. Two years ago, I watched you charge one along the drainage ditch of Baer's Pass because you thought it would scare away the carriages. You almost leapt onto the thing's back. Now you're mostly a dragon, and you're afraid of what? The pony dancing above us? That's as irrational as your fear of heights."

"And you nearly vomited the first time you saw a unicorn pelt and scream at the sight of butterflies," Marani shot back.

"Grey." Javad clucked his tongue like a disappointed parent. "If you can't face this reality, how are Jacks and I supposed to? You've led us for years. You've led Jacks his entire life. If you crumble like one of Liu's butter pastries now, what hope is there for the rest of us?"

With a long, labored groan, Marani leaned back in the saddle and let her head fall back. Her sunset-colored palace friend had been joined by...it looked like six or seven other pegasi of similar sizes. They flew in sort of wing-shaped formation, where the leader would somersault in long backward loops until it made it to the end of the line—the leaf 'stem.' Then another pegasus would push forward, carry the group for a few heartbeats, then repeat.

"It feels like they're playing a game with me," Marani said to the sky. "I don't like games. And I don't..." she struggled over the words. "I find pegasi disconcerting. Not because of the flight, but because it originally took a dragon and a horse to make them. It took *humans* to make them, and our colonization of Yuro. This island was the last refuge of magic and instead of leaving it be, we not only colonized it, we *bred* it. Pegasi are a constant reminder of how much humanity messed up this island and that reminder makes my stomach flip more than the things above us."

"Is it that, or do you just not want to have sex with a horse? I don't think anyone can make you, regardless. Let's find out." Javad stuck a finger and a thumb in his mouth and whistled.

"Don't do that!" Marani pulled a hatchet from her saddle bag. "I will cut your fingers off."

Javad pointed upward. "Look."

The entire constellation of pegasi now floated on the air currents, hovering just above Marani and Javad. Some fourteen pairs of beady eyes stared at Marani, and hundreds of pointed, bared teeth glinted the waning sunlight. Marani's tongue went to her back molars, where her new tooth was now halfway erupted from the gum. It was a fat, pointed thing, meant for tearing flesh from bone. And it was identical to every pegasus tooth she currently saw.

"Go away," Marani hissed. A front tooth was also loose, so Marani yanked it from her mouth and bared her fresh nub of white at the pegasi. "I'm not in the mood."

The sunset pegasus nickered, and it almost sounded like laughter.

"That settles it. They're definitely going to eat us." Marani unsheathed her hatchet and touched it to Javad's dagger. "Can you hit one from here? Maybe that will discourage the rest."

"I'm not going to kill a full-bred pegasus, Grey, and neither are you. I've never shot one, no matter how you've screamed at me. I've told you a thousand times they're harmless, at least to us. Not a single one of your bandits has ever been accosted by a pegasus. They may kill travelers on the roads, but they respect the Common Forest as much as the royalty used to. For fuck's sake, Grey, I fed a pegasus colt from my hand when I was barely thirteen. They've had endless chances to eat us. They eat raw meat, too, and you're smoking like a brisket. Why would they wait until you're even more inedible than normal?"

Marani, having no good retort for Javad's frustratingly sound logic, opted to keep her mouth shut.

Javad brought his horse back in line with Marani's and pointed west. "Look. They're landing."

Half a kilometer down the Harmonic Pass road the constellation landed and promptly started to graze. Only one kept her head up, eyes on Marani—the sunset one, from the courtyard.

"They're blocking our path," said Javad. "They want something."

"Me," Marani said with an exhaustive sigh. "Stay here. If I die, you still have to find Jacks and then go help Princess Nuria."

"You are the most dramatic bandit kingpin I've ever met."

"You're afraid of *butterflies*," Marani snapped back. She nudged her pony forward, patting its neck and silently thanking the castle staff for whatever pegasus-training they'd given the little mare. Ponies were frequent food for wild pegasi, which had always made finding a suitable mount for Marani nearly impossible.

Click clock. Marani's pony cantered down the broken brick road. Every pegasus head shot up from the tall grass. Beady, serpentine eyes focused only on her.

Marani refused to turn back, especially since Javad was watching. *Click clock. Click clock.* She was close enough to throw her hatchet and hit one of the pegasi, if she'd wanted to. If Marani hadn't been grossly outnumbered, she'd have considered it.

Sunset stepped directly onto the road in front of Marani, and took three wing-assisted hops in Marani's direction.

Marani tugged her pony's reins, bringing them to a stop. She was a horse-length away from Sunset—close enough to confirm that Sunset was a mare, and heavily pregnant.

"It's not mine," Marani said flippantly. "I don't have any business with pegasi. Please leave the road. I'm here looking for my brother, not trouble."

Sunset tossed her head, tangerine forelock curling in the air like steam from hot butter. The bulge in her belly rippled.

Had she...offended the pegasus? Marani didn't care for basic human-to-human etiquette. Pegasus formality would never happen. "I'm not a dragon yet. Not all the way. If there are formalities here, I don't know them. I'm sorry. Please move. I'm on a timescale."

Sunset nickered. Her ear flicked west.

"I don't speak horse!"

This time Sunset pawed the ground with her two front feet.

Marani was done. She held up her axe and shook it like cow bell. "I appreciate that you're frustrated, but I need to find my brother and I need to find him quickly. You are in my way so unless you know where the other human-dragon is lurking, fly away!"

Sunset charged.

Marani's once well-behaved pony, reared. Marani lost her hatchet to keep hold of the reins but her pony stayed on hind feet, kicking the front ones at the oncoming Sunset. "Settle!" Marani yelled at her mount. But Sunset was easily four times the size of the hunter pony. The pegasus reared as well and boxed Marani's pony in the head, the force sending them both to the ground and Marani into an inconveniently placed blackberry bramble.

Sunset pawed at the bramble, still horrifically balanced on her back feet, wings beating the air for balance.

"Cut it out!" Marani yelled. She clawed her way up from the bramble, thorns ripping her surface scale away in hand-sized pieces. Her hatchet was underneath her leg, tearing pant but not scale, and she promptly got it reattached to a holster on her back. Her pony got back on its feet, head shaking from side to side, and retreated to the safety of Javad and his much larger horse. Which left just Marani and Sunset, and Javad's smug grin.

Marani tried to step back onto the road, but another ream of blackberry snagged in her pants and she fell to her rear. "Damn pegasi!" she yelled. "Damn blackberries and damn dragons!"

Before Marani could take her hatchet to the blackberries, Sunset settled to all fours, flicked her left ear, then leaned down, chomping blackberry in giant mouthfuls. Marani nearly screamed as Sunset's head came at her ankle, but the mare's teeth grabbed only at branches and thorns. Sunset was fast, her teeth efficient, and in four mouthfuls she'd cleared the blackberry still holding Marani down.

"It wants to be friends!" Javad yelled.

"I don't have friends," Marani huffed as she stood back up and gave her forest-green, gold embroidered traveling cloak a pull to free it. The cloak had been a gift from Nuria that no amount of "Is this really practical for traveling" could dissuade. It was pretty, with the little golden aspen leaves embroidered across the back in tight rosettes, and marginally warm, but Marani's flush-adjacent, newfound body heat had already charred tiny holes through the fabric, and the blackberry had shredded the hem.

Sunset grabbed the decorative hood in her teeth and pulled up until Marani's toes lifted off the ground. Frustratingly, the burnt, torn fabric did not rip apart. Instead, the dragon claw shaped clasps ground into Marani's neck.

"Just because I don't strictly need to breathe doesn't mean I don't enjoy it!" Marani wheezed. She twisted, further wrapping her throat, and kicked at the pegasus' throat. Sunset growled and shook her again, like a cat with a particularly feisty mouse.

Javad's dagger whizzed past Marani's ear. It buried itself in a tree trunk a meter or so from Sunset, so he'd either been trying to distract the pegasus, or he'd missed. But Javad never missed. It had been the reason Marani had recruited him for her forest bandits to begin with.

"This one is feisty," Marani heard Javad mutter as she fumbled for the cloak clasps.

"Kill it please!" she croaked. The six remaining pegasi moved to the road and whinnied in unison. Loudly.

"Javad!"

Javad frowned. He threw another knife, this one dead square with Sunset's mouth. But the blade skewered down, left, slicing instead Marani's hood from her cloak. She fell back to the blackberry and Sunset reared, then took back to the sky in a great *woosh woosh* of creamsicle and strawberry nuisance. The other pegasi followed.

"Asshole!" Marani yelled at the sky, and the nickering ring of pegasi that still circled them.

Marani rubbed her throat as she kicked at torn and crushed blackberry branches. "The literal moment I become a dragon I am going to eat one of them. Starting with Sunset up there. I—" The thick leather heel of Marani's Aspen Grove issued-boots *thunked* as she fought against a particularly persistent bramble. She kicked again, the same hollow, iron sound returning.

"You going to pull yourself out or do I have to drag you?" Javad asked as he stomped over to her. "The pegasi are staying high. Guessing they're done with their games for now and a dragon caught in blackberry is more pathetic than a highwayman choosing a princess over robbing a castle. I say that with respect, Grey, but also I think you're about as intelligent as those pegasi up there." He offered her one of his thick, gnarl-knuckled hands. "Fierce predator my ass. Did you ever consider—"

"There's a tunnel in the blackberry."

"Huh?" Javad paused his rambling long enough to follow Marani's line of sight. An iron circle sat firmly atop a clay mound. Marani's first kicks had sent the lid a quarter of the way off. The smells that came up from the exposed tunnel were earthy—mold, decay, and damp.

"It smells like cave." Marani got to her knees and shoved at the iron. "Help me."

"You're sure it's not a sewage cover?" Javad fanned the air. "It smells like one. Know what the stamp means?"

"We're an hour from the Common Forest boundary. Monarchy drainage systems don't move into the island, they move to the sea. Their covers are all stamped, too. Probably so they know whose taxes have to cover maintenance."

"Yeah, but we know the four crests of the monarchies. That emblem is a...a cow. No cows on Yuro. We use horse meat, horse milk, and horse leather for everything."

"I care more about what's behind the cover. Shut up and help me push."

Javad dutifully got down and added his own weight to hers. In his defense, "sewer" would have been her go-to thought as well if she and Jacks hadn't spent most of their formative years living in the entrance to a cave system. They'd never explored too deeply, not with Jacks' allergies to mold and Marani's general dislike of the damp. But Marani did have a memory—vague—of a tunnel system, of twisting corridors and luminescent walls and walking, on two bare, chubby little feet, across soft stone as she held the hand of a much larger adult with thick brown hair and a dimpled chin.

The lid, finally, toppled off the clay and down to the bramble below. Inside was a sheer drop of unknown distance, the dusk light unable to do more than cast shadows.

Marani tossed a blackberry down the hole. She counted to five before she heard the *splat* of overripe fruit.

"You might survive that fall, but I won't." Javad crossed his arms. "And I want to remind you, we are out to find Jacks, not explore pegasus tunnels."

But Marani could not tear her eyes from the blackness. She leaned and searched the darkness for...she did not know what. Memory? Hope?

"Hey." Javad grabbed the collar of her cloak and tugged. "What's the matter with you?"

The cloak again pulled at Marani's neck, setting another cluster of tiny scale free. They spiraled down the tunnel entrance, reflecting bits of green for seven whole heartbeats before it landed in a perfect aspen-leaf pattern on the ground below, surrounding a rectangle of leather that Marani instantly recognized.

"That's Nuria's notebook," she breathed into the cool tunnel air.

Javad squatted next to her and pushed his head to the opening as well. "It's *a* notebook. How can you tell it's the princesses'?" He pointed down, making a circle with his index finger. "Is it because of this magic shit you have going on right now with the scale?" He paused, his voice turning thoughtful. "I've had a patch of dry skin on my forehead for a decade or more. Think if I scratch that, I'll get a glowing pattern thing, too?"

"Not until you find your key," Marani murmured, only half paying attention.

"Yeah, I've been meaning to talk to you about that. I've got no memory of my life before about six, and from there it's all small-town market robbery, a decent number of public lashings, and incessant hunger. Most stability I had was a nine-month stint as a pegasus shit-shoveler in a Bad Mill rookery—and I got bit so many times by the damn things I had to leave before they took an arm clean off. If my key was stashed in some familial homestead, like yours, I've got about as much chance of finding it as a half-breed horse does of flying. You about lost your mind the first time you saw the comb in the princess' carriage. Did it, say, call to you? You think if I locked myself in a tower or somethin' and concentrated a lot, I might hear mine?"

Marani held up a hand. "Can you stop talking for a...no. Wait." She straightened, grabbing Javad's shoulder as she did so she could look him dead in the eyes. "Soothsayers."

"Bananas. We saying stupid words to avoid dealing with our feelings again?"

Marani punched Javad in the shoulder. "No. Soothsayers. They're the only humans with any sort of control over magic *and* have you used your question? Your one life question? If not, I think you just found it."

Javad sniffed as he rubbed the place where Marani's scale had impacted. "Dunno if I trust soothsayers. Worth a shot though, if we can find one."

"Oh, we can find one. Nuria has one coming to the palace, and it's the same one who helped her write all the stuff in *there*." Marani stabbed the air with a finger, pointing to the notebook. "You have any rope?"

"We've got horse reins," Javad said. "Going to be hard to keep riding though if you repurpose it."

"Bigger issues right now. You help me get back out of the hole, I'll get you before a soothsayer. Deal?"

Javad rubbed at his forehead with the palm of his hand, groaning. "Ughhh yeah fine, Grey. Thought we'd kind of moved beyond a transactional economy, you and I. Go on. I'll be around in a minute."

Javad made his way back to the horses, muttering about leadership and friendship and a whole mess of concepts that Marani had never once thought would come from his mouth. She *almost* regretted shattering his favorite throwing dagger two summers ago, when he'd brought a shire horse into camp and left it staked just outside Marani's tent. Marani had awoken to one massive, solitary wing beating the side of the canvas while the horse grazed on flax. The first thing she'd seen upon leaving her tent was a rounded snout the size of her face looming at least half a body length above her. She'd screamed in a very un-bandit like manner, stopping only when the horse's impossibly long, forked tongue snaked out and lapped at her cheek.

She'd unstaked the horse, fuming and dripping horse saliva, and pushed it from the camp, Javad and Jacks' peals of laughter taunting her from some unseen tree perch.

"He just had to be magic too, didn't he?" Marani threw her legs over the side of the hole and peered down one final time. She had not, historically, had an issue with subterranean heights. Being atop a horse was horrifying, especially when one's feet were half-housed in wobbly stirrups. Being underground was...well, your feet were still technically *on the ground,* even if the ground was also above you. It was semantics, yes, and certainly once Nuria found out it would be the topic of much teasing, but right now, the mental gymnastics worked in her favor.

Marani pushed off the ground and fell.

A screech came from overhead. An eagle? Marani looked up, expecting treetops, but saw only blue sky and the streak of thin clouds. Her feet should have hit the ground, but she was still falling, still screaming, useless fingers clawing the air, fragile feet somersaulting over her head and she spiraled down, down, toward a spiraled, blue and golden unicorn horn held by a woman who—

"What in the name of Yuro are you *doing?*" This time it was Javad's voice that broke Marani from the vision. Vision? Memory? Didn't matter. Marani's ass hit the ground, tailbone cushioned only by the thick pages of Nuria's journal. Thin rock chittered across the ground on impact, her faint dragonscale scattering across the floor.

"Got it," Marani said with a groan as she pulled the book out from underneath and dusted it off. "You ready to haul me up? Wall is too far to climb."

Javad's head popped over the side, his eyes blazing with accusation. "You were fucking floating in the air, Grey. Screamin'. Screamin' and floating and *steamin'* like a campfire that just had a bucket of water tossed on it."

Marani tucked the journal into the waist band of her pants and scowled up at her highwayman. "A pegasus led us here. Nuria's journal, which I tossed out of a carriage an entire country away, is just sitting in a hole in the ground, waiting for me. My skin is made of glowing scale. We've already established a magic problem. Get me out of here."

"If you can float, you can fly."

Marani clawed at a loose patch of scale on her lower back, sending more dim green light to the ground below. "If I transform in this cave, you will be the first thing I eat."

Javad barked a laugh as he tossed a length of leather strapping down to her. It had been a part of a bridle and reins—Marani could still see the indentations from the metal components—but Javad had managed to splice and rebind edges into one continuous length that, as Marani did a test pull, would likely hold her weight. "No knots?" she called up, not because she was surprised, but because it was always good to know just how much magic one was dealing with.

"Never tied a knot in my life, Grey. Got the other end on my horse. Let me know when you're in and we'll start the pulling."

Marani looped one end of the rein around her right foot, tangled a hand farther up, and took one final look around. Her landing, and scratching, had scattered her scale in all directions, giving her a faint outline of the cave's length. The tunnel paralleled the road, running toward the very center of the Common Forest, where Marani and Jacks' ancestral land sat. The air was cool and damp, and soothed the dryness of Marani's scale. As her eyes adjusted to the low light, she could make out imprints in the soft clay of the cave floor. There were cloven hooves, perhaps of a very small, or young, pegasus. There were dozens of bird-like feet, and markings of small scavengers. And in the very center was a set of distinctly human-shaped prints—small, wandering, and with the big toe pointing ever so slightly to the outside, turning the gait wide. The child had been ever so slightly bow-legged, just like Marani.

"No," Marani said to footprints that were certainly her own. "Not today. Later. After Jacks. Maybe after the meeting at Bad Mill. Whatever is happening here," she nodded at the prints, "and here," she tapped her temple, "has to wait. I can handle being a dragon, but I cannot handle it right this second. Too many people still need me. Javad?" Marani yelled upward. "Let's go. I'm done with all of this, at least for now."

* * *

By the time Marani and Javad returned to their mounts and the road, the trailing pegasi had disappeared. Whether their self-appointed task had finished, or Marani's loud, awkward cave exit had scared them off, was unclear. Javad miraculously had the reins sorted back out and onto the horses by the time Marani managed to remount, and the two continued their journey in stoic silence.

It was late afternoon when they reached the boundary of the Common Forest, both humans and their horses overheated by the high sun. They stopped near a small spring, Javad taking the horses to water and Marani pulling out bits of dried meat and fruit for a meal. She was two bites into a chewy piece of mango when the pull of the journal overrode her desire for a speedy lunch. Marani sat, back against a cephel tree, shoved the rest of the mango into her mouth, and opened the journal.

"Princess Nuria of Aspen Grove." Marani traced a finger over the looped, overly ornate name that had been carved into the leather with a seemingly blunt object. By the wiggle to the letters, Nuria had to have been barely pubescent when she'd done it. Amusing, but not critical information. The first page of journal, the first page with thick, creamy paper pressed with flax flowers, was far better.

My Question: Who is the owner of the dragonscale comb?

My Answer: A girl? I did something wrong. You read about it all the time in fairy stories. I thought I had it just right, too. I ran my question past our court philosopher, two knights, and Cook Senna from Two Spires, who knows everything. I didn't ask 'Show me a dragon,' because they're too far dead for me to see anything. I didn't ask about the comb's maker, because that could have been a human. The word 'owner' was so important, because humans can't really own dragons—even if the queens of Aspen Grove claimed to in the past—and so this girl...she doesn't make sense. A living dragon's scale belongs only to the dragon. The soothsayer wanted it so badly! But no queen needs money, and mom gave the comb to me for my tenth birthday. And the scale still shines so I should have been within the time window! If the scale was dead, and not glowing, I should have seen nothing.

So I guess I did something wrong, although I can't sort what. And I've got a girl, in a forest, who can't comb her hair and probably stole the comb, noting how tattered her clothes are. What am I supposed to do with this?!

What a dumb birthday.

Marani flipped the page to the next entry.

I'm half a year older, and the comb is just as bright, and still all I see is that forest girl.

Queen Ndolo says I can have two readings a year if I keep up my studies in A Political Protocol for Non-Human Species. I think she feels bad that my question got wrangled wrong. Maybe she hopes, like I do, that eventually I will see the dragon, and I'll need that fancy dragon language. She said I should keep watching, that the soothsayer and her struck a bargain, and that visions are tricky and I might be too young to interpret. I can't misinterpret there not being a dragon!

But the girl is okay, I guess. She's older than me by a good number of years, which I'm guessing more from her height than her development. She's hungry a lot. She has a brother who looks older than me, too, and he's just a fragile thing. I don't know how she keeps him alive. Today I saw them trying to peddle flax flower bouquets in a rural market. No one was buying and I could feel the girl—her name is Marani—I could feel the grinding of her stomach.

The visions are funny, because I can see what Marani sees but I can also look around, even when she is focused on the sale, or her brother, Jacks. Since the queen said I should write down every detail I remember, I'll note that the market looked coastal, and the air smelled of salt. Jacks and Marani had tattered horsehair clothes and no shoes. They sold one bouquet the whole day and that money bought Jacks a tea. Neither ate. They fell asleep against a rock just inside the border of the Common Forest and when it started to rain, a feral pegasus landed and shielded their bodies with an eggplant-colored wing. They never noticed.

A pegasus had done *what?* Marani re-read the passage. She did not have a distinct memory of the day—she and Jacks had sold bouquets at a dozen markets each year during the spring—but the details about the horsehair clothes, and tearing hunger, those memories were stronger than time.

"Horses need maybe half an hour. Share the jerky." Javad took the packet from near Marani's hip and tore off a healthy amount. "Whafs if say?"

"Irrelevant things." Marani flipped a few entries forward and read aloud, "Queen Ndolo has never struck me, nor ever ordered my nursemaid to do so. When I misbehave I'm not allowed pastries, or am confined to a servant-style room for a week, plus whatever lecture the queen decides I need. Today? Today I watched the girl steal four loaves of bread and a handful of tea nettle. Guess the flowers don't sell well enough. She got caught on the edge of town and the baker beat the bread from her, but she kept the nettle well hidden. I hated her screams. I hated the sounds the rolling pin made when it hit her back and face. I screamed for the pegasi to come help her. I screamed so hard that the soothsayer had to shake me from the vision, so I didn't get to see any more. But I know the nettle is needed for Jacks, now. It keeps him alive.

I can't watch anymore. My interpretation of the visions is that Marani needs help. I'm going to ask the queen if we can send a few scouts with food and supplies. Or if we can bring Marani and her brother here, to the castle. How is she supposed to work if she has a brother so fragile to care for? They don't belong in the forest. I could take care of them both."

"Rolling pin?" Javad said noncommittally. "That had to hurt."

"Jacks was allergic to horse milk, and it was near impossible to find goat or cow milk for him. Only way he could keep the horse milk down was if I mixed in nettle tea. That's all I did for about a year after our parents were murdered. Just…just stealing milk and nettles, and some rice or bread for myself. As he got older he needed less milk, but I kept getting it for him up until he could throw his own knife. Kids need milk, right? He was my baby brother. It was my job to get it for him. Still. It…" Marani shuddered. "Those aren't my best memories."

"Maybe there'll be better ones, later?"

A very bland and conciliatory statement, coming from a marksman. "Undoubtedly. Although I'm left to wonder who else shares them. This was Nuria's notebook, but clearly someone recovered it after my, tantrum, in the carriage. And no one picks up a notebook, places it strategically in a tunnel, and doesn't read it."

"The soothsayer who proctored the vision might know too?" Javad offered. "Can they see the visions in tandem? Guess I always assumed they could. Kept me well away."

A funny little grunt came from Marani's throat. "I'd never thought about it. If so, that royal soothsayer Nuria is meeting with now knows more than she should. She's a liability we will need to wrap up, eventually." She snapped the cover back, stood, and stuffed the journal back into her waistband. "I'm going to need some time with this thing—"

A horse screamed, the sound piercing worse than a blade. "What are they doing up there?" Marani yelled as she looked skyward. "Pegasus death battle?"

"Not the pegasi. The horses!" Javad bolted to the stream, where his horse and her pony were grazing. The tall sedge and the curve of an aspen tree blocked their mounts from direct view, but horses had no natural predators on Yuro, aside from the pegasi. Feral half-breeds roamed every inch of the Common Forest. Marani had never once considered protecting a *horse*. "Get off!" Marani heard Javad yell. "Grey, get over here!"

She'd never heard that particular hitch to Javad's voice—a sort of measured terror mixed with incredulity. She pushed into the tall grass and sedge, pressing toward the screams, when a giant *woosh* of wind sent her backward.

Her head hit rock, breaking the stone and sending another handful of scale across the landscape. When her eyes opened next it was to a pegasus—a full breed, full sized, utterly feral pegasus looming above her.

"Javad?" Marani called as blood *pit patted* from the pegasus' snout onto the front of Marani's jerkin. It pulled back part of its muzzle, exposing pointed teeth half clogged with horseflesh, and squealed.

Marani tried to slap the muzzle away, but the pegasus head was three times that of a horse and would not budge. The scale on her palm did rake across the pegasus' jawline, however, opening a thin line of blood.

"They ate the horses, Grey!" Javad yelled from somewhere above her. "Three bites and all we've left are legs and tail."

"They trying to eat you?" Marani tried to sit up. The pegasus head-butted her back to the ground. Hot air shot through its nostrils, tossing Marani's short curls and heating the scale on her face. "Keep that tongue in your mouth or I will have Javad cut it off," Marani hissed.

The pegasus snorted and tossed its head right, giving Marani a full view of Javad. His pegasus, the sunset one who'd been dogging their heels since Aspen Grove, had her head lightly resting on Javad's shoulder while the highwayman silently read a crumbling bit of birch bark.

"You're awfully calm for having just lost the horses," Marani called out. "Don't tell me Sunset is a courier pegasus. There's no way the one looming over me is tame."

"Neither are." Javad looked up, incredulous. "Note is from Jacks. He wants us to get on one of these things and meet him at your old house."

Javad could read? *Read?* Marani and Jacks could read because their parents had left a stack of Common Tongue primers in the cave during some cleaning event, and thus they had missed the robbery and fire. Javad was a bandit with uncanny aim who'd grown up stealing as much as they had. When had he found time to learn to read?

Another mystery, for another time. "That could be from anyone." Again, Marani tried to push the pegasus away, and again, it tossed her back to the sedge. "Oh come on!" she yelled. "You can't stomp me to death, or bite my arm off. I *can* cut you. What are you trying to accomplish here? Why is it suddenly so damn complicated to travel a basic road?!"

You will listen, said the pegasus.

The forest went dead silent, like the birds, insects, and even nightflies had collectively paused so that words no louder than a breath could make it to Marani's ears. The pegasus' mouth hadn't opened, either. The creature had simply stood there, looming and leering, with only the twitch of a flared nostril indicating life.

"Fuck the world," Marani whispered.

Dragons do not copulate with inanimate objects.

"In a world where pegasi use the word 'inanimate,' I think dragons can do just about anything. Javad?" Marani called, stringing out the last syllable. "Is Sunset talking to you?"

"You wanna get to Jacks, or you want an answer to a stupid question?"

Marani snapped. "*This is not a stupid question!*"

A very calm, yet wide-eyed Javad knelt down next to Marani, Sunset just behind him. With one hand he spread apart the birchbark letter and held it over her face. "Looks like Jacks' handwriting to me. I don't think we have a choice, regardless. This was a purposeful snacking."

The little square punctuation marks and curved diamond accents definitively marked the letter as from her brother, but forgery was not currently Marani's largest problem. "Did you hear the pegasus?" she asked Javad again. "Did you hear it talk?"

Javad's eyes flicked away. "Could have been wind blowin' across the reeds down by the spring. Could have been nightfly buzzing. Could have been a lot of things."

"And you sound like you've got a lot of practiced excuses. Damn it." She could peel apart the Javad layers later. Right now, right now she would deal with a talking pegasus. "I'd listen better if I could sit up," she said.

The pegasus—coat a royal blue with white diamonds down the spine and wings a deep turquoise—took two steps back. That the pegasus had listened to her was just as surprising as the potential communication. Pegasi *could* be trained, sure, but said training had to start as colts and took decades of patience. Pegasi were much like pigs in that regard—not domesticated so much as opportunistic while caged.

Marani took the bark from Javad and held it toward the blue pegasus. "My brother send this?"

A man can request. A dragon may command.

"Uh huh. And when I told you to get off me you just...didn't care?"

The pegasus nickered, and it almost sounded like laughter. *You may command. I do not have to listen. As requested, we have disposed of your other mounts. You must come. The alternative is death.* The damn thing knelt down, and Sunset did the same, wings lowered into ramps, massive heads turned to stare at Marani and Javad.

Death? Marani had thought a lot of things about pegasi over the years. Never once had she thought they'd be dramatic. She was invulnerable, and Javad was made of irritation. The only fears either of them had were the irrational kind.

"What do you think?" Javad asked. "Can you keep your lunch if we fly?"

Did...he sound *excited?*

"You heard their words too." Marani's words to Javad were more accusation than question.

Javad grunted.

That was a damn fine secret to keep. Marani briefly considered that Javad might have used his hidden talent for good, perhaps even keeping the pegasi from the homestead where the highwaymen sheltered, then shook her head. That was far too altruistic, especially for Javad. "How long?"

Javad grunted again, this time accompanied by a mild shrug to the shoulders.

"Now is not the time for secrets. Have you *ridden* one of these before?"

What little color Javad had regained to his cheeks, bled away.

"I get a little scale and it's like the whole world has gone crazy. Fine. You can ride a pegasus. I'm certainly not getting on one." Marani turned back to Blue. "Why don't you fly to Jacks and bring *him, here*? Why not come here himself? What kind of trouble is he in? Because there is no way my baby brother would ever think that I would willingly—"

Only magic could have allowed the pegasi to move as quickly as they did in that moment. Sunset sprang to her feet and tossed her head, muzzle catching Marani between the legs and tossing her across Blue's back. She grabbed fistfuls of mane with one hand and tried to push away with the other, but Blue got to its feet just as quickly.

Marani yelled. Javad yelled, but both voices were quickly drowned out by the *woosh woosh* of turquoise wings. The ground shook, then fell away from Marani as Blue shot up, *directly* up, into the sky where Marani had no desire to ever return.

"Put me down!" Marani yelled. "By landing. Not by tipping." Wind rushed past her ears, and stoked her internal fire, instead of stripping away her body heat.

Blue continued to gain altitude.

"Hoy! Grey, you okay?" Javad's voice spiraled past Marani, direction of origin unknown.

No part of Marani would ever be okay, not ever again. She had both hands tangled in Blue's mane, the pegasus' spine in her armpit, one leg dangling into nothing, and the other barely tiptoed on the base of a wing. It was a horrible position to be in, unstable, and far, far too high off the ground.

"Land!" Marani screamed, although the wind tore away her words.

Fly, returned Blue smugly. The pegasus turned in a tight loop and shot into the forest, hooves just brushing the top of the treeline. *Because you are too young to save yourself.*

"I'm invulnerable!" Although a fall from this height would definitely put whatever magic held Marani's human form together to test.

Blue's wings froze, not in a glide but in a purposeful drop that sent Marani's feet over her head. Her hands stayed in the pegasus' mane, and when Blue struck its left wing out and spun them, then again pushed upward, Marani found herself wrapped back to a proper riding position.

"See you got the seat sorted," Javad said with a snort as Sunset shot past them, Javad low and tight against the pegasus' back.

"I'm going to murder my brother," Marani said, too low for Javad to hear over the rushing wind. Marani swung her feet, desperate for some ground or purchase, but only managed to slide sideways, her knee now clutching where her rear should have been.

You are a very bad dragon, Blue chided.

"Don't you dare drop again. I'll fix it." Marani tugged mane and righted. In the process she got an unfortunate look at the forest below. The cephel trees grew thicker the closer they progressed to the forest center, but autumn was waning, and most of the deciduous trees had already shed their leaves. That gave Marani a clear view of the snaking forest trails and a band of unmarked humans on a direct intercept to where she and Javad had lunched. One man shouted and pointed up at them, but another waved him off. Pegasi were common enough across Yuro, and hopefully beating wings were enough to obscure frantic booted feet.

She could focus on people, instead of her increasing distance from the ground. "They're not mine," Marani said, more to herself than Blue. "But they've swords or crossbows, and two have pistols."

Blue nickered and shot them into a terrifying descending arc that looped back in on itself just as Marani's feet broke off a cephel branch. Marani managed not to scream this time—mostly due to the angle of Blue's descent, and the way the midday sun cascaded down a long, golden *something* strapped to a woman's back. At their very lowest point, when Marani's stomach threatened rebellion and the people below cried and shielded their heads from potential pegasus attack, the woman bent over, the flap of her knapsack flipped up, and Marani lost her breath.

Unicorn horn.

The twirls of sunlight and summer sky were unmistakable, as was the jagged, shattered end where the bone had been sawed from the poor beast. Like Marani's comb, the horn glowed with life and the thrum of unspent magic. It called to her—not the way comb had, but in a soft lullaby of promise.

Blue rose higher, the canopy blurring back to brown. As they climbed, Marani caught sight of other accoutrements: pegasus hair rope threaded with what looked like gold filament. Thin blades that she had originally dismissed as cooking knives, but upon closer inspection were clearly made of spent dragonscale. And at their lead, a woman in a tight purple cloak, who did not crouch at Blue's descent but instead glared up at them, her eyes razor focused on Marani. The clothes under her cloak were a thick leather that hung wrong. Not made from horse, she realized, but cow. An expensive, and unnecessary upgrade for basic clothes.

Marani had been spent most of her life on the wrong side of the law, but more of a sidestep, than a plunge. She and Jacks had stolen to survive, and they'd never stolen from those who also barely clung to life. One of her sharpest memories, one that still gave her nightmares, was of her seventh year, when she and four-year-old Jacks had been caught stealing handfuls of purple clover from a duke's field on the outskirts of Faun's Pass. They'd meant to sell bouquets at the Faun's Pass market and make enough coin for a decent dinner. The duke hadn't run them off, or yelled, or even taken off his belt and whacked Marani—a punishment to which she'd become well accustomed. Instead, the duke had taken each of them by the back of the neck and calmly walked them to his stable. There, he'd proceeded to push both their faces into a full water trough, holding them under while they screamed and kicked and pleaded, until the water had boiled and the man was forced to let them up, or lose his hand. He'd screamed about enchantments while Marani grabbed Jacks and bolted from the stables while coughing up horse water.

They'd gotten away, mostly because the duke had not given chase. But Marani remembered the man's scale-sharp eyes, and the neutral set to his mouth, like their lives were an annoyance he tolerated only because he didn't have a better alternative.

They were the same eyes as the purple-robed woman below, whose expression remained unchanging as the pegasi pushed farther into the forest and Marani, finally, lost sight of her.

Chapter 3 - Nuria

It is a notable misconception that the unicorn stems from the misaligned fornication of dragon and horse. Unicorns were noted independently within the archipelago by early settlers, before the introduction of horses to the islands. Unicorns are one of three magic vessels noted, with harpies being the third. All three groups are untrainable and untamable, and their magic nontransferable by conventional means.

- A Political Protocol for Nonhuman Species, Chapter 2: Magic and Breeding

"You've requested another reading, Princess?"

Nuria scowled at a honey-colored curl that refused to stay underneath her coronet while she debated her next words. It had been just over a year that she'd last had a visit from the royal soothsayer. It had been twenty-seven years since she'd asked her first, and only, question, and seen a vision of a teenaged Marani and Jacks scrounging for mushrooms in the Common Forest as pegasi circled overhead. Everyone was tied to their first question, but the question could be asked many, many times. Hence, Nuria had spent most of her life with a window into Marani and Jacks' hardships and, occasionally, gotten a glimpse of their futures.

The intervening years had been filled with desperate plans held together by hope and unicorn hair, as Nuria planned and plotted a way to eventually meet the bandit woman she could not stop dreaming about. And then there had been the carriage robbery. The Two Spires Ball. Marani's partial transformation.

Nuria's question was no longer the window she needed to her future. The Princess of Aspen Grove was unsure what question *was* best to ask. Especially noting the limited power of soothsayer vision.

"Won't you please sit?" Nuria asked the soothsayer, gesturing to the gilded loveseat upon which she currently sat. Their visits had always taken place in Queen Ndolo's receiving room—a small, private chamber just off the main throne room which housed two love seats, a worn unicorn pelt carpet, and a small table made entirely from used dragonscale. The walls held the more faded castle tapestries and the ones needing sewn repair, which made for an eclectic collection of human-dragon lore. The tapestry just above Nuria's head, for instance, depicted a gold and white dragon charring a forest mid-flight while a girl no older than twelve gaped at the sky. Out of context with the larger set, the scene showed only the human-centric violence that had surely helped lead to Yuro's mass magical extinction events.

"I've never liked this one." The soothsayer—an elderly woman with deep laugh lines around her eyes, sheared white hair and tight brown leathers—sniffed at the tapestry. "Does your mother not rotate them?"

"I don't believe tapestry rotation is high on her list, no," Nuria said, trying not to sound impatient.

The soothsayer turned her head to Nuria and cocked an eyebrow.

"I'm sorry." Nuria took a deep breath and folded her hands on her lap. "I'm overdue for travel and there has been a chaos of events recently. I'm glad you're here, and I could use guidance."

"The dragon. I heard." With a small grin she added, "You saw the same?"

Nuria's skin goosefleshed. "Yes."

"Green and brown? You're sure? The same as your comb?"

"Yes. And I'm...I'm still coming to terms with that, I think. I gave up on seeing my dragon, and fell in love with a bandit, and now I have both and my world is suddenly both abundant and unpredictable. A month ago I had only predictability."

"What will you do now? Follow her? Follow her brother? Help him transform, too?"

"I..." An uncomfortable thought dredged from Nuria's belly. She'd spoken about her visions to the soothsayer from time to time, especially when she was younger and had searched for interpretation. And certainly Queen Ndolo had spoken to her royal soothsayer as well, especially after Marani's partial transformation. These soothsayer's words felt targeted and specific, and Nuria squirmed on the embroidered loveseat. "I don't know what I'm going to do. I had hoped another reading might give me guidance."

The soothsayer sniffed. "With the sheer cost of the readings, you've been given far more than most. If a few decades of visions haven't set you on your path, one more won't change that, princess."

Nuria huffed. "Do you...see the visions you give? Do you understand what I'm working with? It's not simple. Yuro's magic is...leaking. Or Marani broke a seal. Or...I don't know. I know I *should* know. Marani always has a plan, and a direction. I can write pegasus treaties all day but what do I do with a dragon?"

A familiar, bland expression took over the soothsayer's face. "Princess. Let's get to your reading. Where is the comb?"

It was beyond privileged to hope that answers would just materialize from the soothsayer, Nuria recognized that well enough. But she was tired, and her lover was questing without her, and was likely not going to be in human form next they met. Yuro could extend her a little grace. "In the treasury. I don't want my vision this time. I want information. My mother has paid you, correct, for our time? Would you answer questions for me not related to my question? Questions about magic? About Yuro? About Marani?"

The soothsayer stayed just to the side of the loveseat, her face a frozen mask that made Nuria want to scream. Marani was a dragon! The cat was well out of the bag on magic. What good was it to hide critical information now?

Especially from the person the soothsayer had been feeding hints to for years? "Please?" Nuria tried.

"One question," the soothsayer replied in her frustrating monotone. "You know the rules, Princess. You'll need the comb. It's best if you retrieve it."

Nuria would have screamed if it wouldn't have sent a dozen guards into the room. "The comb is gone. Marani is gone. Right now it is just you, and I, and a bunch of worn old tapestries that depict a past I don't want repeated. You're here, and you've been paid, surely. I don't want magic, I want information. Tell me something real. What is your name? You've never even told me your name."

Did Nuria see a softening around the woman's eyes? Or had the flicker been a mote of light dancing through the window and the rosewood branches outside?

"The queen does not, nor has she ever, paid me. I come here as a favor to the crown. Surely you could also get someone in to repair the tapestries."

No soothsayer worked for free. Nuria swallowed a growl. It was games, then. Fine. "Do you have a favorite one?"

The soothsayer nudged a rolled tapestry with her foot, sending it to unfurl along the length of the room. The background was the light pink of daybreak, and the embroidery featured a herd of unicorns being led to slaughter, willingly, by a boy of maybe ten. "I'm partial to the dragon ones. Their scale colors note their family lineage. Did you know that? Even before your visions, I'd been partial to the green ones. The color is wild, like the forest, and untamable, like a storm at sea."

"Marani isn't untamable," Nuria said flatly.

"No queen has ever held a dragon, the way no madam has ever held a unicorn. These are the realms of princess and maids, or even duke's sons and boys before their first draw of blood. Yuro, and magic, has rules. To your question then, Princess?"

"I don't suppose said rules are written down anywhere?"

The soothsayer nodded at a tapestry. "And so very well within your reach. But that is not why I am here. Ask your question, princess."

Nuria had spent hours playing in the tapestries as a child, but she'd not made a formal study of them since her first soothsayer visit. There wasn't time today, but when she got back from Bad Mill, it would be a priority. "I want to see the owner of the dragonscale comb. The one that used to be in my mother's treasury, that she gave to me on my tenth birthday, the same year I had my first visit with you. My question is, who is the owner of the comb?"

The soothsayer pivoted, her knees touching Nuria's in a gigantic breach of formality. "Again I must ask, where is the comb? You've always had it with you, before."

Nuria had seldom let the comb out of her sight growing up. The swirls of brown and green had soothed her worst tantrums, and the gentle striations across the handle had always grounded her when the pressures of heirdom, of queendom, had threatened to drown her. She had brought it to every soothsaying because...well, it was her question. Her fantasy. A fantasy shared, apparently, by her soothsayer, whose eyes were as hungry now as Marani and Jacks' had been in their youth.

"Say the words loudly. Yuro must hear."

"I don't have it anymore. I gave it back. It was her key."

Loud was not possible. Nuria said the words so delicately, like the power of her breath might shatter the air the way the dragonscale comb had shattered the Two Spire's passage wall and broken the spell keeping Marani in human form. The world had turned electric in that breathless moment, and sound had cracked across her ears, as debilitating as staring into the sun. A rainbow of scale had made an impossible dance from the stone, to the air, and then pierced Marani's skin like a hot knife in ice cream.

Now the air of the sitting room held the leaded taste of magic. Nuria felt the weight of it pressing onto her shoulders, thickening her breath and compressing her lungs. "Will you break me apart like Marani?" she asked the soothsayer.

"You hold no secrets, princess. There is nothing to peel back. But there are promises that must kept. Breathe out. Whatever breath is still in you, thrust it from your chest as if the act might blow wind under Marani's unfurled wings. Then breathe in until your lungs scream."

Nuria had long since given up trying to parse soothsayer words. Her breathing had turned shallow in the magic filled air but she compressed anyway, wheezing out the last of her breath and ending with a thick cough. The air she pulled back in afterward was...crisp, clean, and smelled not of magic, but of pending snow.

Tension bled, ever so slightly, from the soothsayer's shoulders. "Yuro is finally moving forward."

"What does that mean?"

The soothsayer held out her hand in invitation. "It is vision time, Princess. Without the comb, it will be different. Prepare."

It was a shame Marani had already left. Nuria's court training forbade her from punching people, but Marani would have had no such restraints. "Yes, of course," she said instead, and placed her hands atop, and they grasped each other's wrists in familiar ritual.

The soothsayer's lips trembled and Nuria caught a hitch to her voice. "Close your eyes. Ask your question again, within your mind. Then let go of my hand."

Nuria wanted to ask a dozen follow up questions, but the soothsayer's nails had already pierced her skin. Pinpricks of red beaded on her wrist as the soothsayer lifted their entwined hands up to her mouth, where she whistled three low notes across the open wounds.

The magic had always been a hot, scalding thing before, with the soothsayer's breath burrowing into her bloodstream and raising a very unprincess-like sheen across her skin. The comb would burn into her free hand, and Nuria would clasp it in a death grip as the soothsayer released her and she fell, unseeing, onto the couch. It was an unpleasant, often painful process made tolerable only by the visions that came after—of Marani's smile, and Jacks' laughter, as they tossed stones at cephel fruit in markets to release the obnoxious smell, or collected flax in meadows dotted with feral, half-winged horses, or, as they all got older, learned how to court women.

This time the sting of magic turned Nuria's nervous sweat cold as ice, not fire, shivered through her. Her vision turned the white of snow, blanking out the pastel pinks of her mother's sitting room and replacing them with the numbness of winter.

"Ask," the soothsayer commanded.

Nuria clung to her question like she had once clung to the dragonscale comb.

Who is the owner of the dragonscale comb?

Time stopped.

Nuria stopped, both in breath and shivers. In a void of vision, between reality and magic, Nuria stood on the edge of a cliff. In front of her was a drop into thin, dark clouds. Behind her, the opening to a wide, dry cave whose interior glittered like amethyst and ruby in the waxing sunlight. The princess could neither turn her head nor pivot her body— acts she had always been able to accomplish before—and so stayed rooted on the crumbling precipice as a dragon landed next to her.

The rock trembled as claws dug in, and wind beat at Nuria's face as the dragon's wings pushed back and up, finally settling along its barrel-chested frame. It—she? He?—was the size of six full-sized horses, both in width and length, with a snout much more equine than lizard. The wings were pointed and leathery, but covered with the down of feathers that looked soft and perhaps ornamental. Two steel-grey horns shot like daggers from either side of the head, and another row of smaller spine-scales rose along the back spine.

"Marani? No, not the right colors." Nuria whispered as she surveyed the fiery orange and green scales, and tried to reach out and touch the delicate, sky-blue feathers.

A squeak followed Nuria's words as a dragonlet no bigger than Nuria's hand slid from under the larger dragon's wing and fell, face first, to the stone below. Blue and gold feathers tangled in the tiniest of claws and then a snout no larger than Nuria's pinkie emerged, pointed upward, and gave an angry *chirrup!*

The invisible grip holding Nuria in place, loosened.

The larger dragon tossed her—surely this was the mother—head and pried the bloody body of a snowshoe hare from under her other wing. She placed the hare next to the dragonlet and blew a soft orange flame at the carcass—singing the fur to brown. Her tongue then lapped down at her baby—blood-red and forked, and washed the feathers backs, removing some unseen dirt and exposing a wash of brown and green scale beneath.

Chi-chirrup! The dragonlet pounced, teeth and claws tearing at the hare in predatory, childish delight, oblivious to the mother's grooming.

"You did tell me you hated cold meat," Nuria whispered as she smiled. "And I'm the princess?"

A funny sort of snort, followed by a puff of grey smoke, came from the dragonlet's nostrils. It stopped chewing and canted its head, turning toward Nuria and looking not through her, but *at* her.

Fear shot along Nuria's spine and would have collapsed her legs if she'd been standing under her own power. Her visions had always been windows to a concurrent timeline in which she'd been an observer only. This one was the past—it had to be if there was a dragonlet—and therefore there was no possible way that an echo of Yuro's history could have heard her. Right?

Scaled eyelids squinted at Nuria. The dragonlet set one feathered paw down in Nuria's direction and hissed.

"I didn't—" Nuria began.

The hiss turned into a belch, and a fist-sized ball of flame rolled off the dragonlet's forked tongue and engulfed Nuria's foot. There was no pain, no burning, but Nuria's foot disappeared from the vision, although she was certain it still existed.

"That wasn't very nice," Nuria said.

The dragonlet shivered. It—no *she,* if this was indeed Marani—curled into an armadillo-sized ball and arched her back. There was a *pink pink pink*, and a line of soft feather scale parted down her back and shoulders, revealing a fresh row of dewdrop green feathers, twice the size of the others.

"You're molting? I...I suppose I never thought about how dragons got bigger. Scale isn't exactly flexible, is it?"

A chubby, triangular face peeked out at her and said, with a proud puff of chest feather, *Chiip!*

Nuria got down on her knees, her lack of foot a metaphor she'd tease out later. "You are the most precious thing," she whispered to the dragonlet. "Can you imagine if we'd grown up together? Not as humans, but as you are now? Because I'd have loved you, Marani, like this, as a dragon, a human, I'd even love you as a pegasus, were that to come to pass."

To speak to a dragon and not get eaten hinged on the deepest formality, as well as a strong dose of verbal submission. Speaking to a dragonlet, Nuria mentally noted, took only sincerity. Marani unfurled and took one adorable, hesitant step toward Nuria, when her mother's tongue wiggled under a cluster of feathers on the dragonlet's shoulder, wrapped around one, and tugged. A thick, almost scale-like feather came off, the blue so deep it looked almost brown. Two tiny drops of dragon blood fell to the stone before the indignant baby reared on her mother and spat the cutest curl of flame.

There was no disappearance this time. The mother grunted a warning, and the dragonlet let out one final *chip!* before it went back to its meal. The mother waited until the dragonlet's head was buried inside the hare's chest cavity before laying the feather just to the left of Nuria's remaining foot.

Nuria, who would not court the crosshairs of an adult dragon, stayed silent.

"The soothsayer is prepared to receive her? The foster humans are trained?"

A harpy hopped from the cave and crouched next to the feather. Her face was lined with wrinkles, her feathers were the color of live coal, but her breasts—Nuria couldn't help but stare—were succinctly pert. She'd never seen a harpy, not even in tapestry, and so she continued to gawk at the eagle-woman as the harpy opened her very human mouth and spoke.

"Darifa waits in the forest with the unicorns and my brethren, guarding the house and the human fosters. Another dragon was slain on Chilliwack Island this morning. We can keep preparing, but there will be no one left to save if we do not perform the spell now. We have a baby born under the right sign, and a fitting one, I think you'll find. Do you have the incantation? I have the horn and harpy magic to tangle within."

The dragon rumbled a response, the sound somewhere between a bullfrog and a horse's nicker.

"The language is irrelevant. The magic will understand whether or not you use your tongue or mine. But if you are concerned, I will say it for you. I cannot make flame hot enough for the transformation, however. You will still need to supply that."

The dragon sniffed in way that very clearly translated as *If you continue to tell me things I already know, I'll eat you.*

The harpy shook one of her wings out in apparent dismissal. "This is not an alliance, it's an agreement for survival. I'll begin when you do."

Flames erupted immediately thereafter, the force of the blow drowning out the harpy's words. The world turned orange, then red, then blue as the dragonfire burned and Nuria watched the same transformation on the feather. Barbs and veins? fused together, folding over each other, thickening and hardening, darkening. The feather curled in on itself and took on a purple-blue patina that turned brighter, brighter, until Nuria had to close her eyes against the shine.

When she opened her eyes again, it was not to dragons and fire and feathers, but to a weary soothsayer whose nails still tinted pink with Nuria's blood, and whose eyes stared as intensely at Nuria as the dragonlet's had.

"Are you alright?" the soothsayer asked. "Magic can upset, even through the echo of memory."

Nuria didn't answer straight away. She let herself breathe, slow and steady, and felt the velvet of the cushion under her backside, and tried to overlay the shape of the curled feather across the dimensions of the dragonscale comb. The colors didn't match. The material didn't match, but her question had been about the comb, and soothsayer magic could not deviate from the petitioner's question.

"Princess Nuria?"

Nuria didn't plan the words that came next, but neither did she attempt to reign them in. "Was that Marani? I command you to answer or I you will sit in a cell until you do. That wasn't a vision, it was a memory. Tell me the whole truth, for once."

The soothsayer replied, simply, "Yes."

"What happened after?"

"She was delivered to the parents she remembers. She was raised in the Common Forest. You know this. You watched it happen."

"And so did you!" Nuria scratched at a nearby cushion. "What game are you playing? You saw the visions, but never helped her. You knew I begged the queen to let me intervene directly, and she always thought I was spinning tales. You could have vouched for me. Instead you, you what? Wove shadows and memories and futures together? *Why!?*"

The soothsayer, with maddening calm, flicked an unseen mote of dust from her leather jerkin and spoke like Nuria was a particularly dim village child. "You could have me sit in moldering cell for three decades and I would not answer your question, princess. You have tasted magic. You have watched magic most of your life. If you cannot see, cannot understand its rules by now, I will not explain them to you." The soothsayer made to stand, but Nuria took her by the wrist and forced her back to the pink velvet.

"She's out there, back in the Common Forest. She's alone, and she's transforming, and I should be by her side. My insides are being pulled like taffy, being apart from her now. But I can't help her grow wings, or learn to breathe fire. I can't even soothe her scale as it burns. I cannot help her if I cannot see the whole picture." Nuria pushed her palm into the soothsayer's sternum. "You did this. You *led* this. You conspired with *harpies*, which were supposed to all have been hunted to extinction a century ago because of their untamable violence. Why do I get this memory now? How does it, or how can I, help Marani?"

For a moment—a shadowy moment of the sun disappearing behind a cloud, and a cool breeze passing through silk curtains—Nuria thought the soothsayer might actually answer. The woman's mouth opened, her tongue touched her top teeth, and she took a breath, preparing words that would finally break apart Yuro's secrets.

But the clouds passed, and the breeze settled, and the soothsayer stood, brushing off Nuria's hand like a feather. "I'll see you next year, princess." She was at the doorway, hand grasping the knob, when Nuria pleaded.

"Please. I love her."

"Dragons love flight, and mountain air. They love waterfalls and gemstones and horses, and tea, but they do not," the soothsayer said over her shoulder, "love princesses. Especially not from lineages responsible for their extinction. You must love the last dragon of Yuro, because that is what it will take to save her. But once she has completed her transformation, once the humanity has boiled off her bones and her skin has cauterized to scale, and her internal furnace finally combusts, she will not love you back. Not the way you need her to." Her voice turned soft and apologetic. "I'm sorry, princess. The rules of prophecy, and magic, are not intentionally cruel."

"You don't know that. The future is always changing. You told me that. Prophecy shows possible futures, not the definitive."

"For those not bound by magic, this is true. But some, like you and I, have only one path. We must walk it with dignity."

"What does that *mean?* Come back!"

The soothsayer pushed from the room, taking with her the faint static of magic and the smell of worn leather, and Nuria's now foolish hope of an uncomplicated future with Marani.

Chapter 4 - Marani

Braeburn suggests in his Treatise on the Sociopolitical Realms of the Unicorn that unicorns form complex social groups based on mane color and decorative arrangement. This chapter argues that original accounts of unicorn socialization were biased, and that unicorns are actually bound by a rigid moral code that has its foundations in sexual purity. This is in direct contrast to the dragon, which has long been known to route its value systems around wealth and power, from both its own species and those cohabitating around it. These two species therefore avoid social interactions, when possible.

- A Political Protocol for Nonhuman Species, Chapter 3: The Unicorn

The acrid taste of memory kept Marani's mind away from flight and dangling feet until Blue's descent into the canopy. What would have been another half day ride had taken just under an hour, from what Marani could sort by sun position. She had a chance, a small one, of getting back to Aspen Grove castle before Nuria even left. Assuming Jacks was lurking at home.

The pegasi landed in tandem in the small clearing that had once housed a handmade, wooden lean-to built by Marani's parents. Marani had reinforced the rickety structure over the years with bits of cephel branches and birch bark, but neither she nor Jacks had used it for a residence in almost a decade. They had housed a few of their keepsakes within, but in the month or so Marani had been chasing Princess Nuria and her comb, the lean-to had blown over, and Marani and Jacks' meager possessions were tossed around the clearing in a pattern that indicated forest scavengers, not bandits.

The pegasi knelt, and Marani eyed hers warily before sliding off a wing. When her feet were once again on soil, she said, begrudgingly, "Thank you. Please don't ever do that again."

"Never thought I'd see the day you thanked a pegasus." Javad gave Sunset's forehead an appreciative stroke. "They did save a good bit of time."

Marani shook her head. "I don't care about the time as much as the hunters we flew over. We'd have been outnumbered and more than just delayed. Did you see them? Did you see all the weapons?"

Javad's eyes narrowed. "The ones on the trail? Heading to the forest boundary? Yeah. Outfitted like an army. Pistols aren't cheap and we don't make them on Yuro. That's a Tchun import."

"Did you see the soothsayer? She was packing live unicorn horn, amongst other paraphernalia. I'm more concerned about the horn."

Javad's stomach contorted and he turned his head away, hand over his mouth. Marani refrained from commenting. She'd battled her own nausea during the flight, and not just from Blue's incessant looping.

"Nuria said hunters would come. It's not that I didn't believe her, I guess I just...thought it would take them longer to organize. They'll have turned back, certainly, into the forest to follow us. We can't linger here."

"Is that what the horn is for?" Javad asked voice muffled by his hand. "Killing dragons?"

"I don't know. Jacks was the one who got into the history books before he left. I was...occupied." Marani eyed a small path of broken ferns that lead to a cave opening, where her family had spent many stormy nights. How many times had she and Jacks retreated to the cave when storms tossed their lean-to, or when Jacks' skin could take no more sunshine or heat, or when they'd needed to hide from merchants they'd defrauded just so they wouldn't starve to death? The protection had always been so absolute, not just in their minds. But leaning past the opening, Marani could see the cave still sheltered the old rosewood bench she'd salvaged from their parents' house. It was missing both legs now, although Marani had replaced them with aspen stumps a number of years ago. The aspen was near rotted out, but the bench top itself remained whole and free of mold. The cave protected. It had always protected. It was home.

"Jacks!" Marani walked to the cave entrance and yelled. "Jacks, you down here?"

"There's fresh tracks in the mud behind your lean to, or what remains of it," Javad said from somewhere behind her. "Made from cheap horsehide boots. Probably men's size. Could be Jacks. Could be Hans or his ilk."

Marani called another "Jacks!" before turning and asking Javad, "Which way do the tracks go?"

"West. To the old encampment. Just one set, come here then turned around and went back. No hoof marks. Man was on foot. Funny, since his note says to meet here."

Against all better reasoning, Marani asked Blue, "Who gave you the message?"

Blue's right ear twitched. *Dragons have always been found here.*

Pegasi were useless. "Well, he's not here anymore." Marani sighed. "I don't have time to confront the highway guild, but I suppose we don't have an option. They're a better choice than dragon or magic hunters any day." Marani gave one final look to the cave. "Those caves go on for ages. We never did find the end. That's an exploration for another day, when I'm not on a princess clock." To Blue, Marani said, "How far does our alliance extend? Would you consent to watching from above as we track my brother? Warn us of the hunters or soothsayers if they get close?"

The old alliance holds until your transformation. We will watch. The pegasi took flight, the power of their wings tossing Marani and Jacks to the ground as they ascended. Marani landed in a circle of soft mud, upsetting a nightfly nest and sending thousands of the little black insects into the air. She batted at them, ineffectually, while Javad laughed.

"I could watch you swat at air all day," Javad said as he gasped for breath. "Fucking dragons. I'd never have believed it, without the scale. You're a mess, Grey. Come on." He offered her a hand up, the nightflies parting for him like a curtain of rain. "Let's go find Jacks."

* * *

"Psst. Jacks!"

Marani tossed a blackberry at the side of her brother's neck. He was standing with his back against a cephel tree, one foot resting against the trunk, head tilted back, eyes skyward. Marani and Javad had managed to approach the camp undetected not due to Marani's grace and gentle footsteps—that would never happen—but because herds of feral horses still roamed the central forest and her former employees had long ago stopped turning their heads at the crunch of leaves and bramble. Added to that was the *woosh woosh* of pegasi wings as Blue, Sunset, and their friends circled overhead—a horrible sort of honor guard.

Jacks blinked but did not otherwise move. Just past him were a handful of Marani's former bandits, lounging on downed logs in a small makeshift camp.

"Jacks!" Marani said, louder this time. She started to stand up, but a short back wave of Jacks' hand kept her low to the ground.

"You say something, little boy?" A man of middling height with a piss-yellow beard spun on Jacks.

Jacks' head fell forward with a snort. The exaggerated movement rattled iron, and Marani made out a shackle around his left ankle, the other side of which was attached to his cephel tree.

"Shit," Javad said under his breath.

"I was debating which direction to piss," Jacks said, his voice as flippant as Marani's. "From here, I might be able to hit the traveling jerkin you so nicely left in range."

"Shut up or I will cut out your tongue," said the blond man.

"Dare you to try." Jacks reached for his crotch. The blond man pulled a knife from his belt and had it at Jacks' throat in two quick steps.

"It's not gonna cut him, Grey," Javad whispered. "Keep it toget—"

Marani leapt from her crouch and barreled into the man's stomach, sending them both to the forest floor. She heard a "Damnit!" then the whistle of Javad's knife in the air as she slammed the blond man's head into a conveniently placed boulder. "Don't fucking touch my brother!" she yelled as the flush descended and her vision turned red.

"Grey, stop!" That was Jacks. Marani ignored him in favor of grabbing the collar of a man with a large axe and tossing him against a tree. The axe hit her shoulder. Scale *plinked* off, scattering droplets of sunlight into the sedge below.

"And your roads are terrible!" That was Javad, somewhere to Marani's right, quickly followed by the gurgling sound of a cut throat.

"Would you two stop!?" Jacks yelled while a high-pitched female voice called from farther into the woods, "Grey returned! But she's...she's...not human!"

From the sky, a pegasus whinnied.

"Why do you have my brother?" Marani sneered at the woman she currently had pinned to the side of a very unconcerned feral horse. The dull orange scales on the mare's rump snagged on the woman's coarse wool dress, the sound searing Marani's ears.

The woman whimpered.

"Talk, or I get out my own hatchet."

"He came here and demanded we leave. This is our home too, Grey. You made it our home and then you abandoned us. Where are we supposed to go?"

"And chaining him to a tree was the logical reaction!?"

"Dragons help us. What happened to you?" The woman underneath Marani's arm slacked. The knife she held patted into the bunchberry below. Wide, childlike eyes turned up at Marani as the woman's fingers bumped along Marani's forearm. Her small scales here had almost entirely shed away, and the solid brown plating underneath was smooth and striated, and far less inclined to shred human skin.

Bandits—many of which Marani recognized, poured from the trees. In their hands they clutched rusting knives, broken pots, and trowels. Her highway guild had gone from boutique robbery to hungry and listless in a matter of months. The decline tore at her heart, but was second to the rage that swelled up when Hans stepped from the forest.

"Magic. I thought the news was out. You leave out the dragon part when you stormed back here?" Marani asked her brother as Javad worked the chain lock with another bandit's dagger. She released the woman and kept her eyes on Hans as he kept to the tree line, rightfully cautious. Above, the pegasi still circled, but they were lower now, their hooves kicking the tops of the canopy. What a pain. The last thing she needed was pegasi exacerbating what was already a ridiculous, if not sad, situation.

"I did not. I was very clear about dragons. But no one here takes me seriously since I'm not the one that flies into rages and eats swords." The lock clinked open. Jacks kicked the iron away, nodded thanks at Javad, and then said, firmly, "Hans. Get over here. The rest of you can leave."

Hans did not move.

Marani recognized the flush as it rose in her brother—the set to the jaw, the rigidity of the shoulders, the pinprick of black in the center of his eyes that kept his focus only on Hans. He was quicker to flush now, too. The same short temper as her own, now that her transformation had begun. Marani's own breath turned ragged in tandem, and fire surged inside her, begging for blood, or fire, or release. Her scale sang in tandem with Jacks' rage, and her throat burned with ash. A little voice in her head yelled that her brother was here, and the sky was here, and her freedom was here if she would just take it...

And Nuria was back at the castle, waiting for her.

Marani was familiar enough with the flush to back it down on her own. The people around her wore tattered horsehair cloaks and horsehide boots patched thrice over.

Hans' beard had consumed his face and neck, and through the tears in his pants she saw spindly legs and still-healing scrapes from blackberry.

"Jacks," she said hoarsely, "he's already lost. There's no point."

"He fucking buried us alive!"

Marani had never seen Jacks kill even a nightfly, but in five long steps he had Hans by the neck while the shorter man clawed and gurgled. Hans' face turned an unhealthy purple and the bandits—none of whom had fled—stared, perhaps too numbed from watching Marani's poor flush behavior over the years.

"What happened to the tolls?" Marani asked the crowd. "What happened to our stores?"

"Taken," said the woman Marani had just released. "Bands come through the Common Forest now, day after day. They wear leathers and carry swords that even Javad couldn't handle. They have pistols and soothsayers. They take without thought for families. They've stripped us bare."

"I left you a functional bandit guild and you...you let yourself get robbed to death?"

"They weren't bandits that came through, Grey. They're wearing cow leather. They've got cloaks, like yours. They're not stealing to stay alive. They're chasing a prize."

They're chasing you didn't have to be said. The message was plenty clear.

From Jacks' hold, Hans gurgled.

"Jacks." Marani put a hand on her brother's shoulder. "Let him go. We've bigger problems, like those monsters in the sky that you sent after me. Remember them? They talk. Put Hans down and you can mock me while I try to ride one again. I rode a damn pegasus here for you, brother. Think about the hilarity of that."

The face that snarled at her was of a wild, untamed thing, whose taupe skin smoked as outlines of scale pulsed beneath it.

"Jacks. Step—"

Jacks punched her in the sternum, a move that, from a human, would have been irrelevant, but from Jacks, sent Marani first backward, then to her knees. He sneered down at her, his mouth filled with still-human teeth. "He is mine," Jacks hissed.

"Javad?"

"I got you, Grey."

Marani rammed Jacks like a rutting stallion, driving her shoulder just under his chin. He released Hans, who fell into Javad's waiting arms, then rebounded back at her, his hands cupped and drawn like he had miraculously grown dragon claws. "Jacks, s—"

Jacks' fist drove into Marani's mouth. She bit down, two of her human teeth lodging into Jack's skin and staying there when he pulled back. Jacks fought for purchase on her scale, his fumbling giving Marani the advantage. They'd grappled like this a handful of times before, although it had always been Marani in the flush and Jacks the voice of humanity. The most recent iteration—when Marani had overreacted to a rude barmaid turning down Jacks' first attempt at courtship—had lead to the complete destruction of an Aspen Grove inn, and an entire town neither Jacks nor Marani could ever visit again.

"Grey," Javad said, his voice tight with warning. "Wrap it up."

"Damn it, Jacks!" Marani yelled as her brother's search for soft tissue finally led to a twisting of her elbow. Jacks' skin smoked and curled back, charring to reveal his green and yellow kit scale beneath. The smell of burnt linen mingled alongside, as spark leapt between Marani's scale plates and singed her clothes. They'd set the entire Common Forest alight if she didn't get Jacks from his flush. Fast.

"Cut it out! I'm trying to help you, damn it. This isn't the time for a transformation, for either of us. Plus, we still don't have your key, so all your skin is just going to grow back. Just like in King Fridolin's study in Two Spires, the last time your flushed too far."

"I'm going to kill him, Grey!"

Jacks again tried to lunge for Hans. Marani drove a knee at Jacks' midsection, thinking she might wind him, when a downward thrust of wings pushed them both off balance.

Blue landed in the clearing, followed by Sunset and three additional pegasi Marani did not recognize. Jacks snarled, one hand still gripping Marani's jerkin, and then let out a throaty sort of warble that sounded more frog than human, but with just enough undercurrent of language that Marani felt sure she heard him say, "Kill."

"Jacks, step *out!*"

Jacks went to his knees, dragging Marani down with him. Smoke bled from him in thick curls, but he breathed, thank dragons, and his eyes focused, and his growls turned back to the whine that had grated Marani's ears since his toddlerhood.

"I'm going to at least punch him," Jacks said after catching his breath.

"Grey?" Javad said her name like a warning.

Marani held up her hand. "You should definitely punch him. You don't need to burn down the Common Forest to do it."

"Grey!"

"Javad, what could possibly be the matter? If you get Jacks going again we will all—" She turned, but instead of Javad there was Hans, looming over her, a dagger with a pearly white blade poised to strike.

"Took it from one of the hunters we managed to down during the last raid. Steel might not hurt you, dragon, but I'm betting horn will."

"Hans," Marani said with a groan. "I only just got this under control. Can your tantrum wait until—"

The blade slashed down, right at Marani's face. Horn split apart her scale like it was warm butter and her blood fell, like hot acid, across Hans' hand, and the forest floor below.

Hans screamed.

Jacks yelled.

The pegasi attacked.

Marani bled. As she bled, she dreamed. The vision dotted in over the carnage, overlaying not just sight, but sound and smell. A pegasus bit through the back of a man's skull and in her vision, a dragonlet nipped at the ear of a dead snowshoe hare. Glittering orange wings with silver tips as sharp as scale sliced through three sets of leathers as Marani grabbed her shoulder in a similar shearing pain—not from a knife, but from some imagined, ripped-out feather. She looked left, for the culprit, and saw Jacks glowing with encased fire, Javad mounting a pegasus and charging Hans with a spear and...a dragon.

The mirage-dragon wasn't in the clearing. Not really. The body was far too massive to fit, even with weaving tail and appendages around the trees. It—no, her—body was more barrel shaped than Queen Ndolo's tapestries had depicted—the snout rounded, the ears tufted. The dragon smiled in a sort of horrible grimace, and her teeth were both pointed and flat—the first row for tearing meat and the second row for more omnivorous purpose. Her eyes were entirely equine—large, round, and the deep brown of river mud. Her front paw was held out, near Marani's side, and held delicately between two claws was a curled, crisp feather.

"That hurt," Marani said, indignant, although she was well aware no one else could see her imaginary dragon.

"What hurt?" a weary Jacks asked from her side. "The horn? Not surprised that cut you. But it's already clotting, like usual."

"Put the feather down on the ground with one of your own," said an ancient harpy with eyes the same brown as the dragon's. "I will place the horn atop, with one of my own feathers. Then we begin the incantation."

"You gonna help out, Grey?!" Javad yelled, more triumphant than angry, as his pegasus landed on Hans and proceeded to prance on the rebel highwayman like an overeager ballerina.

In that moment of split attention, Marani had missed whatever magic words the mirage-harpy spoke. She refocused down, on the whipping ribbons of light that braided through the feather, horn, and scale, pressing them into one another, draining light from the scale into the feather, dissolving the horn, remolding and infusing, until, in the span of a heartbeat, the light snuffed out, leaving the dragonscale comb. *Her* dragonscale comb.

"It does not look like a scale," said the dragon with a cock of her head. "Why does it have spikes?"

The harpy picked up the comb with her mouth and tapped the dragonlet on the head with her wing as she did so. There was pressure on Marani's forehead as well, and she scowled in tandem with the juvenile dragon. "Humans don't have scales. Humans have hair that must be tamed. If you want her to keep the object despite having no memory of its origin, a comb is choice." When the dragon's head remained slanted, the harpy added with a sigh, "She's going to have hair, Kiri. Like a horse."

"She will be beautiful," the dragon said in a long sigh that sent wisps of smoke from her snout.

Marani's nose turned up in tandem with the harpy's. "I'll take the comb to the humans today. Your flight with Marani is on schedule?"

"Three days," said the dragon, her attention only on her kit, who had returned to the snowshoe hare. "You've found a pair?"

"Darifa the Soothsayer continues her hunt. It may be some years yet. This should not be rushed. Magic should never be rushed. Have patience."

The dragon snarled.

"Grey, what the hell?" Jacks' backhand snapped Marani from the vision-memory-thing and sent her to her back on the forest floor. He hadn't hit her cut cheek, which was already knitting back together, but his scale-bare hand still hurt nonetheless. "You dead? I've never seen you skip a fight. Not that we needed you. The pegasi were...thorough."

"Fucking *horn*." Javad knelt on her other side and laid the horn blade on Marani's lap. The bone was a pearlized white with a breath of seafoam green, and a bright red splash of Marani's blood. "If Hans weren't mushed in the ferns I'd cut an answer out of him about the original owner. Unicorn is for healing, not killing."

"But now we know it can cut dragon. That's awful." Jacks poked the horn with a wary finger. "Wonder how many other people know?"

"Every dragon hunter on Yuro, I'd imagine. I—" Marani squeezed her eyes shut, trying to seal every new memory in place. The comb. Her comb. Her key. She was the dragonlet. The harpy, she didn't care about, but the dragon. The *dragon*. That was her...that was her and Jacks' *mother*.

"I told you she wasn't responsive." Jacks shook Marani's shoulders, his rough fingers further chipping away her loose scale. "Grey, what's wrong? The pegasi are done. They really only ate Hans. A few more people have bites, and Gillian has a nibble from her shoulder, but if we get at it we can patch them up, if you care that much. Grey?"

"I'm fine." Marani pushed Jacks and Javad away as she sat up. The horn knife rolled from her lap and embedded in the trampled sedge. "Magic is unraveling more than my skin, that's all." She took in the forest with unobstructed vision, now filled with parts of highwaymen, a lot of blood, and six very smug, very large pegasi. "This wasn't how I saw this going," she murmured. "Did you...did you slap me?" she asked Jacks. "I was trying to help you, asshole."

"Yeah yeah. Not all of us are professionals at flushing. I maybe wanted to squeeze the life from Hans. But you choked plenty of bandits in your day and I generally let you, if you'll recall." His voice softened. "You don't need to protect me anymore, Grey. Not even from myself."

"I thought we were protecting each other? Besides, I'm supposed to be the wild one. You're supposed to keep me from knifing every irritating nobleman I see, or, perhaps more apt, setting a town on fire. Which is why we came. I want to be with Nuria in Bad Mill but I can't go like this. Want to be my safeguard?"

Jacks offered her a hand up, which she took. "Want me to stab you with a unicorn knife if you transform and eat

Bad Mill's ruling body?" He picked up the horn, turned it tip over hilt, then handed it to Javad.

Javad grunted a question.

"I may be Grey's safeguard, but if we're both in a flush, you're next in line. I also think a dragon shouldn't carry the only weapon that can take it out."

Javad gave a strange gurgling laugh and said, "Knew one of you had to have a working brain."

"Would you both shut up? Jacks, let's restart the conversation with where have you been, then graduate to why you were tied to a tree. We can finish with some yelling around why you thought it was appropriate to send pegasi to kidnap Javad and I from the very stable road. Then we can sort heading to Bad Mill."

"You've been in bed the last three days, haven't you?" Jacks asked, not unkindly.

"She also fell into a cave and found some notebook," Javad offered. "It wasn't all sex."

"Stop trying to be helpful," Marani hissed at Javad. "And you," she jabbed a finger at Jacks. "I have been *asleep*. It's hard work growing scale."

Jacks held up his hands and smirked. "I didn't mean like that, although I'm sure there was *some* of that. If I was fate-bound to a princess I'd take full advantage of it, too. What I meant was, you don't know what's going on in the forests and on the roads. They're crawling with hunters, and raiders, yes, but also *soothsayers*. I've never seen so many soothsayers. They're clearly not very good ones, as I chatted with three on my way here and they never once recognized me, but they're out here, crawling the forest, looking for dragons."

"The party on the road?" Javad asked as he used a canteen of water to clean his hands. "The woman with the purple cloak and the dead eyes?"

"Wearing cow leather?" Jacks asked.

Javad nodded.

"Soothsayer attire. The better ones wear cow leathers, because they can afford it, I'd guess. One I passed had a cow emblem for a cloak clasp, if you can believe that. What a waste of resources and design. Thick cotton says more about your wealth than jewelry."

And Nuria was meeting with a soothsayer *right now*. Marani's skin crawled. But she wasn't at the palace. As long as no one was princess hunting, and Marani stayed away, Nuria was safe.

"We could easily avoid them on pega-back," Javad said. "Not sure they're much to worry about right now. They're concentrating in the Common Forest, right? They'd never think to look for you two in Bad Mill."

Jacks wiped his hands across the well-worn sides of his cheap, horse-leather pants. "It's the damage they'll do to the forest while they're looking that has me concerned. They breached the Common Forest boundary before you or I had even left Two Spires, Grey. The first one I met was alone, a youth with a sword and a dream of a hero's journey. He sacked the lean-to and pissed in our cave. I sent him home with a broken arm, took back the few things he nicked, but it wasn't half a day later when a trio came by the homestead with the same idea."

"You're alright?" Marani blurted out, scouring Jacks for any sign of trauma.

"That group had rope and I'm as terrible with a sword as you so no, I wasn't alright. They had me strung up like a wild hog when your previous band of misfits swooped in, actually managed to beat them off, and spent the intervening days debating whether it was better for them to sell me to the highest bidder, or keep me for themselves. They've had a hard go of it too, as you can imagine. I'm betting any villagers within a ten kilometer radius of the Common Forest are getting the same treatment."

Marani groaned. "They're going to starve because of us. Great. I don't suppose we could command the pegasi to attack dragon hunters?" It was a silly thought, borne more out of desperation than actual planning.

"You're welcome to try." He looked skyward. "How did you call them down the last time? I don't see a single one anymore. Do we have to wait for them to be overhead?"

"I didn't call them. They ate our horses, showed us a letter written by you, then tossed us on their backs and brought us to the homestead."

Jacks turned, ever so slowly, to Marani. "Okay, well, I didn't call the pegasi either, and I didn't write you a note. Why would I lure you into a bandit trap when none of those idiots can actually hurt me—unknown unicorn dagger aside. I thought you'd called them with your advanced dragon magic, or whatever you have going on that's making you shed your skin like a shiny lizard." In a very little-brother voice, Jacks added, "What does Nuria think of the look?"

"She thinks you should shut up."

"Uh huh. Any chance she called the pegasi?"

Marani debated that ridiculousness for a moment before shaking her head. "She's meeting with her soothsayer today and then heading to Bad Mill. She doesn't have time to miraculously learn to talk to flying horses. But a human had to be involved, surely. Last time I checked, pegasi couldn't hold a pencil."

"And you said it looked like Jacks' writing," Javad added. "Person wanted you in the forest knew how to get you here. That's more magic."

Javad held up a hand. "Hold on that for a moment. Nuria is with a soothsayer? If the lot of them is out hunting us, the royal soothsayer could be in league. She'd know more about you than anyone other than Nuria, right? It wouldn't be too hard to lure you into the forest."

"Sure," Marani said as she debated storming the Aspen Grove castle in a fiery rage and eating the soothsayer on sight. "But the blue pegasus that carried me said it was saving us from the hunters. Bringing me to the forest was more...a favor?" Marani pursed her lips as she thought. "Timing isn't right, either. Nuria's soothsayer was to arrive just after breakfast. They'd have finished their meeting by now. I suppose it's possible the princess saw something, and asked the soothsayer to intervene? Though why the woman would do so now, and not, say, when Jacks and I were starving, is another question."

"You just believing the best in people now?" Javad asked. "You ever met a decent soothsayer? I say Nuria had a vision, her soothsayer saw your location, and sent us to the forest where all their soothsayer friends could whack themselves a dragon."

Jacks groaned. "And we're just sitting here while they all head toward us. We need to move." The chain that had held Jacks to the tree lay in pieces at his feet and he halfheartedly kicked at the pile. "What the fuck do we do, sis?"

"We could start by not jumping to conclusions. Nuria's soothsayer could, in theory, have known where we were for years. Why would she come at us now, when we are both arguably *more* invulnerable? Your paranoias don't add up."

Javad folded his arms. "You ain't giving us a better theory."

Marani mimicked his stance. "You said Jacks was the brains. Ask him. He's thinking of something. He's got that weird 'V' between his eyebrows."

"You're not going to like it," Jacks said.

Marani kicked her brother in the shin. "I don't like Javad, but he's still here, isn't he?"

Jacks continued, cautiously. "Nuria's soothsayer spent a lot of time grooming a princess and circumstances so that a couple of transformed dragons could emerge, or partially emerge. If she wanted us dead and mounted to a wall, we'd be there. If she wanted us caged, we'd be there. If she's working with the soothsayer guild, she's got a lot more direct way of achieving those objectives than a pega-letter. So. She's driving us somewhere. We just don't know where, yet, or for what purpose."

"You're saying Nuria is a pawn?" Marani asked, her voice unnaturally high.

"Yeah, but no more so than you or I. The only one who isn't being manipulated is Javad. Which is why he gets the unicorn dagger."

"Backhanded fucking gift," Javad spat.

"We have the players. We just don't know the game. And I am out of ideas on that, sis. Short of finding a soothsayer and asking directly. Or finding a magic mirror, which I am mostly certain is a real fairy tale."

Marani let out a long, hot breath that sparked orange. "It's more a window to the past, but..." From her interior jerkin pocket, Marani pulled out Nuria's diary and tapped it on Jacks' forehead. Her brother swatted at her hand, intentionally missing. "The notebook of Nuria's visions. Twice a year since I was sixteen. Probably things in here we don't even remember, and probably lots of possibilities that never came to pass. This isn't the soothsayer's plans, but it would at least put us on a level field."

"I thought you threw that out a carriage window?"

"And then I found it in a cave that a pegasus dragged me to. Pushing against the path magic clearly wants us to take is getting us nowhere, and my plan to race back to Aspen Grove is clearly dead. I'm not going to bring all of Yuro's dragon hunters and soothsayers to Nuria's doorstep. She's going to negotiate the port treaty. She doesn't strictly need me for that."

Jacks just stared at her.

"I didn't say I *like* leaving her alone."

Jacks blinked.

"Fucking say what you're thinking or I will punch you in the face."

"Just want to hear about the plan, sis."

Marani swallowed heat. Another forest tussle with her brother would certainly light the place to ash. "Fine. I say we let the current lead us for the moment, while we explore a little history. Javad? What's the nearest pub to our location that is also the most likely to be deserted?"

Javad, with a similar maddening expression on his face said, in as bland a manner as possible, "You did pubs more frequently than me, Grey. I gave my wife most of my coin."

Marani spat out a human tooth along with a sputtering of flame that smoked before it hit the sedge. "My bars are not the right kind. I have historically looked for ones with a robust clientele and very robust waitstaff. We need...family friendly."

"Gross," said Jacks. "And Javad isn't a eunuch. Why would you assume he's seeking out antisocial bars any more than me?"

"Because he hid a damn family from us for years and if he can hide that, he can hide a shitty bar or two." Marani scowled at Javad. "Well? If you don't know, can you ask one of the pegasi?" With a side eye to her brother, she said, "He's been talking to them for years or some shit. Or they've been talking to him. Digest *that*."

Jacks opened his mouth, but Marani slapped her hand across it. "I said digest, not question. Let the man talk."

"Gods save Yuro from the idiocy of dragons. Bars by their nature aren't solitary. You don't go to one to avoid people. Best I can suggest is a secure one. You've got money now. We all do. There are bars with a cover that provide more discretion. Closest is the Solitaire Bar. It's on the Faun's Pass side of Baer's Pass Road. Nearly a day's walk, but less than an hour via pegasus." Javed smirked. "Never been, but heard stories. How badly do you want to get there?"

Cow fuck a pegasus, Marani did not want to fly again, unless it meant going back to Aspen Grove, stealing Nuria away, and hiding them on some remote archipelago island where no one had ever heard of dragons. But Nuria wasn't in danger. She'd have heard something, surely. There'd have been a pigeon, or pega-letter, or smoke curling from the Aspen Grove sky. Nuria's soothsayer had laid this possible trap over decades, and Marani and Jacks were her targets. And if the soothsayer had planned Nuria as bait, the path of least resistance would have been to just wait in the Aspen Grove castle for Marani and Jacks' return, and capture them there. Or trail Nuria on her way to Bad Mill and spring the trap whenever Marani and Jacks showed up.

Yuro had become nothing but traps, it seemed, in under a week. Even the Common Forest was suspect. Their six still-attending pegasi had made soup of the clearing—with enough noise to send every adventurer and soothsayer their direction within a twenty-kilometer radius. They could march to the nearest town and give their money to besieged townspeople, but that was helping the symptom, not the problem.

They needed to leave the forest, fast, and Marani needed a few uninterrupted hours with Nuria's diary. Then she'd order some cool pettian juice and together, the three of them would come up with a plan that didn't involve flying Yuro's last two dragons back into a soothsayer's waiting arms, or leaving the townspeople of Yuro to starve to death while every magic hunter in the archipelago went on a dragon hunt. Marani tucked the diary away and, with clenched teeth, said to Javad. "Call them back. Have them take us to the bar. And if I don't have a clearer picture of what's going on by the time I'm done with the diary, I'm going to have Blue drop me off a mountain. The only way any of us makes it through this alive, and protects our families, is on the other side of our transformations."

Chapter 5 - Nuria

In this experimental chapter, the authors offer hypotheses on suitable vessels for magical transference from an archipelago native. Putting aside standard options such as horn, feather, scale, and claw, the authors argue that human tissue can retain magic for up to one year if the magic is ingested orally. This chapter also includes conceptual cookbooks and offers grinding tips which the reader may find especially useful for the dense unicorn horn, and thick harpy claw.

- A Political Protocol for Nonhuman Species, Chapter 6: The Human and His Relationship to Magic

Nuria was atop a dappled gelding, pegasus-leather boots laced up to her knees, aspen-green riding dress tucked under sensible cotton pants, when Queen Ndolo stalked out from the kitchens.

The four knights Nuria had asked to escort her to Bad Mill dismounted their own horses and knelt in the stable straw. Nuria merely straightened in the saddle.

"My Queen?" Nuria kept her words sweet. "Did you need anything before my departure?"

"Grey isn't with you." Queen Ndolo hurled the words like an accusation.

"I've four knights, which has always been sufficient previously. Grey went to fetch her brother from the Common Forest. They will meet me in Bad Mill for the treaty talks." With a forced smile, she added, "Two dragons are better than one, right?"

"If they were with you, yes." Ndolo pinched the bridge of her freckled nose. Her tunic was well-pressed silk and her pants a clean linen, but no amount of laundering could hide the strain in her muscles, or drown the frustration in her voice. "I don't suppose you considered waiting for her return?"

"You really think the talks can wait? Yesterday you yelled at us both for not being on the road already."

"Yesterday, you were traveling with a dragon."

Nuria threw up her hands. Her horse's head jerked up as her toes slipped in the stirrups. "I can double the knights. I can take a carriage. I'll take whomever you'd like, but I need to leave. I want to get ahead of the treaty talks, or as ahead as we can be. Representatives from Two Spires and Faun's Pass are likely already at the table with Bad Mill. We can't be the only monarchy absent. If we're not there, then Two Spires and Faun's Pass could end up with ports, leaving just Aspen Grove stuck with intra-island commerce. Our economy will die."

"And with Grey at your side, you think Aspen Grove could land the biggest port? Perhaps the only additional port?"

Nuria snapped a furious scowl at her mother. "I'm not using her. But she is...useful. Even if her and Jacks' eventual transformations may render pegasus transport irrelevant. There will be ships for a good long while, and we need a functioning port, one way or the other."

Ndolo frowned, but in that stretchy way that meant she was about to say something unpleasant. "I've left you and the dragon alone these past two days out of respect for her partial transformation, and in the hopes that we might be wrapping up our side of the prophecy."

"My queen—"

"Your devotion to treaties and ports is admirable, even if you've continually ignored my commands about leaving it be." Ndolo's tone turned curt. "You've refused to listen in the past, so I'm not sure why I think you'll listen now, but at least hear these words. You seek to treat with Bad Mill over their port, and their pegasi breeding program. You fear for the Aspen Grove economy, and pegasi monopolies, and once again I am telling you *these things are irrelevant*. You have a *dragon*, Nuria. You have *two* dragons. One dragon can carry at least a dozen people, and can travel twice as far as a pegasus. Bad Mill can entice pegasi to their fancy imported breed horses but they will never breed as true as dragon to horse. You should not be negotiating with Bad Mill. Bad Mill should be negotiating with us. The other two monarchies are irrelevant. King Fridolin of Two Spires is older than I am, and would never court the ire of a dragon. He will play any game we suggest. The Duchy of Faun's Pass has never had any interest in pegasus breeding, and I suspect will fall in line once we have the first lineage complete."

"I...what!? You...you want me to breed them? Harness them like a common pasture horse and use them to ship, what? Pettian juice throughout the archipelago?" There were no descriptors for the rage that swelled inside Nuria, and for one blissful moment she fantasized what it would be like to have her own flush, and thereby a great excuse to set, say, the royal stables on fire. Horses evacuated first, of course.

Ndolo's voice cracked. "Jacks and Grey are dragons, Princess. They wear the shells of humanity and those shells have slacked. They will eventually shed them like the lizards they are, and your highwayman with the heart of gold will be, unequivocally, a dragon. A *dragon,* princess. A dragon bound to you through prophecy that you have played so very well, for so very long. Except you have let *your* dragon go off alone, back into the Common Forest, whose borders are no longer sacred."

"She's only gone to find Jacks," Nuria heard herself saying—her voice tinny and distant as her mother's words tumbled around her head. Pegasi...pegasi *didn't* matter if there were dragons. *Nothing* mattered if there were dragons, except maybe how to control them, or harness them, or kill them for their magic. Marani and Jacks were dragons, which meant they didn't technically have the same rights as humans and the monarchies would certainly *expect* that they would bend the wing...

"Princess Nuria, get off your horse." Ndolo's words were so sharp that Nuria found herself sliding off the gelding before her mind registered the movement. She landed in the straw with a puff of dust that sent the knights sneezing as they kept their heads bowed. "You've seen the soothsayer?"

Nuria nodded. "Yes. She's only just left."

"Your vision. Tell it to me."

Nuria almost smiled—not because there was humor in her mother's words, but because in the decades Queen Ndolo had gifted her daughter with soothsayer readings, never once had she shown more than a passing interest in their contents. "It was a different kind of vision, without the comb," she said. "I...it was the past. Too far back for a soothsayer reading. I thought they could only go two years either direction. But this was...this was Grey as a dragon kit, and the creation of the comb, and a harpy. There was talk of a soothsayer."

Ndolo grabbed her arm. "Prophecy is funny, sometimes. Magic is unreliable, without the dragons to tether it. Write it down, the same as the others. Then get back on your horse, without the knights. Forget Bad Mill. Head into the Common Forest and bring your dragons back here."

There was a long, pregnant pause as Nuria digested her mother's words. "I...what?" she stammered, when her brain failed to reconcile being allowed to travel to the bandit-laden Common Forest over the well-patrolled streets of Bad Mill. "You want me to go alone?"

"Have you not traveled the roads of Yuro countless times before? Frequently alone?"

There was danger here that had nothing to do with highway bandits, but Nuria ignored it. "I don't understand."

"You have to go get her," Queen Ndolo said again, every word measured and sharp. "There are two dragons in the Common Forest. We know who they are, and one is bound to you. You are best suited to find them and bring them home."

"Firstly, when I did sneak from the castle it was *never* to travel to the Common Forest, of which there are no reliable maps, and secondly, home? Aspen Grove? The forest is their home. They don't belong in a castle, especially not after transformation. Will we keep them in the stables like the horses?"

"I don't believe they would mind that."

"Mother!"

The conversation had become so bizarre that Nuria's only defense was argument. "I don't even think the Common Forest is their home! I saw mountainside caves in my vision, with Grey and her mother. There are no mountains on Yuro, but I know a few larger islands in the archipelago have them. But even if they were to stay on Yuro, Grey and Jacks spent most of their lives as orphans, living near caves. Living in a castle, or a stable, would be like you moving your bedroom to a swamp."

"You refuse, still, to see the larger picture. Leave," Ndolo waved her hand at the knights, who scattered back into the stables. When their footsteps could no longer be heard, Ndolo stepped into Nuria and took her hand, running her thumb over the crescent-shaped scabs on Nuria's wrist. "All of Yuro knows there are dragons," Ndolo said, in the voice of a mother, not a queen. "Bad Mill's pegasi are irrelevant if there are dragons. But those two out there, Jacks and Grey, are juveniles. They've been human longer than they've been dragons. You've seen Grey captured—it doesn't take more than a handful of men." Her grip again tightened. "Do you think the other monarchies don't have people out hunting Grey? Do you not think the entire island of Yuro isn't going to turn itself inside out to find our last two dragons? Do you think Two Spires, Faun's Pass, and Bad Mill, are treating right now? If the situation were reversed, if Bad Mill had a dragon, I would have sent every knight on payroll into the forest to find it."

"I—"

"My darling, nothing matters except Grey and Jacks. Every scheme of Bad Mill, every poisoning in Two Spires, it all means *nothing* if there are dragons again. Those who control the dragons control Yuro and the archipelago, through magic, through force, through fire, take your pick. So hear me when I say you need to find Grey, and Jacks, and bring them here, where we have a hope of protecting them until they complete their transformations. How they are...what they do then, we can sort when they are safe. Here. Read. Before Darifa left, she brought me this." Ndolo pulled a roll of birchbark from a back pocket and handed it to Nuria. An unstable hand had scratched onto the surface:

YURO'S DRAGONS HAVE AWOKEN

REWARD: 50,000 SHIELDS FOR INFORMATION LEADING TO LIVE CAPTURE

ADDITIONAL INFORMATION AVAILABLE AT YOUR NEW REGIONAL DRAGON HUNTER HEADQUARTERS

Nuria found her hand shaking as she passed the birchbark back. Increasingly alarming scenarios played in her head. Marani bound and gagged. Marani bound and gagged while some Bad Mill knight peeled her scales and sold them to the highest bidder. Jacks tortured until he transformed, then chained, caged, and turned into a monarchy pet. The horrible, gut-twisting knowledge that there was one male and one female dragon and that their familial ties would not stop anyone determined to ensure dragons did not once again go extinct.

"I'll need an army." Nuria backed her horse from the stable and eyed the armory across the grounds. "How many can you spare?"

When Ndolo did not respond, Nuria turned her horse back toward her mother and repeated the question. "How many can you spare from the guard? You just said if the situation were reversed, you'd send every knight at your disposal. So send them with me."

The queen met her eyes, but still she did not speak.

"Mother!"

"She's no good to us in human form, Nuria. Neither of them are. They aren't safe, and they cannot be well protected. I need you to bring home dragons, not humans."

"Mother, I am not bait!" Nuria's voice squeaked, making her sound like a youth, instead of a fully-grown woman who was being used to emotionally manipulate a dragon.

"Then take Liu," Ndolo offered. "Although in the end I believe it will be Grey's love for her brother, or for you, that pushes the transformation. Almost certainly you, otherwise why else would you be tied to her? Perhaps you can find another way. You've seen more of her life than anyone. Perhaps there is a kiss that unravels the last bits of magic holding her form, or an enchanted sword that can cleave the magic away." With a set jaw, Ndolo said, "However I suspect that the classics hold true. A virgin calls a unicorn, and royal youths call dragons. And nothing calls a dragon like the peril of a princess. You are technically older than the children used historically, but I think your connection with Grey will override the age differential."

When Nuria set her hands to her hips, Ndolo added, "We cannot escape prophecy, Nuria. None of us can. I tried to keep you safe for years. I tried to keep you in the palace, trained you with a sword, taught you two hundred and seventy-five ways to compliment a courtier—which barely scratches the surface of dragon etiquette—I kept you *alive*. That was my job. This, now, is yours. Find the dragons. Get them to transform. Bring them back here, away from the other monarchies, who I am certain would be plucking scales before nightfall and a juvenile dragon can quickly die if descaled too quickly. I...please wipe the tears from your eyes, child. I love you fiercely, but all princesses, and all princes for that matter, are pawns. For marriage, for dragons, for alliances. You watched Princess Oksana fight her role to combustion. Do not throw your life away. Not when Grey's hangs in the balance."

Nuria turned to her dappled gelding as she wiped at her eyes. She was too old to cry, and princesses did not beg. Throwing up would only upset the horses, and screaming would get her nowhere. She had negotiation, maybe. Could you negotiate with prophecy? "I'm going to need a lot more knives," Nuria finally said. "And more than lunch. Damn it." She rubbed at her eyes again, exhaustion creeping in despite it barely being noon.

"Marani is gone." Ndolo's hand was back on her shoulder. "You will not see her again. But you have a chance to see Grey, a dragon of Yuro. You have a chance to be part of her history. You are a part of Aspen Grove's greater history, too, and our generational bond with dragons. I didn't hang the tapestry of your great-grandmother pulling a dragonlet from its shell in your bedroom, or the tapestry of your grandmother's dragon tea party outside your favorite library, just to have you forget where you came from. Think on those things as you travel."

"It's been decades since either of those women walked Yuro. Dragons have changed, surely. Besides, Grey and Jacks wouldn't know that history, would they?"

"That gives you a right to forget it? Why read any books then, if the people around you might not have read them? Think of the coin I could have saved on your tutors and governesses since all you needed to know came from sporadic soothsayer visions."

Were her mother's words meant to cut? Why was it so easy for anger to slip to tears? "You can protect Grey and Jacks? When they're back here?"

"I'm calling in our reserve knights from the villages. I'm lighting the old tunnels. King Fridolin of Two Spires is standing with us and sending soldiers. Just...get them out of the Common Forest, Nuria. They're fair game there for anyone. Get Liu or don't, but you should leave immediately." With a smile, she added, "With knives, of course. And nettle. As much as you can carry."

Nuria wrinkled her nose. "Jacks' allergies are skin deep. I thought he didn't need nettle tea anymore?"

Ndolo rubbed her temples and said, with an exasperated sigh, "All dragons drink tea, Princess. Especially nettle tea. What do you think your grandmother served the dragon

Stuart in order to tame him? Do you at least remember the formal greetings? Do you remember anything from the one book I required your tutors to teach you?"

At the moment all Nuria remembered from her childhood dragon lessons was that a dragon mouth contained two hundred and twelve teeth that constantly replaced, like a shark. She would not fight her mother's urgency. Ndolo spoke truth—Nuria could feel it deep inside her bones.

Nuria curtsied to her mother, although she could not force the frown from her face. "Of course. And My Queen?"

"Princess?"

Questions warred to be spoken, the words tumbling over each other as Nuria tried to form cohesive sentences. In the end, Nuria managed only, "Thank you."

"Take care, princess." With a short bow and forced smile of her own, Queen Ndolo swished away in a cloud of the most delicate, forest green silks, leaving the stables in silence.

"This wasn't supposed to be how our story went," Nuria whispered to her gelding when she was finally able to convince her legs to move forward. "I've no map for this future, and no guide. If I lose her..." The princess swallowed the rest of her sentence. That future was impossible. She would not let it happen. She *refused* to let it happen. Confidence and luck, and a decent helping of magic, had gotten her this far. No part of that equation had changed, although the magic had shifted more to dragons than soothsayers.

Soothsayers. Nuria was back to fuming. She'd spent a lifetime planning and orchestrating, and knowing she was a piece in a bigger Yuro game only exacerbated her anger. She was her mother's bait, a soothsayer's pawn, and had been living under an illusion of agency her entire life. And there wasn't a damn thing she could do about it in the moment, because Nuria was still a princess and Marani once again needed help.

The formula was the same. Maybe it would always be the same. Maybe she and Marani could change it, later, but for that to happen, Marani had to be not just alive, but free. Which meant it was time to stop whining, get on her horse and save the love of her life from herself. Again.

First, she was going to secure herself a guide.

* * *

"I don't need prophecy to see you're headed in the wrong direction. I wanted to give you a warning. The roads—"

Nuria was close enough to the kitchens that she could hear Cook Senna's barking orders in a tone that indicated either a delivery person, or an apprentice who'd burned butter. Senna had previously been head chef for Two Spires royalty, but with the fallout from the poisoning, and Princess Oksana...well. She'd shown up at Aspen Grove Castle one day after Nuria and Marani themselves asking about a position. Nuria, without asking, had hired her on the spot. What position Senna had worked out with Aspen Grove's Head Chef, Nuria did not know, but Senna was still clearly in charge.

Nuria had her hand on the kitchen doorknob when the royal soothsayer stepped into her path.

"Change of heart?" Nuria asked, not bothering to hide her exasperation. "Decided to answer all my questions? Ugh, don't answer. I don't care, and appreciate that I don't have to track you down." Having just come from the royal armory, Nuria pulled a knife from her boot and leveled it at the soothsayer's neck. "Shut your mouth and come with me."

The soothsayer blinked and took a step back. "The queen showed you the posting?"

A funny tickle went off just behind Nuria's ears—like a connection desperately trying to take hold. "Why not give it to me during our reading?"

"I only wanted to—"

"Give me more cryptic messages that take too long to unpack? Deliver just enough information to shape world events exactly as you'd like to see them? Leave a trail of breadcrumbs that won't get you in trouble with whomever controls you, but are still moderately helpful? No, thank you. I'm on a timetable that I am sure you are familiar with. As of now, you are my prisoner. The queen advises against guards, but not against guides."

If Marani could barrel through life without a thought for tomorrow, or consequences, Nuria was certainly entitled to one or two bad decisions herself. She watched the soothsayer's lips purse and relax, then purse again, until the woman finally clasped her hands behind her back and nodded. "As you say, Princess."

Nuria slid the knife back into her boot. "Don't make bind you," she said, voice insufferably haughty as she continued toward the kitchen. "Follow."

It was just before lunchtime, and the royal kitchens were packed with cooks and servants as they organized the meals for the various palace staff. A steaming game hen sat atop a silver platter near the west door—clearly meant for Queen Ndolo's lunch. The smell of potatoes and rice mingled with the sweet smell of pettian, all of which Nuria ignored. "Liu?" she shouted into the din. "I'm looking for Chef Liu."

"Here!" A thin arm raised from behind a wooden rack filled with cupcakes. A round face peaked around the corner, dusted with flour, apron stained with a rainbow of frosting. "Is it pressing? I'm working on roses."

"When the princess calls, you just say 'yes.'" Senna grabbed Liu by the back of her apron and hauled her—not unkindly—in front of Nuria.

"The icing will harden," Liu said with a sniff. "Best I'll be able to do is leaves if this takes more than a minute."

Senna's eyes closed. As she wound up for an admonishment, Nuria cut her off. "No more cupcakes. Get a bag together while Senna packs another set of meals, and meet me at the stables." Nuria let the command set in for a moment before adding, "It's Grey. She needs us."

Nuria had expected the statement to stop any argument from Senna or Liu. She had not expected the entire kitchen to unanimously stop all movement. Every face turned toward her and every ear listened for any kernel they might discern, of Yuro's new dragon.

It was Senna who spoke. "Provisions for how many?"

"Just two more. Liu and the soothsayer."

Senna eyed them both, then said, "You want Darifa? Not guards?"

Darifa. Her mother had said the name minutes ago, when handing Nuria the wanted posting. And Nuria had heard it...in her vision. Right? There had been the harpy, and she'd said, what? That Darifa waited with unicorns? In the forest? Gah, this is why Nuria had always written her visions down right after viewing them. The sharp details had already melted like Liu's frosting, into the inaccessible corners of her mind.

With Senna still looking at her expectantly, Nuria said, "She's not being given a choice."

"Ah. Well then." Senna found a knife and piece of unaffiliated meat and began to cut thin slices onto a piece of waxed paper. "Lunch isn't cancelled because the princess is going on a trip," she yelled. "Get back to your work."

But the kitchen staff did not resume work. Every adult and every child stayed rooted to the cobblestone floor, staring at Nuria.

"Grey in trouble then?" Liu asked Nuria as Senna continued to slice.

"I'd be happy to discuss details with you outside." Nuria took Liu's hand. "Please go pack."

"But is she safe?" The question came from a young man feeding wood to the cookstove, who couldn't have been much older than nineteen. "If you need riders, I volunteer."

"As do I," said a middle-aged woman kneading bread. "I can have a horse saddled in five minutes."

"And me!" chirruped a girl of about six who'd been sweeping the floor. "I know how to ride!"

The kitchen dissolved then into shouts and pleas to accompany the princess, the volume so terrific that Nuria had to cover her ears as she backed from the room. "I have sufficient escorts," she tried to yell over the din. "It isn't safe for you all. I thank you for the offers but—"

"Shut it, all of you!" Senna beat her rolling pin across a wood cutting board so forcefully that the board split in two. The resulting *CRACK* silenced the kitchen. "Liu, out. The rest of you will stay. Princess? Here." Senna handed Nuria a bag heavy with food. "And a bag of dried nettle in there too. You'll need to visit the apothecary for more."

"Thank you, Senna," Nuria said as Liu wordlessly brushed past on her way to her chambers.

"You bring her back here, Princess," said Senna, her voice almost as commanding as Ndolo's. "Her and Jacks. And you be careful of protocols. She's more dragon every day and there's going to be a point where what you say matters more than your clothes, or what's under them. You remember your history lessons, and you remember those tapestries and the nettle tea, and you stay alive. Every peasant knows the history of Aspen Grove's queens and their taming, and breeding, of Yuro's dragons. We all know how that ended, too—with the death of magic across the archipelago. Prophecy and legacy don't own you. Do you understand?"

"I understand. And I promise." Nuria kissed Senna's flour-covered cheek—an affection she'd not practiced since her childhood, when Senna would sneak her butter cakes at afternoon tea when Nuria was visiting Prince Toms and Princess Oksana at Two Spires.

"Thank you again, Senna." Nuria snapped her fingers for Darifa to follow, but as Nuria exited the kitchens, Senna took the soothsayer by the shoulders and violently whispered into her ear. The soothsayer scowled but nodded, and Senna then pushed her back to Nuria.

Dragons may have protocols, but they cannot possibly have as many secrets as royalty, Nuria mused as she marched Darifa to the stables. *And I have a feeling that*

*those secrets, and those protocols, and all the buildup that
has the castle feeling like a combustion engine, won't mean
a damn thing to a reformed highwayman, dragon or not.*

Chapter 6 - Marani

There is no recorded successful pairing of unicorn|human or dragon|human, although Cao and Shuster argue that the genetics of dragons are sufficiently broad to crossbreed with most advanced life. These pairings would be more likely to occur were the human to be a magic user or magic vessel. This chapter offers theoretical mathematical equations broken out by all macro species across Yuro, along with anticipated outputs of the viability of the offspring.

- A Political Protocol for Nonhuman Species, Chapter 2: Magic and Breeding

"Password?"

A very bored, elderly man greeted Marani, Jacks, and Javad at the splintered wooden entry door to the Solitaire Bar. At his feet was a rusting broadsword far too heavy for him to lift, and there were no locks on the door itself, as far as Marani could see. In terms of security for a supposedly elite establishment, she was not impressed.

"This isn't another geriatric situation, is it?" she asked Javad, making no effort to lower her voice. The bar was situated under a grove of old, disfigured pettian trees, and the shade, as well as the fancy embroidered, hooded cloak Nuria had given her, had kept Marani's identity well hidden. She'd hoped that arriving on pegasus might help the lot of them pass for royalty, however the bar bouncer seemed not only unimpressed with their entrance, but mildly disgusted.

"Money?" Marani pulled a pouch from her belt and jingled it at the bouncer.

The man rested his head back against the pettian sapling that grew just outside the bar door. Was it pettian? Marani squinted at the pinnate leaves. Not a pettian. Hickory, maybe? If she didn't know better, she'd have sworn walnut, but walnut trees were extinct. Of course, so were dragons, in theory.

"Got plenty of money. Password, or you can take your disgusting horn, get back on your flying horses and go somewhere else."

From behind, Blue whinnied. An orange and silver pegasus kicked a gnarled tree with his back hooves, sending a cascade of what was unequivocally walnuts, to the forest floor.

"Keep it calm or I'll make glue out of all of you!" the man snarled. "Damned half breeds."

Blue nickered back—the sound echoing human laughter.

"You let a pegasus talk to you like that?" the man asked Marani with a hefty finger waggle. "You let them talk like that and they'll turn and eat you one day, you mark my words. That one has too much horse and not enough dragon for any sense. Real fifty/fifty mixes at least spoke the Queen's Tongue."

Did the horse-like grunts Blue was making count as speaking? Blue certainly *could* speak, but the nasally nickers currently stuttering from her muzzle surely didn't count. If he was speaking to a tavern bouncer, that was a whole different set of issues.

"Ideas?" Marani asked Jacks and Javad as Blue made a round of indescribable noises with her mouth and the bouncer cursed back. "Javad, can you get the horn under your shirt? Carrying it in the open just makes us look like soothsayers. Which we are not," Marani said, pointedly, to the doorman. "Although we would love to know more about the supposedly extinct walnuts here."

"Wouldn't tell you if I could," the doorman returned.

"This bar cannot possibly hold a secret bigger than dragons," she muttered.

"Your scale?" Javad said in a low voice to Marani and Jacks. "If they don't want horn, it's the only card we hold. Unless you want to sell Jacks."

Jacks snorted. "I kept Marani from running you through in Cayan when you lost that drinking contest with the husband of the nettle farmer and Marani's bulk nettle deal fell through. If anyone is getting sold, it's you. And for that matter," Jacks' nose wrinkled. "How *did* you lose? I've never seen you drunk. Not once."

"Boys, please." Marani gripped each of their shoulders. Hard. "Dragon exposing seems risky without knowing who is inside. Anything else?"

"Threaten?" Javad tapped his chest. "I've got six knives here, another twelve around my person. A little knife has gotten us a lot of places."

It wasn't the worst idea, and from the look on Jacks' face, he didn't hate it, either. "Just try not to actually *use* them," Marani said. "Nuria doesn't like it when we stab people."

"Ugh. Soft. All of us." Javad slid a hand-sized knife from somewhere under his jerkin and approached the door man, who currently had both fists balled and was shaking them with jittering rage at the pegasi. "Let us in or we cut you," Javad said. And then, perhaps out of newformed habit, he added, "Please."

"Yuro has frozen over," Jacks muttered. "I've never heard than man ask nicely for anything."

"Does it count as nice if it involves a knife?" Marani countered.

The doorman eyed Javad's knife, then the horn strapped to his back, Blue's backtalk momentarily forgotten. He focused then on the knife's cheap bronze hilt. He flicked a fingertip at a patch of rust near the blade's base, then moved his attention to Javad's finely stitched but mud-covered jerkin, then face. "You'll not do much convincing with that," he said. "Why so small? And again, you owe me some answers on the horn. That better be yours."

Javad sniffed. "It's mine now, since the guy I took it from is dead. Blade though? I've bigger ones. They cut all the same. Let us in."

The doorman shrugged. "Password. Or I've got some pegasi of my own you can be fed to."

Blue let out another round of whinnies as she pushed herself between the humans and leveled her massive head at the doorman. Eyes boring into the man, her muzzle dangerously close to his crotch, Blue grunt a string of irritated breaths before ending with a loud *chomp* of the teeth.

"I *see*." The doorman turned his attention to Marani and Jacks, who both still clutched their hoods like the shade might poison them. "You're sure? How come I can't tell them about the walnuts then?"

Blue let out a long neigh.

"I suppose that makes sense, since the older one is still in human form. Going to be a slow magic decay, is it?"

Blue's head bobbed.

"And *him?*" he pointed at Javad. "If he's a dragon, I'm a harpy."

Another string of indecipherable nickers.

"Well don't that beat all? I had no idea. Still can't let them in, however. We've protocol, which, as you just noted, I can't talk about until the magic sloughs a bit more."

Blue made another lunge for the doorman's crotch.

"Alright, alright!" he said, jumping a healthy distance away from pointed pegasus teeth. "Dragons it is then, at least until Starlight checks them out. He'll run you right through if you're lying."

Blue folded his wings in, nestled into the ferns, and looked decidedly smug.

"Can't believe I'm doing this. Get on in then. All of you." He pushed the door open, spilling a rainbow of light and music onto the shaded forest floor.

"Thank you," Marani said, overly sweet. As she crossed the threshold she asked the doorman, "What was that about decaying magic and walnuts? Surely you can tell a dragon, right?"

The doorman growled. "Magic that binds you binds all our tongues, too. Stop pressing and get inside."

Marani decided that pettian juice and rice were more important than arguing with a doorman, and pressed forward. There were plenty of patrons inside she could question, once she had a snack.

"Did a pegasus just vouch for us?" Jacks asked as Javad led them inside. "Also is this how you felt with Nuria? Like everyone else had a guidebook and you were being led around on a leash with blinders on?" Jacks shuddered. "I don't like it. This bar isn't visible from the main road, and there's no clear path to it. There isn't a village for kilometers in any direction. How do people find this place? Who are the target clientele?"

Marani pushed her brother into the bar with a loving but firm smack. "You're a dragon. A pegasus just threatened a man and *didn't* eat him. The doorman knows about magic binding spells and we're in a walnut forest. There's weirder events in the world than a likely bandit bar. Follow Javad and don't eat anything you haven't sniffed first. I just need an hour or two with the diary, then we can leave. We can handle anything for an hour. Maybe you can spend the time seeing who *will* talk to us about magic."

"You can't handle nightflies for more than ten minutes," Jacks muttered back, but dutifully kept walking.

Marani gave a final glare to Blue, who smiled back at her with a full set of pointed teeth. As every rule of her reality had been left firmly behind, she said, "I appreciate the help, but you're willfully withholding information. I could eat *you,* you know," she hissed at the pegasus. "Post transformation. Next time I ask you a question, how about you give me a direct answer?"

Threats mean very little in human form, Blue returned. *Find your fire, and we will see if you can roast me.*

"I think I'm going to be sick," the doorman said with a mock gag.

Marani very nearly retorted, until she realized that this type of banter, were it between herself and a human, would have been considered high-level flirting, and that the doorman was possibly privy to both sides of the conversation. "Sorry," she said as she followed Jacks inside. "I'm not like that. With pegasi. I've got a girlfriend."

"Please never speak to me again," said the doorman.

"There." Javad punched Marani's shoulder, then pointed to a bow-legged table in the far corner. In any other bar, a corner would have been the perfect place to read. Every self-respecting pub owner in Yuro kept their bar corners dimly lit and grimy so that people of Marani's caliber would have secure locations to do business. But aside from the shoddy joinery, there was nothing dark or grimy about any part of the Solitaire Bar. Every wall contained at least three fake, backlit windows—none the same size or shape—and in each window hung at least one prism. Tiny rainbows danced over countertops and chairs as servers purposefully tapped the prisms as they walked past with tall glasses of pettian juice and a variety of liquors.

"You don't see a lot of cow decorations on Yuro," Javad said, his voice more wonder than disgust. Marani couldn't blame him. She'd spent several decades in banditry, and knew that unicorn pelts and dragon scale were the decoration of choice, not just for the elite but most of the middle class—what little middle class existed on the island. There were no cows on Yuro although they frequented many nearby islands, but their import was expensive and heavy with Bad Mill tariffs. They tended to succumb to illness within a month or so of their arrival to Yuro as well, and were a favorite prey of feral horses. As a ranching opportunity or stable milk source, the cost and risks were simply too high, and Yuro was stuck with pricey imported butters and cheeses, and a reliance on horse steak.

Hence, while cows weren't *rare*, they were certainly *expensive*, which made the choice of cow pelt rugs, mounted steer heads, and a...bronzed disemboweled cow carcass on a central table with a plaque that read *Archipelago Buzkashi Champion, Year of the Fern* make a weird sort of sense.

Well, the carcass didn't make sense. But as Marani sat and squinted at the ribbon collection on the wall to her left—*Regional Buzkashi Champion, Year of the Watermelon; Second Place Buzkashi Regionals, Year of the Clover; Fifth Place World Buzkashi Participant, Year of the Blueberry*—she at least didn't feel uncomfortable.

"It's a sports bar," she said to her brother, whose eyebrows had gone so high they'd disappeared into his fringe.

"A rich sports bar?" he responded as their server placed crystal clear water on the table, along with a beveled, crystal dish filled with roasted peanuts. "Should we know what a buzkashi is?"

"These complimentary?" asked Javad. "I didn't bring a lot with me and am not sleeping with royalty."

"Brethren eat and drink free," returned the squat, gender-nondescript server. Their hair was a flat, chestnut brown, their face symmetrical but unremarkable, their hands large but fingers thin. If tiny rainbows hadn't been dancing across the bridge of their nose as they spoke, Marani would have forgotten they existed the moment they left the table. "You do not need coverings in here, friends," said the server.

Jacks already had his hood down and was taking an experimental sniff of the peanuts. "What's a buzkashi?" he asked as he licked the top one without picking it up.

"Jacks!" Marani hissed. "We're dragons, not children. Pick it up at least."

Jacks turned to Marani, head still low over the table, a look of absolute bewilderment on his face. He blinked once, twice, then slammed back straight into his chair. "I am so sorry. I don't...I don't even know what that was."

"You're leaking magic," said the server, their tone gentle, but curt. "Aston Harper Murray says the archipelago's magic is unbinding in a chaotic way. But you know pegasi. Flighty, at best." Before Marani could ask, the server pointed back toward the door. "Ashton is the blue pegasus outside who is still yelling expletives about our lack of adequate stables. He's brought you here and thinks he is entitled to treatment above his station. Our doorman, Herb, will sort him out. As for you lot." The server slipped a finger under Marani's hood and pushed it just behind her ear, exposing a cheek that was now a solid sheet of brown scale. "Dragons, huh? We all thought it would be another few years, but your people never did understand time. Bet that hurts, the peeling. Your bodies are reaching their expiration. We're all thrilled about it, of course, but I assume it isn't pleasant for you."

Marani tugged her hood back. "You have a lot of information about something that isn't your business. What do you know about dragons? What do you know about the walnuts out there?"

"I know about buzkashi!" the server continued, brightening. "It is a globally recognized sport of goat ball, although recent animal cruelty laws have changed from goat to cow. Once considered the international sport of unicorns, the island of Yuro has placed numerous times on the world stage. Our last team had qualified for the global finals in the Year of Squash. Who knows how far they'd have gotten if the Collapse hadn't come!"

The server finished in a breathless squeak of excitement. Marani, Jacks, and Javad, collectively, stared.

"In its current state, a human rider atop a horse must carry a headless cow carcass to their team's circle to score points. The other mounted team tries to regain control of said carcass. When played historically by unicorns, there were no riders, and a goat was skewered on the horn to carry it." The server leaned in and conspiratorially whispered, "No rules, really. Horns were routinely shattered. That one you've got there," he pointed to the horn dagger still attached to Javad's back. "That's thrice broken. Break like that would be common in buzkashi, too. Is that historic?"

The server tried to inspect, but Javad slid from his chair, to under the table, and did not bother to pull himself back up.

"Oh. How...fun," Marani said after an overly long pause in which the server looked excitedly to each of them for enthusiasm validation, and neither she nor Jacks could do more than open and close their mouths like fish. "Could we have three of whatever the house special is, and pettian juice? And a thanks for your hospitality."

"Of course. And if you'd like to learn more about unicorn sporting events in general, or buzkashi, we have a small museum in the back near the toilets." They bowed, then pushed back into the smiling crowd of other pleasantly nondescript servers and patrons.

"I'm gonna die, Grey," Javad moaned from under the table.

"Not unless you're a secretly transformed cow. Get up. Your stomach is just empty."

A hairy hand slapped Javad's chair seat, but the rest of him remained on the ground.

"Is...is it a real sport?" Jacks asked. "There's too many awards to be made up, right?"

"I'm not sure this bar is real, but we're here, and we're sitting, and no one is trying to stab us. No one is really talking to us, either, which is a different problem to unravel. Right now though, I'm taking the moment. Can you two maybe...just, watch for trouble?" Marani set Nuria's notebook on the table and flipped to the first page. "Ignore the cow lovers and their teasing information. Or go question a few of them once there is food in your stomachs. I think I need to start at the beginning with the notebook. I'll read, you two watch. We eat, maybe we question a few people, then we make a plan. Okay?"

"What are we watching for?" Javad's head appeared, although his eyes were set on the bronzed buzkashi trophy. He was, however, high enough on his knees to simultaneously grab blindly for the peanut dish.

"Arguments. Sharp objects. Dragon hunters. Soothsayers. Talk of magic that isn't a giant riddle. The usual shit that keeps us from living basic lives filled with butter and breasts." Twirls of smoke began to curl from between Marani's scales, and bits of her cloak darkened in response.

"No reason to set the place on fire." Jack's human-soft hand covered Marani's. "No one is coming for your butter or breasts. Not that you have them, anymore."

"Your face is puffy," Marani shot back. "You're allergic to peanuts."

"But they sure aren't going to kill me, are they?" Jacks grinned like a twelve-year-old and dumped the remainder of the dish into his mouth. "Know wfa I ate yefterday? Stwafberries." He swallowed before continuing, his grin even wider. "Laid right in the patch, too. I swelled up bigger than a pufferfish, stopped breathing, got so unreasonably angry that I punched a tree, then the swelling started back down. I was still upset enough that when Hans' crew found me, I laid a few out before they had me in rope, but I *ate strawberries*."

"But you didn't find your key?" As much as Marani wanted to grin with her baby brother and delight in a world no longer restricted, she was simply stretched too thin. The fourth and fifth pages of Nuria's journal had a pastel rendition of Marani and Jacks' lean-to, from right around the time Jacks had been born. The linework was wobbly and the colors muted by magical distortion and childish interpretation, but Marani recognized the two adult and one child-sized wooden rocking chairs, the low table, and the horsehair bed mats. There was a clear time skip between the previous two drawings and this one, as the one Marani currently looked at also contained Jacks' crib and a rosewood bench near the door where the family had sat to remove their shoes upon entering. Jacks had arrived shortly after the new furniture, and the raiders that had slaughtered her parents had followed the next fortnight.

Those events had happened well before Nuria had been born. Soothsayers could give visions of the past, sure, but not the far past. There were six years between Marani and Nuria, and Marani had been only three when the raiders came. There was no way the soothsayer could have given Nuria a live viewing of the murders.

With the pastels, and the chalky borders, and strange fixation on objects that would have been head-height for a three-year old...This was Marani's memory, drawn on the woven cotton paper. A dream, maybe, that Nuria had shared when she was no more than a child herself.

Jacks' voice tugged Marani back to the present. "No. Sorry. I wanted to take the bench at least but wasn't sure how to get it on horseback. You fixed it well enough last year that I couldn't bear to cut it up, either."

"And you don't think the bench is your key?" Javad asked after emptying his glass.

"A bench?" asked Jacks. "Marani got a scale comb. The bench is made from rosewood. And wouldn't a key be portable?"

"Maybe." Marani turned the page and found, finally, not drawings, but looping childish handwriting.

Marani is having dreams again. I don't like sharing them. I like when she picks flax flowers, and when Jacks learned to pick pockets. I wish I didn't have to hear her screams at night, when she watches her mom and dad die. I wish I didn't have to watch it with her, over and over—a trauma that is almost mine with how often I've seen it. I wish I didn't have to feel the pain in her belly when she gives Jacks her food because there isn't enough to go around. My stomach has never been empty. Hers has never been full.

She stole a pie today, from a baker in Aspen Grove that my mother once took me to. She wasn't caught, and tonight both her and Jacks' bellies aren't growling, but she was so close to the castle. I told the queen but she was too busy to take me. She said the guards couldn't take me, either, on a wild pegachase chase for a girl that existed only in visions.

She's so close to me. That hurts more than her hunger. It sears worse than the dreams.

I don't have enough money to go to her. Maybe I can sell the soothsayer the comb my mother gave me for my birthday last year. She always asks to hold it. Maybe it's worth enough to visit Marani. Maybe I can buy her some food. Maybe I can see if she wants to come live with me at the palace.

If that doesn't work, I will get money to her, somehow. She'd never take it from me. She hates charity. She doesn't trust people because they're always trying to take her and Jacks. But she likes girls, especially tavern girls. I could send the money through one of them. Maybe. I'd just have to find the right one.

"Glad you didn't sell the comb," Marani murmured. "Even if it would have meant a night of cow steak and a princess." The next four pages were more drawings—Jacks and Marani staring at the night sky as they lay at the mouth of their cave, Jacks with a pilfered bag of rice and a shit-eating grin, Jacks swollen and floating in a nettle bath while Marani cried. The linework steadied with each progressive picture, as Marani and Jacks fought, and stole, and aged, blissfully unaware that a princess watched them.

The fifth page, finally had more writing.

I won't let it happen again.

The queen has relented to giving me pocket money and free roam of the capital city, provided I disguise myself. At twelve, this is overdue. I've pinched from the treasury for years now and I have enough for a bar, and a plan.

This morning I had my second reading of the year, per my regular birthday gift from the queen. This morning, I got to watch a woman give Marani a bag filled with wooden pennies, while Marani fumbled out a "Thank you."

The vision is old, and I know it is from the past, but Marani needed those pennies. I can tell she didn't want to take them. I've never seen her look embarrassed. I've never seen her shake. I don't know what happened the previous day, but she took those pennies she wasn't proud of and spent them all on nettle for Jacks' tea. And I think about if, if she's doing things she doesn't want to do, for money? Stealing she enjoys. I see it in her smile. She's always kind about it. She never takes from children, or those as disadvantaged as herself. I've never seen her be disgusted over coin. Until this morning.

I'm buying the bar at the west end of Aspen Grove, in the town closest to the Common Forest. There's a woman there named Suba. I've seen her in my visions. She'll help Marani. Quietly. In a way that won't make her mad. She can make sure Marani and Jacks have food, and nettle, and clothes, and that Marani never has to take pennies she doesn't want, again.

I wish I could buy her more than tea. I'm glad such a small thing can make her, and Jacks, happy.

That was not a memory Marani wanted to revisit. And it still wasn't helpful.

"Anything?" Jacks asked when Marani let her head fall back.

"I'm only a few years in, but it feels more like Nuria was fed a curated glimpse into my life, instead of truly random events. For all she poked and teased, this," Marani thumped the notebook, "is a sterilized version of our history. No action, just," Marani searched for the right word. "Just feelings. Aftershocks. Drama."

"Well, if you want repeat business, I guess you don't show eating dinner, or picking flax, or the half of every day when we're sleeping. But soothsayers can't control visions, not as far as I know."

"Thought you only saw one twice, and bungled it both times." Javad had found his chair and, while still ghost pale, was at least upright.

"Yes, but the rules of soothsaying are posted outside every commercial hut. As a kid I was too eager to read but trust me, I've read them now a hundred times over. You're paying for a soothsayer to channel magic, not manipulate it. That would cost more than a handful of silver shield coins."

The server returned with three platters of steaming cow steak surrounded by the tiniest potatoes, and dishes of buttered corn. "Best of the house," they said. "For new family."

"Cow?" Marani slapped the diary shut, then poked experimentally at the beef. She and Jacks, and most of Yuro, had grown up on horse. Cow butter she'd stolen enough to get a taste for, but the idea of eating the thing that produced the butter seemed...counterintuitive. She'd do it though, especially if it meant a break from memories she had no desire to revisit.

"We don't serve horse in this establishment," the server said when they caught the slight curl to Marani's lip. "The owners find the meat distasteful. We understand dragons have different appetites, but I'm hoping this will work for now. I'd suggest you eat it, as you will want the energy in the coming hours."

The next person who made even a tangential horse sex reference near her was getting stabbed. "We weren't planning on staying more than two hours. Just a bite to eat, a bit to read, and then we have to head out."

"That isn't advisable."

"You say that like you're going to stop us." Javad placed a sheathed dagger on the tabletop.

"*Why* is it inadvisable," Marani asked.

The server blinked at Javad, then canted their head assessing him from boot to nose. "I thought...you really don't understand do you? Any of you? What's going on? The magic?"

"You could *tell us*. Then we would understand."

"Is it more than being dragons?" Jacks added. "We got that."

"Of course it's more than that," their server stuttered.

"Out with it then," said Marani. "Thus far, everyone with more information has stayed maddeningly silent." She shoved a spoon into the buttered corn dish. "Besides, I thought we were safe here?"

"You are," said the server. "And know that we will keep the door barred as long as possible. We've doorman here for a reason. But scouts report three bands approaching, one from the west, one from the east, and one from the north. All monarchy funded, led by soothsayers and I suspect all are coming for your heads. And you two kits haven't even begun to leak true fire. You—" They coughed, rubbed their nose, and then with a toothy smile said, "Enjoy the butter. If you'd like to play a round of buzkashi later, we have a quarter-sized arena out back. I will inquire what information may be shared. If you are still hungry after your steaks, flag down any server and we will bring you more. But do not leave, dragons. Not like you are now."

"Sweaty?" Jacks said as the server gave a half-bow.

"Irritated with your teasing of information?" Marani added.

"Human," the server said. "Your humanity, all of you, is a liability."

Jacks snarled, "Information would make finding my key a lot easier. And we don't know what's keeping Grey with legs and arms."

"It's a..." the server searched for words. "A binding spell. You...are bound. I'm bound. We're all bound, in different ways. Until the binding is undone, you'll get no more answers." The server bowed again, then scuttled back to the kitchens.

Jacks called after them. "Hey! Come on, friend. Why does this have to be so hard? You could have us transformed before all these soothsayers get here, we could crisp them, and then get back to our lives. Why does this have to be such a damn secret!?"

Marani wiped butter from Jacks' elbow with one of the heavy linen napkins. The shirt he'd taken from Two Spires stayed on his shoulders through sheer spite, and Marani counted at least seven holes big enough to shove a pettian fruit through. The smoking skin beneath those holes was enraged, blistering, and in some cases clotting, but it was still skin.

"Jacks," Marani cautioned. "If it really is magic—"

He slammed his fist on the table, charring his palm into the wood. "I fucking hate this! This isn't a puzzle. It isn't a game. It's a horse-damned tease!"

"And there's nothing we can do," Marani said. "Except wait. And read. Get your anger under control, or go play a round of buzkashi. Raging at a bunch of fancy people who think they're under a spell will burn time we don't have. Let the soothsayers come. If it comes to fighting, I'm sure tongues will loosen with a blade to the throat. Right now, I'm going to eat rich people steak and read a rose-colored version of our childhoods."

Chapter 7 - Nuria

Although numerous studies have proven a dragon's magic to be held in living scale, there is an argument to be made for their flame as well. It births from a specialized chamber directly above their stomach, where secretions from the muscular lining mix to create fire. This fire burns continuously within a living dragon, seemingly without fuel, and is expelled at will. With no noted fuel source and no apparent link to ingested foods, a strong hypothesis can be made for the involvement of magic. Discussion of such mechanisms directly with dragons is, however, not recommended.

- A Political Protocol for Nonhuman Species, Chapter 4: The Dragon

"You'll want to take Baer's Pass when we get there," Darifa said to Princess Nuria after a long stretch of silence punctuated only by the even *clip clop* of horse hooves.

"Hmm?" Nuria registered the words slowly as she fought yawns and heavy eyelids. With Liu in the lead, they'd set off along Harmonic Pass alternating walking and trotting—fast enough that they had some hope of finding Marani before nightfall, but slow enough that Nuria could keep *A Political Protocol for Non-Human Species* propped across her lap. After visiting the kitchens, she had gone to the apothecary for more nettle, and an overly helpful apprentice had handed her the same copy of *Protocol* that Nuria had been made to study as a child.

Nuria had confirmed prior ownership by opening to the third page and finding, in shaky writing, *Why would anyone talk to unicorns when there are dragons?* She'd lost riding privileges for three days after her tutor noticed. It had not endeared her to the book, but she'd been forced to study it for over a decade, regardless.

She flipped to a fresh page and read,

Lo! The Dragon waketh at the zenith of the sun and must first send the Morning Flame of Burning

Embers in response. This empties the Dragon's gut of nightly churning and allows for the freshest of starts. Next shall the Dragon consume flesh and fruit in equal quantities, ignoring all fibers which are consumed by ruminants. Indeed, to even suggest such nutrition is an offense worthy of Flame, and should the eager scientist find cruciferous or monocotic forage, he is encouraged to discern if a Horse might be in the vicinity. For while the Dragon is carnivorous, he is also amorous, particularly to the petite Sorraia horse, which he keeps in his caves for a multitude of carnal needs, including but not limited to—

Nuria swiped a thick ream of pages over, having no desire to read about dragon and horse pairings while currently on a horse. The section she read next, clearly by a different author, was still on breeding, but at least was about dragon to dragon.

It is unfortunate to report that the conditions necessary for dragon reproduction are highly environmental, requiring magmatic incubation for two and a half years, then an early diet of cephel fruit for the kit to grow his first feathers. Courtship nests have been observed to be made only of walnut branches, which are assumed to be more heat resistant than other woods. This is a benefit during dragon mating rituals, which have never been closely observed due to the excess fire production involved. What has been noted by this researcher, as well as Traden et al. and Cabbat et al., is that dragons do not adhere to mammalian sex distinctions. Verified reports note apparent female dragons paired to produce eggs, as well as male pairs. Traden et al. has noted one verified instance of throuple production. The sexual pairing does not appear to significantly

*affect egg numbers or offspring fitness, however data
are limited due to incubation times and—*

"Princess?" Liu asked. "You look pained."

"That is...yes. Yes, I think that is true." Nuria pressed a smile to her lips as she looked at Liu. "It's not my favorite read."

"Why bother?" Liu returned. "Grey hasn't read it. She's not going to know that stuff."

"No," Nuria said with a long sign. "Not as a human. Maybe some of this is instinct? Maybe there are more dragons? It's good to be prepared. Grey taught that in the Highway Guild, right?"

"Yes." Liu's nose turned up. "But she also said boredom is our enemy. And you're bored."

Nuria couldn't argue with that. The text tasted of her mother's lectures, and the orations of Faun's Pass senators at the All Yuro conference held bi-yearly for the ruling monarchies of the island. It did not help that her governess had used passages from the same book to help her fall asleep during her insomniatic teenaged years, and she found no new excitement in the sentences now that she was older and, in theory, wiser.

"It's faster to take Harmonic Pass straight through," Liu said, loud enough for Darifa to hear as well. "It bisects the Common Forest and cuts right through Marani and Jacks' homestead."

Darifa shook her head. "Which would be lovely, if they were still there."

"Where else would they be?" Liu shot back.

Nuria slipped the book back into a saddlebag. Aside from her most recent skip, she'd made it all of two chapters in. Chapter one covered the colonization of the "feral forests" and made a cursory discussion of dragon and unicorn species divergence, hypotheses of harpy off-branches, ancient common ancestry, and pre-human territory lines. Chapter two was entirely reproduction, with diagrams. The mechanics of how dragons and horses could interbreed to birth pegasi *should* have been interesting, if not downright fascinating, but the comma spliced prose and excessive adjective use managed to turn inter-species sex from biological wonder to a treatise in mathematical probability. It was also impossible to read Chapter Two and not wonder how anatomy lined up for, say, human to dragon, which seemed a very, very weird inevitability.

"They're not just going to stay in their well-known homestead. They're being hunted. Think, Baker."

Liu fluffed her hair and huffed. "Excuse me for not having command of magic. Butter is a more powerful tool."

"I'm done with the book," Nuria said, loudly. "You both have my full attention. How do we know Marani is no longer in the preserve?"

"Because I've been paying attention."

Nuria considered growling, but princesses, especially of her age, did not growl. Her irritation still overrode her decorum. "Do you sign a contract when you become a soothsayer wherein you are only allowed to parcel information? If so, is it hourly? Daily? If I offered you, say twenty gold leaves, would that be enough to get a straight answer?"

"Princess, I am giving you as much information as is safe, and I'm not tracking, I'm paying attention." Darifa looked up and Nuria followed. A full constellation of pegasi flocked overhead, their lead pointing south, toward Faun's Pass. Farther to the west Nuria saw another constellation headed in the same direction.

"Oh," Liu said. "But how do you know its Marani?"

"Because pegasi are drawn to magic." Nuria tapped the book through the saddlebag. "They're drawn to the source, which is dragons and unicorns. It's like...like going home I bet. Like a homing beacon." She looked at Darifa. "I'm certain it says something about that in this book."

"Men wrote that book, Princess. You can see their bias in every sentence—trying to have science make sense of magic, and straddling magic with human norms. You don't need it. Everyone and every thing with an ounce of magic feels the bloat right now. The corset of Yuro is strained to the point of breaking. When Marani broke the comb, she cracked a valve. The pressure building behind is too great for the opening. It will swirl, and build, and push like water over a clogged drain, until the drain is opened, or the sink breaks. *That's* what the pegasi know. That's where they're going, and where we are going, too."

"Are you sure you didn't write part of this book?" Nuria asked. "You and the authors share a love of hyperbole."

Liu patted her satchel. "I brought twelve muffins. If I'd have known, I would have put stones in them. I'm afraid that's as useful as I am in a battle with magic. I'll fight for Grey, obviously. And you too, princess."

"Noble sentiment, but Grey is fine. It's humans that are in trouble. Anyone with sense would be leaving Yuro, not riding into the mouth of a newborn dragon." Directly to Nuria, Darifa said, "Liu shouldn't be here. This isn't her prophecy."

Nuria nudged her horse up alongside Darifa's. "Grey is human as much as she is dragon, no matter how much she transforms, and you are not abandoning her."

"I didn't say I was going anywhere. You and I, princess, do not have a choice in this." Darifa nodded at Liu. "She does."

Liu waved a dismissive hand. "Whatever you two are arguing about, it isn't me."

"Astute," said Darifa. "Especially for a baker. Have you ever asked your question?"

"Five and a half years ago I asked to see how the best baker on Yuro gelatinized a lime pie. She used condensed cow milk, not gelatin, which is useless information if one is too poor to get cow milk. I did not see dragons. I didn't even get to see a cow. I have also never had a chance to try the recipe."

Darifa humphed.

Their horses continued down the road, the pace smooth and even, as pegasi continue to fly overhead. One constellation turned to two, then four. A fifth formed in the east, then pushed south as well. The sky swirled in a tornado of pastel scale and feathers, and eager nickers fragmented in the wind, reaching Nuria as reedy whispers of feral excitement she did not share.

Their pace had been more for Nuria's reading comfort than anything else, back when she'd been under the assumption that Marani might need a bit more time to sort herself and Jacks before a soothsayer and a princess arrived. Time was not, however, currently working in Nuria's favor. "It feels like preparation might trump speed, and this book won't help us if Marani is being picked apart by pegasi. I've memorized a poem greeting for a middle-class unicorn, and three generic greetings for young dragons. Unless Marani also got protocol lessons as a kit, and those memories resurface with her wings, I think this is sufficient."

"A canter would be wise," Darifa said. "A gallop, unnecessary. Birds are still in the trees. Rabbits are still in the ground. The forests do not burn. The dragons remain human."

Liu shivered. "You're so creepy."

A pegasus flew overhead—her stomach distended, her body a tangerine orange. She was lower to the ground than the rest, but being that pregnant, Nuria surmised, made it a lot more work to stay off the ground. She turned southwest then disappeared amongst the treetops, her belly jettisoning autumn leaves across Harmonic Pass.

"You're not helping things," Nuria muttered at the sky. She was just about to nudge her horse—a purple and white dappled appaloosa with green wing stubs—to gallop, when he bobbed his head and cantered entirely of his own accord, ahead of Liu. He whinnied, and Liu's white and grey criollo with quarter-wings responded in kind. Darifa's black, wingless cob nickered, and all three turned off the well-laid brick road and into the fern and sedge fields, loosely following the direction the orange pegasus had flown.

"Hey," Nuria said with a tug on the reins. "Clover. Back to the road. We're headed toward the magic, but on a road, please. All our boots are new."

Clover swung his head back, eyed Nuria with the closest look to murder that she had ever seen on horse, and then broke into a gallop.

"Clover!"

Overly full saddlebags whacked against Clover's sides in tandem with Nuria's legs. The princess grabbed at the saddle and shrieked. Similar sounds came from Liu, whose horse ran parallel to Clover and was similarly headless of the uneven ground. Darifa and her cob followed closely behind, but it took only a quick look back over her shoulder to confirm that the soothsayer, while dead quiet, was exactly as terrified as the rest of them.

"Clover, stop!"

The orange pegasus shot from the canopy like a firework. She managed a sagging loop-de-loop—belly keeping her more on her side than her back—nickered, then shot directly south.

Clover continued the gallop, pacing the pegasus and clearing fallen trees like she'd been born to the wild, instead of bred in the Aspen Grove stables for demure carriage pulling.

"Should we jump?" Liu yelled.

"You'll break your neck," Darifa wheezed back. "I was perhaps wrong on the timeline."

Nuria briefly considered the shock value of screaming, but decided being thrown from her horse was the not the sort of peril that her mother had been after—and Marani was likely too far away, regardless. Much like her history lessons, the best way through was to just hunker down and breathe until her teacher, or the horse, tired himself out. None of the palace horses had been trained for hard riding. Besides, when magic pulled, surely one followed. Even if one had not packed the appropriate footwear.

Thus, Nuria spent a very unpleasant hour clinging to Clover, occasionally whispering pleas into his ear about how yes, his pegasus blood gave him more stamina but that didn't mean she also had such stamina, until all three horses stopped, without warning, at the edge of a sickly tree grove. In the stillness of stationary horses there was a charge to the air, and a heavy taste of lead that Nuria now attributed to magic. Behind that was the smell of sweating equine, the tang of molding feathers, and very light hint of butter.

Liu promptly slid from her horse and sank to the ground on wobbly legs. "That was atrocious," she whimpered. "Although the cream I brought may be halfway to butter by now. I suppose that's a bright side."

"I don't see the orange one anymore," Darifa said, pointing to the sky. "But there are plenty more up there now. Six constellations or more. They're swarming like hornets."

"Or like a school of fish near a predator," Nuria murmured. Did dragons eat pegasi? Was that cannibalism?

"Are we to keep going?" Nuria asked Darifa. "Or wait? Is this the convergence? Where is Grey?"

"I can't say, princess. I'm your hostage, not your guide. Note that our hurried pace turned us into prey as well."

"You're almost as infuriating as Grey." Nuria dismounted—her legs just as wobbly as Liu's—and hobbled to the edge of the grove. The trees were spindle-thin, their stems curled like a tortured oak, their leaves brown and crisp in a way that spoke not of autumn, but decay. What bark remained was thick and grey, and raised up in diamond patterns. "As we were hurtling toward these, I thought they were burnt pettian. But...walnut?" she muttered. "How? Walnut trees have to be fertilized with dragon dung. The last walnut tree on Yuro died before I was born."

"I'm fascinated by your knowledge of trees, but your disinterest in protocol." Darifa had snuck up beside her. Nuria started, then scowled.

"Don't do that. Go back and stay with Liu."

"What would you have us do with the riders approaching from the north? Would you like to meet them, or press into your walnut forest? Proper greetings might save you in there, but they will not on the road. Or in the clearing, as it were."

"Damn you, soothsayer. If I'm supposed to go into the forest, just tell me!"

Darifa gave a toothy smile. "It is in Yuro's best interest if you don't die."

"Princess!" Liu's sharp note of warning cut the air.

Nuria stomped her foot. "Do you know where we are?!"

The benefit of age was that wrinkles could hide a berth of emotions. Hence Nuria could not tell if Darifa was being glib or just...soothsayer-ey, when she said, "A walnut forest, inside the boundary of Faun's Pass, two hours from what could have been their port if Bad Mill hadn't sent pegasus half-breeds to sack it twenty-two and a half years ago."

"And do you know who the riders are?"

"By our location, militia from Faun's Pass. Dragon hunting, without a doubt. A princess is excellent dragon bait."

Enter into an impossible walnut forest or start an international incident? *How is there a walnut forest? Maybe it just takes a generic magic creature poo to fertilize? Harpies might still fly, according to my vision. They could be responsible? That is the simplest explanation. The worst explanation is that this forest is a mirage, or held together by magic, and crossing into it is going turn us into frogs, or snakes, or cephel fruit.*

"Hold!" yelled a husky woman's voice, although the slight hill they'd come up still blocked the riders from view. "Hold for inspection on order of Faun's Pass."

"Decide, princess," Darifa said.

"Dragons and politics don't mix. Forest." Nuria took Darifa by the arm and shoved her past the first walnut tree. When no magical enchantment loosed, and the ground failed to open at their feet, she called back to Liu. "Can you bring the horses? Liu?"

In the intervening moments between dismounting and forest contemplation, the riders had crested the hill and now swarmed the baker. No hands grabbed at Liu's heavily embroidered dress, but Nuria had no doubt that once the troupe realized none of them were dragons, that robbery would be the next objective. "Princess," Liu called out. "Run!"

"Shit. Darifa, could you—" Nuria turned back but found herself speaking only to shaded understory.

Of course she'd run. Damn soothsayers. "Hold on. I'm the one you want. Please leave her be." Under her breath she added, "Although neither of us are dragons so you're wasting your time." Nuria stomped back toward the horses, still muttering, "This isn't how this is supposed to go. I swear once I find Marani I'm going to—"

"Princess, was it?"

A man dismounted and stepped into Nuria's path. He was comically tall, as if his body had at one point found the wrong end of a taffy puller. His beard was white, braided with sparkling beads, and his head-to-toe leathers were a sort of berry-purple with fine, even stitching, and stamped at the joints with the emblem of a cow. Behind him were a handful of rougher-looking men and women in similar purples, though cotton instead of leather. They had the horses now, and Liu, who had dismounted, looked more disgruntled than afraid. They still hadn't so much as wrinkled her dress, and had allowed her one hand free to hitch the hem from the dirt, which was both endearing, and baffling.

"You bear neither the colors, nor the banners of Faun's Pass, and you've got my pastry chef," Nuria said to the man. "Why?"

"A bounty is a bounty, princess."

"And a ransom is a ransom?"

The man laughed. "Whichever monarchy you are from, they don't have enough gold stars to beat having a living dragon."

"Liu isn't a dragon. Neither am I. Leave us be."

From his pocket, the man pulled a delicately folded sheet of paper and handed it to Nuria. "I fear you might be behind in current events."

Nuria scowled. When she refused to take the paper, the man unfolded it himself and again held it out.

BOUNTY
Any persons with ties to the Common Forest dragon
5000 shield reward for capture
200 shields if information leads to capture

The text was followed by crude drawings of Nuria, Javad, Liu, and Jacks.

"If it helps, we will not be cashing in on this bounty. I do my own live baiting. I trap harpies on Tchun, which is nasty business. I know my way around feathers and claws, and the pleas of maidens." The man refolded the paper, slipped it gently into his breast pocket, and smiled. "Have you ever been bait before, princess? Not the royal kind, where you sit on couches and sip dandelion wine, but the kind where you are strung over a pit by your ankles? And would you say you have a commanding voice? How well would your screams echo in a ballroom or, say, a forest?" He smirked back at his team, then winked at Liu. To Nuria, he bent down and whispered into her ear, "Shall we find out? Smile now, little princess. Just like this. You'll be seeing your dragon again, very soon."

The man's smile was half-rotted teeth. His breath smelled of cabbage and his leathers stank of cow. Nuria did not care for his smile *at all*.

"Stay out of my head!" Marani's words from their shared carriage ride to Two Spires rang in Nuria's mind. For the first time, Nuria understood the rage. Marani had lived day-to-day with starvation and beatings and courted her and Jacks' death with every new flower. Nuria had come along with promise the world would be fine, that Marani and Jacks' suffering was a chapter in an all-knowing book that Nuria alone controlled. Nuria could be calm, because she'd had a soothsayer, and certainty, and money. Marani had...Marani had survival and a consistently unknown future.

Now the royal soothsayer's visions had run dry, and Nuria still had her dragon to save. She no longer had a map, or a plan. And an unknown future? An unknown future was *terrifying*.

Chapter 8 - Nuria

A dragon protects what it loves, but a dragon cannot love a human. To do so is to prompt an investigation into the very core of dragon culture. The act, even the academic question, posed to a dragon, has documented disastrous results. The monarchies of Yuro have begun long-term studies in dragon taming through courtship, and it is this researcher's opinion that such relations will lead to the destruction of the species.

- A Political Protocol for Nonhuman Species, Chapter 6: The Human and His Relationship to Magic

"Consider, princess," said the man. "We do have options. You're an educated woman. I respect education. I'm an educated man. As we are approaching a magical impasse, if you provide me a location and the trapping is successful, we can avoid the bait phase. This would be in your favor if you're prone to holding in your screams. I see the little aspen leaves embroidered on your bodice. Princess Nuria, is it? Such a delight to make your acquaintance. Give us a scream, please, or a location. An Aspen Grove princess is certain to have tamed her dragon in short order."

"There haven't been dragons since my grandmother's time." Nuria continued to hold her firm, stern pose. The man certainly wore enough leather to indicate income. How well did harpy hunting pay? Had he...gone to a school for it?

"Queen Ndolo would never let the old ways wither. She must have known that dragons still walked among us. How else would her daughter have snagged one?"

Nuria waffled between laughter and suggesting the man copulate with an equine. Queen Ndolo hadn't said more than two sentences to Nuria about dragons her entire life, save very recently. Every time Nuria brought them up, Ndolo sent the conversation to tapestry embroidery, or tea recipes, or the proper placement of adverbs.

And this man. What did Nuria know about the man who thought he knew everything about her? His teeth were bad, but his clothes, nice. He wore leathers stamped with cow emblems, and there were no healthy cows on Yuro. He traveled to other islands to hunt harpies. He had at least some magic training and...ugh there was something about that cow stamp. There was an appendix in the back of *A Political Protocol for Non-Human Species* that dealt entirely with magic-borrowing species. Although it had been several years, Nuria had read that chapter front to back many times. Who wore the cow stamp? Not hunters. No, it was—

"You're a soothsayer," Nuria shot back. Darifa had always worn court attire when at the Aspen Grove palace, but the guild of soothsayers had a cow crest. "Can't you divine her location?"

"That would seem the logical step, wouldn't it?" He snapped his fingers and the two men holding Liu brought her forward, still very careful with her dress. "It would be common sense that a soothsayer could pay a villager for their life question. In Two Spires in particular, there are plenty of hungry children who would ask anything for a handful of pennies. What is fascinating," he pulled a fragment of dragon scale from his hip pocket and twirled it between two fingers, "is that dragon-related questions don't fall under soothsayer purview. I've tried at least three dozen versions of "Where is Yuro's dragon?" and reports always come back as simply, nothing. Tragically even a dud question does use up that person's chance, as well. With the binding spell uncorked, I'd thought that might yield better results, but alas. Five questions we've asked this morning alone, all to no result. Now a princess with a royal bond to a dragon? A royal bond that is part of her *blood?* I'm willing to bet she could have any dragon vision she wanted."

"Maybe. Or maybe you're just a bad soothsayer." Nuria put on her best highborn court voice. It's true my maternal line tamed dragons, but we did that with tea and politeness. Have you tried asking the question nicely?"

The man raised his palm to slap her.

"No point in making me cry if there's no dragon nearby to hear. Or do you just like slapping unarmed girls?"

His open hand met her cheek, the leather of his gloves wet enough to hide Nuria's whimper under a *thwock*.

"Call the dragon."

Nuria straightened, silently cursed the uninvited tears, and said, "I can't help you."

Again, he slapped her. The same cheek, welting the skin. The same leather glove. Nuria's head shocked to the right. "Where is the dragon!?"

"You don't have the temperament for this."

Thwock.

Nuria would not move. "Not my fault you threw away your question. Or the questions of those villagers. What education did you say *you* had again?"

Thwock.

Nuria fell to her knees, ripping her arms from the men who held them, and soaking her green skirt in wet sedge.

"I can slap you just as well in the sedge, princess."

Tears continued, salt burning her bruised left cheek, as she tried to focus. Keeping him engaged with her kept him off Liu. That was all that mattered right now. That, and what he'd said about soothsaying. Nuria was aware there were rules, but she'd been ten years old the first time the royal soothsayer had come around, and had just...assumed the woman would correct her if she attempted a faux pas. But her question had worked—in a roundabout way—and had been working since, despite definitively being about a dragon. But Nuria had been schooled with *A Political Protocol* since she could walk. She knew how to ask a dragon question, and she'd had Marani's comb. Clearly, that had been the right combination.

"Maybe your question is wrong."

This time the soothsayer barked a laugh. "Do you speak from experience? Tell me, princess. Have you ever seen a soothsayer?"

"Yes," she answered automatically, defiantly, before her brain registered the danger. Her eyes still tracked the bit of used scale playing between the soothsayer's fingers. It had lost its sheen and most of the marrow, but a faint blue still showed on the striated surface.

"Mmm. And what was your question?"

"Let Liu go. You don't need her."

The soothsayer's attention turned to Liu. "Madame Pastry Chef, have you asked your question?"

Liu, who had spent at least a decade as one of Marani's Highway Guild bandits, looked decidedly unimpressed with both her captors, and the soothsayer. "If all your previous attempts have failed, forcing my question speaks of desperation. In addition, if you ruin my dress I will murder you."

The soothsayer laughed. "Well, we are in a bit of a desperate situation, dear, and two screams are better than one, should your reading fail."

Nuria considered, darkly, that at least this was the peril her mother had wanted. Which was useless, of course, if it was being leveraged by others. At least this wanted poster didn't mention Jacks.

"The clearing here is delightful. I'd like to take time with this magic source, in the grove of"—the soothsayer squinted—"walnuts. No wonder the pegasi are flocking. Pastry chef, to your knees, please, along with the princess. We don't need a sprained ankle during the reading." He winked back at Nuria. "You, I'm sure, are quite used to being on your knees. I've heard the rumors about Aspen Grove's queens and their dragons."

Nuria pushed the image of her grandmother and a dragon in a...romantic...position, far, far from her mind. A month ago she'd have found the idea horrifying. "Crass. Subtle insults are more effective. Crass insults often speak to jealousy. But there's only one dragon to seduce, and I've already got her."

As the soothsayer turned the pink of his beard beads, Liu yanked her arm from one of the men's grasps. "Leave her alone. We are following the pegasi migration, the same as you. The dragon you're chasing used to be the best highway bandit on Yuro and as sure as yeast makes dough rise, if you even suggest harming Princess Nuria, she will skewer and eat you, transformed or not." Liu released her skirts and sniffed. "And I'll bake what remains into a pie with a braided crust and with two little aspen leaf cut outs on the top, which is a very basic design because you are very basic bandits. Kneel in the dirt? The *dirt?* I am baker, and a highway bandit. I am not a thug."

The woman with the deep voice—who had called out to them on the hill—chortled. A few of the men exchanged incredulous looks before resuming their hold of Liu, not so gently this time.

"Now they're wrinkling Liu's sleeves," Nuria pointed out. "You're prepared to court an angry dragon, but I don't think you're ready for an angry pastry chef."

"This doesn't have to be violent, princess," said the soothsayer, although normal color had yet to return to his face. "Any more so than it has been. Consider your options."

A few slaps and the ringleader was trying to deal again? The very concept of a dragon had everyone around the bend. "Right now, I'm considering why it takes such very big men to take down a pastry chef and a princess." With a sugar-sweet smile up at the soothsayer—which hurt her bruised cheek—she said, "You are considerate, for all your threats of using me as bait. I am not terribly familiar with the rules of soothsaying, but I'm wondering if consent isn't a part of it? Obviously, that isn't needed if you want me to scream, but that does no good if the dragon can't hear. My dragon, in particular, is a stickler for consent. So. We don't consent, and you're not scary. What'll it be then? We're very busy and as you note, I have a dragon to seduce, and I don't appreciate having my time wasted by journeyman soothsayers and their hired hands. Make your move, or go away."

Another scale emerged from the soothsayer's leathers—this one an effervescent pink that burned with life. It was palm sized, like the last, and Nuria finally pieced together that it wasn't dragon scale she was looking at, but pegasus scale.

Possibly feral, cross-bred horse scale, of which Yuro had an endless supply. The soothsayer pressed the scale to his lips, closed his eyes, and mumbled. Pink wicked from scale to his skin, staining his moon-white cheeks a child's magenta. A shock of rainbow wicked through the walnut grove, and a *snap-hiss* of magic? electricity? lifted the fine hair on Nuria's arms as the man sucked magic from the scale, his eyes closed, his stance waving like a reed in the wind.

Nuria kicked the soothsayer in the stomach—hard, with the pointed end of her fashionable traveling shoes that the royal tailer had studded with the tip of used unicorn horn for traction.

The heel parted a leather seam like pegasus wings and lodged into the soft belly beneath. The soothsayer screamed. The scale dropped, half-bleached, half still burning pink. Nuria kicked it farther away, into a clump of ferns, then landed another heel to the soothsayer's temple while he gasped for breath. There was blood then, and men grabbed at her arms but only for a moment, as Liu's lacquered, perfectly oval nails found first ears, then eyes. A well-placed muffin temporarily blinded one of the men, and another Liu wedged so far down a man's throat that he doubled over, gagging.

Even with targeted heels and muffins, there were still six men and two women against them, not counting the soothsayer, which did eventually lead to Nuria's hands being bound. A knee found the small of her back and she fell to the dirt, coughing and sputtering, but still refusing to scream. She'd consented to be bait, but she'd be bait on her own terms.

"Dirt? Really?" Liu, having no such restraint on her own voice, screeched at the women that held her shoulders. A mustached man grabbed for her delicate little wrists but she slapped him away, the man more startled than hurt. "You have *stained* my *hem!*" Off to their left, the muffin man continued to gasp for breath.

"Liu," Nuria said as rough hand pushed her further down, onto her belly, her mouth kissing the sedge. "Maybe not the item to worry about at the moment."

"This was the last bolt of Seashore Opal silk coming to Yuro this year. I didn't ruin clothes when I was a bandit, and I am not going to have them ruined *by* bandits."

"Watch the muffins," said the throaty woman. "She might have more in her pockets."

"I'm not going to pat her down," said the taller woman. "I know how much Seashore Opal costs. Dragons have killed for less, even if the finery is on their pets. I'll hold her hands, but that's it. Mazen, you alright?"

Nuria caught the subtle tensioning of Liu's body as the taller woman released her shoulder and, with the irritated caution instead of urgency, fished for Liu's hands.

Mazen the soothsayer growled as he got to his feet. He held a palm to his right temple, where Nuria's heel had broken the skin. The other hand held together the front of his leathers, which had stained a deep rust red. The pegascale remained on the sedge, dim and lifeless. "Princess." The soothsayer's exposed skin sparkled from nose to fingertip in a seashell glow. "Princess," he seethed.

Liu pounced. From an unseen fold in her gauzy skirt, she pulled a massive kitchen knife and, without a moment of hesitation, sliced two of the woman's fingers clean off.

"She's got a damn knife!" yelled Moustache. "Hold her."

"Liu, be careful!" Nuria yelled.

"They *ruined* my *dress!* And Senna just made me learn to field dress a horse because I used the last of the butter for an experimental croissant instead of the queen's dinner. I'm supposed to practice!"

Nuria was momentarily forgotten in the flurry of soothsayer shouting and bandits changing tactics from 'subdue two court women' to 'weapons have been drawn.'

Liu would lose far more than her dress if they didn't get away. Nuria rolled over, kicking at the looming soothsayer's knees. Her boots were new leather, the horn-heel plenty sharp, but Mazen was high on pegasus magic. He hauled Nuria from the ground by the clasp of her cloak then slapped her once, twice, across the same cheek. "Scream, princess," Mazen commanded. "Let's see if there are any dragons nearby while we murder its pet."

Another slap, this one catching Nuria's nose. Blood ran thickly now, down her chin and neck, and under her collar. But she would not scream. She was a princess, but she was not a victim. "I bet you dance like a little boy," she said as droplets of blood stained her lips. "I bet you step on girls' feet and talk endlessly about your mid-tier sword collection and expect them to be overly grateful when you bring them a cup of wine."

The soothsayer raised his hand, this time not to slap, but to strike.

A blue pegasus dove from the sky, the wind screeching around its wings, its mouth pulled back in a predatory sneer.

Mazen released her cloak. Nuria, having had a solid year of feral pegasus training required before she was allowed to ride horses, immediately dropped to hands and knees and covered her head. Liu screamed, the bandits screamed, and the soothsayer cursed and ran. Hooves clapped to the ground so hard Nuria fell over, and after a shrill yell the pegasus grabbed the soothsayer by the neck of his leather jerkin, shook him back and forth like a cat with a mouse, then bounded back into the sky, over the walnut grove, and out of sight.

"What the *fuck?!*" exclaimed a man with a cleaver-sized gash across his cheek.

Liu's knife was still in her hand and so she brandished it in a wide arc at bandits who stood, gaped-mouthed, at the sky. "That's for eating all the muffins!"

Nuria pinched the bridge of her nose with one hand while brushing off the front of her dress with the other. The clasp of her cloak had caught the front of her dress when the soothsayer had picked her up, and what had been a slight dip near the front had torn to expose a very unprincessly amount of cleavage. If she ended up on a galloping horse again, she'd have to ride one-handed or risk hitting herself in the face. Further insult was that the white fabric bodice had grass stained an unfortunate shade of green that did not match her dress at all. It would be easier to blend in with townspeople now, although the profession she now best represented would not win her points with Marani. "Are we done here then?"

"It just came out of the sky," said Moustache. "Do you think it's coming back for the rest of us? Do dragons control the pegasi?" He fell to his knees and tugged at Nuria's skirt hem. "I'm sorry. Tell your dragon I'm sorry!"

"Get away from her." Liu repocketed her knife and flounced over to the princess, with a haughtiness Nuria downright envied. "Horses ran when the pegasus came down and I don't think you want to waste time chasing them. Enchanted forest then, is it?"

"So sorry," murmured Moustache.

Nuria appraised the man at her skirt, a woman still gaping at the sky while the other cradled her bleeding hand, and decided she and Liu had won, if only on a technicality. They'd gotten lucky with this first batch. Seasoned soothsayers and proper hired thugs wouldn't be quelled by courtly insults and delicately sugared muffins. Their best bet was to find Marani, fast, and work toward a transformation once they were all together. "Yes, into the forest. Maybe we can follow Darifa's trail, since she ran off the moment I was distracted." She touched the hem of Liu's skirt with her boot tip, dislodging Moustache in the process. "Sorry about the dirt. If we're walking, there's sure to be more. I'll be sure you get a replacement the moment the next silk shipment comes in, regardless of tariff cost."

Liu returned a warm smile. "That's a better deal than Grey ever offered. Off we go then. If the pegasi ended here, and there's maybe a hidden bar somewhere in the grove, then there's a perfect chance Grey is there, too." Liu's smile turned to a girlish grin. "And with the cut to your bodice, I'm sure she'll be very glad to see you, too. Do we, do we need to do something about them? Should we stitch your cheek?"

Eight bandits stared back at them. Three bled from knife wounds, one was slowly turning blue as another pounded on his back, and the three remaining looked ready to piss themselves. "My cheek is fine. Can you imagine what this lot would have done if a dragon had actually shown up? Let's tie them to the closest tree and head in. At least if they're under the forest canopy they can't get picked off by another aerial dive. The pegasus would have to land and peck them apart."

Moustache whimpered.

"It's funny," Nuria said as she took the taller woman by the arm and led her, without complaint, to the closest walnut tree. "My exposure to bandits is limited to my visions, and you, Marani, Jacks, and Javad. That appears to have been a very selective view."

Liu drove the bleeding men to the same tree with a point to her hemline, and a caustic glare. "She never had to recruit, if that's what you're asking. Couple of us she asked to join, like me. Some she beat up and never left, like Javad. There's a lot of us out here looking for something, Princess. We look for food, for shelter, for family, for belonging. Grey and Jacks, they built a home for us in the Common Forest. People that came to join the Highway Guild, they never left. Jacks was mostly useless, and Grey's temper could get you impaled but they were...like shepherds in a way." Her brow wrinkled. "We served them the way your people serve you. Like they were king and queen of the forest. How do you think it'll be when they are dragons again? Will the monarchies bow to them? Are they supposed to serve the monarchies?" With a snort, Liu said, "I don't see Grey doing that, no matter how torn your dress is. Forget what these kids would do with a dragon if they caught her. Have you thought about what *Yuro* is going to do? How hard would it be for Grey and Jacks to just burn down all the settlements, eat the residents, and take Yuro back?"

Nuria had failed to find any rope with the horses gone, so she settled for tying the bandits together through the loops in their knapsacks as they linked arms around the base of the walnut. Muffin man they'd left on the ground. He was breathing again, thanks to a final whack to his back, but with the way he curled on the ground and sucked at the air, he had little chance of walking soon. As she worked the knots, Nuria let her mind wander to scenarios she'd refused to think about during the ride. What if they found Marani and she was already transformed? What if they found her human, but she transformed halfway back to Aspen Grove? What if they did get her back to Aspen Grove, and she transformed at the castle, and didn't want to stay on the palace grounds? Did she *need* protection, as a dragon? How high could arrows fly? And would a transformed Marani remember enough of her previous life to not, say, just eat every human in her line of sight?

Nuria finished the knots, dusted off her dress, and stood. "I guess we hope that a little bit of humanity stays after the transformation. Without it, none of us will fare well." She took Liu's hand and guided her through a boundary of ferns, following a trail of crushed stems.

Liu winked. "I wouldn't put money on humanity, but I would on Grey's love of breasts. You underestimate your value to both Grey the human, and Grey the dragon. If we stumble on a tailor, I have some ideas on a cut that would make better use of your assets."

Chapter 9 - Marani

In the battle of dragon versus unicorn, calculations suggest that the dragon would surely win. There must be a natural pecking order amongst these beasts, yet no scholar has of yet, discerned one.

- A Political Protocol for Nonhuman Species, Chapter 7: Courts of Magic

"Okay here, what about this passage? It's from just a few months ago." Marani put a full glass of pettian juice on either side of the notebook to hold it open, then read, "My visions are increasingly destructive. I've begun editing the version I give to the queen. This time I saw Aspen Grove's fledgling port on fire. Ships in our harbor flew Bad Mill flags and the sky was so thick with wings I couldn't see the sun. All around I hear shouting, but now my sight is frozen ahead, at the flames, and the choked skyline. Marani isn't in this vision, like many of late, but the soothsayer won't tell me what that means. I still, to this day, do not understand what any of this has to do with that old comb. You'd think I'd asked about pegasi, for all the wings and horses I see."

"There are another few lines under it," Jacks said, craning across Marani's lap.

"They're irrelevant."

Jacks smirked. "Are they? You asked for help, and everyone at this table is an adult." He took a long drink of pettian juice, then said. "Read it, and I promise to lay off strawberries for the next month. Or I can read it." He reached for the diary with puffy, strawberry-stained fingers.

"You just claimed to be an adult." Marani scooted her chair back, keeping the notebook from her brother's sticky hands. "It says, Two years ago, both my readings were intimate. I still giggle over her face when I dream of her robbing my carriage, but I kiss her instead of giving her coin. The second reading I had that year, dragons help me,

I fantasize still about the callouses on her fingers as she ties me to my bed and commands I stay quiet, even though she's just brought me a bouquet of flax flowers in a handmade vase and asked if I might like to have a different kind of adventure."

The next lines, which Marani did not read, were much too intimate to share with anyone, much less a brother: *I was so wet after that reading I had to change clothes once the soothsayer left. The visions engage like life. Her hand grasps my thighs and push them apart. She's so insistent, unless I hesitate. If I hesitate there are only butterfly kisses and delicate words meant to soothe. If I comply, oh, if I comply there is a heat to her tongue that feels inhuman when it enters me, and burns a soft fire across my belly and breasts. I have never wanted like this, not for food, not for sun, not for monarchy freedom. I am hers a thousand times over and she knows that when she kisses me, and when her fingers thrust inside my folds. She ties me down but that is never needed, for I am an endlessly willing participant. I tell her so, and it drives her as high as a pegasus. She does not relent until I beg her for release. I screamed too, in the vision. I pray to every dragon that ever lived that I did not make that same kind of scream in real life.*

"Why'd you stop? It was just getting interesting."

Marani glared at her brother. "It's just her babbling about pegasi."

"You brought her flax flowers?" Javad, who had been uncharacteristically silent to this point, regarded Marani. "Women are a lot like dragons, I suppose. They like shiny things, and pretty things, and sex."

"In her vision I brought her flowers. That particular entry has not, at least to my memory, yet occurred. Regardless, I'm not reading any more out loud. Here." Marani tossed the notebook to Jacks. "Good luck parsing it. Half of the current entries read like the near future, while others revisit pasts that are close to, but not identical, to what actually happened. I'm nude in a disturbing number of them."

Jacks mimed choking himself. "Sounds like soothsaying to me. Half of it has to be guess work." He opened the notebook to the last few pages and scanned. "Sex. Sex. Kissing. This one, ewww, no. Whips? Really? Why?"

"That would be one that hasn't happened yet," Marani said to the floor.

"Thank dragons for small favors." He skipped three pages. "Ah, a page without boobs. This one and"—he flipped a page over—"the next one has 'wings in the sky,' and a lot of things on fire." Jacks rubbed his nose, then looked back at Marani. "Wings could be dragon, but even if you and I transform, and, say, Javad goes dragon as well, the three of us wouldn't block out the sun. You'd need thousands of dragons for that. And while the future is fluid, this is implausible."

"You don't think there could be more like us?" Javad had settled back into his chair, hands clasped comfortably across his overly full belly. He belched, and their waiter glared from across the bar, but no one said anything directly. Which was—again—strange, as a bar with door staff, passwords, and crystals would not generally tolerate rude, dirty travelers, no matter how high quality their new clothing might be, or how many horns they were packing. Then again, sports bars had their own unspoken rules, and any bar with a bronzed cow carcass was outside her normal genre.

"You don't think we would have found them? Even by happenstance?" Marani took the notebook back from Jacks and shoved it back into her jerkin. "I've thought about this. A lot. Invulnerability would make a person a natural thief, or natural soldier. Yuro has no armed conflict, either on-island or within the archipelago. And we know all the bandits, either through the Highwayman Guild or the alliances we had to make with the smaller bands to keep off our roads. Jacks' grace might have led to a career in dancing maybe, but the allergies would have made most of the performance wear impossible. A talented enough child might have been shipped off-island, but stealth dragons on other islands are outside of our preview." Marani nudged Javad's foot with her own. "Marksmen like you? Again, it speaks to military, or assassin, and we just don't have need of that sort of thing. Maybe they'd hide out in a traveling skill show? But Jacks and I have seen plenty of those, especially when he was young. We've never seen *anything* like you, Javad."

"Doesn't mean they couldn't be out there," he snorted, although Marani caught the acquiescence in his voice. There was no way, with all the robbery, and arrests, and general mayhem the three of them had been involved in across their lives and across their very tiny island, that they'd have missed another magic-touched human. Maybe said human couldn't talk about their abilities, assuming a binding spell was in play, but they would have *shown* their abilities, eventually. Like her, and Jacks, and Javad, there was no way to keep their skills hidden on an island where few outside town walls slept with full bellies.

Maybe they'd all just been hanging out at the Solitaire Bar, and Marani, Jacks, and Javad's invitations had been eaten by pegasi. Still. Dragons had been extinct for a generation, the same with unicorns. The Solitaire Bar patrons hadn't spent the last fifty years inside a walnut forest. That was ridiculous.

"Could just be pegasi, too." Jacks finished the last glass of pettian juice and reclined in his own chair. "With the way they're flocking to us. Maybe Marani gets mad and sets a few ports on fire after Bad Mill talks go bad?"

Marani sighed. "I can barely light a candle. We're smoke, you and I, not flame. At least right now. And that vision you just read? Other than telling me that Bad Mill will be chaos, and Nuria might be in trouble, it doesn't help. Except that Nuria'll be in even more trouble if I arrive with several constellations in tow. But. Ugh." Marani slapped the tabletop. "I'm not just going to hang out in a bar, either, just to prevent...whatever, from coming to pass. Especially if everyone here knows about magic and refuses to talk. It's a great bar, the crystal shiny, the steak juicy, the butter thick, but no. Ugh." Reluctantly, Marani set the notebook on the table. "Jacks, you want to have a real go at the notebook? Maybe you'll find a nugget I missed. Just promise you'll skip over any of the naked parts. Nuria had...quite a show on several occasions. She didn't need to write it down with so many details, and yet..."

"I would rather pluck my eyes out than reading any of those. You want to start the questioning or—"

"I said you may not enter!" The familiar voice of the doorman boomed through the small tavern. All the patrons, including Marani and her crew, turned their full attention to the east wall. A woman in a green traveling cloak stood with crossed arms, her grey hair windblown, as she glared up at the doorman. She wore leather pants, a leather jerkin, and stamped on the right breast of said jerkin was a cow hoof outline.

"Herb, you want me to call Starlight?" asked a woman in a corner.

The doorman snarled. "I thought you already did, for the dragon lot? This time, call the whole tootin' council. If a human woman got past the magic barrier, the clock is ticking faster than it should."

Four women left their small table and exited through a door behind the bar.

"Get away," Herb growled. "This isn't your place and you know it."

The soothsayer stayed rooted in the entry, her hands high, her ancient face oddly smug. "The world is broad and our time small. I seek to enrich and not to enrage. I bear no weapons nor malice and swear my fealty to Yuro and its queens."

"Just kill her," called a man from the back.

"I beseech you, please—" Her words ended with Herb picking her well off the ground. What she managed to squeak out after, turned pleading. "You have Grey and

Jacks here, do you not? The dragons? If you bring Lord Starlight, I can prove my credentials."

What little, curious conversation the bar had held, died. Marani, Jacks, and Javad all stood, although Marani had no memory of them doing so. Javad's hands had already found blades, Jacks had small paring knife of his own, and puffs of smoke had already begun to escape from underneath Marani's cloak.

"*Human* woman," Javad whispered.

"She's a soothsayer," Marani whispered back. "She has magic. Betting that's what got her across. I think this whole lot of patrons is the same. Magic calls to magic, and where's there is one soothsayer, there are a dozen."

"This one hasn't got a blade on her," Javad said. "I can tell from here. Doesn't look like she was expecting trouble."

Jacks nodded. "She's definitely a soothsayer though. She has that heavy metal smell to her, like loose magic. Her cape is a thick cotton, like the kind Nuria wears. I'm not seeing embroidery. She's well paid but not working in a court. But she sure has angered the magical cow lovers. She's not one of them."

"Huh. Hunting us, then? I suppose we should deal with her. It isn't the Solitaire's job to dispose of our baggage." Marani reached for her hatchet. The soothsayer peered across the threshold.

"Marani! Grey!"

Well-dressed, and working for a court. The last time a well-dressed nobody had known Marani's birth name, it had been due to prophecy. As Nuria was not here, that left a very real possibility that this soothsayer was *her* soothsayer, which meant Marani couldn't quickly punt her to the edge of the woods and go back to her steak.

"There are no dragons here!" said Herb. He stepped outside, soothsayer still dangling from his hand. "Close the door and bolt it," he called back to the patrons. "Send Lord Starlight when he arrives."

A thin man bolted the door shut behind him. The patrons sat back in their chairs, their chatter resuming, but the tension refused to bleed from the air.

"You two stay here," Marani said, although she did sheath her hatchet. "I'm going to get information. Jacks, you're still on diary duty."

Jacks rounded on her. "Soothsayers don't travel roads alone, sis. If you go alone, you get captured, then we have to spend the next few days chasing you down and killing everyone responsible instead of sleeping in soft inn beds. So no, you aren't going alone."

"Jacks," Marani out her hands on his shoulders and tried to push him to the side. "Come on—"

Javad came round her other side and pressed the tip of his better blade, ineffectually, against her throat. "You're outvoted. Don't think with your dragon brain. Think with the brain that wants to live long enough to see your princess again and use that saucy little whip."

Marani wrapped her hand around the knife and pushed it down. "You could just ask to come, although I think the three of us against one royal soothsayer is overkill."

"We don't travel alone anymore," said Jacks. "Dragons flock, just like pegasi."

"She's just a soothsayer," Marani said, but did not object further as the three wound their way around the tables and to the door. A beefy hand slapped hers down when she reached for the deadbolt.

"Herb said to keep it locked." A woman with tinsel wound through a double braid glared up at Marani from her seat, hand poised for another slap.

"I've business with that soothsayer," Marani said, in as mild a voice as she could manage. "Unless you'd like to distract me with information about the nature of this walnut grove, or why there is a magical barrier around it that humans cannot pass?"

"Door is stayin' closed, just like my mouth." She snapped a lock on yet another previously unseen deadbolt, then sat back down and crossed her arms. "You've rooms for the night. They've already been sorted. Go back to your table."

Marani caught the distinct smell of burning leather coming from under the door. "You people are maddening. We've no intention of staying the night in this circus."

"Not that we're not grateful," Jacks added. "You took a chance, housing dragons, and it's natural to want us to stay, but we need to speak with that woman, who does seem to *want* to give us information. Let us out."

"She can't give you the information you want, the same as us." Their server returned, voice dripping apology, but a stance that clearly expected physical argument. "We are asking you, dragons, to please sit and let us handle this soothsayer. If your skills are needed, we will request. Until such time, it is best if you remain indoors."

"What kind of inn did you say this was, Javad?" Marani asked over her shoulder.

"Last time I was nearby it was just an exclusive sports bar with nice rooms. Hey friend, we aren't requesting." Javad's blades were back, one now at the server's sternum, the other imbedded in the door, just shy of the server's ear.

"Last time you were here, brother, you didn't have dragons. And we are not requesting, either." In a move that directly mirrored Marani's, the server clasped Javad's blade, wrapping fingers tight enough to sever, and pushed the marksman's hand away. "Dragons. Please. To your table, or to a room. Is there one you would prefer?"

The server released Javad's blade. Javad's kitchen-sharp, royal steel blade.

There was no blood. Not on the floor, not on the server's hands, not on the blade itself.

"Yuro take this, are you all a mess of dragons?" Javad spat. "That's the kind of thing you tell people when they visit. Fucking magic everywhere!"

Blood rushed in Marani's ears. *Trapped* echoed in her mind. She shed her cloak, smoke licking from her scale and setting the cotton alight before it hit the cobblestones below. But it was Jacks who said, in a deep, guttural voice as he grabbed the server by the throat, "Let us go."

The smell of burning skin shocked Marani from her flush before it had a chance to fully take hold. As her mind snapped from *trapped* to *improbable,* she registered the flames from her cloak, the balls of sparks that rolled from her scale, and the smoke that crested from Jacks' hand as it burned the soft, chalky skin of the server.

Underneath Marani's clothes, scales loosened and fell into her boots. Sharp teeth cut at her gums, pressing against what remained of her human molars. A lock of hair fell in front of her eyes and when she brushed it back it came away with her fingertips.

Every day, every minute, brought their tempers higher. Every flush brought them closer to scale and wing, and fucking *dragons*. Marani wasn't ready. Jacks wasn't ready. But they would not be trapped, either.

The server clawed at Jacks. Blood did well then, at the meeting of nail and skin, as Jacks' fingers ground down.

"Jacks stop!" Marani grabbed her brother by the wrist and pried his fingers away. "Do not release the blood. You know the consequences."

"We're *trapped,*" Jacks's cold, empty eyes turned to Marani. He snarled, a sound that Marani felt through her bones. Echoing around it was a *whump* from the other side of the door.

"But we don't kill," she said. "Not like this, anyway."

Jacks hissed, "It won't kill them. You saw the knife. Maybe they're a dragon, and that's why they can't talk to us. We're all bound up in this magic."

"Then we shouldn't be able to talk about it, either," Marani hissed back.

"This isn't the correct path," gasped the server.

"I also see the server's blood dissolving your skin. More caustic blood is a great addition to our troupe. You won't win this fight, so why not talk instead?" Marani took Jacks by the chin and forced his focus back on the server. The person—dragon?—was brave, she'd give them that. The server still stood between them and the door, hands curled into the loose fabric of their pants, mouth gasping for breath as boils swelled and blood dripped, hot and red, from fingerprint-sized patches where their skin had adhered to Jacks' fingers.

And Jacks' fingers. His human skin fit like a torn glove now, exposing sharp lemon-colored scale. Hints of green shone along his jawbone, where the skin pulled back of its own accord. His pupils were wide and amber, not black, and Marani swore she saw protrusions on his forehead—where horns might one day erupt.

They could not do this here.

"They can't be a dragon, Jacks. They're bleeding."

The flush continued to hold. "We bleed, under the right circumstances. If dragons can injure themselves, surely dragons can injure other dragons."

That was a theory they'd never tested. "Their blood disappears. Ours just kills. If there is magic inside them, it is like Javad's, and we don't have the time to tease that out."

"We have to know—"

"What if they're human, Jacks? A human just touched by magic, like a soothsayer? Like Javad? We don't know what kind of drugs they have. Where did the magic of the walnut grove come from? Who controls it? Has it infused into its inhabitants? What if this is just a human trying to protect us and you, what? Want to sear their head off for that?"

A firm knock came from the door. Everyone ignored it.

"They won't let us *out!*"

"Gods help me with two of you," Marani heard Javad mutter. "If you both flush at the same time I'm diving into the nearest body of water and drowning myself."

"Unhelpful," Marani snapped. "If we both flush, we'll bring the inn down, and you'll never make it to water."

"I won't be trapped. I won't be caged. I'm a fucking *dragon,* and maybe they don't deserve to have a head." Jacks, oblivious to everything but his target, raised his free hand, fingers wide, ready to peel the server's face off.

Marani shoved herself between them and kneed Jacks between the legs.

"*Marani!*" Jacks snarled, his voice more feral than human.

"If you want to hurt someone, hurt me. Let's test your theory. Take your time. Crushed balls at your age can't be pleasant. We cannot flush in here, Jacks. These people are irritating, but they're unarmed and generally pleasant. Magic-kissed doesn't make them our enemies, no matter how secretive they are."

Jacks growled up at her, and through his curled lips Marani noted two missing back molars.

WHAM WHAM WHAM.

"Herb?" the woman who'd locked the door yelled. "That you?"

WHAM WHAM WHAM.

"Sure doesn't sound like Herb," said another woman at her table.

"Any chance it's one of ours? Sicorro and Cirrus are on forage today."

"We have a password for a reason, Glitter."

"Would you be able to hear it through the oak though?" Marani asked. "What does an inn full of buzkashi enthusiasts have to be afraid of?"

Glitter shot her a *don't be daft* look.

Marani still wasn't sold on the dragon front. Their server was on their knees alongside Jacks, their neck wounds already healed. There wasn't a trace of their blood to be found—Marani's never disappeared—although unmistakable evidence remained in Jacks' fingers, where the peeled skin had cauterized and failed to grow back. His jaw, too, remained exposed. If they had his key, one sustained flush would finish his transformation. Ugh, they were so woefully behind. The soothsayer drama needed to wrap. More magic nonsense they didn't have time for.

WHAM WHAM.

"I suppose stabbing them is out of the question?" Javad asked.

"Has stabbing me ever gotten you anywhere?"

"It's cathartic, and is doing more than standing by a door and reminding your brother he isn't in charge."

WHAM.

Marani's own flush rose again, simmering just under her carefully sutured human veneer. Again she shot it down, swallowing the rage that would, along with her dragon-strength and impenetrable skin, lead to a mess of bodies and no more answers than she'd had before. "That's a lot of knocking and not a lot of sieging. As a reformed highwayman I can tell you we didn't tend to announce ourselves if we were looking to engage in crime. I'm going to open this door now. It is in all of your best interests not to stop me. Jacks and I are under control, right now. If we both flush, you won't have a door, or an inn, to protect."

"No soothsayer has ever been anything but destructive." Glitter helped the server to stand. "Find Starlight. Now."

The server nodded and slipped away.

"Choose your next words carefully," Marani said to her. "I'm not in the mood. You know what we are. You know what we can do. Please. Open the door."

"Dragon." Glitter said the word so definitively, like Marani was already a flying lizard, and not just a painted, scaled human with lizard aspirations. "You're cute, but you do not know the game."

"Then fucking tell me!" Heat surged from Marani in an ellipse, blackening the stone floor and charring the soles of dozens of leather boots. Blood thrummed behind her eyes, pulsing and narrowing her vision. The acids in her stomach roiled. *Calm down,* she commanded herself. *This isn't the time. The inn is too small. The patrons are too strange. We need a soothsayer, not a battle.*

"Grey." Javad's sweaty hand fell onto her shoulder. "Jacks is unavailable as your safety trigger. Consider what you're doing. The words never work if I say it, or Liu. Nuria works, but she isn't here."

Jacks got back to his feet, his flush settling but his eyes still wild. "No more talking. I'm going to fucking kill—"

They couldn't both be wild things. Yuro would never bear the destruction. Marani forced herself to think of cool pettian juice, and her parent's hugs, and the cool silks of Nuria's bed. Her blood still pulsed, and her muscles still tensed, but her voice gave only a hint of waiver as she said, "Step out, Jacks."

Marani caught her brother as he collapsed, keeping his head from hitting the polished stone below. "There we go," she soothed as his eyes fluttered through the waterfall of emotions that accompanied a sudden break from the flush. "You were very ferocious. At least three of the inn patrons squealed."

"Shut up. Did you have to kick me?" Jacks pushed Marani away but stayed seated on the floor, his head between his knees. "Next time, just use the phrase. I want to have children someday. Or, kits. Ah shit, Grey." He turned a horrified face to hers. "These people had better be dragons, because I am not doing, that, with a horse."

"I think if you can't say the word sex, you don't get do it at all. Think of this as payback for the several hundred times you've done the same to me. Welcome to dragonhood."

WHAM. With her hearing back to normal, and Jacks no longer set to attack, Marani made out a faint "...message and you need to...princess..."

A lead weight dropped in Marani's stomach, turning the acid to boil. The pounding began in her ears again. *Woosh. Woosh*.

"Dragon," Glitter said, this time physically barring the door. "Be patient. Be smart. You're not just pretty scale. That woman out there is a soothsayer. She looks half-out of her mind on dragonscale. She shouldn't have been able to make it past the boundary. We have to investigate that, first. If the boundary has fallen that protects the grove, the only stopgap left is this door."

Woosh. The flush rose again, insistent and unrelenting. This time, Marani would not hold it back.

The door was between her, and Nuria.

"Javad."

"Jacks?"

Jacks grunted an assent.

Without a word, Javad tossed Glitter to the floor, arms pinned under her back. Another patron made to stand, but Jacks' kicked his legs out from under him.

"Grey." Jacks' voice came low and steady. "Is it worth it? You don't know it's Nuria. You don't know there's anyone in danger. Soothsayers lie, the same as anyone."

Jacks' vice grip on her upper arm helped Marani wrangle a modicum of thought that wasn't *kill the door*.

"What princess?" Marani yelled through the keyhole. *Not Nuria,* she begged through her flush-addled mind. *There are at least four other princesses on Yuro. Let one of them be in danger this time. Just not Nuria. She's supposed to be safe. She's supposed to be on the road to Bad Mill.*

Unless this morning's soothsayer visit had given the princess reason to change course.

"Marani!" The soothsayer had her own lips pressed to the keyhole, the scratch to her voice a clear indicator that she'd been yelling. "At the boundary. Nuria and Liu, and dragonhunters."

Jacks' arm did not loosen. "She could be lying. Grey—"

There were other words, but Marani ignored them and shook Jacks off. Another patron came to the door, but she flung him aside as easily as a soiled tunic, tossing him into Glitter and sending them both into the bar. The inn erupted into shouts, and in her periphery Marani noted several men lunge at her, only to be leveled by Jacks and Javad.

"Didn't we just play this game with you?" Javad said.

"Yes, but she's been doing this longer, and is stronger than both of us combined, even without the flush. As long as she isn't burning down the inn, maybe we let it run its course. Or you can try kicking her abdomen and see if she takes it as well as I did."

"Don't you dare say it. Just come with me." Marani snarled, throwing open deadbolts and, when the last snagged, embedding her dagger-like nails into the wood and ripping the metal clean off.

"It's not safe out there, pretty dragon!" Glitter yelled from atop the bar, where Jacks had her pinned. "Just because we cannot talk to you does not mean we cannot protect you!"

"Feels a lot safer than here." Smoke leaked from Jacks' nostrils as he too, flirted with another flush. They'd both be useless tomorrow, but that was a problem for later Jacks and later Marani.

Marani snorted her thanks, threw open the door, and rammed directly into the soothsayer—her hand raised for another whack at the door.

"Where!?" Marani demanded.

"She's just outside the protected grove. If you can get her past the tree line, the other soothsayer and her band will not be able to follow."

Javad yelled from across the inn, "You made it through."

"Because the princess brought me through. Do you want to stay here and get a treatise on Yuro magic, or do you want to save your princess?"

A deep, more reflective part of Marani's mind noted that soothsayers did not generally work in such a straightforward manner, that she had no proof Nuria was either A) outside the grove nor B) in peril, and that there was a substantial likelihood that this was a trap. The flush side of her mind, the vocal majority, insisted that if there was even the potential that Nuria was in danger, she had to act.

"Take me to my princess," Marani said. "And if she's alive, I might let you live."

Chapter 10 - Marani

Although the unicorn and the dragon have uniformly colonized across the archipelago, the harpy keeps to the highland caves of Tchun and is rarely spotted elsewhere.

- A Political Protocol for Nonhuman Species, Chapter 5: The Harpy

"I've got your back."

Jacks was more snarl than words as he buoyed himself across the tavern and landed next to her on the packed dirt of the inn's entryway. "Javad is holding down the pub."

"Keep it in one piece," Marani yelled over her shoulder. The only benefit of frequent flushing was that at least Marani could almost hold a conversation in the midst. "You hear me, Javad?"

Instead of Javad, a petite patron with cornsilk hair yelled from deep inside the bar. "No, *he* can go back there, surely. It's just those two that can't."

To which a tall, willowy man answered as he ducked around Javad and a brandished chair, "Protocol doesn't matter if soothsayers are coming. I'd rather have dragons in the horn room than humans. But we're supposed to keep them all here. Can you hold this one and I'll go help wrangle the *oof!*" A chair leg made of cephel wood connected directly to the man's midsection.

Javad hooted. "You can stay here. Got plenty of chairs for all of you!"

"If he's fighting with furniture, we've got time. Nuria?" Jacks all but danced on his toes, his skin smoked to sparks, his cropped hair curling with unshed heat.

The princess had not left Marani's mind, but neither had the state of her baby brother. "Your eyes," Marani said. "You're supposed to be my failsafe."

"How about I be your backup, instead?" His smile, through the flush, was a grotesque thing, with lips curled and nostrils flared and a mirage—faint—of green bottlenosed dragon with lemon rind striping. He spat teeth to the ground and when his eyes again met Marani's, his pupils had stretched into the serpentine. "Where we go, we go together. Where we fight, we fight together. From here on out."

Who needed keys? Marani nodded.

They ran.

Marani was well used to the soundlessness of the flush, and the narrowed vision, and the hyperfocus that all too often called for blood. But as she ran through the meager undergrowth along the game trail, her brother pacing her, eyes just as focused, muscles just as tight, Marani registered, for the first time, other sounds. Jacks' breath came even and deep, though their pace was frantic. He scratched at his chin, peeling away skin, and Marani heard the scrape of scale.

She noted the syncing of their gait, and breath, and when she caught sight of honey-colored hair and a leaf-green bodice, Marani and Jacks stopped in tandem, their fingers entwining like they could not bear to exist anymore as separate entities.

It was a flush, yes, but with two sets of eyes, two sets of lungs, and an entire island waiting for them to reach out and claim it.

"Princess?" Marani called out. They'd stopped near the base of a giant walnut whose trunk could have hidden four women with ease. There was a break in the trees ahead, the ample sunlight indicating a clearing, and the end of the grove. Nuria, or what appeared to be Nuria, idled just beyond the tree line. Marani would not rush, in case it was a trap. Her brain was not so dragon-addled that she could not sense human danger. "Nuria? Speak to me!"

"Grey! Jacks!"

The green-clad figure waved them off and so it wasn't Nuria who greeted them, but Liu, her dress dirt-stained and her face showing every ounce of corresponding irritation. She bounded to Jacks and Marani from around another large walnut and offered them a tight, but genuine, smile.

"We started in, but one of the wannabe-bandits broke through their satchel and tried to run off. We figured you'd want to talk to them, so the princess chased him down and brought him back. We were still sorting how to resecure him. You didn't bring any rope, by chance?"

"Jacks," Marani said under her breath. "I cannot."

Jacks squeezed her hand. "Liu, take me to them." He broke from Marani—the loss of his hand as painful as losing a limb—and ushered Liu back the way she'd come.

Liu said, as they walked away, "You're a handsome dragon, Jacks. I love yellow. You wouldn't happen to have a cave filled with silk of a similar color, would you?"

Marani returned to her solitary goal. She stalked now, toward the honey and lime that still fussed near a tree "Nuria," she growled, the name rumbling in her chest.

"Grey?" The figure turned to Marani and waved, like they were greeting each other for afternoon tea. "Oh! I thought we'd meet you in the forest. I'm just finishing up here. Give me a moment."

Although the distance made Nuria's face indistinct, the lilting, girlish voice was unmistakable. Marani broke into a run and it took a handful of heartbeats before she exited the grove and found her princess standing over five kneeling, disheveled, terrified men, and two slightly less terrified women—although one had a heavily bloodied scarf around her hand. Nuria's dress and traveling cloak were just as stained as Liu's, and her bodice had a gash down the front that looked as if, at any moment, her entire chest might spill forward. Clutched under one arm was a massive, leather clad book. Her face...*her face!*

The flush flared higher, narrowing Marani's vision and choking her words.

"Who hit you?"

The princess looked composed, if not dirty, and there was only clotted blood near her nose, but bodices didn't rip themselves, and she'd a bruise the size of a horse hoof on one cheek. And bodices—Marani kept flitting from face to chest—they were next to impossible to rip by hand, as

Marani had learned in her early twenties, when she'd managed to entice a duke's daughter at a harvest festival but had been able to remove her bodice without the aid of a pocketknife.

"Oh?" Nuria gingerly touched her cheek. "He's gone. Pegasus took him and I think we just have his right leg left. I'm fine, and I'm glad you're here." She made no mention of her clothing. "We were going to leave them after a pegasus took their leader, but Liu brought up that they could easily just regroup and follow us, and try another attack. Then we thought we could tie them and bring them with us, but the pegasus encounter spooked our horses and we've lost all our supplies except my book, which broke through the bottom of one of the saddlebags. *Then* one of them had to urinate and I tried to drag him into the grove so at least Liu wouldn't have to watch, and when he hit the boundary he got tossed two meters backward. He's the one on the far left, with the crispy hair." Nuria smiled prettily at Marani, then got to her tiptoes and kissed the highwayman's cheek. "I'm glad you're not a dragon yet. How has your morning been? Tense?"

"Nuria," Marani began, her voice still deeply in the flush, her eyes unable to move from the princess' chest. "What happened, here?"

"Can you find my eyes, highwayman?"

Smoke clouded Marani's vision. The hem of her tunic charred to ash. "No. Who touched you?"

Nuria gave an irritated sigh as she patted out the flame. "I have been slapped before, and the only thing hurt is my pride. My bodice can be repaired and I promise, no damage was done to your favorite pillows. Now darling. Please." She put a finger under Marani's chin and tilted her head up. "You are within your rights to stare at my breasts all you like. What I wanted to see was...mmm. Your eyes have changed. And"—she looked down—"most of the small scale is gone. It's moving more quickly now, isn't it? The transformation? I can feel your heat, even, without touching you."

The only thing moving quickly at that moment was Marani's heartbeat.

One of the men on the ground moaned.

"Nuria *what happened?!*"

"That's a complicated story. You didn't run into a soothsayer in that grove, did you? I brought mine. Which is again, a complicated story. Is that Jacks?" She waved. "Hello Jacks. It's good to see you. Did you find your key? You look almost as feral as Grey." To Marani, Nuria whispered, "*Did* he find his key? How is his transformation holding? He's browning the sedge as well."

Marani's foot pawed at the ground, sending an arc of heat that browned the ground around both of them in a wide arc. "*Nuria.*"

"Grey, I don't...oh. This again?" Nuria tilted Marani's head left, then right. "The way your temper has been I can't differentiate between flush and dragon. But I'm not in any danger, I just came to take you back to Aspen Grove. Step out, Maran-."

The whistle that cut Nuria off came not from pegasi this time, but arrows. They arced over the hillside, sparse and blunt, and clearly meant to panic more than hurt. A full constellation of pegasi shot from the grove, their wings beating the air so furiously that Nuria fell into Marani as they ran for the cover of trees.

"DRAGON!" came the charging cry of what appeared to be a gaggle of adolescent boys waving rapiers.

The pegasi circled twice, then fled north.

"To the grove, Jacks!" Marani yelled. "Get Liu back. I've got Nuria." To her princess, she said, "Run. Now."

"Hold on." Nuria, maddeningly, stayed put. "The island has lost its collective mind over you and Jacks," she said as an arrow struck the branch above them. "I want to take you both back to the castle, where we can protect you. And the castle is east, not west into a magical walnut grove. Besides, we don't need to run from *that.*"

Boys ran down the side of the hill, tripping over their feet like excited puppies, yelling "Charge!" like the children that they were. Behind them marched the woman in purple that Marani had seen during her pegaflight—her hood still up despite the midday sun. A row of women followed with bows. They arced their arrows high, not aiming for the humans, Marani realized, but the clearing itself. Behind the women were the men she'd seen on the trail, armed with swords, pistols, and three more reams of unicorn horn.

Marani's bones ached. She reached for Nuria's shoulder and heard the *clink* of scale splitting apart—the sound like fracturing ice. It *hurt*. Her changes had been disquieting, yes, to this point, but they had never been painful. "I'm trapped," Marani breathed. "In this clearing. In this body." *Clink*. Then another arrow embedded itself into the bark above her head. "The grove is closer, princess. The castle is too far." She'd never make it to the castle. Marani wasn't even certain she'd make it back to the inn.

"We can make it past one soothsayer," Nuria said with a sigh, oblivious to Marani's clenched teeth. "We may just have to go the long way around. Unless the pegasi want to intervene again." She set Marani with a queer look. "Did you call them?"

Marani barely managed small talk when she wasn't flushed. The best she could manage at the moment was flick of eye contact while snagging the arrow lodged above their heads. She needed to just...grab Nuria and run. Jacks called to her from inside the grove, but Marani's feet felt as stationary as the tree roots she stood upon. "I've spoken to one, but never called one. Nuria please. The grove. Padded or not, arrows pierce."

"Tip is a ball of spun flax," Nuria said as she took the arrow from Marani and inspected it. "Why?"

The smell wafting from the flax was unmistakable, especially in a flush. "Pegacide," Marani said. "There will be no help from above."

The first of the boys stopped just shy of them, sheathed his child-sized rapier, and waited. The next boy queued up beside him, then the next, then the next. The soothsayer continued her pace, and the arrows continued to dot the clearing.

"Liu's bandits are secured." Jacks jogged up to them, his face filled with the confusion that Marani felt to her core. "Are we standing here courting capture for a reason?" His fingers laced with Marani's again, his kit scale snagging on the thicker plating of hers. "Snack? You know your elbows are bleeding, right?"

Because the scale is too tight, Marani screamed into her head. *Because my forehead pulses with pressure. Because the fire in my chest wants freedom but flares only when Nuria is around. Because I want to run but Nuria is…binding me and I can't get enough rational words out to explain any of this to her.*

Nuria spun around, likely to chastise, but said instead, "Both of you? They're children. Dragons don't eat children." She waved her ancient book at both of them. "It's somewhere in chapter six. You've an alliance with the unicorns about it."

And once upon a time, a dragon made an alliance with a soothsayer. I want to know why.

"Kid who is old enough for a sword is old enough to be eaten," Jacks replied blandly. "And I didn't make any unicorn pacts."

Jacks' hand soothed, blunting the fire-edge that threatened to split Marani's scales right down the center. Nuria was, maybe, partially correct. The danger was not in front of them. No, instead, it was inside Marani herself. "I'd cook him first," Marani said with a small grin. "Germs and such. Your digestive system is delicate."

"Definitely wash your claws. Hunger is no excuse for poor hygiene."

"Into the forest. Both of you." Nuria tugged Marani down the trail of crushed ferns, and her feet, miraculously, followed. The boys paced them, and the soothsayer in spitting distance now. Marani felt each soundless step as it crushed the sedge beneath it. She felt the rub of cape cotton on well-worn leathers, and could smell the waterproofing linseed oil that coated all the woman's clothes.

Soothsayers.

Marani hated them.

She had no reason to.

Logic was irrelevant. She *needed* them, or at least, the information they held. Which meant running, whether to the inn or Aspen Grove, was not an option.

"You all well?" That was Liu, from just beyond the tree line. Smart, to stay safe and out of the way. Which was exactly what Marani needed Nuria to be.

Jacks got there first. "Liu?" Jacks said, his hand melded to Marani's. "Take the princess down the trail just behind us. Far enough you're out of immediate harm, but not so far that Marani can't see her. Stay inside the forest boundary, where the soothsayer cannot follow."

"Go," Marani said, before Nuria could voice protest or utter another command that would lock her back to the dirt. "Do not argue. We've business with soothsayers. Old business."

In an act of true magic, Nuria placed a hand on Marani's hip and said merely, "Be safe," before allowing Liu to lead her back into the grove.

The soothsayer broke through the line of boys.

Jacks wiped blood from Marani's chin.

"You're not looking your best," her baby brother said.

"Maybe killing a soothsayer will help," Marani said, in a voice that rumbled like thunder. The two of them backed up, step by slow step, until the first line of walnuts grazed their shoulders. Marani felt the magic barrier this time, in the way it softened the sharp edges of her flush and whispered to her about quiet ferns and moonlight.

"Don't want to question her first?" Jacks' voice came in the same rolling timbre.

"Why? You think she would tell the truth?"

"No, but she might be useful as bait. I've been having dreams, sis. Volcanoes. Soothsayers. Horse-fucking harpies. I get piece after piece, but I don't understand how the puzzle fits together. I can't keep up with the changes and the flush—the longer it lasts the more, well, the more of this." He held up his bloody thumb. "Did Nuria bring answers? Is that what the book is about? Although she's been about as forthcoming as the soothsayers. No offense meant."

"Nuria is my problem. I suppose I could kill the soothsayer tomorrow," Marani said. "But I'm still going to tear at least one arm off. We can let her babble first."

"Ah. Excellent. Dragons."

The boys parted into two tight lines for the soothsayer, opening like a drawbridge. The archers remained at the hill crest, bows loaded, waiting. There were easily three dozen arrows littering the clearing already—the smell of the pegacide so strong that even the ferns had begun to wilt. It would be days before pegasi returned to Faun's Pass, magical gathering or not. With luck, the smell would keep horses, and therefore riders, away as well.

The soothsayer stopped just before the tree line—her body so close Marani could have traced the cow imprints on her leathers. Strapped across her back was the longest, intact unicorn horn Marani had ever seen. It twirled teal and gold, but the colors were muted and almost grey.

"Soothsayer," Jacks and Marani said in tandem.

"Hiding? I suppose that is what dragons do best. Unicorns were never afraid, which is likely why they're gone, and you're still here. Shall I send the boys in for you?"

"Do you want them to live?" Jacks replied, his voice deadly even.

A smile curled at the edge of the soothsayer's mouth. "We're that far already, are we, into transformation? Sending them in after your humans won't help much then. Shame. Tell me," she leaned against a walnut tree, her skin immediately blistering, her cape turning to bright red embers, yet she did not pull away. "Have the cravings started yet? The yearnings? Do you dream of flight?" She pushed back off the tree and leaned toward them until her nose sparked off the invisible magic boundary. "Do your wings furl under your skin and beg for release? Do your scales shred themselves as your form struggles against your human shells? Has your fire yet formed in your bellies? You will not find release in a walnut grove, dragons. This is a cage, and no dragon yearns for a prison."

"But we will find release with you?" The woman smelled like wet clay and manure. And she hated how, when the soothsayer picked at the curling, burned skin on her hand, rich, red, human blood flowed. She was a monkey in boots and a cloak, and Marani *hated* her.

"I know the spell that bound you. I know the spell to free you."

There was the bait. The promise. The prize. "And you have my key, I suppose?" Jacks said. "You offer us nothing that we cannot find ourselves. We have no use for you and your stolen magic."

Gods, Jacks had always been aces at lying.

"Your key?" The soothsayer swallowed an incredulous laugh. "The bottle is open. The magic is leaking. You are beyond your key, little dragon man. You must break the bottle, or die trying. And you will die." Her voice turned sharp. "A human body cannot accommodate wings, or tails, or horns. Your frames can accommodate only so much growth, your mouths only so many teeth. Your fire will burn you from the inside out. If you attempt to transform while magic still holds you to humanity, those bodies will split apart and the last dragons of Yuro will die."

One of the boys behind the soothsayer sniffed.

"Quiet" the soothsayer snapped.

"You didn't say they might die," another boy said. "I don't wanna see a dragon *die.*"

"It's an unfortunate wrinkle in the spell. Or a fortunate one I suppose, if one wanted to ensure one's dragons were controllable before they regained their form. Let me help you. Let me help you out of those forms so you can truly be free."

"You know your spell would work?" Marani asked. "Thus far our transformations have not been cumbersome. We have no reason to believe they would continue in any other way." Such formal, stilted language she had all of a sudden. Lying had never been Marani's skill set. She'd always been far better with flattery.

Because Nuria was incapable of listening, she came up behind Marani, book open, and read, "Magic exists not in a free state but only bound. It generates in the living creature—unicorn, dragon, harpy—and may be extracted at a price, but never bottled. Humans are poor magic vessels, requiring frequent transfusions and while they may be adequate targets for spells, their bodies are sieves, not cups." She slammed the book shut. "Chapter Six: The Human and His Relationship to Magic. Whatever magic she has, it's nothing like yours, Grey. Don't let her use you."

Marani snapped. "We belong to no one."

The soothsayer waved a dismissive hand at Nuria. "If that were true, you'd have been able to shuck your final bindings. Step beyond the boundary. Let me do a reading. I can help you, dragons. It's not power I wield, but knowledge. I can help you transform, help you rule not just Yuro, not just the archipelago, but the world, if you desire. But first we must break your biding spell."

"Just so you can saddle them and suck their magic? You're as transparent as a courtier." Nuria took Marani's free hand. "Grey. Here isn't the place. It isn't safe. You have to transform, but not here. Not like this."

"When, then? Everyone has an opinion, but no one has any facts." Jacks turned to Marani, his eyes holding the same question she was asking herself. Who could they trust? Nuria, obviously, and Liu and Javad, but none of them knew anything more about dragons than Jacks or Marani. Did they need trust, even, or just a human who had some idea what they were doing? Would they die, truly, if their transformations continued without intervention? Transformation here, or transformation in Aspen Grove's borders? If they were going to have wings, did borders matter?

"How long do we have," Marani asked the soothsayer. "Safely, in these bodies? You earn trust with information."

The soothsayer bowed, low to the ground. "I'd need your hand, dragon. Yours, not his, for you are farther along. The boundary will not allow you to eject without consent, and I have no weapons." She dropped her cloak and the half-spent horn, and patted her legs, although the leather was too tight to conceal even a toothpick. "A reading only. I promise."

"Don't." Nuria tugged Marani's hand. "Darifa is in the forest. If you want a soothsayer, we can use her."

"Darifa?" The soothsayer snorted laughter. "She has as much power as you, princess. If the dragons had wanted her to have real power, they'd have given it to her along with the kits. Now she clings to prophecy, hoping to be dragged along with it, back to relevance. Darifa is useless."

Marani head snapped right.

"It was an interesting reading," Nuria said with an apologetic smile. "I will tell you every detail, in private. I promise."

Later was not a concept that sat well in a flush.

"Dragon?"

What Marani wanted was Jacks' input. Which her brother gave, in the form of, "Hurt her and I scatter your body across the archipelago."

The soothsayer offered Jacks an almost maternal smile. "You cannot outrun a harpy, you cannot lie to a unicorn, and you cannot break a promise to a dragon. Allowing you to mature with the poorest of humanity has done you no favors. Your education is lacking, but that too, can be amended." To Marani, she asked, so very, very gently, "Your hand, dragon?"

"Grey *don't*," Nuria pleaded. Pleaded, not commanded. It was a distinction that mattered. Besides, what did Marani have to lose?

She thrust a cracked, scaled, bleeding arm beyond the tree line and waited, hopefully, for answers.

Chapter 11 - Marani

There exists a tenuous truce between the unicorn and the dragon, born more from a common enemy than a desire for peaceful cohabitation. Early Yuro surveys found no overlap in territories between the two species, although there was significant overlap between harpy nesting rooks and dragon caves. Two surveyors noted that all three species are capable of communication, and this shared language appears to be not sound based, but rather a part of the magical fabric of the archipelago.

- A Political Protocol for Nonhuman Species, Chapter 7: Courts of Magic

There was no spark, or tug, only a bracelet of wind that circled her wrist at the interface of grove and clearing. The soothsayer's hand lay atop of Marani's and she instructed, "Close your eyes."

She'd already taken a giant chance. What was one more?

"I want you to think, please, of flight."

The first thought that popped into Marani's mind was flailing on Blue's back as they bumped along the canopy of the Common Forest. When that memory threatened to spill her lunch across the grove, Marani tried to envision herself as a fully formed dragon riding the thermals of a volcano. That turned her legs wobbly.

"An older memory?" the soothsayer prodded. "What brings you to flush other than anger? You've flown before. Remember."

Marani's dream flooded her mind. She was a kit with soft, oversized, eagle-like wings. Her talons were sharp and new, and she could spear fish with them and bring the fish back to her nest, as long as they weren't too heavy. On clear mornings when her parents still slept, she would sneak to the cave mouth and dive down, straight down, through the clouds and the shrieking hawks and the insect swarms, crashing into the ocean below. Then she would beat her wings and push up, breaking through the waves, slicing the air, and scream with lungs too small yet to roar.

Standing in the walnut grove, one hand threaded with Jacks, the other grabbing the soothsayer, the scale on Marani's back itched and cracked, and burned with anticipation. She opened her eyes to sapphire sky, and the heavy autumn breeze that teased of winter, and the unshakable certainty that Yuro was her birthright.

The sky is mine, came a savage voice inside Marani's head. *The wind is mine, the trees are mine. The caves and dirt, the cephel and walnut, are mine. The humans are mine, and the monarchs will honor their oaths of a child, and the dragons will return to the archipelago.*

"She's bleeding again," said an accusatory Jacks. Marani heard the *pitpat* of his kit scale shedding to the sedge. "No, wait, it's flame? Blood and flame? Is that possible? Whatever you're doing, stop it."

"Oh." The soothsayer dropped Marani's hand like it was actually on fire, although the seeping fireblood concentrated along Marani's jaw. She turned accusatory eyes to Nuria. *"Oh."*

Jacks tugged Marani back across the barrier, to the safety of the walnuts.

"Well?" he growled.

The soothsayer continued to study Nuria the way a nightfly studied a rotting cephel fruit.

"More memory," Marani said. "Flying. Living with our parents. Garbled emotions about hoarding. Nothing fundamental. If our transformations are based in desire, I don't need soothsayer vision to want freedom." She scrunched her shoulder blades. "The pain is edging to the unbearable. Sparks and smoke I can handle. Fire in my throat is the worst heartburn."

Jacks rounded on the soothsayer. "You tricked her!?"

The soothsayer held up her burnt hand. "Patience, kit. Or you'll lose your sister the same way you lost your parents." She turned her focus entirely on Marani. "Listen to me, dragon. You count your life now in hours only. The magic of Yuro ties through you. Only when the binding falls, will you be released. Your brother will follow. You must undo the binding spell."

"You're as bad as the royal soothsayer," Marani said. "Use nouns. Proper nouns."

"I...cannot." Frustration sparked in the soothsayer's voice. "The binding magic won't allow it. Your brother is bound to you, and you are bound to... Yuro, and that same magic binds me. A deal was made, a bargain struck, and your hourglass is near empty." Again, she held out her hand. "Come with me. I can protect you. We can unravel your bonds together. We can release the fire. I may be able to transfer the focal point. But I can't help you inside that walnut grove."

Marani, said, in a voice tinged by exhaustion as the flush began its ebb, "Why does a dragon need protection?"

"Because you cannot yet fly?" the soothsayer responded, irritably. "Because your true forms will destroy your bodies and release your souls if the magic isn't done properly?" She craned her head and sighed. "Because you travel with real humans who mean nothing to scavengers and yet they are as bound to this prophecy as you are. Now come here. Please." A childish lilt lacquered her words. "Please, dragons. I can help you break away. You don't deserve to die. That...woman with you," her eyes again went to Nuria, "you do not want her to help you. Not the way you need. You don't have time to travel back to Aspen Grove. You don't have time to visit the queen. You have only now. You have me, and my promise that laws and spells and promises mean nothing if our dragons die. I will toss them all aside for you. I will transfer the binding spell to myself and die here, in this clearing, if it will save your lives. Please let me help you."

Jacks' hand trembled in Marani's and the world made sense, maybe, in a queer sort of way. Nuria bumbled around magic as much as they did. The royal soothsayer was playing a game neither Marani nor Jacks had any interest in. But this soothsayer...this one might not have answers, but she had a plan. She loved dragons—Marani could hear it in her voice. Maybe it was time to align with a human who actually knew what the fuck was going on.

Liu had joined Nuria at the boundary line. "Don't go past that line, Grey," she said. "I've never seen you seduced before, don't let this be the start. You don't need what she's peddling. You have plenty of magic on your own. We know Javad is a part of this. We have always known. She's grasping at crumbs, but we will have the full butter tarts."

"Stay out of this," snapped the soothsayer.

Liu stuck out her tongue. "You offer ingredients. We have a recipe. We just have to follow it." To Marani, she said, "Right? That's how prophecies work—just like cooking with Senna. She gives you ingredients, she gives you directions, and you have to trust the process. You don't get to see the pie before it's done. You skip steps and your floating crust sinks into the filling. You have to follow the steps, Grey. You have to trust that whomever stuck you and Jacks in human bodies had a plan to get you out because if they wanted you dead, it would have been a lot less work when you were both eggs."

"Does it hurt, Jacks?" Marani asked her brother.

"I feel like a chick emerging from a shell with unformed bones. I feel like soft clay under a highwayman's boot. I feel like shit, and yet I would rip away this human form with my bare hands if I thought I would survive it."

"I won't risk your life on a hope."

Jacks glared. "But you'll risk yours? It's both of us or neither."

Damned brothers. She hadn't kept him alive for forty-odd years just to toss him to the first soothsayer with big promises. "We will think on it." Marani's fingernails—more tiny claws now than anything—dug into the remains of her brother's skin, scratching down to scale. A familiar tremble ran up her legs. In his questioning eyes she caught the twitch of his own fatigue.

Dragons help her, she was exhausted. Too exhausted to play with soothsayers, and archers, and hopeful, scared little boys with swords.

Inside the grove, there was no imminent danger, only desperation. Until their bodies shattered, they had respite. And she and Nuria had notes to compare. "We're going to the inn," she said. "To eat, to nap, and to strategize." To Jacks, she asked, "Okay?"

He stared at the purple-clad soothsayer for a long moment, weighing his exhaustion against the heavy question of their existence. Finally, he nodded. "Yeah. I think it's the right call. It's not like she won't be here later if we change our minds."

As the group turned, the soothsayer called out, "I promise I will be here when you emerge, along with, I am sure, many others. Remember my offer. And do not dawdle, dragons. Yuro needs you alive."

"Yuro could have thought of that before it bound us in magic and threw away the spellbook." Jacks managed to mutter a "But thank you," before he and Marani ushered Nuria and Liu to the path. "You want to leave the ones Nuria and Liu found?" he asked, pointing to the ream of humans still bound to a massive walnut. "They're inside the barrier, which makes them our problem, but also not fodder for bored soothsayers."

"I am too tired to care about humans I do not know."

"Harsh words, but very dragon. And I completely agree."

Marani chuckled, then checked Jacks' eyes. His pupils were still the shape of ovals, the skin around them made of thin yellow-green scale. *Will we leave this flush?* Marani wondered as the group continued in bloated silence along the thin path. *Or ride it to a doomed transformation, since we have neither Jacks' key nor the mechanics of the binding spell?*

Nuria waited until their view of the clearing was well blocked by walnuts before slipping her hand back into Marani's. "Are you alright?"

"Flush is waning but not leaving." Marani tried, and failed, to swallow a yawn. "I'm not sure it will, this time."

"I don't want it to," Jacks added. "I like how sharp the world feels. I like the smells on the wind. I like the power."

Marani snorted. "You don't sound like a disaster waiting to happen at all."

Jacks barred his teeth at her—half human, half dagger-edged dragon. Marani barred hers back. "Don't forget who bottle fed you, and picked the Common Forest clean of nettle, and got whipped—"

"Grey?" Nuria's wrinkled her nose as she peered at Marani's mouth. "Did you lose more teeth? You stink of sulfur. I suppose you look more like a proper highwayman now, but that will take some getting used to. I don't even see any human ones in there anymore. You're very fierce. Both of you."

Her words were light, and meant to brighten, but the thought of teeth brought Marani right around to their conversations that morning. "Nuria," she said. "You were to go to Bad Mill. What happened?"

The princess waved her hand. "There was another soothsayer and a small handful of bandits."

"And pegasi," Liu added with a shudder.

Marani glared down at her. "Where were your guards?"

"We handled it." Nuria's free hand went to her hip in a movement that was certainly supposed to convey authority, but only made her look haughty. "I've handled plenty of highwaymen, Grey. You're all very gruff but basically made of butter on the inside. A very small percentage are dragons, but I think I've flushed those out."

Jacks spoke before Marani could form her exasperation into words. "You handled it, but you shouldn't have had to. I'm all for empowerment, but you and Liu on the road together, without guards or even an escort?" He tripped over an old walnut branch. Liu tried to catch him, and they both crashed onto their sides in the leaf-littered understory.

"I've never seen you trip before." Liu sprang up like a twenty-year old, and helped Jacks to his feet before Marani could even shuffle over to him.

"He's exhausted. We both are. It used to take days of built-up frustration to send me to flush. Now it feels like it can be brought on by a spilled glass of juice."

Nuria let out a long, princessly sigh. "All the more reason to get you back to the palace. Although didn't you bring Javad?"

"He's at the inn, waiting for us. We aren't going anywhere until we've collected him." Marani considered the badgering soothsayer and her fawning adolescents, the rumbled, ruffled Liu, her exhausted baby brother, and a princess who had more confidence than sense, at least when it came to road travel. A royal bed *did* sound amazing, but the amount of fighting, and talking, they'd have to do to get there would kill Marani and Jacks well before their transformations could. "I don't think we'll be able to travel, princess. At least not me. This...situation is going to have to ride out here, in the grove."

Nuria looked helplessly from Jacks to Liu. "Jacks?" she asked. "Liu? Transformation in a magical forest is not sound, politically or safety-wise. There's bound to be another clearing on the back side of this forest. We can call the pegasi and be home in a few hours. Where you can safely transform."

"Sorry, princess. If I flush fully again, I'll be passed out for days," Jacks said. "At the inn, at least we can rest."

"Liu?" Nuria pressed. "Help me talk sense into them?"

Liu stroked the silk at her hips and said, very carefully, "I lived before silks, and I can survive without them for a time." She gave Marani a tight smile. "You just cannot die, alright? That's my only stipulation. I'm not ruining my wardrobe just so you and Jacks can bumble around with prophecy. Get this sorted, Grey, get transformed, and then get us home."

Marani kissed the top of Liu's hand. "I promise, pastry chef."

"Grey," Nuria began. "I have to insist—"

Oh no. They weren't courting that magic again. Marani cut her off, hopefully before Nuria realized what power she'd inadvertently stumbled upon. "Back to the Solitaire, which is that bar ahead with the hay-thatched roof and the cascading nettle in the hanging baskets. If the magic of the grove does filter out the unwanted, it will give us a reprieve and a chance to regroup. I want answers to the magic of this grove, and the bar, before we leave. Jacks is right. If we go back to the roads, we will never make it to the castle."

Nuria stopped walking so suddenly that Marani slipped forward, staying upright only by virtue of Jacks being right in front of her. "Grey you are not listening to me."

Marani swallowed a snarl. "I am, but I can also barely keep my eyes open. Did you hear anything that purple-clad soothsayer said? Do you see how tired we are?"

"I did, but I wonder why you believe it. I've got, well, I had, mountains of dragon history books and my own soothsayer, who has watched your life just as much as I have. My only interest is keeping you, and Jacks, safe. Her interest goes well beyond that."

Marani was too tired to hide her irritation. "And negotiations with Bad Mill are easier with a dragon. You inferred as much this morning."

Nuria clenched her hands. "I would never use you like that, Grey. If you want to fly off Yuro and go nest in an old volcano, that's fine. But...if you do stay, you could help, yes. You've seen the damage the pegasi do. You've seen the monopoly of Bad Mill. With you and Jacks, we have a very real chance of equalizing. But that's not why I want you at Aspen Grove. I want you there because it's safe, and these woods, these roads, are not. You're about to be a *dragon*. And if that soothsayer is right, and there's a spell that must be unwound, there'll be more information in a royal library than a," she squinted ahead, "sports bar?"

"Liu? Why don't we walk ahead," said Jacks. "This conversation isn't for us."

With an appreciative nod, Liu said, "Yes. Thank you."

Marani waited until Jacks and Liu were out of sight before taking Nuria by the wrist and demanding, "Why are you here? Without guards. Tell me the real reason. If you have information I don't, now is the time to tell me. The purple soothsayer was right about at least one thing—my body won't last much longer. I need answers. I need them *right now*."

"I don't have answers," Nuria said through pursed lips, "just more pieces. What I want to do is protect you and Jacks. There's larger issues at play, as you probably gathered. Queen Ndolo thinks the safest place is with us. She set out a plan and I agreed. But she also knows that it would be a lot easier to protect you and Jacks if you weren't so...easy to tie up. And a dragon can be tied up just as easily as a human. We have four tapestries on it in the palace you may have seen. At Aspen Grove, in the palace, you'd have a host of new weapons at your disposal, as dragons. We also have a whole library we can use if the soothsayer out there is telling the truth, and your key isn't enough for this transformation."

"That still doesn't explain why she sent her only heir, with a pastry chef, into a bandit-laden highway system."

Nuria looked sheepishly at the ground.

"Damn it, princess. I want honesty. You were attacked less than ten minutes from me and I still didn't know. I cannot protect you if you won't tell me what's going on. Sending you and Liu out on the roads makes it looks like you *wanted* to be attacked."

"Well, maybe not quite so early on," Nuria murmured. "And we didn't know about the binding spell. That complicates things. But my book probably knows a way around—"

"No." Marani tossed Nuria over her shoulder, ignoring the princess' shriek of protest.

Nuria's book thumped against Marani's back as the princess clung stubbornly to the old leather. "Absolutely not, Marani. I will be put down! Carrying was necessary at the ball. There is no reason for this current indignity *at all.*

You can't argue that each time you flush, it brings you closer to dragon. If you wanted to stay human, it would be one thing. But you're dreaming of flying, and all but purr when I scrub your scales. I've caught you staring in the mirror, naked, flexing and snarling. You're a *dragon*, Marani. I've accepted it. All of Yuro has accepted it. If it's what you want, you have to accept it, too. Which means we have to do what is right for the island and make sure you don't get captured. We have to get rid of any spells that are holding you and Jacks together. We cannot do that *in a walnut forest!*"

"Shut up." The words were harsh, so Marani softened her hold. "I am done with everyone else deciding when I transform."

Nuria wiggled. "Marani, you have to—"

"*No.* And keep any further commands to yourself." She resumed walking, Nuria bobbing on her scaled shoulder, which had to be a very chafing experience. Nuria was well-padded, however, and could handle a few minutes of discomfort while she mulled the chain of incredibly poor decisions that had led her to the grove.

"Dragon, please. You aren't safe here!"

"And you aren't safe on the roads. Right now, the safest place for you is with me, and the safest place for me at the moment, is a weird little sports bar in a magic walnut grove. Be quiet and be patient, and use our travel time to consider how I might react to *anyone* who suggested using you as bait."

Chapter 12 - Nuria

Nuria had limited education in magic, although that was not for a lack of asking. She'd participated with all the royal children of Yuro in *Frequent Fundamentals of Mysticism*, which consisted of traveling scholars making monthly visits to all four monarchies to teach out of *A Political Protocol for Nonhuman Species*. The course eventually moved to more advanced texts, but Queen Ndolo had chosen a permanent governess for Nuria instead, and had her focus on etiquette and dagger work.

Nuria had asked, and then begged, for more magic content, and had gotten twice yearly soothsayer readings instead. The queen had said the cost was the same, and the soothsayer was less disruptive. Nuria hadn't argued again, not after her first vision of Marani, but now that she dangled at the threshold of a sturdy inn, hidden inside a magical walnut forest, she concluded either the gap in her education had been on purpose, for whatever prophecy she and Marani were entangled in, or Queen Ndolo simply had no appreciation for how much magic still lurked inside Yuro's boundaries.

No amount of cursing, pleading, or book thumping had convinced Marani to set Nuria down during the mercifully short walk from the clearing. Halfway through their trip Nuria had settled into silence, which had earned her a condescending pat on the backside, and after fuming about that for a few minutes she'd spent the remainder of the trek mulling the forest, and her educational inadequacies.

A boundary traversable only by those without magic. Or, rather, by those whose magic was their own. An inn so far off the road that it could not possibly have sufficient clientele. A forest of trees that could only be grown with dragon poo as fertilizer, growing straight and strong in a patch of forest that was on no map she'd ever seen, accessible by roads that had no names.

It reeked of extinct magic. It rang with answers to questions she'd never been allowed to ask. Nuria could not *wait* to unravel its secrets to save her dragon. Assuming Marani ever put her down.

"Cute inn," Nuria said when Marani finally eased her to the ground. "Surely carrying me didn't help with the exhaustion."

"Don't make ill-informed decisions, and I won't be forced to do it again," Marani snapped back, although fatigue took the sting from the words. "I'm exhausted, and I'm frustrated. You're playing into Ndolo's games *now?* Why? What could your soothsayer possibly have said to you?"

That stung. "This time, the queen is right. You and Jacks need to be in Aspen Grove so we can protect you."

"I don't need protection!" Marani slammed her fist into the inn's wooden door, denting the fibers. "I'm an invulnerable dragon. Jacks is an invulnerable dragon. He and I can transform and burn the island down, if needed. And we were fine here, with Javad who, if he gets captured, can take care of himself. But now we have you and Liu, who are *not* invulnerable. Now I have liabilities. Now if I burn an inn to the ground, people I love might die. Did that factor into Ndolo's plan at all?"

Nuria refused to lose her temper. Marani couldn't see reason because she was flushed. Arguing wouldn't get them back to Aspen Grove, but guilt might. "I thought we were partners, Grey. In this, magical whatever, in life, not just in the bedroom. Did you forget that I'm part of this, too? You can't just leave me behind now." Nuria twisted her voice, cautious not to command. There was no need to trigger a deeper flush. A dragon Marani might be, but Nuria would not lose her lover to scale and temper and poor planning.

Marani put both hands against the inn and let her head fall forward. "I know, but you've complicated everything. I don't need complications right now. I just want fucking answers."

Nuria had no answers, but she did have a giant book, and one new vision. If that wasn't enough motivation, well. Maybe she could bribe Javad to tie Marani and Jacks up again and she could cart them back to Aspen Grove. And the siblings would fume and rage at her, and probably spit fire, but eventually they'd see it was for their own damn good. "Take me inside and buy me a drink and I'll tell you every detail of my last vision. It has your parents in it. Your real ones."

Marani put a tight grip on Nuria's forearm. "It's Grey," she said as she slapped the door. "Open up."

Marani's scales were the hot of steaming bathwater, and Nuria's skin reddened underneath. Which didn't make any sense. The highwayman could barely hold her head upright. How was she still holding the flush? "I'm not injured, you've found Jacks, and yet it seems like your month of court training has evaporated during a five-hour reprieve from the palace."

"We aren't at a palace. We're in the woods. These are woods manners. Please, be quiet for a moment. We will talk later."

Her words were so dismissive. So void of humanity. Nuria needed a dragon, yes, but she needed Marani to still be a part of the thing, even if deeply buried. A battle-ready dragon would not do, and wasn't canonically accurate anyway, according to *A Political Protocol for Nonhuman Species*. Nuria bristled and wound up for a retort about how dragons were notorious sticklers for manners and etiquette and that she would *not* be quiet, when a man pushed open the thick slab of walnut. He eyed Nuria, frowning, but still stepped aside.

"Thanks, Herb," Marani said with a half-salute.

"Loot doesn't belong here, Dragon. Nor do humans, but the one that came in with your brother has already endeared herself to our cook, so I've got no say with her. This one"—he closed then bolted the door after Marani pulled Nuria across the threshold, her grip only tightening—"brings trouble and magic."

"I'm aware," Marani returned. "But I can't send her home, and her magic is mine. We're an entangled mess. I'll vouch for her."

"I do not need vouching for!" Nuria went to straighten the front of her bodice, remembered the horrific split, and said in a much quieter voice, "I will acknowledge that I might not look the most stately at the moment."

Marani blinked and her head slowly, deliberately, turned back to Nuria's chest. The heat of her grip turned...silkier, somehow, the pain morphing to a tickling prickle. *Still a flush,* Nuria considered, *but one I have a bit more control over?* The tightness eased from Marani's eyes and she licked parched lips that seemed fuller, in the lamplight.

"We have to stay focused on your safety," Nuria whispered.

Marani's desire turned back to the burning heat of the flush. "I don't suppose anyone here is a seamstress?" Marani asked the doorman. "She at least needs to deal with, that"—Marani made an awkward motion around Nuria's chest—"before she heads back out."

"Dragons," Herb the Doorman muttered. "Dragons and princesses. Wait here."

No one else came to guard them, but the eyes of every patron stared and every piece of cutlery pointed in their direction in a deadly promise.

Nuria's arm burned from Marani's touch, and the ripped fabric of her dress kept slipping from her fingers. "Grey?"

"I know where my eyes are. Thank you."

Nuria sighed. "It's everyone else that concerns me."

Marani whipped around to face the bar, her lip curled up, a growl birthing deep in her throat. But not one of the patrons had any interest in Nuria's breasts. Their knives pointed quite clearly at her throat.

"I'm unarmed," Nuria said to the patrons. "I'm not here with trouble. I'm actually trying to take trouble back home with me." She'd meant the nod to Marani as a joke, but no one so much as smiled.

"Stand with me for the moment. They're funny here, and we're leaning on their hospitality. Must be something about humans."

As in, they're not humans? She let herself look around. The place was definitely more inn than tavern or bar. Nuria spotted the differences immediately. The corners were well lit with electric lamps, the bar top granite, not wood, the chairs uniformly carved. The plates were porcelain, the tableware silver, and the dedication to prismatic rainbow décor spoke of intent and a deep purse. The owner was well traveled, as buzkashi had not been played on Yuro since the unicorns went extinct, but was a favorite sport on more cow-friendly islands, like Tchun. The patrons were, not richly dressed, but comfortable, their clothes coordinated, their leathers worn but polished, their jewelry unobtrusive. Nuria saw wealth that didn't want to be recognized, and comfort that sought protection.

She also saw her royal soothsayer bound to a chair with a knife to her neck.

"Steady, princess," Marani said, her hold still firm on Nuria's arm.

"Why is she bound?" Nuria was careful to keep her voice low, but it carried regardless.

"Soothsayers aren't welcome," said a pink-haired man to her left.

"Neither are princesses," said another man. "Though your cook we can work with."

The doorman returned with taller, thicker man with rose-colored hair and a freckled, aspen bark-colored complexion. "As I said. Another one." Herb indicated Nuria. "We're not set to accommodate this many humans. I'd say back out the door with her. She can idle in the grove, where it won't tax the spells."

"She's mine," Marani said in a voice so feral that Nuria shivered. But Marani spoke not to the doorman, but the taller one, whose laugh lines grooved otherwise unmarred cheeks, and whose eyes sparked the same as the window prisms.

Among other options, this man had to be the inn owner. Nuria knew a dominance challenge when she saw one. They never ended without at least one piece of broken furniture. If this was a unicorn-themed sports bar, Nuria was willing to play along.

"Sir." Nuria managed as deep a courtesy as she could with Marani's hold. "I apologize for the intrusion. I swear upon my familial crest and lineage that I am unpolluted and without blemish. I seek to ask a favor and will do so only within the bounds of what I can equally pay for." The words weren't quite right, noting that Nuria was no longer a virgin and therefore had no right to even make such a request, but politeness never hurt.

"We can make an allowance for a dragon's princess, Herb," he said in a coaxing voice. "It's only the one, correct?"

"It had better be," Nuria said before she could stop herself.

"What did you say, princess?"

"I said that I've come to bargain for my soothsayer, and for the freedom of the dragons." Nuria managed to pry her arm from Marani's death grip, which she immediately used to pull the ripped line of her bodice together. Not that anyone was being inappropriate, which put her even more on edge. Not because of the patrons, but because Marani hadn't said a thing about her bobbing breasts, or that one of her nipples was threatening to dive out the front. Instead she was glaring at a pretty, yes, but otherwise soft inn-owner who, Nuria assumed, bore the wrong equipment for Marani's usual interest.

"Send the sisters to the outer grove for the ones tied up there," the inn owner said to Herb. The inn owner ticked his head left, and four women of middling height, with long silver hair wrapped in high buns, stood and headed for the door.

"And to you, dragon. I apologize for my friends, and for your troubles accessing the inn. We saw the pegasi. We knew you would come, but I admit that we doubted it would be this quickly. The magic felt strong, still. We assumed we had weeks, perhaps months. Now I see we have perhaps an hour or two, noting your physical contortions. You need to relax into the magic. It was right to bring her here." He gave Nuria a small smile, taking careful note of Marani's hand, and the burned imprints that ran along Nuria's arm.

"We will begin again. A proper introduction. I am Starlight." He knelt before Marani on both knees and said, in a voice as dry and serious as Nuria's dragon book, "I honor the bonds of our magic. I honor the history of your lineage. I own no lands that are not first yours, I own no property which cannot be freely claimed. We are siblings in magic, but the Lord of Clover will always serve." He rose with the severity of a courtier who knew he would never rise above his station. He stood in front of Marani with the rigidity of a third-born prince in a peaceful kingdom. And Marani…just…glared at him like he was late with her dinner.

Oblivious highwaymen. Lovely. Maybe if Starlight had a ripped bodice, Marani would have clocked that he was leaking magic like a soothsayer run through with an arrow.

Nuria deeply regretted skimming the unicorn chapters in her book. She nudged Marani. "Your line is, 'I thank you for your fealty and will honor our bond as long as dragons fly,' I think. It's something close."

"I am not saying that," Marani said. "How about, you've got another soothsayer at the boundary, and a few dozen humans at her command. She says she's holding them for now. I'm guessing others aren't far behind. So. Thanks. For the shelter. Once we rest we'll take the conflict back to the road."

"You are welcome here, dragon, for as long as needed."

"She needs to go back to Aspen Grove."

Starlight ignored her. "How can we best make you comfortable for your transition?"

Marani scoffed. "You really want it here? You want your inn to get burned down?"

"I want to do my duty."

He was so polite. Everyone was—from the doorman who grumbled but never put a hand on them, to the woman who was holding out a glass of cool, sweating water to Nuria. *Why?* Aside from fundamental, cross-species protocol, that was. There were plenty of mystics clubs across Yuro, some of which specialized in dragons or, as was clearly the case here, unicorns, and many of them dabbled with magic, the same as soothsayers. Nuria had just never seen it taken to this level of dedication. The inn was more shrine than clubhouse, and the patrons performed better than an acting troupe.

"Rest, Grey. Maybe while you eat, Starlight could help me gather some pegasi on the non-poisoned end of the wood. I don't want you sliding off mid-flight."

Mercifully, Marani had reached the stage where she was too tired to argue. "Alright," Marani yawned. Another few minutes of courtier-level small talk and she would fall asleep on her feet. "Um. Thank you. Can I get a steak?"

The knife had still not come away from Darifa, and Marani clearly would be of no help. But the inn had the feel of a place a low-ranking noble might design as a 'rustic' getaway, and if Starlight had enough history to properly address a dragon, and travel to buzkashi tournaments, he was high born, and educated, and thereby just as much of a danger as the soothsayers and bandits...just a better dressed one.

One of Starlight's eyelids twitched. "Were you not offered food? You have my deepest apologies. How many would you like? Cow, I assume? We do not have horses here, but would be willing to capture a pegasus if that would be of more interest? For...food, I think?" Again, he eyed Nuria. "Your princess is sufficient in other areas?"

"You don't have to stick *that* close to history," Nuria muttered.

In the back of the inn, Javad laughed.

"I'm going to sit down," said Marani. "Whatever this nonsense is can wait. Jacks? You wanna order us another round of cow steak? I don't hate it."

"Grey, wait. Please."

Marani grumbled but stopped walking.

Nuria addressed Starlight directly. "Forgive me. The dragon Grey is tired and needs rest. She...I'm here to help. The transformation is hard on her human form and her desire for formality is short. If you would release my soothsayer—"

Starlight spoke to Nuria in that polite, forced way that Nuria reserved for her embroidery tutor. "Your soothsayer will stay here with us, for a while. She broke our boundary, and we will know why."

"I pushed her through," Nuria said.

"And that should have killed her, not sent her directly to us."

"But—"

"Princess," Starlight said. "You are no maid and therefore have no power here that does not come from your owner. As to your property, I promise we will not kill the soothsayer. That isn't our way. It would, however, be very helpful if you could take the dragon to nap, hmm, after she eats? We have rooms available." His eyes went, very deliberately, to Nuria's torn bodice. "We need time to repair the magic boundary, if possible, or to plan our best road to defense. The dragons won't be able to leave the inn without incident, and they must be rested and fed before then."

Gods, why did they have to be unicorn fanatics? There had been a section in *A Political Protocol for Non-Human Species* that had dealt with princesses kidnapped by dragons, but it was over halfway through the book, and Nuria had not thought it a relevant section to prioritize. With the way the rest of the book had gone, the text would have been more painful than titillating, but even a dry rendition of how a princess was supposed to act around a dragon would have been useful in the moment.

"Dragon?" Starlight said. "Room or table? Dragon lust is a fickle thing."

"Room," Marani said. "And if you look at her like that again I will kill you."

"I'm good on steak, and princesses," said Jacks from the back table, boyish humor tangling with fatigue. "But I can take a room as well if you need time. Grey, I'll keep going through the notebook. Seems only fair if you get the source."

Jacks brandished a notebook with two interlaced aspen leaves embossed across the front. It was definitely Nuria's notebook—the one she'd religiously recorded all her soothsayer visions in.

"Give that—" Nuria began.

Marani put a hand over her mouth. "Thanks. See you all in, say, twenty minutes? An hour?"

Starlight nodded. "We dare not press more than an hour, not with the way your scale cracks. We will have steaks brought to your room and will tend whichever humans you leave in the commons."

"Mmmh!" Nuria said.

"And when the next soothsayer comes?" Marani asked. "Or when our transformations truly begin?"

"Soothsayers cannot breach the walnut forest, dragon. Although they were certainly mass at the boundary. You and your brother will not leave the grove without a fight, but here at the inn, you are safe. We have a small arena out back you can be brought to when your bodies begin to break down. We have oil and fire for your new scales, and balms for areas that are too stubborn to close.”

“The soothsayer outside said...our bodies can’t handle the change as they are now. That there is another spell to undo. Can you...can you see it? Do you know of it?”

“MUPH!” Nuria yelled.

“The ones who made you and your brother’s binding spells have long since died. Anyone who tells you they know the particulars is lying. Now,” he gestured to a man of maybe thirty years, with deep midnight eyes and hair the color of autumn leaves. “Amethyst will show you to our guest rooms behind the bar.”

Amethyst? Starlight? Herb? The dedication to the façade was nauseating. Any bar, or inn, any gathering of people was bound to have one offbeat name. And Herb wasn’t uncommon. Together...Nuria reconsidered her assessment of the inn. The rainbows. The table linens. The little bells that were woven into bears and braids, and the slow, gentile way the patrons sipped their juice, or touched each other’s knees.

Amethyst bowed first to Marani, then Jacks. “If you’ll follow me, dragons.”

“Don’t you dare,” Nuria said as Marani’s hand dropped from her mouth and reached for Nuria’s waist. It was unlikely Marani could carry her even if she’d wanted to, but that wouldn’t stop her from trying. “You can hold my hand like a gentleman...gentledragon, or I’ll walk on my own.”

Amethyst, in complete seriousness, said to Marani, “We have restraints we can bring to the room if you’d like a reprieve from your princess.”

Nuria decided the world had turned completely upside down. Her gaze locked with Darifa’s across the inn, who gave her a funny sort of nod and, with bound hands, tapped the center of her forehead.

“Seriously?” Nuria mouthed.

The soothsayer shrugged.

"She's capable of listening, she just doesn't like it. I have it under control." Marani took Nuria's hand, lacing their fingers into a grip so strong Nuria thought it might stop blood flow. "I'll have a talk with her when we get to the room. Please lead on."

Chapter 13 - Nuria

Power belongs to the dragons, but magical skill will always be the preview of the unicorn. Harpies trade in secrets and words. To these creatures a human is at best, a vessel, but more often, simply a snack.

- A Political Protocol for Nonhuman Species. Chapter 6: The Human and His Relationship to Magic

With the door closed and the windows decorative, Marani's shed heat turned the small inn room to summertime in a matter of minutes. The cushions on the pink embroidered love seat crisped to brown and arcs of black cracked across the stone floor as Marani made her way through six cow steaks, two carafes of pettian juice, and an entire bowl of brown rice.

As she ate, Nuria studied. She watched the plate scale slide past one another at Marani's joints, and the way she grimaced through the gristle of the steak, the pressure on her new teeth clearly painful. Her jaw wasn't big enough—Nuria could see that clearly—for the double row of tiny white daggers that had erupted behind what remained of her human molars.

Worst was that the cushion upon which Marani sat was pink again, from the slow drip of her blood from an unseen cut. Her body—her human body—was dying, and it clearly hurt.

"What about a short nap?" Nuria asked as Marani wiped pettian juice from her mouth with a tattered sleeve. "Then maybe we can revisit the Aspen Grove conversation?"

"No time, and I'm fine." Marani waved her off. "Food does wonders, and the flushes aren't as draining now. They're a part of me—the dragon part I'm sure—and I swear they feel more real sometimes than this does. Right now, I want to discuss how we get you safely back to Aspen Grove before...whatever is set to happen here."

Nuria took another sip of pettian juice to drown out a laugh. "Marani, I am not going home without you."

"Yes, you are."

Nuria giggled, despite her best efforts. "Highwaymen don't get to order around princesses."

Marani stared back at her with cool, focused eyes. Her response, when it came, was Marani's voice, stripped of its humanity. "What do dragons do with princesses?"

"I..." Nuria's autumn dress was too thick a cotton for a dragon's gaze. "The queen has a tapestry in the mending room with a dragon burning a princess on a pyre. I believe they were also used as snacks or, um, kept like trophies or treasure. From what Starlight inferred, they may have had other uses of a more intimate nature. Which we do not have time to explore."

"Starlight didn't seem concerned about the transformation. I'd think you'd be more concerned about arguing with a dragon."

"Is that what you are, Marani?"

Dragon eyes stared back at her, unblinking, from Marani's still very-human head.

A chilling reality settled over Nuria. The moment was too delicate for even court training. She needed her book, which she'd dropped near the door, but in lieu of that option, strung together courtesy as best she could. "I don't mean to challenge. I made a mistake. You have my apologies, dragon." Nuria took Marani's hand and added, "And you have me. I came here to help, not to fight. I was there with you, remember, in the tunnels at Two Spires Castle. I was there when your skin powdered in the sunset of King Fridolin's sitting room. You were transforming, and you asked me to stop it, and I did. I've only ever done what you've asked of me. I just want to ask this one thing of you. To have your transformation at Aspen Grove, not in a strange forest bar. To have it where we can protect you."

"No."

There would be no arguing, not with the dragon who wore her lover's face.

"They'll come for you. The hunters. The soothsayers. Every inhabitant of Yuro is going to come for you and Jacks. They're going to come to this grove. The magic boundary will stop the soothsayers, but not the hunters. Not the children with their bows. You can't fight them like this, dragon, exhausted, blistered, and bleeding."

Marani said, without inflection, "I will transform."

"*How*? You peel apart, layer by layer until, what? You're in pain. Your blood—your *deadly* blood—is all over the forest. Your transformation wasn't like this in the castle. You peeled off those kit scales like they were dropped rice. In this forest it feels like your transformation is a fight. At the castle, it just," Nuria stumbled for the right words. "It just *was*."

Marani blinked, and a very human tremble came into her voice, "I need it to end soon. I need it to end here. Aspen Grove is too far."

"You're sure? Because at the castle—"

"Enough. Please."

Nuria took Marani's hands in hers and kissed the palms. No castle. She could regroup. It was the transformation that truly mattered—and keeping Marani sane through it. "Let me help you, love."

"By getting captured and tortured?"

"If that's what it takes, yes."

"Fuck that."

"Marani." Nuria said her name in a singsong sigh as she scooted and, careful to avoid any open wounds, laid her head on Marani's shoulder.

Marani pushed back into the brightly upholstered chair and scratched at the velvet armrests, shredding the pinky fabrics. "You won't go back to the castle without me, will you?"

Nuria smiled cutely up at her. "Nope. We're just going to have to figure this out together." She kissed Marani's chin. "You don't frighten me, dragon."

Dragon eyes blinked back at her and deep inside Marani's chest, Nuria swore she heard a purr. "Maybe I should. What if the soothsayer at the border is telling the truth?"

"She has nothing to gain by telling the truth and everything to gain by lying. Once you cross that boundary, you're hers, and she knows it." Nuria kissed her then, a long, lingering kiss that ignored the sharpness of scale, or that Marani's tongue had developed a mild fork. Marani's clothes were shredded and stained, and the princess' fingertips skated through gaps in the fabric to caress newborn scale. The blood had dried. The scale shimmered. Marani's flush waned, at least for the moment. She was stable. She was happy. She was, for a delicate moment, still human. "You found your key, love. There is nothing holding you back, if dragon is what you want."

Marani mumbled, "What if I want you as well?"

Gods, how Nuria had missed this. Did dragons joke? Did they banter? If this was the last time Nuria got to play-bicker with Marani-the-human, she would savor it. "Mmm." Nuria pushed herself onto Marani's lap. "I've given that thought. Do not let me be the one that holds you back. I love you as a human, and I will love you as a dragon. I don't...strictly know how it will work, but we weren't bound by prophecy just so I could dump you over a tail and a pair of wings. You'll still have a tongue. I'm sure you'll figure out how to use it."

"You're sure of yourself."

Nuria pivoted and arched her back, her breasts straining against the ripped bodice. A quick movement, even a giggle, and they'd be in Marani's hands. "A queendom has assets."

"Indeed it does." Nuria savored the warmth of Marani's hands as they slid between breasts and fabric, sliding away the remains of the bodice. "How do you control the heat?" she asked as fingertips circled her nipples, then stroked the supple underside of her breasts.

Instead of answering, demanding, insistent lips pressed to hers. Marani's fingers tugged at the sides of the bodice and, when it stayed firmly attached everywhere but her front, raked up the sides, searching for clasps, ties, or any opening that her rough scale might worm its way through.

"The tie...is in the back..." Nuria said when Marani's hands began to pull at the fresh tear in silk. "But Marani, we need to get back to Darifa, and if we're kissing you aren't transforming, and hey! You'll tear it even more and it barely holds my breasts in as it is. Shouldn't we—"

Marani's mouth returned to Nuria's. Her tongue pressed into the princess's mouth while the highwayman sorted the back lacing. Nuria's bodice loosed, then fell to the ground, the covering replaced entirely by Marani's hands.

The room was hot again, but not the scalding burn of the flush. This softer warmth radiated from Marani's kisses, and the swirls of her fingertips, and the clasp of her hands that directed Nuria's knees apart.

"Marani," Nuria gasped as a sharp fingernail tugged at the hem of her panties. "We have to talk."

"After," Marani whispered as she nipped at Nuria's jaw. "Right now, you do what I say."

Nuria started to object, to say that she loved role play as much as the next princess but that Marani turning into a dragon had to take precedent, when the sparkle of scale caught her attention. A handful of smaller scale on Marani's jawbone dusted to motes. Underneath was more of the brown plate scale, the striations thick in the pale lamplight. While Marani tore her undergarments, Nuria explored. The striations moved. They...they pulled apart, no, spread apart, as the plate expanded down Marani's neck. Without cracking. Without blood. Without pain, just a delicate heat that smelled like hearth fire.

That was a lot of mechanics and magic to sort while a dragon shredded your clothes. Had the transformation continued when they started kissing? Had a flush arisen when Nuria had attempted to put up a fight? Was she going to be able to think about any of this once Marani's fingers found her clit?

"Spread your legs," Marani commanded, her voice halfway to dragon.

Acquiesce, or object? Dragons take her, how many times had Nuria dreamed of this? How many times had she wandered into this fantasy during a lecture from her mother, or an etiquette lesson from her tutor? And while this was not her and Marani's first play at intimacy, it was the first time Marani had not been overly burdened with concern, or guilt, or Nuria's unintentional maidenhood. There had been, Nuria realized, a subtle fading of Marani in the days since her partial transformation, replaced by...the dragon, she supposed. Or maybe not replaced, but melded with. Like the easing of Marani the human had given Grey the Dragon room to stretch her wings.

A feral sort of growl escaped Marani's throat as she gathered Nuria's skirt and wrapped it up around her waist. "You are not listening!"

"It's...an awkward position. I am favor of continuing, but do you want to go to the bed?" There was no reason to delay things. She was already soaked, but there was an answer here, somewhere potentially between lust and love, dragons and breasts, that she needed time to tease out. "It would free your hands for, oh!"

Marani pressed two long fingers inside of Nuria, choosing to push aside the remains of her undergarment instead of removing it. Nuria whimpered—not in pain, but at the suddenness, and the pressure of Marani's palm pressing against her clit, and the *fullness*.

"Marani," Nuria mumbled into the highwayman's neck and her fingers slid out to fingertips, then pushed back inside. Marani's scale grabbed at Nuria—buffered by her moisture but adding a friction that made Nuria wiggle.

"You were supposed to go to Bad Mill."

"I...oh! I was going to, but Darifa came and then my mother said-*oh!*" The thrusts were insistent. Commanding. Nuria's body followed as she clung to her dragon, any attempt at rational thought lost to pull of scale and heat.

"You're mine," Marani said, her voice dangerously low. The fine hairs on Nuria's arms rose as Marani again slid her fingers out and back in, pressing sharply at her entrance until Nuria squeaked.

"That...was never in question." Nuria let her head fall back while her hips pushed forward, aching for more contact. "Marani, I. Please. I don't know what you want. I'm sorry plans changed. I was going to explain, but you didn't give me time. I want to talk about all these changes, I want to help with all these changes, but dragons aren't good at communication."

Marani's grip between Nuria's legs softened. She exhaled, the breath whistling through her nose. The fingertips inside Nuria turned from pressing to circling, teasing Nuria's clit with a gentle pressure that brought another whimper to her lips. In tandem, the glow left Marani's exposed scale.

"I'm sorry," Marani whispered as she kissed Nuria's lips, then her cheek, then pushed up her left breast and kissed its nipple. "I'm not sure what that was. Let's go to the bed. That way I won't tear your dress. You're right. This can wait. What did you want to talk about? Not Bad Mill. Your soothsayer?" Nuria caught the suppressed grumble in Marani's now very human voice. "Your new vision? What was it about?"

Marani's fingers continued their slow twirls. Nuria's body screamed for release, and her heart screamed for the slow, lingering kisses between her legs that Marani had perfected over the past few days. But the scale at Marani's jawline was moving again, subtle fractures developing that leaked clear fluid that would surely turn to blood.

Not about location, Nuria thought as tension built between her legs and her thoughts muddled. *Not about the flush, not entirely. Not about sex, at least not completely. Heat? No, that's under her control. What's the overlap?*

"Nuria?"

What was the question? About her reading? "I saw the binding spell of your and your mother's feather, made into the comb. It was a strange thing. Not the ritual, for I've nothing to compare it to, but the vision. I swear you saw me, Marani. Like it was a lucid dream more than a voyeuristic fragment of your past."

Marani's fingers stalled for a moment. A pinprick of blood dotted the junction on her chin where scales met. "That's not how soothsayer visions work. That's too far into the past."

When Marani still did not move, Nuria rested her head back on the highwayman's shoulder, enjoying the static fullness that still pressed between her legs. "I don't believe any of my visions worked the way they were supposed to, and I think that's because of Darifa. She wasn't there, but her name was said. She's a part of your past too, love. Which is why I'd prefer she not stay alone down in the inn."

"Damned soothsayers." A flush rose, entirely unnecessarily, within Marani. Scale clinked to the floor and the dots along her jawline became a stream of boiling blood that she hastily wiped away with the edge of her cloak.

Nuria shifted, seeking to avoid the blood and the death that could follow. "Darifa should be questioned, I agree. But I think our main priority is—"

"Stop wiggling, princess," Marani snapped.

Her blood clotted, then smoked to ash. Instantly.

Nuria went still. Not out of fear, but a sinking realization that the more risqué visions of herself and adult Marani might have had oddly prophetic value. At least one vision, since around seventeen, had been of her and Marani in bed. Or something akin to bed. Nuria pulled at the "memories." There'd been the softest kisses paired with exploratory pinches across nipples and backsides. There'd been delicate bruises raised on her neck and inner thighs from teasing lips. There'd been Marani tying her to wooden headboards, metal post headboards, the carved, wooden feet of loveseats, and once, a stable door. Nuria couldn't begin to count the number of props that had been employed over the years, including feathers, fur, scale, unicorn horn and, with great care, a padded leather strap that left behind the most perfect pressure.

It was fantasy that she enjoyed, yes, but it was also...it was also a script. Just like her visions. There was a prophecy, and there were roles. Hers was a dragon's princess and if that was what it took to get Marani safely through her transformation...

"I'm sorry, dragon," she said, very, very politely. "I did not mean to offend. I'm here to serve, as you desire."

A definitive flash of *something* sparked across Marani's face. Tints of grass and emerald sparkled across her scale. "I thought you wanted a conversation?"

What Nuria wanted, other than the return of Marani's fingers, was a dragon. "Remember what you told me in my bedroom? That I was terrible at behaving?" She pulled the hem of her skirt higher, putting herself in full view. "I want to do better."

Marani's breath hitched, and her eventual exhale sent embers into the stagnant air. One hand still cupping Nuria's breast, the other grabbed at the soft skin of her inner thigh and squeezed. A question. A question from the human part of Marani that was holding the dragon back.

Marani had to let go, or the dragon would tear her apart.

Nuria could seduce a highwayman.

Could she seduce a dragon?

"Shall I take off my dress?" she asked, her voice as light as a summer cloud. "So it's not in your way?"

An affirmative sounding grunt came from Marani as her hand slid from Nuria's chest. The lower hand stayed clasped, firmly, on the princess' thigh.

Nuria tugged what remained of her bodice up and away. The back clasp of her seafoam skirt she unhooked, then said, "May I stand?"

No answer this time, from Marani, but scale slid across her eyes, narrowing the pupils.

Nuria slid off Marani's lap, the highwayman's hand tangling in a cascade of silk and cotton that snagged on her scale. Nuria waited, patiently, for Marani to untangle herself before letting her skirt drop to the floor. She pushed what remained of her undergarment down as well, then shed her boots and socks, and the few bits of jewelry she'd put on that morning. "Where do you want me to go?" she asked. "May I sit? I could"—her formality slipped as she scanned the room—"I don't see any rope, but the rug looks soft and isn't made of unicorn. I could lay there? I can be as still as you like. Or I can go to my hands and knees and try to escape, if it would please you?"

There was no natural light in the small room, no fire in the fireplace, but in the corner, where Marani sat, was as bright as sunrise and as warm as an autumn afternoon. Marani's scale shone like polished gold and Nuria had to clasp her hands behind her back to keep from reaching out and touching real, living, singing dragon scale.

Nuria had dreamed of dragons her whole life. She'd seen every dragon tapestry in Aspen Grove. Nothing compared to the way Marani shone now.

"Dragon," Nuria whispered. "My dragon. Oh, Marani. You're so close. What am I missing?"

"Nuria?" A husky version of Marani's voice managed to say.

There was still too much Marani in the equation—too much human concern for an act that was, at its heart, animalistic. Marani needed to lead, but Nuria was going to have to prime her for it. The princess stepped into Marani and straddled her leg. "This is what dragons do to maidens, isn't it? Claim them? Find their vulnerable areas? You just also happen to have the benefit of consent. I am *yours*, dragon, and I understand what you are capable of. I know what you want. Fuck me here, bind me to the bed, or spread me on the rug, it does not matter. You claimed me as a kit. Do you remember your fire on my foot? Do you still have those memories? It could not have only been a vision. I am *your* princess. You are a dragon. You own this island. You own the archipelago. You own me, and I am not afraid as long as we are together."

There were no words then, only Marani's hands on Nuria's hips, turning her around so she backed into Marani's chest. The highwayman lingered on Nuria's breasts only long enough to roll her nipples against scale before sliding down Nuria's belly. With one arm around Nuria's waist, another hand buried itself in honey-colored curls. Two fingers slammed back into Nuria, pushing and stroking and sending the princess over the edge of orgasm before her next breath.

"Harder, dragon," Nuria murmured, through the pleasure and sting of Marani's thrusts.

"You should be afraid," the dragon whispered into her ear. "Even good girls should be afraid."

Nuria began to speak, then cried out when Marani's fingers retreated. She had to clap a hand over her mouth when Marani grabbed her hips again, turned Nuria around so she lay across Marani's lap, and smacked her backside. "You were supposed to go to Bad Mill. You disobeyed me."

"Ow!" she cried, her voice muffled by her hand in an attempt to not shake Marani from her ministrations. "I'm sorry. I should have listened. I won't disobey you again."

"Princesses," the emerging dragon muttered. "So dramatic."

Slap!

"*Ow!* I'm doing my best. Please excuse my outburst but being spanked by a dragon is not exactly—"

Soaking fingers slicked down Nuria's backside, between delicate folds, finally resting on her clit. Here the dragon paused. Nuria whimpered and wiggled, the fire between her legs hotter than dragon breath.

"Princess," the dragon cautioned, low and dangerous.

Nuria froze. Spanking, stroking, licking, she didn't care. She just didn't want Marani to stop.

The feather touch on her clit turned to a rhythmic stroke. "D-dragon," Nuria began. Was begging the correct next move? Was she capable of anything else? "Again. Please?"

"Shush," the dragon commanded, before a gentle pinch caused Nuria to yelp. "You disobeyed, and there has to be punishment. Mind your manners. There are many sensitive places that can be spanked, if needed."

Nuria would combust before Marani at this rate. When the highwayman's fingers returned to their sharp strokes, Nuria let her hips sync to the rhythm. When Marani's other hand left its command position on her waist, spread her further, and slapped, she let out only a soft "Oh gods, dragon. *Please*." Marani reddened her backside, alternating cheeks, stroking her folds when the heat burned too brightly. When Nuria came a second time, and then a third, and finally collapsed across Marani's legs, her only thoughts were of the erotic sting of Marani's touch, and the fire of Marani's kisses, and if the future of Yuro was the eclectic needs of dragons, there were a lot worse ways to go.

Chapter 14 - Marani

Since the colonization of the archipelago there have been seventy-two reported abductions of royal children by dragons. Most are from the royal line, however sixteen are noted from duke and lower standings. Gender of the kidnapped has no correlation, however age is significantly related to outcome. Those kidnapped before the age of majority have a one hundred percent return rate without injury or trauma. Those kidnapped after the age of majority, and their experiences, are detailed within this appendix.

- A Political Protocol for Nonhuman Species, Chapter 9: Promises, Prophecy, and Profit

A woman with coal-colored hair balanced Marani on her hip. She patted the fur on Marani's head and tutted at the unicorn whose horn tip was centimeters from Marani's belly. "How much will she remember?" the woman asked the unicorn.

"Nothing," the unicorn sang in response. It had a mane of jay-blue and a coat of marbled sunlight, and the wind threw its hair softly away from its eyes, which sparkled like dragonscale. The things were a hideous conflagration of color and human dreams. Humans were stupid, and irrelevant unless they were serving you. The only color that mattered was the thick honey-gold of the sun in deep summer, and the living greens of a forest that bore cephel fruit.

Marani's tiny, human stomach, growled.

Dragons weren't *supposed* to eat unicorns, but maybe there was an exception if said unicorn had taken your wings.

Marani reached for the tip of the horn but the human woman took the chubby human hand in her own. "Not while she's working, my love."

Marani turned and growled at the woman, but the sound came out an indignant cry instead. Not a hint of sulfur, or smoke. She tried again, louder, and this time water clouded her eyes. *Water.* The complete opposite element! This was...this was *horrible!* She squirmed and, when the woman's hold refused to break, she kicked. She had no claws, just soft nail, but Marani reached still for the woman's face. Maybe she could at least take out an eyeball. It would be a good snack, later.

"Darifa, can you help me?"

A soothsayer came then, her clothes made of cow hide, her face as irritated as Marani felt. "Dragon!" she snapped. "You're embarrassing yourself and your cave. Enough."

Marani roared. Or she tried to roar. The resulting sound was much higher pitched, closer to a harpy scream.

"Shshhhh, baby." A man with brown hair took her then—his arms thicker with fur as well—and held her close to his chest, where her little hands and feet hit only woven leather armor. "Andra, would you get the comb?"

"The magic requires consent," the unicorn sang. "Or at least, the absence of rage."

Marani did *not* consent to be a monkey. She screamed again, stretching her lungs and demanding her mother, her wings, her fire, and the freedom of the sky.

"Marani. Marani, look." Over the man's shoulder and just out of reach, the woman held up a piece of Marani's scale. So close to the unicorn it radiated magic, and home, but it was also strangely deformed. It had tines now, like little teeth had been carved into its edges. It was her scale, Marani had no doubt, and it was still alive—not shed—but it wasn't a part of her. That was wrong!

"Will it hurt anything if she holds it?" the man asked.

The unicorn's horn probed the back of Marani's neck while Marani reached over the man's shoulder for the comb. "No. That transformative spell is settled."

"Here then."

Her fingers grasped the scale. She closed her eyes, ignoring some strange mammalian desire to shove it into her mouth, and wished as hard as she could for her body. She wished for her cave, carved into the lowlands of...and island. She wished for her mother, whose scale was...who had...

"Marani's binding spell is done." The horn tip backed away. Marani still clung to the comb, because its light was pretty, and because it was hers. The rest of the world though, had gone fuzzy. "It is the soothsayer's job now, to set the false memories. You have sufficient magic, Darifa?"

"I do. And I've one segment left of donated horn for the final enchantment. Once Marani's memories are set I will continue to monitor the monarchy births. Is there," the soothsayer stumbled over her words, "a moment here to gauge the future? Any information about this dragon's preferences will aid me in my selection. I don't, rather, it would be unfortunate for the comb to find its way to a battle-ready prince if this dragon will prefer a pretty wallflower."

Boring, Marani thought to herself. The man's shoulder was warm, so she rested her head on it.

The unicorn walked around the man, her mane swishing like little bells, her hooves soundless on the sedge. She regarded Marani with slow blinking eyes and in the reflection, Marani saw faces. A boy with sunrise hair and dimpled chin holding a thin rapier. A scowling girl carrying a thick leather-bound book, wearing a floor-length dress and heavy circlet. A child in loose pants and a form-fitting horse-hide jerkin with a gapped-toothed grin. A parade scrolled inside the reflected irises and Marani watched, underwhelmed, at the bland people in blues and purples, that she did not know and did not care about. She turned her attention to a nearby cephel tree and chased a memory of honey-sweetness.

"None that are yet born," the unicorn said. "I suggest frequent pegaletters to Andra and Ian here, in the Common Forest. Watch how the dragon's personality manifests in this human body as it grows. Dragons love a challenge, but not a fight. They love power, not conquest. They love submission freely given. You must pair the royal child properly, or Marani is as likely to kill the thing as bond with it. I wish you luck, soothsayer."

As the unicorn began a slow fade into dew and sunlight, an increasingly panicked Darifa called out, "Your Highness! Where will you go? How can I contact you once the bond is complete? King Unicorn! Please! What if one dragon isn't enough? What if she gets lonely, or isn't controllable? What if—"

* * *

"Dragon?" Nuria's voice melted Marani's dream. "Marani? Can you hear me?"

"Yes?" She propped herself up off a rug made of thick wool—sheep, maybe, imported from Tchun, which she'd heard about in concept from a merchant at a Bad Mill market when she was thirteen but had never had the pleasure of touching. A sheep rug was puzzling, but not as puzzling as her dream, or Marani being fully clothed—sans scale tears—and Nuria being next to her, nude, flushed, with her hands tied behind her back with a strip of her skirt.

The room smelled of fire and sex, which filled in only some of the gaps.

"How do you feel?"

About the dream, or the sex she'd apparently just had? Marani rubbed her jaw. It had been sore and cracking for most of the day, but now the scale was as smooth as butter. The same was true of her arms and thighs, although there was a tightness still to her back that persisted. "Polished?"

Nuria giggled. "In so many ways."

"It would be funnier if I could remember what led to this." She pointed to Nuria's bound hands.

"Flip me over. I'm certain your handprint is still on my rear."

Submission freely given? Well done Darifa, I guess. And thanks for not binding me to Princess Oksana, who I would have indeed killed. Marani reached over the princess and as she undid her restraints, confirmed that yes, a very familiar outline tinted across the royal backside. *Freely given?* "Are you hurt?"

"Not any more than I wanted to be. And the payoff was amazing. Do you want to go again?" Nuria put her hands back together and moved her knees apart just enough to tease Marani with a glint of wetness.

In any other scenario, in any other moment, that would have been an outstandingly silly question—much like asking if one wanted more butter on their corn. But a now too-familiar twinge hit Marani's gut. It was the same feeling she'd had in her first carriage ride with Nuria, when the princess had confessed the scope of her journal. It was the same feeling she'd had when she had stumbled around the subterranean tunnel under the Aspen Grove castle, and when the Two Spire's clock had struck its maddening chords. It was the twist of magic, and prophecy, and a destiny that Marani had no control over.

Nuria noted Marani's hand on her stomach. "We could eat first. I could have more cow steak sent around. Let me get my skirt and I'll run to the kitchen and ask."

Nuria had her skirt halfway on before Marani gathered her thoughts. "Nuria. No. I don't want...I don't *remember*. I don't remember any of this. I think even kissing is off the table if it...I mean, if we can't predict how I'll respond. I...it's not safe." *I don't trust this transformation, either, or my lack of memories.* But saying those words would mean discussing her dream, and time felt too sticky short for a devolution into her childhood.

Nuria gave Marani her best, 'you're a highwayman and not in charge' look. "There's no mirror here, but surely you can feel the difference? It can't just be external. Your eyes are the green of ferns, and shaped like a serpent's. Your kit scale is gone, and your plate scale glows underneath, like the scale that lines the underground passages of the palace. Like it did when you first emerged in King Fridolin's study and the sun burned away your skin. Before I made everything stop. You're almost there, love. You're so close."

"I still don't understand why a process that should be natural has to hurt so damn much." Muscles cramped in her lower back as her scale continued to tighten. She ran her definitively longer tongue across her teeth. There were three rows now, all long, pointed things, her molars gone. Her fingers were longer, the nails thickened and curved to chocolate-colored claws. Marani ran those claws through her cropped grey hair, and her fingers bumped along delicate ridges of bone that traced from the back of her skull to the bridge of her nose. She looked more dragon-shaped but her mind, for the most part, was just Marani.

Again, Nuria misread Marani's silence. "Mm-hmm. Sex calls the flush, and the flush pokes the transformation, as far as I can tell, but there are iterations there I can't yet parse. If I invite, you are more dragon, but more at ease. If I request or command, you don't hesitate but your scale starts peeling. We will have to work on it more. You fell asleep when the"—Nuria pointed to Marani's forehead—"cresting started to erupt. You probably just need fuel. Let me get it and we can finish this."

"A transformation tied to sex can't be right. What about Jacks? What if I'd never found you? Besides, I'm not using you like a—"

"Bar maid?"

Marani scowled. "Like a princess. I saw those tapestries, too, when I was casing the palace for loose coins. You're my...our relationship isn't ownership, by one party or the other. Queens thought they could seduce and own dragons. Dragons stole royal children. Back and forth, and onward to our extinction. We play at power here, in the bedroom, but I don't want historical reenactment."

"We are bound by prophecy, and I'm afraid there's no getting around that." She took Marani's hand in hers and kissed each knuckle. "Sex is useful because it calls the flush. I'm sure there are other workarounds. The only one fighting the prophecy right now is you. That's what will destroy your body, I'm sure of it."

Marani's stomach growled again. "My body can shred. If I'm touching you, I demand to be a part of it. Horse tits, Nuria. I could really hurt you. Somewhere Jacks is laughing his ass off, but sex isn't the answer."

Nuria rolled her eyes as Marani stood and tried to straighten her pants. "That's just the hunger talking. Come on. You can accompany me to the kitchens. I want to check on Darifa anyway. I...am not comfortable with her tied up like that in a unicorn bar."

Marani whipped her head around so quickly she overbalanced and landed on her elbow, hard, on the sheep rug. "I'm sorry? A what?"

Nuria, having recovered her torn panties, sighed and offered Marani a hand up. "You really hadn't noticed? The décor of rainbows? The silver jewelry, the tablewear, the names? Have you ever met a human named Starlight? There are a few unicorn enthusiast bars around. Same for dragons. Patrons dress up, read stories, act out little plays, try to recreate a culture they barely understand. Except there is real magic here. There's a magical boundary and walnut trees that are somehow still alive despite needing magical fertilizer. The inn's name is *Solitaire,* which would be too subtle for a club. They've got real buzkashi trophies, which is a real sport played by mostly men on horseback *now,* but not a single patron here has the shape of a jockey. I think there's a decent chance at least one unicorn lives here. What sport would a unicorn play, if they played sports? I think they'd be very adept at stabbing a goat carcass, or cow I suppose, and carrying it across a field."

Marani just stared at her as she tried to imagine the unicorn in her dream—King Unicorn, which could have been a title or a name—using her cornflower blue horn to spear a cow. "Unicorns played sports? Team sports? Sorry I'm trying to imagine it but I can't hold any image that silly in my mind."

"I don't know! Maybe I'm wrong. Lots of people on Yuro are obsessed with extinct magic. Maybe this is just a group of unicorn enthusiasts. Maybe the bar was founded by unicorns before they went extinct and these people are the caretakers. Regardless, they know more about magic than us, and they have my soothsayer, and seem very keen on keeping you and Jacks inside. And—" she scowled down at Marani, the jut to her hip sinking her panties to an exposing height. "And...are you going to take my hand, or not?"

The edges of her vision blurred. Marani screamed at herself to calm down, to think of buzkashi, or cow pelts, or literally anything other than invitation in front of her. A voice far deeper than her own said, from Marani's mouth, "I like the view from here."

"This island is not ready for dragons, I swear. I thought you were hungry. I'm already up off the ground. Why did you wait until my undergarment—which is barely holding itself together, was already back on? If you're going to do further violence to my wardrobe, now would be the time. Once the rest of my clothes are back on they are *staying* on for at least twelve hours, or unless a fully-formed dragon tears them back off."

Marani had reached a stage so far past exhaustion that the heat that came to her barely registered. Her stomach rumbled. A headache threatened. But Nuria's panties split perfectly along a leg seam, the gathering of fabric accentuating Nuria's mound.

Nuria hooked a thumb into the right corner of her undergarment and tugged it below her hip, exposing just enough to quicken Marani's heart and condense her emotions down into a singular lust.

"If you want this, dragon, come take it. I promise to behave."

The bits of humanity that had cobbled themselves back together after her last round with Nuria promptly shattered. Her lip curled, exposing dagger-teeth that would have sent any sane person running. Marani had yet to remove any of her clothes, and as she coiled herself upright the tight fabric grabbed on the scale of her back and shoulders. Muscles swelled. A hot tickling rose underneath and Marani's vision slipped between the tease of Nuria's slit and darkness. Fire churned in her belly, and crept up her throat. She was losing control. She could not lose control!

"Take them off," the dragon commanded.

Nuria shook her head, and took exactly one step back, her thumb holding the undergarment in that maddening, tantalizing, half-exposed position. The top of her slit. The petal-soft skin of her mound. The tightness of—

The pressure in Marani's back turned to jabs—not of pain, but like how popcorn had to feel when finally released from its shell. Marani watched through spotty vision as her hand shot out, grabbing Nuria's thigh and hauling her forward. Seams popped as she did so, not on Nuria's panties, but on Marani's cream colored shirt.

"I need to eat," Marani managed to growl.

"Anything you'd like," said a very acquiescent Nuria, in a voice that sounded nothing like it should. The still-human part of Marani's mind screamed that this wasn't a game. That she refused to disappear into...whatever curled underneath her scale. The dragon part had already pulled Nuria's panties to her knees. Yuro help her, the princess was shaped so perfectly here, like a pear at full ripeness, juices ready to burst into Marani's mouth. She spread Nuria with thumb and forefinger, then grinned up, triumphant and saw...not coyness, or arousal, but...wonder.

Humanity rammed its way to the forefront. Marani froze. "Nuria?"

"I'm sorry. I didn't meant to distract. It's just...I've never seen dragon wings before. I didn't realize they'd be iridescent. The tapestries don't do them justice."

"Wings?"

"Your back. Right there, between your shoulder blades, where the fabric ripped. Can you feel it? You're bleeding again, which must be my fault. I must have said the wrong words. But it's alright. It doesn't look like you're in pain. Can you feel them? They're right—"

"Don't touch!" Marani shrugged off the remains of her shirt and stared, transfixed, as cherry-red blood mixed with a sheet of skin shaded hellebore green.

"Here." Nuria handed her a delicate, silver hand mirror. "There's a full-length mirror on the other side of the bed. Go look." As Marani stood, she asked, "Does it hurt?"

"It didn't a moment ago. Now..." The lacerations stung in the open air and the pressure built, unrelenting, like a million sharp horse hooves vindictively dancing along her spine.

The mirror showed blood beading in two long lines that ran parallel to Marani's backbone, the skin underneath mounded and taunt. Historically, Marani's open wounds knit together in seconds, but the breaks in scale here stayed open, blood oozing out and eventually, forming thin rivulets that ran down her tailbone and stained her pants.

"I'll get you a new shirt. You can wipe it away until it stops. Then we can find a fireplace and burn it. I'm sure the inn has spare clothes. The rest of your wounds healed quickly. This one is sure to as well. But we could keep going, too. Stopping now," Nuria bit her lower lip. "Maybe it's better to get it over and done with? I can probably avoid the blood."

Events were unfolding far too rapidly, and sexily, for Marani's comfort. "Leave the shirt. Get Darifa. She has to undo this. I can't keep...I can't keep splitting apart. There has to be a spell that ties me back together. Pegasus balls, this *hurts.*"

Pit pat. Marani's blood slid off the now saturated hemline of her pants and landed on the cobblestone floor. The grey and brown stone was polished which only made the blood shine that much brighter.

"But Marani—"

"Nuria. Please."

Nuria nodded, then sadly but necessarily reclothed. "Alright. I'll see if can free her without giving too much away. The last thing we need is zealots finding out we have fresh dragon blood. And I'll get a few more steaks sent up, too."

The unicorn bar thing. Right. Marani reached around her back, wiping a drip before it hit her already ruined pants. The blood was still thin and bright, with no sign of congealing. It fizzed on her scale, as if it sought to dissolve everything it touched.

Pit pat. Pit pat. A wave of nausea washed over Marani. She lost her balance and groped for the bed, little dots swimming in her vision. Nuria was somewhere behind her, finishing the lacings on her half-corset, but Marani didn't have the energy to turn around. "Nuria?"

"It's just the end of the transformation, love. It has to be almost done. Just rest."

There would be no rest, not with the way the muscles in her back balled, and the way her scale tore itself apart. Marani curled into a ball on the bed, stretching the skin of her back but easing the churning of her stomach. She heard the *chink* of scale shifting, heard the ripping of cotton as she tried to turn and the raw scale of her back tore at the sheets now heavy with her blood. Everything hurt, not in the way it had in the Two Spires tunnels, where magic had infused her body and reformed it like a caterpillar in a chrysalis, but like her human bits were struggling to hold on to an obsolete form already set to decay. Nuria's kisses had soothed for a while, but there would be no soothing wings. "This shouldn't hurt. I'm not a pig bladder being filled with air, I'm...I'm an accordion expanding. Right? Agh!" Another seam ripped down her back and warmth soaked the sheets, sticky and sweet. "This isn't right. The transformation isn't right. I'm tired of guessing. I need a soothsayer. Now."

* * *

It wasn't a soothsayer who banged opened Marani's door, but Jacks.

"What the hell happened?" Jacks' cool hands were a welcome relief on Marani's shoulders as he turned her over to inspect her back. "Marani, there's bone protrusions."

"Is that a fancy way to say wings?" she groaned back. "It won't stop bleeding. Where's the soothsayer?"

"Our hosts won't release her. She's still tied up, and I asked Nuria to stay downstairs since there's blood. I don't think this is all bone, either." Jacks' fingers pushed down the edge of severed scale and Marani had to swallow a scream. "Yeah, connective tissue. I'm betting scale comes later, or maybe feathers? Pegasi have feathers on their wings and that had to come from somewhere. I know the illustrations usually show a more leathery material but—"

"Jacks!"

"Well excuse me for finding the mechanics of our bodies fascinating. I have to go through this too, you know. You could whine a little less. It's not like you're dying. Right?"

Why was he here? Not physically in the room with her of course, but bound into a human prison. Dream-Darifa had spoken about needing another dragon...if things went wrong? Was this what was wrong? What if they had to transform at the same time? What if they had to battle, or gods, what if they had to fuck the same person? Marani would rather die. "I will try very hard not to, but this...situation, isn't right. I feels like my body is in a vice. Every time I expand too far, or too fast, it tightens, crushing me that much more. My insides burn. My throat is all ash. I'm a fire in a bottle. I can melt, or I can crack, but either way, do I survive?"

"I can press towels to you until you clot, but otherwise, I don't know what to do." He took a deep breath. "You can't die. You probably shouldn't transform here, either. Want me to take you outside? What *do* we do, Marani?"

"Unbind the magic of Yuro that has strangled us both?" Marani said, unhelpfully. "In the next hour or so? There's no caterpillar inside me, Jacks. There's nothing to emerge. I either transform properly, or I'll be a pile of charcoal."

"I'll get right on that." And because neither one of them had ever been good at serious conversations, instead of getting a towel, Jacks prodded an exceptionally tender area under her ribs. Marani screamed.

"Yeah, that's definitely a feather outline." With a bop on the top of her head he said with mock glee, "Congrats, it's wings!"

"I should have drowned you in your last nettle tea bath."

"Can't say I miss thrice-daily nettle tea at all, although you could use a cup right now just to calm you down. You're clotting, by the way." He passed her the hand mirror. "You've got scabs over the bone protrusions. With a cloak on you might just look like a hunchback." Jacks took a wet cloth and wiped it gently down her back. "It stopped. It's done, for now. Why don't we try sitting up? Then discuss where we can go that isn't an inn filled with guys named Starlight."

Marani bit pointed teeth into her lip, scratching the scale. "It could hurt less, but I suppose clotting is a good start." When Jacks paused to wring out the cloth, Marani sat up and prodded as best she could at the offending area. It did hurt less, now that Nuria and her panties were outside the room. "I don't understand why it keeps stopping and starting. Why do I get pieces of a transformation? What purpose does this serve!?" Marani hadn't meant to yell the last sentence. As a familiar heat rose in her chest, and the flush threatened her eyesight. She doubled over, expecting another stab in her back, but nothing came.

"Damn it I just had it cleaned up." Jacks pushed her back flat and pressed the soiled cloth down. In a voice that sounded more like her father than her little brother, Jacks said, "Keep your damn temper if you don't want wings. You've got...huh. Okay, nothing new, but that was a fast flush. Probably not enough time."

"I wasn't angry earlier," said Marani through clenched teeth. "Not ten minutes ago I was thrilled."

"Thrilled, or aroused? And while I beg you to *not* give me the specifics"—Jacks paused his ministrations to point at the door—"was this a 'I've not seen you in hours lets smooch' thing, or an 'I'm upset you aren't where you're supposed to be so I'm going to do some kinky power play' thing? Cause one of those is going to be a lot closer to flushing you than the other." Jacks flung the bloodied washcloth into the fireplace, where it landed with a heavy *splat*.

"What's going on?" Marani asked. "Did you get too much of my blood on you? Feeling ill?"

Jacks tossed a new shirt at her from some unseen drawer. "You are *the worst* when it comes to women, and I am tired from a long two days of key searching, pegasus diving, and brigand smashing. Having to rescue my sister from the manipulative advances of a princess has worn on my last nerve. And there's shirts in here, but no jerkins. Your cloak is downstairs and I'll go get it for you if you want, although I don't think anyone here is going to judge your ridging."

"Manipulative?" Marani eased to her feet, swallowing a string of curses as the muscles in her back pulled and threatened to split. Again. "I all but pinned her to my lap and shredded some of her clothes. I'm the problem. Not the princess. Why—what is that look for?"

Jacks tried to smooth his expression back to neutral, and ended up looking like a spooked owl. "Pressing this means discussing more about your sex life than I want to. Let's try a different direction. Do you *want* to be a dragon, sis?"

Marani blinked at him. "That's a moot question at this point, surely."

"No, it's not. Magic kept us in these simian bodies, and it can probably put us right back. You have a choice. We still have to understand what's happening, and we have a history to uncover, but the end of this game doesn't have to be 'Yuro gets two dragons.'" His voice softened. "Maybe you want to be a princess consort the rest of your life. Maybe you want to keep chasing every barmaid you see. Maybe you want to reign fire from the heavens on unsuspecting townsfolk. I don't know. I can make that choice for myself. No one can make it for you. That soothsayer in purple said magic is keeping you a human, but what if it's just *you?* If Nuria wasn't here, if I wasn't here, if the world was fresh and new and you could make any choice you wanted, what would it be?"

Marani sat on the edge of the bed and chewed the inside of her lip. She ran her fingers down the length of her forearm, bumping over the striated scaling. "I love this new body. I love its power, and its heat. I love its surprises, and its pain, and the way I can suddenly shut down my brain and revel in basic senses. But I love the softness of skin and the taste of butter, and the joy of picking flowers and chasing my little brother with them around a clearing. I don't... think I'd mind being a dragon I just thought...the change would be more gradual. That I'd have time to get used to the phases along the way." She laughed. "That sounds so naïve."

"It sounds like a perfectly fine reaction to being a magical lizard. What I'm trying to say though"—Jacks kicked at the door to their room—"is that every person out there, except for maybe Javad and Liu, is invested in dragons. Not Marani and Jacks the outlaw peasants, but *dragons*. And that includes a princess who left very important treaty talks and deliberately put herself in harm's way. And when harm didn't work, I'm assuming, and *please* do not give me specifics, opted for a 'oh woe is me I'm a damsel in distress no please don't do weird things with your tongue there.'" Jacks mimed fainting, then retched.

Marani was about to argue that her and Nuria's sexual preferences were no stranger than at the palace, even if she had definitely been more forceful than previously. She opted to keep those thoughts silent however, in deference to Jacks' continued gagging.

"I'll keep an eye on it," she said instead. Talking with her brother soothed the tension from her back and faded the cuts and stings to a mild irritation. "Promise. But what about you? Do you want to be a dragon?"

He sighed. "Fair deflection. Is it a load off my pustuled shoulders that I'm not actually allergic to the world? Yeah. Do I want to go through whatever is going on with your back? Absolutely not. I'd settle for just being a regular human. Find my own princess or barmaid or pastry chef. But I want the *choice*. And I don't get that if I can't find my key, or if we get captured by soothsayers. So." Jacks sat next to Marani on the bed and poked her arm. "I skimmed the notebook. It's creepy, how much of our lives the princess saw, but it's the passages that don't seem to have anything to deal with us that I'm more interested in. They all have to be about you, don't they? Isn't that how the magic of soothsaying works? If we can unravel those visions, I think we will have our answers. Although I think we can toss out any tea-related ones, since those were probably about you trying to get nettle tea for me."

"That would make sense."

"So." Jacks again poked her in the arm. "Let's start easy. We need to leave the inn, no? It's decent construction, and clearly magic, and I'm sure the thumping I keep hearing from the roof has a bland explanation since no one is panicking. But you transform here, you destroy it."

Marani had not paid attention to anything but Nuria since returning to the inn—but there was a low thudding from the ceiling. Bizarre, and currently irrelevant. "Did Nuria tell you her theory?"

Jacks snorted. "Briefly. Unicorn zealots makes me less concerned about them. It's like having a mess of historians right at our fingertips. They might be able to fill in events from the notebook. If we ask the right questions, maybe we get more information about the grove, or whatever magic might be binding you. If they're real unicorns, well, we're all fucked."

Marani laughed so hard she snorted. "Why would a magic spell strip our dragon memories but leave an entire pub of unicorns intact? And how would they have stayed hidden for these centuries? Sure, the inn is protected from soothsayers, but not treasure hunters and general highwaymen. Come on, Jacks. We knew everything that was going on across Yuro less than a month ago. Did we ever hear so much as a rumor about unicorns, or even mystical humans? No. And the way the pegasi flock to magic, why aren't there constellations of them constantly overhead?"

Jacks looked like she'd decapitated his favorite stuffed bunny. "Yeah," he said heavily. "I know you're right."

This time it was Marani's turn to poke Jacks' shoulder. "They don't have to be unicorns to be useful. Maybe they think they are, even. We don't have any business shattering illusions if they're offering protection. I'm stable, for now. Yes, we need to leave, but let's get as much information as we can about the magic of the grove first from someone who hasn't taken a secrecy pact, then see if the clientele have suggestions about how to handle the oncoming soothsayers. Maybe if the soothsayer starts the conversation, the fanatics can fill in. If anyone can explain the rules of Yuro's magic, or tell us how to get around your lack of key, it's going to be a bunch of bored historians in a unicorn sports bar."

Chapter 15 - Nuria

None of the archipelago's magical creatures are prone to conversation. However, long-term studies of unicorn hierarchies suggest that, unlike with dragons, there exists a solitary head of state, supported by an unknown number of regents. These regents are tied to both islands and what appear to be unicorn-fiefdoms, whose borders do not follow any river, ocean, or natural land formation. Further study is required.

- A Political Protocol for Nonhuman Species, Chapter 3: The Unicorn

"I said leave her be!" Nuria pushed at an unreasonably tall woman wearing a double braid, shimmering shorts, and a shirt that barely covered her stomach. "Darifa has served my family loyally for years. She's a *royal* soothsayer, and Grey the Dragon requests her presence. Now let her go!"

Her voice was more shrill than Queen Ndolo would have ever allowed, but Nuria was pressed for patience. No one at the inn seemed to care where Jacks went, even though he was as much dragon as Marani, but her court soothsayer they wouldn't budge on. Nuria had tried asking, then bribing, then offering to outright buy the soothsayer back. Buzkashi enthusiasts were clearly very stubborn, and so Nuria had resorted to yelling and threats to eventually burn down the bar.

Not one of the sweetly smiling, outlandishly dressed patrons had yielded. Starlight had called a meeting, and now, *now* she yelled at the braided woman, a man sitting on the bartop, and Darifa. Darifa had been hung by her ankles from a low rafter, had bits of the foul smelling cephel fruit plugged into her nostrils, and swung in a lazily circle while a woman poked her with a forked stick.

"I think a soothsayer deserves far worse, actually, but we can't release her until she tells us how she got past the barrier."

Nuria stomped her foot. A *whump* came from the roof—a sound which had nothing to do with her current issue and thus, she ignored. "I pushed her in! Now let her go or I'll...have Grey burn down this inn!"

"Princesses do not, nor have they ever, commanded dragons. We've heard the soothsayer's version of events, and of course yours matches." The man atop the bar—short, in purple suspenders and milk-white skin, leaned forward. "You'll forgive Glitter and I if we don't believe you. The soothsayer barrier hasn't been breached in one hundred and twelve years. If there was a workaround as simple as 'getting shoved through by a princess,' we would have known in the first decade."

"Have you had a dragon's princess through before?" Nuria challenged. She had been brought up in rules and prophecy. Crazed unicorn fanatics paled next to the court historian, who'd drilled the names of Nuria's maternal line, as well as their legacy to Yuro, into her head until she could recite her entire lineage forward and backward, even while drunk.

The man's eye twitched.

"It's the truth," wheezed Darifa as she swung in a slow circle. "Majestic Glitter. Radiant Apple. As I said previously, I have critical information to share but it cannot go through the court. I need to see King Unicorn. If she is not here, the Vice King would suffice."

"Pssht," said the woman—whom Nuria assumed was Glitter by the overdone tinsel in her hair. "Found a unicorn history book, did you? Or"—she grimaced—"did you read that horrible tome *A Political Protocol for Nonhuman Species?* You'd think humans would read books *by* unicorns if they really wanted to understand them. No human speaks with King Unicorn. Especially not a human who has made her living snuffing horn and belching out magic visions."

Booomp. Whump fump! Maybe it wasn't the roof, but Marani and Jacks? Could Jacks be transforming? The sounds were impact, not breaking, and no screams followed. Whatever it was, Jacks was better suited to dealing with Marani in her current state, and Marani could certainly shepherd Jacks through the start of a transformation. Nuria had a different job.

"She's here because I made her come," Nuria added as she gave a confounded look to her soothsayer. She'd skipped over all the book's chapters on unicorn pleasantries, and that was about to bite her like a pegasus to the ass. "If it's coin you're after, I can get you plenty. Just let her down. You'll never get more than riddles from her anyway. I've tried for years. Trust me."

Apple barked at her from the counter, "That's because your prophecy muddles magic. It—" He coughed on his next words, then stuttered, "Nope. Barrier hasn't unwound enough for that, apparently."

"This magic, this prophecy, I had nothing to do with creating. If Darifa did, she certainly can't undo it when she's bound. My... Lord Glitter, would you *please* let her down? It's much easier to talk when your feet are on the floor." Lord? Did unicorns have lords? Ladies? They had kings, apparently. Lords and ladies had to be a given.

Glitter considered as she swirled a heavy bottomed glass on a tabletop. Empty of liquid, the glass turned a perfect circle without teetering, then set silent flat against the wood. "Apple, do we still have a princess room? We used to, right? For when the dragons came around? The soothsayer speaks even less with Nuria here. The binding magic strengthens when the princess is near. She smells like red clover."

Apple crossed his arms with a sigh. "She smells like Aspen Grove's queendom, which is the whole problem. I'd love to remove them both, but you stick that princess in our broom closet and the fledgling will take your head off. Ask Starlight when he gets back. Until then let's just get them both into chairs. Maybe if the princess isn't screaming at us she can tell us something about the roof."

"I wouldn't mind taking a rest from the interrogation." Beefy hands picked Nuria up by her shoulders then set her, gently, down into a wicker chair. "Stay," said Glimmer. "Behave. If you're good, I'll cut your soothsayer down, too."

"Glimmer," Apple said with a sigh.

"Starlight said to keep them busy. I'm keeping them busy!"

Nuria had been nothing but courteous to this point, although she was ready enough to be done with niceties. She wasn't selfish enough to wish that Marani would enter and set things to rights—growing wings was a much larger problem than cephel nose—but it had been a long day for her as well and she did not have the stamina for quirky historians right after multiple orgasms. "Whatever it wrong with the roof, I'm certain Javad can fix it."

Glimmer booped Nuria's nose. "Javad is with Starlight and the council. Your baker we might just keep—she made a strawberry tart that I won't recover from. It's just us for now, Princess Hazelnut."

A *whack* came, definitively, from the roof, followed by the tinkle of broken glass. From an adjacent room, a woman who was not Marani let out a string of pegasus-themed curses.

Unicorns had absolutely no sense of urgency. Likely because they'd never had to grow wings. "Don't do that. Please." Nuria's nose wrinkled. "My name is Nuria of Aspen Grove. Is everything...alright?"

"Starlight will deal with the pegasi, your eyes look like hazelnuts, and Aspen Grove is not a monarchy that sits well with the council. It was certainly a wild choice for Yuro's last dragon to align with, but I suspect that alignment will come to an end the moment she leaves her human shell." Glimmer leaned in to inspect Nuria's neck, then forehead. "You're very cute, even when bruised. Although I'm guessing not a virgin. If you are, Grey is a particularly poor dragon."

Pegasi on the roof? Why? What glass was there to break? And was it Marani doing the breaking? Nuria took a moment to consider which disastrous avenue she'd try next, especially since there did not need to be any further discussion of her and Marani's bedroom escapades. With the ensuing silence, she did hear a quieter *thunk thunk* on the roof—which could have easily been walnuts falling from a windstorm. Pegasi should have been out of the equation, noting the pegacide arrows. What was maybe still on the table, was flattery. Or at least, false acquiescence. "Will you please let Darifa go to the Dragon Grey?" Nuria tried with her best virginal voice. "And I'll stay for as long as you like?"

Glimmer grinned. "Oh, I do like her. The dragon has taste. Feisty pets are always more fun. I think this princessly selection was pure lust. That prophecy could have been tied to any royal child. I vote for lust, or a very fantastic sense of delayed vengeance." With a mischievous grin, Glitter asked Nuria, "Virginity aside, does she fuck you, too, the way royalty fucked all the magical creatures of Yuro? Or is she into the more classical horse? You're from Aspen Grove, so I have to assume you spread your legs for her at least once. No dragon ever resisted an Aspen Grove pooch."

"Ahhh look how she shut up!" said Apple. "I knew it. I told you they had a range of appetites. What good is a princess if you can't fuck her? Any princess can fall in love and lose their virginity, but a good fucking? That's dragon skill there, that is."

Glitter shrugged. "I'm sure princesses have other attributes. They're pretty. You could keep them around on a shelf, like pottery or a shiny necklace. Look how adorable she is when she wants to bite us but her training won't let her. Not like a harpy." Glitter scowled as a magnificent screech came from the roof. "Nasty things."

Nuria had to pull on every ounce of her court training to find her calm. "Perhaps we could trade information?" she asked through clenched teeth. "You could let Darifa down and I'll answer every question you have if just let her go to Grey. And maybe if I'm good," Nuria swallowed a revolted cough. Playing cute for your fated lover was one thing.

Playing cute for overly confident historians was disgusting. "You can answer a few simple questions of mine?"

"A mighty proposition," said Apple with a *twang* of his suspenders. "Maybe we should get princesses, once the dragons have resolved. There's precedent for that, right? We don't have to stick to village maidens and virginal boys."

Glitter ignored him. "*Every* question, princess?" Glitter stuck her tongue between her teeth and grinned. "Such as how you got the dragon to take a nap?"

Nuria would not blush. She would *not*. "Every question." And because there did not appear to be such as thing as overkill at the moment, Nuria added, "My Lord. If you let Darifa down."

Glitter beamed. "What do you think, Apple?"

The man behind the bar flashed a thumb. "Down with the soothsayer! Yes to princesses!"

"Consensus!" Glitter cheered as she slit the rope holding Darifa, sending the soothsayer to the floor. Darifa *oofed* just as another scream came, this time from the other side of the west inn wall. Nuria tried to run to her, but Glitter's hands had already pressed back to her shoulders.

"That'll be a hunter," Apple said with a complete lack of concern. "Hitting the roof. Or at least, a human. Maybe they're being dropped in? Pegasi aren't usually so accommodating, especially to anyone after a dragon."

"Leave Starshine to it," said Glitter.

"Princess," came the nasally groan of the soothsayer as Apple gripped her under the armpits and slung her onto a chair. "These two are not your enemy. They're just irritating."

Irritation was exactly the emotion Nuria currently battled. "She can go to Grey? If you've got hunters at your walls, we're out of time."

Apple shrugged. "Humans aren't the problem, and there's nothing keeping her here but her own two horn-licking feet. She's not nearly as entertaining as you are at the moment."

Darifa slid off the chair and coiled in on herself, no doubt fighting a pegasus-sized headache. She needed time to recover, which meant Nuria needed to be more than a pretty distraction. "Do you know a dragon's favorite position, my lords?"

"I do *not!*" Glitter spun her chair around. Apple stood in tandem with her, hands on cocked hips, heads canted ever so slightly to the left. Their frames were wildly different in both width and height, their hair and skin polar opposites, and yet it felt very much like Nuria was looking at the same person.

"Well?" Apple demanded.

Nuria straightened, straining the remains of her bodice. The white linen stretched, uncovering a decent amount of areola. Marani would have a meltdown when she eventually saw it. "On horseback. It gives more options."

Two pairs of utterly mesmerized eyes went wide as Glitter and Apple nodded in tandem.

"The position needs a name," Glitter said, almost reverently. "We can call it...we can call it *The Dragon's Whored.*" Her cheeks puffed with contained laughter and then both of them doubled over, giggling like courtiers over a mismatched petticoat.

"Perfect sense," Apple managed between gasps. "I heard they can go for hours. That's why dragons have egg clutches. Each one of those things has to be individually fertilized. Oh. Oh!" He righted and sucked at the air. "Are you having sex with one or both of the dragons upstairs? Will that mean one egg clutch or two? By the gods of Yuro how many dragonlets are we talking about for next season? I want one!"

Glitter smacked his arm, her grin as wide as the archipelago's ocean. "You don't know how to raise a dragon! Besides, they're going to want different pairings. No one wants dragons too closely related. Jacks'll get his own princess or prince."

"Yeah, but *this* princess is the one tied to the prophecy. Maybe he *has* to fuck her. Or, oh! She fucks the princess, but then he has to eat the princess? Princesses don't make it out of this alive, I'm sure."

"Oh. Yes. Good points all around. But what if he likes men? They're a different flavor. Or any of the minor genders? They're downright exotic. And if he doesn't need to eat them, maybe he does need to mate? What if princesses *do* live, but only long enough to breed? Dragons don't need alternating genitals because they're not mammalian. The fertilization is external. An egg would kill a princess though. I guess she dies either way. Shame."

They both sobered then as they very seriously considered dragon breeding. Nuria...sat and tried to do the exact opposite.

It was Glitter who finally said to Nuria. "Both of them? Yes?"

Nuria said, very regally, "No. Just the one known as Grey. Eggs have not been discussed because she's still human."

With a groan that Nuria hoped only she heard, Darifa got to her knees and removed the cephel from her nose.

"Hah! Told you, he gets his own!" Apple crowed. "Ooh that'll be fun after his transformation. Maybe we can talk him into a Faun's Pass royal or three. I wouldn't mind if he wiped out an entire generation."

"We all lost family during the Shuttering," Glitter said, her mood souring. "Faun's Pass didn't suck any more horn than the other monarchies."

Apple glowered. "Their duke still wears a unicorn horn crown!"

"Could I ask a question?" Nuria asked, her voice butter soft.

"What!?" Glitter snapped.

Darifa leveraged the chair and managed to stand on her feet.

"Why can't soothsayers enter the grove?"

The roof had, for the moment, gone silent. Nuria strained for screams, or scuffles, but heard only Glitter and Apple's excited shuffling.

"They're humans with magic, and that goes against the natural order." Glitter said. "Don't ask stupid questions. How did you meet the dragon?"

Darifa took her first tentative step right onto a creaky floorboard. Nuria added a grating amount of whine to her voice. "That's hardly an answer."

"And you're hardly in a negotiating position. How did you meet the dragon?"

"In a carriage. She robbed me with a blackberry blow dart then rifled through my panties. How does the magic barrier work?"

"Ooooh!" Glitter's foot tapped the ground in hyperactive delight. "I told Starlight they were with that bandit gang that organized the roads. Didn't I tell him, Apple?"

"They were too well organized," Apple said with a nod. "Too successful. Had to be the dragons." Apple said to Nuria, "Did you know she was a dragon?"

Darifa made her way, with pained footsteps, around the bar.

With manufactured patience, Nuria said, "It was your turn to answer."

"Oh, fine. It's not like the magic is going to matter much in a few hours." Glitter clasped her hands behind her back, and Apple did the same. "Let's see how degraded the barrier is. King Unicorn was otherwise occupied so there had to be an assigned spell crew to handle the magic cooperative. I believe it took twelve unicorns, four incantations, and three sacrificial soothsayers to get the spell to recognize who to keep out. Humans can't hold large amounts of magic without turning to ash. That's why soothsayers have to consistently ingest. It rots their teeth, though. That's how you can tell they're magic consumers. Your turn."

"Five soothsayers," Apple said. "Small groups were still getting through for a few years. The spell kept out all humans, originally. But that level of magic is exhausting to hold and one set of brigands got through and caused absolute havoc. The spell needed a booster and they had to call in a second crew. After that the parameters narrowed. Humans aren't generally a problem on their own. *Soothsayers* should all be shot on sight."

"Ah, you're right. Memory fades after a century, as you might imagine. Doesn't fade as fast as the binding spell appears to be though. Your *turn.*"

A century? Or maybe decades, if they were talking about the bandits that had sacked Marani's homestead. Since learning about the dragonscale comb's origins, Nuria had assumed that the death of Marani's parents—however upsetting—had been a critical component of getting the comb to her, and thereby starting the prophetic visions. Glitter and Apple's version of events didn't sit with what Nuria knew. A purposeful obfuscation, or maybe unicorn historians weren't actually as good as digging up the past as they thought? Or. *Or* King Unicorn and Darifa, were playing at intrigue like human royals played at court. If that was the case, Marani needed Nuria far more than as a transformation tool.

"Princess!"

Nuria blinked. What was the question? Had she known about Marani? She'd been flippant but truthful so far. Too much truth, with these two, might be more trouble later. "I knew of her, from the visions Darifa gave me. I knew she was an orphan, and a bandit. I didn't know she was a dragon."

"But she kept you alive anyway. Very fascinating. Did you know, soothsayer?"

Darifa was no longer in the main room.

Glitter cursed, the tinsel in her hair glinting with the harshness of her words. "She can't be wandering the inn. Go find her. I'll get this one to the princess room and come help after. Good bet she's gone to the baby dragons." Glitter hauled Nuria up by her armpits. "You're a delight, princess. We can play fetch later, alright? Maybe I'll rebraid your hair."

Taunt fabric around her arms meant Nuria's bodice split down the center. She pulled back against Glitter's enormous hands, but the effect was only a jiggle of Marani's favorite assets. "I can walk just fine on my own. What is it with all of you and carrying!?"

"Leave her alone!" A still-human Marani all but flew from the hallway and had Glitter back against the wall, sending Nuria to the floor in the process. "You don't touch her. You don't talk to her. You don't *look* at her. She is *mine*."

"Guess that binding spell is still holding a little," Glitter said gleefully despite the arm at her neck.

"Grey, calm down. She doesn't look hurt." Jacks held up a hand to block his view of Nuria's breasts, then knelt next to her. "You're not hurt, right? If so, could you tell her that?"

Nuria fussed with her bodice, but the fabric refused to rejoin. "I'm not hurt, but the woman holding Marani could use a time out," she muttered.

"Does she deserve to die?" Jacks said. "Coming into the main room with your boobs out and a woman leering over you isn't a good look to a half-transformed dragon."

Darifa reappeared and Nuria let her thin fingers draw lacing from behind the bodice and weave it through the front—creating a temporary hold for her chest. "They are not our enemies," Darifa whispered to her. "We are here to save them, you and I. Princess, you must play your part."

"Well it would be easier to do if anyone had bothered to tell me what that part was!" she hissed back. Louder, Nuria said, "Fair point. Grey, we were only talking. You were aching a moment ago. This can't be good for your back."

"Dragon, we would never hurt your princess." Apple walked to them and smiled, slow and wide, showing no concern whatsoever about Glitter being pinned to the wall by a human-dragon chimera who could, at a whim, leak fire from her joints. One of Marani's arms dug thick nails into his shoulder, but Apple still managed to cup her elbow. Not hard—more of a gentle grasp like a lady might do to a child who had set her teacup down improperly. In that touch, the fight bled from Marani and her tense muscle smoothing back to rest.

"She's mine," Marani said again, although the rage had gone from her words. Stress lines fractured her face as the flush receded, and fatigue took its place. "Fuck, I'm so damn tired."

"Won't you sit? Here. Princess? Give the dragon your chair."

What in the magical nonsense was going on? Nuria stood and watched, dumbfounded, as Apple led Grey to the chair. Once she sat, Apple took Nuria by her wrist and tugged her back, until Nuria was once again sitting atop Marani's lap.

Nuria winced at the electric tingles that skated across Marani's still-fresh handprints.

"There now," said Apple. "See? You can pet her while we wait for Starlight. Or we could chat? Do you know much of spells, dragon?"

"We've been half-dragons for almost four days. A turtle knows more than we do about magic." To Nuria, she said, "Do not wiggle."

"I'm tired of the half-answers. Can we wrap this up before Grey and I explode? Do you want dragons, or flesh sacks? If you've got answers, give them to us. Otherwise we are taking our Javad, our princess, and our baker, and leaving." Jacks ran a hand through his thinning hair. The short strands stayed erect, like they, too, wanted to take to the skies. "Grey isn't stable. She needs to be outside. Outside and far, far away from people."

"Where would you go, dragon?" Glitter brought a second chair up and motioned for Jacks to sit. "Out to the soothsayers that gather at the boundary? To the other monarchies who would chain you? You are exactly where you are supposed to be, you're just muddling through a magic timeline you can't control." She sniffed. "We all know how that feels. The binding spell will unwind soon enough, and we will all leave. Together. Except for you. Get over here." Glitter slammed the soothsayer back into a chair then wrapped a rope around her stomach. Her attention was clearly elsewhere, however, and the rope sagged across Darifa's lap.

"Probably for the best to have them all in one place." Apple took Glitter's hand and kissed the top. "Two dragons. We haven't had this much excitement since King Unicorn let us eat the longboat crew last week."

"That was over a decade ago, Apple," Glitter chided. "Or maybe last century. When King Dragon was still alive and before she named her heir."

Apple flashed a ragged smile. "But it was delicious. And we got to blame it on the pegasi. Please, dragons. Relax. There's a handful of minutes left. You don't need to do anything. Wait for Starlight. He can answer questions we can't."

Darifa shrugged out of the rope, putting a finger to her lips with Nuria looked her way.

Jacks refused to sit. He stood instead behind Marani's chair, scaled hands digging into the wooden back. "Why not help us find a safe place to transform? Why not help us understand the magic? Dragons don't *wait*. Come on, Grey. We're done here."

She couldn't worry about Darifa *and* Marani concurrently. Nuria slid off Marani's lap—the pressure to her backside becoming untenable—and was halfway to offering her dragon a hand up, when Javad walked back into the main room. Dozens followed him, representing the widest variation of humanity Nuria had ever seen. Just behind the marksman was a mountain of a man with braided ponytails and a tightly fitted leather vest and pants. Fanned out behind him was a man no taller than Marani's favorite pony, his hair close cropped, his pants frayed, worn linen. Then came a group of women whose skin and hair combinations looked like nature had spilled her watercolor set across a nursery. There were plenty whose gender Nuria could not discern, but all were unarmed, unless one counted bleached leather or hair baubles as deadly weapons. Several were, however, blotched with blood.

The inn patrons made no sense. Groups of people developed culture, and mores, and at the very least, tended to share fashion. Everyone at the Solitaire Inn looked like they had been let loose for three minutes in a different market, told to pick the nearest ten people, and splice together a look. The colors, fabrics, and hairstyles were an afront to good taste, national pride, and somewhere, Liu had to be having a fit.

Darifa edged from her chair and, when no one noticed, slunk to a dark corner of the inn.

Marani pulled Nuria back down. Firmly.

Nuria squeaked.

"We're leaving. Get Liu," Marani told Javad, although she made no move to rise from the chair. Her voice held a tightness probably only Nuria and Jacks could hear. Leaving the inn was the logical choice, noting how much they just didn't know, but could Nuria protect both dragons once they started transforming? Pegasi help her, could she protect them now?

It was Starlight who responded. "My apologies, dragons, for the delay. I trust you have sufficient time to enjoy your princess? We have dealt with the immediate threats, but more are arriving, a group of which we are unprepared to deal with." Starlight's otherwise blemish-free face clouded and lips puckered like a man being forced to smell cephel fruit against his will. "I apologize, too, that we cannot be more direct with you. The magic binds us all. It has loosed, as you can see from your scales and the budding of your horns, but not enough for the answers you want. You found your princess, and you found your key, and I believe the magic will let me tell you that you have every component needed to remove the binding spell. Your agency has always been your own." Starlight cast an apologetic glance at Jacks. "With my apologies to your brother, who was an unexpected addition to plan, and whose fate is tied to yours."

Was this how common people felt when they visited the palace? Like they were accessories? Or ornaments? Nuria couldn't help her growl. She tried to stand, but Marani's arm tightened around her waist, and a second hand, which had been on her knee, found its way under her dress and halfway up her inner thigh. Nuria kept her mouth shut, while simultaneously plotting how much she would enjoy gallowing everyone who discussed her like a piece of furniture.

"If I have everything I need to finish this, send out Liu and we will all be on our way. That should relieve you of your defense, too. We didn't intend to bring pegasi to your inn, or soothsayers for that matter."

"Flyers for you and Jacks have gone up across Yuro with bounties. Soothsayers are the ones who know how to track dragons, but anyone can track a soothsayer. They're magicians first, not trackers used to hiding their footprints. We have fifteen soothsayers spotted at the grove boundary, and another twenty within an hour of arrival. All have bands accompanying them. There are some four hundred soothsayers across Yuro, with varying degrees of competence. They will be clogging the roads, with their hired hunters. There is nowhere for you to flee, save up, and that direction has also complicated. I'm afraid this moment is your final one."

"We're *dragons,*" Jacks snarled. "Give us our people. Now."

With a heave of shoulders, Starlight nudged Javad.

"Liu is safe. I promise." Javad took a chair, turned it backward, and straddled. He'd changed his clothes to a matching orange tunic and pants, and no longer carried the horn-dagger. His skin had gone a sallow sort of grey color, but his eyes sparkled more than Glitter's hair. He looked like a man puffed with importance, but bloated with weight. "Grey I...I'm not telling you what to do. It wouldn't work if I did. I'm asking now, if you would, please, listen to this giant next to me with all the bulges? Half of these guys dress like harlots, the other half dress like deranged children, but you need to listen to what isn't being said, okay? They can't tell you certain things because of magic, but they told me *all* the things and there's some *big ass things,* okay? All that is outside this inn, is battle. And you'd suck at battle. It took me under five minutes to bind you last time, and that was just me and two guys. You and Jacks go out there without being fully committed to transforming, and you're going to get pounded like that dough Liu is working on. Humans have swords, and arrows. Soothsayers have some kind of magic, and harpies." Javad whistled. "Damn, is that a creature made of dead leaves and spite? That's what they sound like."

Harpies? Nuria twisted in Marani's lap, but the dragon's arm held her firm. "A new player on the board means a new strategy," Nuria murmured, hoping Marani would hear.

Whatever Marani would have said was drowned out by Jacks. "What the hell did you do to him? Javad, man, you sound like a man at sword-point. Are you okay?"

"I will be. You will be, too, but maybe too much information at once is not really digestible. You know? And uh," Javad let out a loud puff of air and shook his head. "Man, there are a *lot* of things happening right now. Like the roof. You been hearing that?"

"It's not pegasi," Jacks said. "The grove is covered in pegaside."

"Pegaside keeps the pegasi from landing in the grove, but not circling. Archers were shooting pegasi out of the sky, or trying to. The pegasi were using the roof here for a launching pad since it's high enough from the ground to not stink, but that ended half an hour ago. They're not the only thing with wings on the island, as I've noted, and the harpies prefer launching humans at roofs directly, particularly spires. Right now it's the hunters, with the hope they might flush you out. Once they get desperate?" He started ticking off fingers. "Consider. Basically every magical creature on Yuro is in or above this little grove, which is making it a beacon that the magic can't hide. Every soothsayer, magic hunter, regular hunter, and royal with a gun is either here, or on their way, following a trail of chaos that can only be caused by dragons."

"A canon would have been less obvious," Nuria said, which got her a "Shush!" from Glitter and firm pat from Marani.

"I am not a lap pet," she hissed in Marani's ear.

"Fine, but please don't be a liability," Marani returned.

"I would like to offer protection for your humans while you and Jacks finish your work." Starlight unwound the ribbons that ran through his braids, letting the silver hair fall in waves down his shoulders. The entire action was so very unnecessary, just like keeping all them talking in circles while soothsayers and hunters amassed at the grove. "If you do not go to them, they will come to us. To the dragons. And they will destroy every structure, and every person, that gets in their way. Leave your people here, and go to the clearing. Fulfill your prophecy. Retake your heritage."

Marani stood, finally, using Nuria's shoulder for balance. "Deal. I'm more than ready to bring this to a close. Jacks, can you give Nuria back the notebook? We're done with it, and it is hers."

Nuria spun on Marani, sending her dragon stumbling back into the crowd. Angry murmurs rose up, about unruly princesses and human bonds and *war*. "Damn the notebook! I did not travel highway roads without guards just for you to do this alone. I did not let a man slap me just to be left behind. I am part of this, Grey. I am part of you. You do *not* leave me behind."

Jacks stepped forward, slowly, like a cat to prey, but Marani waved him back from Nuria. Instead it was Marani herself that took Nuria by the arm and shoved her into Starlight.

"Grey!"

"She stays," Marani said, her voice beginning a descent Nuria was quickly coming to dislike.

"As you say, dragon." Starlight bowed. "She is not yet needed."

Jacks tossed the notebook onto a nearby table.

"I'm part of the prophecy! I'm part of the magic. You can't leave me here. I'm part of this, Marani! I've always been part of this!"

Marani took Jacks' hand. "This game isn't yours to play," Marani said, so quietly that Nuria almost didn't hear her. "At least not this part. Please be a storybook princess, just for a little while. What did you tell me, at the Two Spires palace, when I lay half dead on the ballroom floor? That we both had to be alive to be married? Now it's my turn to fight, and your turn to rest. You do not command me, princess."

The voice sounded so much like the old Marani. So much like the girl in her visions begging for scraps of food, or a sip of nettle tea, or to be afforded basic human dignity. Nuria stayed silent, letting Javad offer her support she didn't realize she needed, as Marani and Jacks walked out the inn door and into the walnut forest.

Chapter 16 - Marani

Even from the first census taken just after human colonization of the archipelago, unicorn numbers have dwindled to dozens. Dragons are similarly affected. It is only the harpy, nestled in her mountain rookeries, that appears unscathed by human hunting. New data emerging suggests this is less due to the location of harpy nests and moreso due to hunting preference for higher-density magic creatures over the comparably bland magic of the harpy. Interest in harpy hunting is expected to grow in the next decade, as unicorn and dragon populations dwindle. As humans press into harpy territories, a new and exciting adventure awaits to decode yet another unique culture of sentient, non-human animals.

- A Political Protocol for Nonhuman Species, Chapter 9: Promises, Prophecy, and Profit

Marani stared, mouth agape, at a row of braided tails and horse backsides. Five different breeds of horse—including a Brabant colored in dappled smokey buckskin and a high-tailed, chestnut colored Arabian—were tied in an arc just on the edge of the grove, all facing back toward the main road, giving anyone emerging from the walnut trees a clear view of horse ass.

"Fuck all of this," Marani snarled. "Is it written somewhere that dragons are whores? Not that I'm shaming a decent line of work, either, but come on." Marani pointed to the haflinger horse nearest her, whose crimped blond tail stood at sharp contrast to her cherry coat. "They know I'm not transformed. What do they think is going to happen?"

"That you'll be tempted." Jacks said, grinning. "You visited plenty of tavern women, before Nuria. You have a known appetite."

"Yeah, but you don't. This is stereotyping."

"Or they're just playing to what they know. I'm not the famous dragon, remember?" Jacks pulled her down, low in the ferns, scanning the clearing beyond the grove. They crouched along the base of a walnut that was easily a pegasus wide, not counting wings. It wasn't the edge of the grove as there were four other decent sized trees beyond, but they had a clear view, and plenty of canopy cover. "I don't see anyone out beyond the horses, but these things didn't materialize from nowhere. And it's way too quiet. What happened to that overeager soothsayer in purple? I thought we were coming out here to do some glorious battle? Right now everything looks calm."

Marani pointed to the worn rows of trampled sedge and softened mud. "Looks like we missed at least a partial one. There have been more than just these horses through here. I count at least six trails. And look at all the feathers." The clearing had been mostly sedge, fern, and blackberry bramble when they'd first arrived. Now the ground resembled a royal child's birthday cake where the cook had been challenged to create as many colors of frosting as possible. Feathers of rose and chestnut littered with tangerine and mustard in one pile, while a trail of amphibian green and mint twitched in the wind against blackberry bramble. The feather shafts were too long to be from half-breed horses, and there were far, far too many for just the five that grazed before them.

"Does it look funny?" Jacks reached just beyond the boundary and plucked a blueberry-colored feather from the ground. "The rachis here, at the base of the shaft, is barbed. I've never seen that." He ran his thumb against the area and his scale split, red blood steaming into the air.

"No pegasus feather has ever cut me." Marani repeated the process on her own thumb, to similar result. "Dragons have feathers early on, but none of mine were barbed, either. Nuria was right. A new player does mean new tactics. I don't think soothsayers and hunters are our biggest problem. Keeping them all from the inn is still our goal, though."

Jacks groaned. "What do we attack? The horses aren't bothering anyone. You want to just walk into the clearing and wave our arms around? Hope we don't get shot by arrows made of"—he waved the feather—"whatever this is?"

"You have a better idea?"

An eagle landed in the clearing before Marani could answer, turning its back toward Marani and Jacks. Its wings were the color of buttercream with a hint of olive, its talons a sharp black. Eagles this size had been known to carry off horses, but none of the tethered options in front of them even flicked an ear.

"You want to charge the eagle, just to get things moving?" Jacks asked, only half joking.

The eagle's head swiveled. Its claws dug into the sedge as the thing pivoted, revealing an ample human chest devoid of feathers, and the face of a grinning Subadhra.

"Grey?" said the human voice of Marani's once very human lover. "Won't you come out?"

"Is that—" Jacks began, but Marani clamped a hand over his mouth.

"Oh Grey. Jacks is here too. Wonderful! It's probably too much to hope for Nuria, but time is tight. I need you to come out of the forest now, little ones. We have magic to attend to."

Absolutely not. Marani was not prepared to deal with harpies. She'd never even seen a living one, and what little she knew about the creatures came entirely from children's gossip. What she did know was she and Jacks had known Subadhra for over thirty years. She was a Faun's Pass native who always managed to pop up when Marani and Jacks were desperately low of coin, and options. It had been only recently she'd learned of Nuria's involvement with Suba, but the harpy business had been left clean out.

"Is it Suba?" Jacks whispered through Marani's hand. "It's her face but, you know."

"It's her breasts, yes, if that's what you're asking," Marani returned.

Suba's head canted. "You never change, Grey. Come along. Jacks too. No one means you any harm. Everyone in this field is invested in your change. There is no benefit to a half-dragon bandit woman and her flower-delicate little brother. Yuro is united to see our dragons again. Now please. Out of the grove, where your wings can unfurl and dry properly."

Jacks pulled Marani's hand down. When she scowled, he said, "She can hear us even at a whisper. No point in my slobbering on your hand."

"You don't have time for committee!" Suba pawed at the ground and made a sound distressingly close to a chicken cluck. "Come out, dragons!"

"Why don't you stay back? No sense in us both going into a trap."

Jacks refused to release Marani's hand. "Together, or not at all. Stop fucking protecting me."

"Come out!" squawked Suba. "Come out come out come out!"

"It's less appealing every time she says it." Marani stood anyway, hauling Jacks along with her. "Most of this road stretch is flat. The Highway Guild ran it for half a decade. There are a few small hill crests but nothing that hoards of dragon hunters could hide behind."

Jacks followed her line of sight, and bit into his lower lip before he spoke. "I've never known a soothsayer to keep quiet, either. The one in purple promised to wait for you. Where is she?" His voice turned low and dark. "Where are those boys?"

Caaawk! Amongst the familiar sound of wings came the shriek of something both feminine, and inhuman. Marani knew it would not be a pegasus, for the grove was so deeply infused with pegacide that even she wanted to vomit. It was horrifying, nonetheless, to watch wine-colored wings beat the sky and then circle lower, lower, until another harpy landed in the clearing. This one again wore the face of a woman, and the chest of a barmaid, but her wings were not just wine, but also the color of autumn leaves and her talons tinted of old blood. Her hair was the color of cornsilk, and Marani could not help the exhale of relief that she did not recognize her at all.

"The dragons?" the new harpy asked Suba.

"Stubborn. As always. And still clinging like apes to their human bodies. Further stress will be needed. You've come to assist?"

"Don't I always?"

"Marani?" Jacks' voice was back to a whisper.

"Using humans as bait is low. Ready to rip some wings off?"

"Marani."

Marani turned and wrinkled her nose at her little brother. "What? They're harpies. We're dragons. If you're going to turn into a scared pegasus about this now, then go back to the inn and wait for me." She frowned, then pinched his chin. "What's wrong with you? Your skin and scale have gone an off yellow."

Jacks, his eyes as wide as the twelve-year-olds who'd recently threatened them with toy swords, said, "That's Micha."

Marani wracked her memory for the name. Jacks had so few friends, and all of the ones she could name were still back with their old bandit troupe. He'd had even fewer girlfriends, though not for lack of trying—the perfumes many barmaids wore closed up his airways, which made performance difficult. Marani did remember three distinct occasions where he'd come sulking back to their lean-to in the middle of the night, smelling of lavender and musk, asking for nettle tea and no questions.

"Micha," Jacks prodded. "The tomato heist from Bad Mill's port?"

Marani's nose remained cinched.

"Her skirt was about here," he made a sawing motion just below his crotch, "pleated, with little roses embroidered on the hem? I had welts for four days?"

"Her?" Marani almost laughed. "She was the first you...er. At least the first you ever mentioned to me."

"She's a fucking harpy, Marani! It feels like all of Yuro is unravelling."

"Gre-ey," came a singsong voice from the clearing. A screech of harpies landed, each with progressively larger breasts. Their faces blurred for a moment as wings flushed and settled, but as Marani's eyes focused, she recognized women from bars and taverns across Yuro that she had known, in one way or another, in intimate settings.

Suba hopped to the front, her eagle-body within spitting distance of Marani and Jacks. "We only want to make things easier for you both. Please come out. Don't make us come in."

"Where are the boys?!" Jacks stepped fully into the clearing, Marani just behind.

"Safe and waiting for you," Micha responded from the edge of the harpy line. "We moved them farther away, to be safe during your transformation. All we want is for you two to be safe."

"You're a fucking liar, wearing the face of Micha!" He tried to take another step, but Marani held him back. She remembered very little of Micha—having clearly focused far more on her shorter attributes—but what had imprinted was a confident young woman with a delicate stutter. She'd just enough vulnerability for Jacks to not be terrified, but with enough intelligence to help him lift a crate of Tchun tomatoes from a dock without getting caught. Jacks was, of course, allergic to tomato pollen, which covered the fruits and the shipping box. This hadn't stopped either of them from celebrating their heist in what Marani hoped was an isolated section of forest. Jacks had welts when she'd found him, yes, but those welts had been decidedly pollen-green and hand-shaped.

Granted, there were at least two decades between that encounter and their current situation, but a girl who let a boy's skin boil just to get laid was not intrinsically interested in safety.

Jacks turned flushed eyes to her. His fingernails had dug into her hand during her musings, but her scale was harder than his fledgling talons and she'd not felt so much as a pinch. "We need to go out there. No more waiting."

Suba belted a *cawk!* and Micha hopped to her. Having pulled at the memory, Marani did remember her now—a girl of maybe seventeen with a sharp constellation of freckles on her cheekbones and wild grey eyes. Marani stared now into those same eyes, the edges devoid of laugh lines, her lips still as full and pert as they'd been after a night of tomato play with Jacks.

"No no, Jacks. The boys are fine. Come. I'll show you. Or shall I bring them to you?" Micha flapped a wing at Suba. "Yes?"

"Yes. And Grey perhaps made plans with a soothsayer? One in purple? She spoke to me. She's across a different hill. Come, dragons. Let us see if her magic can help ease your burden."

Jacks yanked his arm away from Marani, so she took his hand instead, her grip a vice he'd, hopefully, not be able to shake off. "Where?" he demanded.

"Jacks." Marani kept her voice low and even. Hysterics only fed a flush, and neither one of them had enough energy to flush again. Logic, too, could bounce right through a flush-addled brain. Jacks had to find rationale on his own...although Marani could certainly leave breadcrumbs. "You're turning forty years old this year. Dock girls see a lot of sun and Micha was, to my memory, paler than an imported eggshell."

Jacks took another step forward, tugging Marani along with him. They were still within an armspan of the grove— close enough to dive back if needed. "Harpies wouldn't age like humans and we have to get to those boys."

She'd given him points for logic while in a flush. Marani was even willing to accept the omnipresent Suba as a harpy, or at least muddled up somewhere in the same prophecy she shared with Nuria. But there was no way that every sexual choice she had made from puberty onward had been...a harpy disguised as a barmaid. Marani had not been particularly discretionary in her late twenties and early thirties and with magic in the state it was across the archipelago, there simply weren't enough harpies to cover her every liaison.

A far simpler explanation was magic and disguise. Unicorns couldn't lie, dragons couldn't break promises, and while she was unsure what magic rule bound harpies, it wasn't going to be redundant with Yuro's other magic creatures. Jacks of course, was in no position to hear any of that.

Micha waddled forward. She spread her fire-colored wings just shy of the foremost walnut and said, "You're safe with me, Jacks. You and the boys are safe."

"It's a trap," Marani countered when she refused to take another step with Jacks. "The boys, the soothsayer, anyone else who arrived while we were at the inn, they're the bait. You don't know they're over the hill. They could be up in a rookery being fed to chicks."

Jacks turned to her with a furious smile. "Then I get my wings and I go to them. Who is going to free them if not us? I'm a dragon, not an asshole. They're our responsibility."

"Really? An hour ago we joked about eating them."

"Not the *kids*," Jacks hissed at her. "Did you see them? Did you see their stick legs and their brittle hair and the darkness not just around their eyes, but in them? They're *us*, Grey. Us just a few decades back, hungry and scared and looking for any way to turn coin." Jacks' voice went as tight as his grip on Marani's hand. "We don't know shit about my life before this human skin. We don't know shit about my prophecy, or my key, or if maybe I have some fated love out there in the archipelago. Know what neither of us have? Purpose. Once we are dragons we have nothing. No script. No plan. But I'm making one right now. No more hungry kids. We're going to get those boys to a castle and get them fed, then I'm going to torch any monarchy that doesn't put its most vulnerable, first. But to do that, sis, I have to leave this grove." Jacks dropped her hand, but held her gaze. "Come with me. We can fuck up some harpies together."

Marani met Jacks' dragon-toothed smile with one of her own. Heat rose across her skin, bled through the joints in her scale, and sent sparks across her tongue.

"Yeah?" Jacks took another step onto the flattened sedge of the clearing. Marani came along in tandem. Step. Step. Too far now, to retreat. Close enough to the harpies that they could have plucked a feather. A chorus of harpy shrieks scratched the otherwise silent forest.

Despite her smile Marani stuck out her tongue. With a chuckle made of fire she said, "I'm glad I don't have to do this alone."

"You never had to do anything alone, but we can talk about that once we have wings."

Chapter 17 - Nuria

In her doctoral dissertation Humans and Magic: A Hypothesis of Vessels, *Dr. Najad Vasshir argues that humans might be capable of holding magic long term if a magical field is also in play that can either counter the pull of the archipelago, or offer a 'fill' site of a kind, when said human regularly encounters it. While Dr. Vasshi's hypothesis is interesting, it fails to consider the proximity said enchanted objects would require to maintain the magic field. Could there, for instance, be one placed per island? Would there need to be multiple across Yuro, to allow for triangulation, or perhaps the magic held by these theoretical objects is so weak one would need say, five just in a given room? Without a means of testing, these theories remain no better than wishes, which a declining unicorn population is certain to ignore.*

- A Political Protocol for Nonhuman Species, Chapter 6: The Human and His Relationship To Magic

Jacks slammed the inn door closed as he left. The ancient wood cracked, then split along growth rings, the pieces falling to the floor in unnatural oval discs.

"I heard that sniffle. She's going to live. They both are." Javad patted Nuria's shoulder, and she shrugged him off.

"You're suddenly experienced in the ways of dragons? You're a bandit! And I can't believe you just let them walk out. I can't stop them, but you certainly can!"

"Not going to do any good though. Can you fight harpies? Can you outwit soothsayers? No, you can't. I can, maybe, but they're gonna fight a lot better if they know you and Liu are safe. So they live longer, maybe long enough to transform, if I stay with you. Got it?"

Javad made maddening sense, which just flared Nuria's temper further. "Where did you go while we were in the bedroom? Jacks was here in the bar when I came back out but you definitely weren't."

Javad shrugged. "They called council. I tagged along."

"And they just, let you do that? A bunch of unicorn historians?"

"I had a horn. An old horn. It was enough?"

"That's a peasant-level sidestep, Javad."

From the back side of the bar, Darifa, halfway into a bottle of whiskey, coughed, "Princess, if a determined royal could shake the secrets from the Solitaire, it would have happened decades ago. Have a drink. The dragons are outside, where they belong, battling magic and prophecy and probably political rifts as old as they are. If you want to join them, you'll need to do more than yell at Javad." She hiccupped. "Never thought I'd see you following orders. Thought Queen Ndolo raised you better than that."

"I thought I was supposed to follow the prophecy? I do not *want* to be here! Prophecy would not have brought Marani and I together if we were meant to be apart. Grey cannot transform without me." Nuria hadn't been sure of the words until she said them, but there was a finality to the air, once they were spoken, that settled the unease she'd carried since the morning. Marani's transformation progressed with her, or around her, or because of her. She'd flushed her whole life, but her transformation had only begun after their lives had entangled.

Javad again patted Nuria. She growled at him, because the last person who got to treat her like a pet was the man who'd buried Marani alive. "Stop it. You know I'm right."

"Never said you weren't," Javad returned.

Starshine reached for Nuria's head as well, but pulled back when Nuria set him with her "I do know how to use a sword" look. "Relax, princess. Your anger gets us nowhere. You charging into a harpy screech leads to your death, which does not lead to dragons. We are short a final piece to this transformative puzzle, and would like to spend a touch of time with you before you join your dragons in the clearing. There is no sense sending you out there without the final key. Perhaps information sharing can be made more friendly by our spirits." Starshine pulled a cup from the bar and slid it across the wood. "Care to share?"

Darifa poured a sloppy shot and slid the glass back. "Try your best. I've poked every workaround possible with the princess already. I'm bound by promise, she's bound by prophecy, and Javad is a complication I was never informed about."

Starshine rubbed his temples. "I don't want the dragons out alone any longer than possible. There must be a release. There must be a safety. What about Jacks? Can we discuss him? Or Yuro? Do you know where his key is? Or the island's key?"

Darifa shook her head, and Nuria swore she saw a glint of water in her eyes. "Nuria came to me with the comb. I knew it from...history, and therefore knew my purpose with Nuria, but I've never found another object like it. No one has. Every soothsayer I've ever met has read and searched. I..." she battled with her words, her lips forming syllables that magic refused to let live. "I was involved only with Marani—Grey—and Nuria. I was informed of Jacks. I...argh! My magic is not involved, by design, so that I cannot undo anything."

Whump. A man screamed once—loudly—then stopped.

"Harpies changin tactics," Javad murmured to her. "Nothing you can do yet. Stay steady, princess."

Another *whump*. This time, a woman's yell, then a plead, then silence.

Whump whump.

The chandeliers shook. The glass tinkled. No one looked up.

"My mother gave me the comb as a present, because I saw it in the treasury and she knew I loved dragonscale." Nuria swallowed and said, with a deep breath, "You don't think Queen Ndolo—"

Apple laughed. "She's not a key. She's a toy, as much as you are. Royals are the favorite toys of dragons—though one could argue dragons got too invested there at the end. Don't look so crestfallen. Humans can't hold magic. That's fact. If they could, Darifa wouldn't have horn breath." Apple leaned in and sniffed. "And don't think we can't smell it on you."

Nuria straightened, although nothing pointed out her petiteness as much as standing next to Starshine. "A toy? That comb allowed me visions outside normal soothsayer norms. I've seen futures not yet come to pass. I've seen the far past. I saw, just this morning, a tiny dragonlet getting a feather pulled from her and handed to a soothsayer. That has to be the comb. That dragonlet was Grey, I'm sure. She looked at me. She chirruped at me. She *knows* me, as a human, and a dragon." Nuria slammed her foot down and pointed to the shattered door. "But the comb is broken. The spell released. It can't still be the comb."

Starlight downed his shot in a soundless gulp. Darifa took hers like a horse at a water trough. "That's what we're hoping to discern. Just a few more questions princess, if you would? Might only be just a few questions between us, and having true dragons. Just a handful of minutes, to earn a lifetime more."

Nuria sucked down her dragon-level rage, folded her hands on her knee, and said, "Yes, of course."

"Your introduction to Grey led to a partial transformation?"

Whump. Whump-thump from the roof. The cries of children this time, not cut off but allowed to seep through the wood walls, sending shivers down Nuria's arms.

"That was the comb, again. Recently the changes have been occurring during flush—which, as far as I can tell, is when they stop pretending to be human and let the dragon part bubble up. But"—Nuria cleared her throat—"lately Grey has flushed during...non battle times." She put a hand across the loose seams of her bodice. "I played into it, willingly, and it did progress but not enough. Marani is adamant that sex isn't the key and, maybe she is right. But submission...that has to be part of it. I can't tease it out. My nudity certainly isn't what Jacks needs. Is," she swallowed, "Is there nothing we can do about the roof?"

Starlight nodded at a group of women to his left, who ducked out of the main room with grim smiles. He then smoothed the front of his overtight pants and returned, calmly, to Nuria. "Not battle rage. Not sexual tension. There are shared components in these. Passion. Heat. Submission seems an unlikely mechanism. If she is tied down, it is a physical thing that holds her. Could we need destruction? Of an object? The comb is gone. What in the physical ties both Marani and Jacks?"

The notebook. Nuria's soothsayer notebook held visions of their past and their future. Of course.

The doorman slammed in from the main entrance, his hair sticking straight up, his bright purple jerkin tangled with blackberry as he kicked away the wood shards of what had once been the door. "Dragons at the barrier, pulling harpy feathers. Don't know what is going on, and it isn't my place. Looks like the harpies have all the humans in range, muddled up in groups around our barrier. They're just picking them up, one after the other, flying them around, and dropping them on us. It's messy."

"The soothsayers?" Starlight asked.

"Two haven't been harpy caught, and one of them already found a way through. They'll be less interested in destruction and more on magical mischief." With a nod to Nuria, the doorman said, "It time yet? Is she broken?"

Darifa snorted into her shot glass. "The last person who tried to break Princess Nuria got a sword through the chest. *We* don't get to do anything. *She* either fixes this, or we're all, if you'll pardon my whiskey talk, as fucked as Nuria was ten minutes ago."

"*Darifa!*"

Darifa giggled and slid in a wavy stupor, down beneath the bar. "Fucking magic," she giggled as she sank. "Gods help us all. I'm afraid our princess is useless."

Nuria needed to be in the clearing, with Marani. She could burn the notebook here, in the inn's firepit, but that wouldn't be enough. Magic had been in the comb, but the notebook was a symbol. Burning a symbol only worked if it was seen. Nuria slammed to her feet. "I know how to both naturally and artificially inseminate a horse with pegasus sperm. I know the basic, assumed mechanics of dragon/horse interactions and the perils of first generation pegasus birth. I know the minimum length of unicorn horn before it is 'worth' cutting for its magical properties. I know the best joinery for building with dragon scale, and how to brush dragons to remove as much scale as possible without harming the animal beneath. And I know, not from reading, that there is a correct way to stroke dragon scale so it does not cut your hand. I also know that if you want me to undo magic, I need to be *near* the magic. I'm taking my notebook, and I'm going out there, unless you have a better idea."

Starlight sighed as he straightened. "A moment please, princess, while I discuss with my court." The inn patrons shuffled into a tight ring, with heads bowed and arms interlinked, saying absolutely nothing.

Javad eased Darifa up from the floor and settled her next Nuria, on an overstuffed armchair patterned with pettian leaves that had definitely not been in the inn a moment ago.

"Did we win?" Darifa asked, her eyelids only half open. "Has Nuria fucked the dragon yet?"

Nuria helped Darifa hook her ankles over the chair's arm. "Take me out of here, Javad. I can fix it. I can save them both. It has to be the notebook."

Javad grunted, "Just give them a moment. They're conferring. Unicorns don't vote. They require consensus and they're debating the best path forward. They cannot abandon the inn, nor the grove, nor can they ignore a direct order from a dragon. They won't take orders from anyone," he paused, considered, and squeaked out a, "deflowered, no matter how much they want to help."

Nuria set Javad with a stare that was meant to melt irritating courtiers into puddles.

"We have reached consensus," said Starlight, as he and the other inn people broke from their strange trance. "The Solitaire is history, and community, but no further good can come of remaining inside it. Half of us will head to the border of the grove and defend the dragons as they can from there. The other half will remain behind to guard the treasury and archives. Soothsayer, you are free to go. Princess? Take the notebook. Go to your dragon. If there is a key, or a key to this spell, it is you who holds it."

Finally. Nuria smoothed her skirt and tried to retwine a curl near her forehead. "I am no sheltered thing. I was raised in a castle, but also in the Common Forest, along with two little dragons. Like a wildflower, I have developed thick roots. I am a dragon's princess. I can be what she needs, and I can destroy what needs destroyed."

"Brave little princess," Glitter said, approvingly.

"Didn't even try to slip out the back way, like the soothsayer just did," Apple added. "I do hope she lives."

"Do you want an escort?" Starlight asked. "You'll take Javad of course, but Glimmer and Apple can take you to the battle's edge, likely at the grove end. You'll need to be seen, or heard, to be effective. Javad will have the tools to destroy the notebook, once you're in sight of Marani. Once the task is done, retreat to the walnut grove. Do not be near when the transformations alight. Dragons are far larger than any tapestry can depict."

Javad muttered unintelligibly, but gave her an Aspen Grove knight salute all the same—three fingers to his forehead, then three fingers to his heart.

Just like that, then, it was decided. All the waiting, and all the talking, and all the attempts to circumvent prophecy still ended with her in a field, forcing Marani into her heritage. "Yes. Thank you." Nuria took both Apple and Glimmer's hands and smiled, as sweetly as she could, at Starlight. "I won't let you down, Starlight. I'll bring you back a dragon."

"From one royal to another, I doubt your success, but not your intent. Good luck, Princess Nuria. And Herb?" Starlight said as he finally did pat Nuria's head. "Gather every horn you can find. We're going to need them."

Chapter 18 - Marani

A dragon, without fire, is a unicorn without horn. Horses are useless things.

- A Political Protocol for Nonhuman Species, Chapter 4: The Dragon

"Pretty. And soft. I never thought scale would be soft." Micha stroked Jacks' arm as she led him into the clearing, Marani still by his side. The harpies did have hands, of a sort. They were tiny, vestigial things set under the feathers, near the apex of their wings. There were no arms, but Micha lowered her wing enough that the hand sat on Jacks' shoulder, guiding him. To the some thirty harpies now in the grove, she called, "Look what I have. Dragons. All pretty and ready to transform."

"Are they?" called a tall harpy. "They were plucking feathers a moment ago."

Micha flapped a wing. "A brief scuffle we have rectified."

"The children. Where are they?" Jacks demanded.

"Over the hill. And the soothsayer is on the other side of the inn, on the other side of the barrier. Which will you go to? Will you walk there with me? Marani can stay with Darifa then. They will have discussions."

Micha tugged Jacks' arm, but he jerked away. "We stay together."

"I don't mind coming to see the boys. Is the purple soothsayer with them?"

"She's with a different group." Suba wrapped a wing around Marani's waist—an echo of the smoothness that human Suba had used to soothe a younger Marani. "This way, Grey, to her."

"Together." Marani growled the word. "As Jacks said."

Micha shook her head, sending hair and feathers tangling in the wind. "Not possible. Come away Jacks." Her hand was more insistent this time, but Jacks had spent a lifetime tearing away from defrauded merchants, port slavers, and angry blackberry brambles.

Marani just hated being touched without consent. They pulled back in tandem, the human-like hands unable to properly grasp living scale. Jacks pulled a short knife from his boot and Marani unsheathed her hatchet.

"My vision is going," Jacks said to her, breathless though they stood still. "There's fire in my stomach, burning worse than any hunger. I'm tired, still. If we flush, what then?"

Suba held up her 'hands,' her wings wide, blocking any movement forward. "Dragons. We are only trying to help."

Marani didn't know the answer, so she spoke instead to Suba. "Show us the boys. Now."

"Jacks first. There are rules, dragon."

"Fuck your rules," spat Jacks, flame mingling with spittle and smoking the sedge.

The flush would take them both, with or without their consent. The same heat rose through Marani, pushing the air from her lungs, drying the fragile scale-skin of her eyelids, and filling her eyes with hot salt instead of hydrating tears.

"Calm." Micha pet Jacks with a cherry-red feather. "Fires must burn slowly, or they burn out their fuel."

Jacks' fingertips were heated like firepokers now, and smoking against Marani's scale. "The boys! Now!"

"Just over the hill. But if you come with your sisters, you will decimate the clearing. Separation is safer. You were not born together. You do not need to flush together. Your spells are not twinned."

"She's my horse-damned sister and if you pull her again I will cut your wings off."

Separation was impossible. Marani settled into the flush like she had between Nuria's leg, welcoming the intensity of heat and fragrance of power.

"They're too hot." Micha's wingtips shivered.

"We do not need a chain reaction. The island cannot take it. Clawdia! Messica!"

Two harpies, one colored gold and green, the other the most delicate eggshell blue, lit from the ground. Gold flew north, along the road, and the sank below the small hill. Blue turned south, toward the inn, letting loose a *skreeeeeeeeech* that made Marani wince.

"Follow her," Jacks said, pointing north. "No children are dying today." He took off before Marani could respond and Marani stayed with him. They slid deeper into the flush, heart beats syncing, breath puffing in the same steam-filled gasps. Suba's wings beat at them, and Micha's useless hands grabbed, but Jacks and Marani ploughed across the clearing and toward the hill, sending more harpies to flight.

They ran, the wind beating Marani's face like in her dream. The breeze cooled the scale that patinaed with fire and for one precious moment, Marani knew only Jacks and the sound of the wind.

"Grey!"

It was a human voice—terrified, female, and a touch nasally—that came distantly from the south. Marani kept running but craned her head enough to see the purple-clad soothsayer dangling from harpy claw above the walnut grove. She was low enough to be heard, but high enough that the fall would snap her neck and any number of other bones.

Marani stopped.

Jacks spun on her. "We have to go this way."

The harpy shook the soothsayer like a worm on a hook. "This one is yours, is she not?"

"And here!" The second harpy rose above the hill, a boy with walnut curls dangling from her talons by his ankles. He cried as he screamed—big, long sobs choked with pleading as the harpy hovered at the hill's crest.

"Separate and save them both," Suba said from behind. "You have my promise they will not be dropped. Just separate."

Lose her brother, or lose a soothsayer? It should have been an easy choice.

"The kids," Jacks pleaded with her. "But without you, here, as this happens. I don't know if I can."

"The entire spell has to be lifted!" the soothsayer yelled. "You don't get to pick and choose the parts. Play *your* part, dragons!"

"I want my mom!" screamed the youth.

There was no further discussion.

Marani and Jacks ran with feet in sync, free hands batting at the air like wings. They growled, together, and the sound came thick as molasses. Another shriek came, from the boy, from the soothsayer, from the harpies as they all took to the skies, dropping whatever they carried and diving upon Jacks and Marani.

Harpies piled upon them. Talons tore at her remaining clothes. Human mouths ripped at her ears. Jacks roared as talons sunk through soft scale and pulled the dragons apart, sending them tumbling down the hillside.

The wind now, was too loud. Marani boiled up blood, Pain stabbed her side, her stomach, her throat, as her fire ricocheted inside her human shell.

"Now!" a human man called, and through the battlement of feathers and claws that insisted upon tearing her human flesh from dragonscale, Marani watched hunters emerge from the walnut grove—armed with rapiers and single-bullet shotguns, swathed in cheap horse leather armor.

"Get them back!" Suba screamed as her talons pierced through Marani's free hand. Marani swung the axe and connected with a rose-pink wing, shearing through bone.

"We can't and hold the dragons from one another," another harpy responded as Marani's victim cried pitiful, human tears and limped back. "Do you want the dragons contained, or the humans?"

"Jacks?" Marani yelled. "You okay?"

"I've never stabbed so many things in my life. Where are you?"

"Buried under a pile of harpy." Again Marani swung her axe, but this time a midnight blue harpy grabbed the handle and shot directly upward, leaving Marani defenseless.

"Get off them!" a man yelled. A pistol fired. Then another. The air turned rank with the unholy wedding of gunpowder smoke and pegacide.

"Clawdia and Messica, drop the humans off a cliff if you have to. The rest of us can hold the dragons."

The harpy piercing Marani's ankles chirped, "They can spend the next four days picking them up one by one and dropping them back down, but it won't help. Look west. The soothsayers. And from the forest come the fucking unicorns. Once they're here, we're omelets. Forget control, Suba. Do you want dragons at all?"

"Get off!" Jacks yelled. "Ow! Skin doesn't come off like that. What do you think you're going to find underne-*ow!*"

"Jacks!" Marani threw her weight left, then right, but talons held her to the ground and wings clouded her vision. Harpy hands with their delicate fingers reached down and peeled away the remaining tiny scale and, when that was gone, began to work underneath the larger plate. "Stop. That's still attached. *Ah!*" A finger slid underneath a pale green scale the size of a dinner plate across Marani's collarbone. The finger tugged. The tendons underneath the scale screamed and so too, did Marani. A magma-like substance leaked from her wound and boiled the ground beneath her.

"Transform," Suba shouted at her. "You don't need this body."

Riiiiip!

Jacks howled from the bottom the hill. "That's my pegasus-damned leg you're pulling apart, fucking vultures!"

Pop!

More gun smoke, and there was one less harpy atop Marani, but no less pain. "I can't, Grey," Jacks screamed. "I can't get them off. I can't see. I can't breathe. They're going to pull me apart!"

"Fire!" yelled a woman who sounded like the purple soothsayer.

Fire would destroy them from the inside out. Right now they were being pecked from the outside, in. Was one better? Less painful?

Fire couldn't be directed. It couldn't be put back away. It would destroy the harpies, the humans, the sedge, and the grove.

Two more *pops*—one, a gunshot off to her left. The other, the entire sheet of scale that spanned Marani's upper chest. She was being fucking flayed alive.

"Fire!" Marani yelled, at the harpies, at Jacks, at any living thing that thought it could fucking touch her. Nuria was safe at the inn, with Javad and Liu. Her brother was fireproof. Everything, and everyone else in the clearing, was expendable. "Fucking fire!"

Jacks roared.

Marani let her body go slack, took a long, deep suck of air, let it churn and roil and roast in her belly, and then, with no thought to direction, exhaled.

Chapter 19 - Nuria

A dragon holds no humanity. This is an inalienable fact.

- A Political Protocol for Nonhuman Species, Chapter 4: The Dragon

"Control her!" Javad screamed at Nuria. "She'll never forgive herself. Neither of them will, if this fire takes the humans!"

"Working on it." Nuria's heels dented the ground as she pressed forward, the ground turned to the waving delicateness of a bog mat that could, at any moment, puncture and send an unsuspecting person beneath. Smoke curled from tiny, pocked sinkholes that spat lava. Live fire engulfed the sedge and licked the walnut trunks, sparked in erratic lines that lengthened but did not widen. Through this maze Nuria walked, notebook clutched to her chest, her dress a torn, tattered ruin. Her feet squelched on hot mud amongst the shrieks and cries of the hunters, and the pleading of the soothsayers, as Marani and Jacks snapped arms, tore wings, and breathed the most horrible destruction.

The patrons of the Solitaire Inn, led by Starlight, charged the clearing, and the harpies writhing, brandishing shimmering horns and battle-glittered faces.

"Marani." Nuria called to her dragon from the west side of the clearing. "Marani, to me love. Please."

An arrow hit Jacks' shoulder, scratching his scale. He roared and incinerated a soothsayer standing to his left, muttering incantations. Marani embedded her hatchet into a harpy pelvis and did not turn around.

"Nuria, come away!" That was Liu, pleading with her from the edge of grove.

"You should have stayed back at the inn!" Javad stalled, halfway between the two women, unsure who most needed his protection.

A pistol fired with a *pop* and Marani fell in an arc of flame, onto her left knee.

Nuria laughed to herself. Protection. It was where they had all gone wrong. Dragons didn't need protection. Dragons needed to be *free*. And how could Marani be free when Nuria had her past, and her future, spun up in paper and leather?

Liu continued to yell. "I won't be left behind, and you could have consulted me. This idea stinks of cephel fruit, and there will be no sweet underpinnings. A notebook cannot bind a dragon, the same as a comb cannot bind a dragon. Stop fucking with ingredients!"

Javad used the shoulder of his jerkin to wipe away sweat. "Unless you've a better idea, baker, she might as well try. The dragons are a bloody mess and we're not far from a volcanic event."

"Don't do it," Liu pleaded. "Think, princess."

"Marani." Nuria said her lover's name as she came up behind her. Marani stumbled to her feet, the axe in her hand dripping harpy blood. Flame dripped from her chin. She snarled a horrible, inhuman sound as she assessed Nuria with eyes no longer green, but yellow and predatory. But she still had two legs. Two arms. A human face, and hands that stalled their violence.

Nuria held out her notebook. "This doesn't belong to me."

A blink of humanity flashed across Marani's face. She took the notebook, spun it on her palm, then spat a dollop of fire between the two stamped aspen leaves.

The leather burned. The paper browned, curled, and powdered. The remains fell from Marani's hand to the liquid earth at her feet and she stared at Nuria, eyes still wide and hungry.

Another roar from Jacks as he pulled claws from his still-human throat. The puncture wounds on his kit-scale bled a deep red, but still he did not transform.

"Stop using ingredients!" came Liu's shrill scream from the grove.

How could it not be the notebook? Was the flush not deep enough? Or was it that Marani and Jacks weren't together? What connection was she missing? For all of Liu's talk of baking, Nuria was still missing the damn recipe. What else was left? The magic of the comb was gone. Any magic the notebook had, also gone. Nuria had no more artifacts, just her own body, and a promise she'd made to a dragon, of love.

The dragons were armspans apart, Marani watching her and Jacks watching them both, coiled and predatory, bleeding and burning.

A harpy came at Nuria. She ducked, instinctually, and the claws caught Marani's scalp and opened a gash as long as Nuria's forearm.

"This dragon is protected by the crown of Aspen Grove!" Nuria jumped on the harpy's back and tried to scratch her face, but the harpy ducked, and Nuria's hand connected instead with Marani's nose.

Jacks roared from her left and tackled Nuria to the ground. Marani impaled the harpy with a fist, then had hands to Jacks' throat a moment later, just as he raised a fist aimed at Nuria's face.

"Say the fucking words!" Javad yelled. "We need a new plan and nothing works if you're dead. What are you doing?!"

The siblings rolled away in a ball of dust and flame. Harpies came again, and a pistol fired into the mess. Nuria propped herself up on her elbows and shook her head. "No."

"Fuck the prophecy and fuck the magic. Grey. Jacks. Step out!"

Javad's words were loud enough, but neither sibling took notice. Ignoring the talons that ripped and bullets that spliced, Jacks and Marani tore at each other, Marani ripping skin from Jacks in eccentric patches, Jacks chipping cracks in Marani's plate. They snarled, and screamed, and lava rolled from the breaks in their skin where blood should have beaded.

"*Step out!*" Javad yelled again.

"It only works when they say it," Liu yelled. "Or Nuria commands. Magic calls to magic It's the bond of princess and dragon. You know that, Javad."

Marani bit into Jacks' neck, stripping his skin down to scale. Jacks pulled away the remains of Marani's jerkin and shirt, revealing the two ridgelines that burst with forest-green feathers. Marani snarled, but it was the sound of a wounded, feral thing, not an emerging dragon.

Nuria stood, ignoring the tears that welled in her eyes. "Please don't die," she whispered. "I don't know what else to do."

"You have to say it!" Javad rounded on her, his face a mask of fury. "They can't hear me, but they will hear you. Stop them, before they tear each other apart! Or do, whatever it is you were designed to do. Just don't stand there!"

"I *have* done everything I'm supposed to do. This is dragon magic we are interfering with. There is nothing left to bind Marani. Better they pick themselves apart than the harpies or the hunters. I've stopped this before. I won't again. My meddling messed this up once. Not this time. Whatever magic is in me, it won't help."

Liu picked her way through the fire lines without a word to how the smoke singed the colors on her skirt. A pegasus shrieked overhead. "I'm not a part of magic, but I've been around it plenty. Let me tell you what I see. Jacks clings to Grey. Grey once clung to her comb, but I don't think that's true anymore. Smells can imprint, when say, cinnamon has been stored too long next to nutmeg. Does she cling to humanity? Or does she cling to you, princess, perhaps even, what sits inside you? To reach adulthood, the dragons had to pass for humans. But no dragon cares for human lives. No dragon loves, not like us. Dragons are fickle, and they are collectors. A true disguise needs a focal point. It needs a beacon. To keep Grey human, she was bound to one. It is that binding, that touch of magic, I think, that Grey must reclaim."

No. A *whump* sounded from the clearing and Nuria turned to see Jacks throw Marani against a walnut snag. His arms shook as he did so, and Marani sat, dazed, for a moment before launching herself back at her brother. Jacks had as much scale as Marani now, and their fire had set the grove alight, but both gasped at air like land-drowned fish, and their scale flickered like dying candlelight.

"Fire's in the grove," Liu said. "Barrier must be down. Tongues will be loose, but that binding doesn't matter. Open the oven. Put the bread in. See if it rises."

Did she hold magic? Nuria certainly held Marani, perhaps from the moment she'd first seen her. Marani flushed during sex, yes, and it helped along her transformation, but only when Nuria could only speak in gasps, and plead for release. Only when Nuria turned away from coyness, and seduction...and when she stopped trying to drive, and control, the situation. When they were two people, two bodies, two souls entwined, without the muddling of prophecy or power.

Willingness. Consent. Marani was always so mindful of it. Magic, too, required consent. Breaking spells, maybe, required the same?

"Javad? You were with the historians during their conclave. Did they speak about Aspen Grove's queens and their dragons?" Nuria asked.

"No, but I've seen the tapestries. You lot rode them like pegasi, and chained them like dogs. There's embroidery of youths being offered to dragons while the queen watches—not a trade, I think. Bribery. Enticement. Queens bound the dragons of Yuro and yeah maybe it was love sometimes, but that consequence was the same. Grey is your dragon. You've said it. She believes it, and she loves you enough to bow to you, even in this. You wanted a human lover, you two probably spoke of marriage and babies and such, and none of that happens with a fucking dragon."

"Dragons are wild," Nuria said, mostly to herself. "Dragons are fire—warm when contained but always aching, and always a force of nature when allowed free." *I was so excited to see her. So excited to see a dragon, and for it to be my dragon, and now she...*

"I always thought I was the solution. I got her coin when she needed nettle. I got her food when her cheeks grew too hollow. In the inn I, I only wanted to help."

"You did," Javad soothed. "You were there when she needed you. But she is no dragonlet anymore. Let her go, princess."

Nuria giggled, the sound swallowed by the snapping fire of burning walnut. The princess cobbled together every bit of confidence she still had, and said, "Please wait here. All of you."

"Nuria," Liu began. "There are a hundred ways to make a pie."

Nuria smiled at the pastry chef. "Right now, only one stands out. It'll be alright. Yuro is going to have dragons again. Promise."

Javad grabbed her arm. "It *will* be alright, princess."

"One step at a time. That's what we have right now." Nuria winked at Liu, nodded to Javad, and walked back into the clearing.

Her footsteps were loud this time, across the burnt understory and the lack of screaming humans—most of whom had the sense to run once the dragons found their fire. Jacks and Marani still tussled and harpies still circled, but the dragons were on hands and knees now, swiping at each other like crawling babies fighting over a toy. The ground streaked bubbles of lava and blood, feathers and skin, and two dragonlets in a caustic battle to their mutual death.

Nuria knelt down next to them. Twin sets of dragon eyes glared back at her. Jacks growled.

A nervous laugh escaped her throat. "What am I going to do with two exhausted dragons?"

Jacks snorted. Marani stayed in position, her muscles bunched, like a cat ready to spring. "Nuria," she rasped. "Princess."

"I love you, Marani. But I also want you to be free. I'll always be here for you, waiting. If you want to come back. But right now, what I want is for you to be a dragon. A real dragon. The dragon I've dreamed about and wished for since I was born. I want that, but the choice is yours." She held out her hands. "Take what belongs to you and be free."

Marani's hands clasped hers—the scale scalding. Nuria wanted to scream, but the questioning in Marani's eyes kept her silent. "I'm okay, love," she whispered.

They stood together, in the center of the clearing, the ground blackening in a widening, perfect circle around them. From the hills beyond, pegasi emerged, their wings kicking up a breeze that fanned Marani's skin to outright flame. She burned as hot as the sedge, her scale alight with greens and browns, dancing and sparkling brighter than any unicorn horn.

Nuria turned lightheaded from the heat, and pain of the touch, and the smoke-choked air, but still she gripped Marani, refusing to let go. "Take me," she commanded. "You have to. For Yuro, and for us."

Marani's hand cupped her cheek, flame cauterizing the soft skin. Nuria's cry was cut short when Marani kissed her. Her lips were a moment of cool relief before fire poured from her, down Nuria's throat, into her belly, and around what felt like her soul. Her body was an explosion barely contained in too-tight skin. She closed her eyes against the pain, and the dryness in her eyes. Nuria's hair caught fire as flame leaked from her pores like sweat and still she held Marani's hands, gripping tighter and tighter, wondering if her failing grip was because her own skin had burned away.

"Nuria."

The name was a gust of wind, or a whisper of a cricket at dusk. Nuria's eyes flew open as her hands closed in on themselves, on nothingness, on her own charred skin. And there was still the pain, and fire, but there was also Marani.

She stood a handspan from Nuria now, her face skyward. The edges of her body blurred in the sunset as her arms thickened, her shoulders broadened and wings pushed, fully formed, from her back. The weight of them drove Marani to her knees and she roared from deep in her chest—the sound not of crushing bones and ripped scale, but of decision.

Her fingers came together, five becoming three, lengthening with her hands and growing claws larger than Javad's biggest dagger. Her boots—her only remaining article of clothing, split at their seams as her feet followed suit. Nuria's next breaths ran together as Marani shifted, broke, fused and reformed—her scale elongating to cover thick musculature, her wings expanding out, out, until their breadth covered the clearing from grove to game trail.

Flame still danced, and the ground still roiled, but there were rainbows now, across solid plate scale, and the most delicate feathers at the edges of damp, emerald and grass-colored wings.

"Marani?" Nuria spoke the name into shocked silence of the grove. She fell to her knees, without pain, without acknowledgement that her own body was changed as well. A dragon head turned sharply to her, yellow eyes narrow, forked tongue licking the air. Marani's scales were a rich, earthen brown that shimmered green when they caught the light. The delicate, fingernail-sized feathers on her wings settled to a dusky lime. In her dragon form she was the size of three full-grown, thoroughbred pegasi, her head alone twice the width of Nuria's small frame. "How do you feel?" Nuria asked the dragon. "Are you alright?"

Two stacked rings of smoke puffed from Marani's nostrils. Her head then swung to Jacks who still stood on two feet, grinning wildly at his sister.

"Now," Javad commanded Marani, his voice thick from smoke. "As the princess is to you, so are you to Jacks. Do it now."

"Wait, do what now?" Nuria called out. "Javad—"

Marani's mouth yawned lazily open. She drew breath, expanding her lungs and rumbling the earth. Then she exhaled a blue-red stream of fire that engulfed first Jacks, then the walnuts behind him and finally, the entire grove.

"The inn! The forest is, Marani, stop love. It's too much."
Nuria stood and reached out, thinking she might touch a
wing tip or feather, but Marani cut the blaze, swung, and
snapped at her—a clear warning to keep her distance.

Nuria stumbled back on numb feet. Her dress had
melted to her skin in places, and while the fabric pulled and
her skin stretched, it did not hurt. It would be a nightmare
to explain to her mother. "I'm sorry. I just wondered if we
could talk about...I mean one step at a time maybe or..."
Nuria was babbling, which every history book she'd ever
read had noted that dragons did not have time for.

Marani sniffed at her and, with three hard flaps, pushed
off the ground and into the sky, joining the circling pegasi.

"Or fly before we get things sorted." Nuria tried,
unsuccessfully, to scold herself into a calm. Marani was not
hers to command. She closed her eyes, counted to ten, and
when that failed to settle her shakes, she shifted her focus
to Jacks, and the burning walnuts. The magic was released.
Marani was released. The next step was to sort Jacks, and
then put out the fire, and then maybe deal with the harpies?

"Marani, maybe," Nuria started as she opened her eyes.

Jacks was gone.

The walnut forest beyond, gone. Not burned to carcasses,
or cut to stumps, simply replaced by dew-covered sedge
and softly rolling foothill.

There *was* Liu, eyes fixed to the skies, hands balled up in
her palace silks that had lost all their dirt. Nuria looked
down, and there she was, her skin as unblemished as the
day she was born, her bodice unripped, her green dress
pleated and pressed and smelling of marigold soap.

She blinked once. Twice. And then there were...*there
were dragons.*

Jacks, Nuria recognized instantly—his yellow and green
scale unmistakable along with the mischief that still
twinkled in his now equine eyes. He too huffed at Nuria,
nudged his snout at Liu, then joined his sister in the sky.

As he ascended, so did others—breaking through distant
canopies, crossing the horizon—filling the sky with bright

jewel tones of pinks, reds, yellows, greens, blues, and purples. They flocked in diamond formations, the pegasi trailing behind them, Marani in the lead, circled, and flew south.

"They're leaving Yuro," Liu said, as she came up next to Nuria and took her hand. "All the hidden dragons, and taking the harpies and the pegasi with them. Who knew there would be so many? Who knew there *could* be so many? Good baking, princess."

Leaving. Nuria let the finality of the word simmer in her mind. She did not prod, and she would not disassemble. Not here. Not now. "Is it any safer for them out there, than here?" Nuria asked. "Or do you think they have family out there, that have been released as well?"

Liu shrugged. "You can't know every herb. The sky is filled with two dozen dragons and that's just the ones we see. Marani and Jacks will have a reckoning, I suspect, if their parents are still alive. Perhaps later, a reckoning with us as well."

"And Javad?"

"Not up, princess. Behind." It was Javad's voice that spoke, but Nuria turned to a dappled white and gold unicorn, whose horn held the most delicate shade of blue at its base. As Nuria stared, other unicorns came into focus and she recognized them immediately. Starlight—long and lean, Glitter with her tinsel hair, Herb—a draft-horse framed unicorn with white hair that curled at the tips.

All of that magic could not possibly have been inside her.

"I don't understand. Was it the fire? Did it break the magic of the grove and that released...everyone? Because I saw...I saw dozens of dragons take to the sky right now. And as I stand here, there are dozens of you winking in and out of focus. How...Javad, was it the horn you had? Did the unicorns, the dragons, the harpies..." The remaining words aborted in Nuria's throat. *How,* was all she could think. *How could we have been so wrong? Where were they all hiding, these dragons bound in human skin? How did*

Marani never find them? What she did manage to say was, "Was I everyone's magic?"

Starlight approached, his tail high and proud, like an Arabian horse. His horn was the color of rose-kissed moonlight and new tears came, unbidden, to Nuria's eyes. Marani was beautiful, as a human or a dragon, but gods, unicorns were *breathtaking*. "Every good spell has a backup. What would the dragons have done, if Marani had never found her comb? Darifa made sure she would find you. You were Marani's key, but Marani, she was ours. It was a brilliant spell in its simplicity. To bind every magical creature separately would have taken hundreds of soothsayers, and months of time that we did not have. Instead, the release for the magic was placed in one dragon kit, and her key, entwined with a princess."

"And if we'd never have met?"

Starshine whinnied and shook his head, sending nut-colored ringlets cascading across his back. "Darifa would have never allowed it. Her magic sealed Grey to you and she was determined to see her task through. I've never seen an altruistic human before, present company excepted."

The delicate tip of a sky-blue horn tapped the side of Nuria's cheek. "Thank you, Princess Nuria. I know you didn't ask to be a baker, but you did a fine job."

Nuria managed a pained smile. "Thank you. And Javad. You look...very stately."

"He is another question to unravel. But we have time now. Thank you, princess."

Javad reared with sheer equine delight, kicking his golden hooves into the air. "I'd had a hard time picturing myself as a dragon, I'll admit. My wife thought I might be a harpy, and we had a good laugh over it, but this? I'm fucking beautiful, princess." In a whisper, he said, "Memories got locked with that magic, too. I've some big ones coming, I know it." Slightly deflated, he added "This'll be a fun conversation with the wife."

"Is there a way to contact her?" Nuria asked Starlight. "Grey, that is. Or any of them?"

"No one can call a dragon, princess, and you gave up your ability to command. A maiden can trap a unicorn, and a hunter can snare a harpy, but dragons follow no laws and care about no land. She will find you, if she wishes. Until then," Starlight nuzzled her neck. "It is best to let her, Jacks, and the others, finally, be free."

Epilogue

Nuria sat in the shade of spindly rosewood trees and stared up into the night sky. The trees she'd planted after a particular visit from Darifa, and a vision of her first meeting with Marani, were barely a decade old. Their crowns were sparse, their bark fine, and their leaves all dropped with the change of seasons. There were better places in the Aspen Grove palace grounds to stargaze, and Nuria had tried them all. The south tower was too cold, the rose garden too sweet-smelling, the courtyard too barren. Her bedroom, and her bed, still smelled like Marani, whose shed kit scales still littered the floor.

Here, in the tiny plantation of rosewoods, was the only place Nuria could sit and think without crying. Or yelling. She'd done plenty of both in the last three weeks, both when alone, and, very unfortunately, occasionally during high council meetings when being pressed about how *many* dragons she'd seen, what *kind* of unicorns, and did she know about their plans, or where they were hiding, and if the pegasi and harpies were in league with them all, was it more of a worshipful league, or a 'take vengeance on the humans who enslaved us' league?

"I planted all of these for you," Nuria said, still staring at the stars. "Because a rosewood penny was supposed to lead you to me. I thought I was being so clever, but...I understand now, your rage in the carriage when you threw my notebook away. Your life was never your own, and I didn't fight to free you. I just...played a part." Nuria laughed. "Ironic, coming from a princess who also got very little say in her life." Nuria's words turned to whisper. "Are you happy, out there? Do you miss butter, or arguing with the maids about pants? Do you think you'll come back, Marani?"

The slow chirp of crickets and the *brrrrap* of a lone frog were her only answer.

"Princess?" a guard called from around the castle wall. "Princess, the queen would like to remind you that even dragons sleep."

"I'll be right in." Nuria dabbed at her nose as she sat up, the soft skin there chapped from the emotions that seemed to endlessly bleed from her. She wove her way through the small plantation, hands tapping trunks as she passed, as she wished each a silent goodbye.

"And goodbye to you as well, Marani." Nuria turned back around when she reached the castle wall and gave one final look to the night sky. "I hope you find what you're looking for, you and Jacks. Be safe."

"She'll be back, Princess." From inside the plantation, the shimmering form of Javad emerged, his horn glowing like a solar flare in the moonless night. Around his horn lay a woven circlet of violets and pearls that shone every bit as bright as the moon. "Grey never could stay away from women very long. You do not bind her anymore, but she will remember the love she had for you. The love she certainly still holds, somewhere in that furnace of a belly. No scales or firebreath can change that."

Nuria ran to the unicorn and flung her arms around his neck, burying her face in the soft down of his coat. Javad knelt and Nuria sank to her knees in tandem and they sat, princess and unicorn, as Nuria swallowed screams of *I want her back* and *This isn't how our story is supposed to end!* Javad smelled of clover and sea breeze, and childhood. Sobbing to a unicorn in a plantation of mostly extinct trees should have been magical, but Nuria could cling not to the moment, but to Javad's coat, and memory, and a promise that had been broken.

Not broken, Javad said, the words sounding inside Nuria's head. *Delayed, so that more questions might be asked. Why bind a dragon with human love? Why bind a dragon to human form at all? Patience, little princess, while plans far older than you play out.*

"I have been patient enough for a lifetime."

I'll stay here with you until she returns. Not in the stables, or with the guard, but nearby. In the rosewoods, or the royal forest. There's a herd of us there. Far enough to not be seen, but not so far we cannot hear. If you call, I will answer, maiden. No unicorn can command their king, but none of us could ever ignore the crush of heartbreak.

"Javad." Nuria finally straightened and said, in all seriousness, "I am no maiden. Grey made sure of that. And you a...king?" She giggled. "You've gone to riddles now, like a soothsayer, haven't you?"

Javad nickered. *You're as bad as she is, making everything about sex. Don't argue with a unicorn, princess. And go to sleep. I'll be here in the morning, and every morning thereafter, until Grey returns. Tell Liu, too. If she needs me, I will come to my family. Grey is not the only one touched by humanity.*

"I will. Thank you, Javad. Unicorn."

Friend.

Javad dissolved around Nuria, his coat feathering into starlight, his horn fading like the dying flash of a nightfly. The grass where he had laid was upright and unblemished, and it was only the scant white hairs that clung to Nuria's vest that convinced her he'd been real at all.

"Don't be too delayed then, Dragon," Nuria whispered. "The world has waited for you, and you've a promise to keep. If not to me, then Yuro itself."

ACKNOWLEDGEMENTS

Books are never written in a vacuum. Books with a decent sex scene require, at least for me, a lot of moral support. Thank you, as always, to my Reading Excuses writing group, who put up with all kinds of weird sex questions without any context. Another huge thank you to Katie Cordy, knower of all things horse, who advised on the breeds and tack (and helped me select the "sexiest" horses in...those scenes). Thank you in advance to my Wednesday Night Chili Cookoff friends who are already helping me brainstorm the spicy scenes in book three—you are all surprisingly well versed in human/dragon relations. I feel like I should be scared but it's too late to turn back now.

ABOUT THE AUTHOR

J.S. Fields (@Galactoglucoman) is a scientist who has spent too much time around organic solvents. They enjoy roller derby, woodturning, making chain mail by hand, and cultivating fungi in the backs of minivans. You can find their books at www.jsfieldsbooks.com. To read more in the Ardulum universe, and more of J.S.'s work, join their Patreon at http://www.patreon.com/jsfields

Please take a moment to review this book at your favorite retailer's website, Goodreads, or simply tell your friends!